KING's Odyssey

BY **JAMES WALSH**

KING'S ODYSSEY

Copyright © by James A. Walsh, 2018

This book may be ordered at Lake Effect Snow Publishers:
by telephoning: (727) 367-9631, or
by mailing to: James A. Walsh, P.O. Box 8292,
Madeira Beach Post Office St. Petersburg, FL 33738, or
by visiting: **www.JohnTKWalsh.net**

This is a work of fiction.

ISBN: 978-0-578-20797-1

Library of Congress in Publication Data

Cover & Text Layout by: Eli Blyden
www.CrunchTimeGraphics.com

Printed in the United States of America

Lake Effect Snow Publishers
St. Petersburg / Kuala Lumpur / Tierra del Fuego

Caveat

This is a work of fiction, and the product of a warped mind. All characters and situations are imaginary. Any resemblance to persons living or dead, or to actual places and events, is purely coincidental. Mind you, the author has been known to lie about other things as well. Anyone who sees him/her-self in any of these characters or situations is clearly delusional and should seek immediate psychiatric attention.

In fairness, the author confesses that there is an exception to the statement that all characters are imaginary. Phred, the fixed, feminine feline, was quite real. So, too were all but one of her exploits recounted here. For fourteen years she lived with the author and his wife, and she herself was a constant source of amusement and wonder.

Other Books by James A. Walsh

Fiction

Death Comes For The Provost

Nex Pro Bono

Occasions of Syn

Clerical Errors

Resurrection

Two Tales of The City

Non-Fiction

The Lamb Shank Chronicles, Volume I

Dedication

This work is dedicated to my wife Ann. She is, *inter alia,* my first reader and my most forthright and fearless critic. She is my moral compass, my keel in stormy seas, my rudder in shifting currents, and my safe harbor in distress. She is the love of my life. Too often, I have neglected to tell her this. *Mea Culpa!*

IN MEMORIUM

Dr. Harry C. Nash
24 March 1927 – 16 December 2017
Professor of Physics
John Carroll University

Harry was a truly remarkable person in so very many ways.

He was married to the late Ann Nash for 65 years. Together they raised 12 children, 11 of whom survived him.

He was a member of the Physics Faculty at John Carroll University for over fifty years.

He was a teacher, a researcher, an advisor, an administrator, an author, an editor, a genial colleague, a trusted counsellor, a valued friend, and, when the occasion called for it, a courageous critic.

He was one of those rare men who was completely unafraid to speak Truth to Power, even when he knew that it would not be well received.

It will be a very long time before anyone comes along who can fill those big shoes.

I freely admit that my fictional character, Hubert Reo, the Faculty "Father" at Thornton University, has more than a little bit of Harry in him.

Harry, you served well. Rest in peace, my friend.

Table of Contents

PART TWO
THE PROFESSIONALS

Dramatis Personae

Arnold P. King, Associate at the Investment Firm of Boyd, Hunter, & Gould

> (B, H, & G), aka Artemus C. Scott

Gloria Hearney King, Arnie's wife

Senior Partners at B, H, & G

> Harold Boyd, Founding Partner
>
> Stephen Hunter
>
> Jeffrey Gould

Nicholas D. Gestas, Junior Partner in B, H, & G

Carleton Dunn, Partner in the law firm of Gray, Arnold, and Young

Alf Whitman, an Associate at Gray, Arnold, and Young

Fingal O'Flahertie, aka "Oscar", History Professor, Thornton University, aka

> Aristotle Tipper, aka Inspector Grimshaw
>
> Constance O'Flahertie, Oscar's wife. Previously known as Sister Margarethe, SSS

The Amateur Hit-Men

> Barry Marsh, former race car driver
>
> Hiram Cassidy, disgraced Ethics Professor, Harrison Community College
>
> Enoch Harris, former baseball player, now a truck driver

Maxwell Greenfield, CEO of Greenfield and Associates, a wealth management
     Firm, Atlanta, GA

Ms. Ani Mameum, Max's Secretary
Selena, clerk in the Registrar's Office, Thornton University
Wilberforce Malone, The Broker, Las Vegas, NV
The Moneyman, the person paying for King's death
Bergen Sawyer, Sociology Professor, Thornton University
Montego O'Higgins, Chemistry Professor, Thornton University
Three of Oscar's Honor Students at Thornton:
     Parker Birchwood, Wesley Colby, and Baxter Gilbert

Katie Carey, aka Aphrodite Burke, aka Aunt Marcy
Byron Carey, Katie's brother-in-law
Ed Franklin, Professional Problem Solver, God's Judgment
Mason, Caretaker and kennel supervisor for Montego O'Higgins
Phred, a fixed feminine feline, who helps Mason
Tobias Woodford, Manager, Bidleman's Restaurant, Pittsburgh
Salvatore Stavola, one of Woodward's henchmen
Marty Harold, a foot-soldier in the army of God's Judgment

KING's Odyssey

KING'S Odyssey

Part One

THE AMATEURS

Chapter 1

King's Predicament

Arnold P. King was a careful man who, over the years, had developed "take no unnecessary chances" into a core religious belief. His co-workers pigeon-holed him as "risk adverse". He disputed that assessment. He would take risks but only as an inescapable last resort, having exhausted all other options. He did not gamble, not even to play the State Lottery. He wore both a belt and suspenders. When he bought a new suit, he always ordered two pairs of pants and insisted that the inside jacket pocket have a zipper closure. When he married Gloria Hearney, he required that she sign a prenuptial agreement. His brother-in-law has never forgiven him for this affront. His personal transportation, a 2016 Lincoln MKT Town Car, has not one, but two, spare tires in the trunk. One can never predict all future problems, but for any that had ever crossed Arnie's mind, he tried to make allowance. However, not even his core religious belief could have prepared him for his present predicament.

Given his mind-set, his choice of profession may seem to some to be counterintuitive. King is an Associate in the Investment firm of Boyd, Hunter, & Gould, located in Harrison. Arnie manages the investment portfolios of a dozen affluent clients. The total value of their holdings at the end of the most recent quarter was well into nine figures. His performance reviews are all consistently first-rate and his clients are uniformly pleased with his work. His direct supervisor is a junior partner, Nicholas D. Gestas.

He first became aware that he had a problem when he checked his portfolios after the close of the markets in New York, something he does every Friday without exception. The value of the combined holdings was low by eight million dollars, even though this had been an up week in the markets. He double-checked the calculations and could find no error. Incredible as it might be, eight million dollars had gone missing on his watch. The iceberg in his gut was beginning to grow at an alarming rate. He fought down the first wave of panic. *There had to be a rational explanation.*

After calling home to tell Gloria that he would be working late, he analyzed each of his portfolios line-by-line focusing on activity during the past week, searching for discrepancies. In each portfolio, he found a withdrawal of between six and seven hundred thousand dollars, actions for which he had no prior knowledge and that he had not authorized. *Someone was stealing from the cookie jar.* The missing funds had been channeled into a group of off-shore banks and holding companies.

It was quite late when he shut down his computer, locked his desk and his office, and headed for the parking garage. The route home was one he had travelled so often that the driving occupied only a small part of his mind. The rest of his consciousness was working to find an explanation for the missing funds. He was so intent on his problem-solving that he had cleared a major intersection before he realized that he had just run a red light. Fortunately, there had been no cross traffic and no cop on duty. But, it was a sobering reminder to pay a little more attention to his driving. Even though the traffic was light at this late hour, a traffic accident would not help to solve his problem. It would only add to it.

The Interstate leading to Harrison's western suburbs was sparsely travelled and he settled into the middle lane at close to the speed limit. *To begin, I know that I did not embezzle those funds. Now, whoever did was able to access my computer. In house, there are only four people who have access to my login ID and the individual passwords for my twelve accounts: Nick Gestas, my supervisor, and the named partners, Jeff Gould, Steve Hunter, and Harold Boyd. While I can't rule any of them out, it's hard to believe that one of them is guilty of grand theft. They are all financially well-off and thus lack motive. Moreover, they are my friends, for God's sake. If the attack was from outside, then a hacker has breached our security. With our firewalls and the level of data encryption, I would have thought that this was impossible. And, while hackers do become more skillful and daring day-by-day, this explanation strains credulity. However, if we rule out the outsiders, then we are left with only my colleagues.*

He exited the Interstate in the suburb of Boulder Creek and headed southwest on the state road toward Airely. His own home was further west in Nailor. In the western part of Boulder Creek, the road skirts the north side of a large retention pond. Just before he got to the pond, a white SUV sped past him and then pulled into his lane. *That damn fool passed me on the other side of the double yellow lines. What is so urgent that this idiot can't wait for a safe stretch to pass?*

No sooner was the SUV back in his lane when it slowed to match his speed. At this point, a black panel truck appeared in his rearview mirror and approached aggressively until it was riding his rear bumper. *What are these two clowns up to? I'm tired and it's late. I'm not playing this game.* He eased off the gas, looking for a place to pull off the road. But the low guard rail around the retention pond would not allow this. He was boxed in.

As if on cue, a Ford F-150 truck pulled up next to him and hovered there as if checking him out. *What the Hell is that monster up to on this road at this hour? It looks hungry and angry.* This was starting to look like an ambush and he was trapped. He began to get a sick feeling in the pit of his stomach. The Ford backed off until it was even with his back bumper and it drifted left toward the opposite berm. The escort cars, front and rear, gave the truck a little more room. Then the truck driver gunned the engine and swung in hard against Arnie's car. The kiss was executed with such skill and artistry as to be reminiscent of the legendary Willie Hoppe during his reign as Billiard Champion. When Arnie lost some of his forward traction, he tried to correct. But, as so often happens, he overcorrected. When he tried to compensate, he lost it. The force of the collision rolled the Lincoln up and over the guard rail and into the retention pond.

The airbags all deployed, as they were intended to, and the car settled into the pond and began to take on water. Arnie fought down the panic that was starting to develop. He pressed the release for the seat belt/shoulder harness. Nothing happened. With his left hand, he fished into the door pocket and found the sharp hunting knife that he kept there. He punctured the air bags and then quickly cut through the straps of the harness pinning him to his seat.

Next, he tried to lower the driver's window. Again, nothing happened. The panic was energized and tried to reassert itself. Again, he fought it down. Delving deeper into the door pocket, he found the ballpeen hammer that he had acquired for just such an eventuality. The water was now up to his waist. He knew that time was running short. Putting all his muscle behind the blows, he worked on the driver's window. The window bowed on the third blow, cracked on the fourth, and finally yielded on the fifth. As the water poured in, he cleared as much of the remaining glass shards as possible.

From the shrinking air pocket at the roof of the vehicle, he filled his lungs. Cautiously, he exited through the window, avoiding most of the residual glass, and made for the surface. His jacket and shoes slowed him down, but he was reluctant to discard them. If he survived, he would need them. He broke the surface as quietly as possible and replenished his air supply. All was darkness. Then he did the breast stroke, heading away from the undertow of the sinking car, and making for the opposite shore. In college, he had been a member of the swimming team.

He had been a strong swimmer, although not particularly gifted with speed or grace.

Quietly, he dragged himself from the water and lay still in the grass, letting his pulse and respiration return to normal. Meanwhile, he observed activity across the pond. Three vehicles had returned and were grouped beyond the collapsed guard rail, angled so that their headlights shone on the water. Three men were arguing but he could not make out what they were saying. For a while, they watched the place where the car had sunk to the bottom of the pond. Then they began to search along the shore. Arnie was processing the information. *There are no flashing red bubble lights, so these are not part of an emergency rescue team. The three vehicles matched the number that had ambushed me. It was possible that these are my attackers. Until proven otherwise, I should do nothing to call attention to myself. Of course, these might be good Samaritans who just happened to be driving by and stopped to see if they could render assistance. But, given the hour and the paucity of traffic I saw on the road, this doesn't seem very likely.*

After about five minutes, the men abandoned their search, got in their vehicles and left. The larger vehicle, presumably the Ford, headed back toward Boulder Creek and the Interstate, the direction from which all three vehicles had come. The two smaller vehicles, most likely the herding cars, headed west toward Nailor and Airely. Arnie waited a few moments to be sure that they did not return. Then, he got up, brushed himself off, and walked around the periphery of the pond, back to the road. *Clearly, this was a deliberate attempt to kill me. But, I can't think of anyone that I've pissed off enough to warrant murder. So, my problems have doubled. There is the thus far successful grand theft and the failed felony murder. The timing suggests that this is not likely to be a coincidence. And applying Occam's Razor, the simplest and most logical conclusion is that they are two parts of the same, bigger problem.*

He stepped over the crushed guard rail and started hiking back toward Boulder Creek. *Presuming that I am being targeted, going home is a bad idea. It would put Gloria and the children at risk.* For the first part of his march, his shoes squished. Eventually, they were quiet. He kept clear of the road and whenever he saw on-coming headlights, he took advantage of whatever off-road cover he could find. Although the idea of hitchhiking was tempting, he reckoned that it would raise the risk to an unacceptable level. He set a brisk pace, burning off the adrenalin that had surged during the "accident". Meanwhile, his mind was busy with what the next few days might have in store. *Someone is certain to report the damaged guard rail. This will lead authorities to discover the car and they will pull it out of the mud onto solid ground. With no drowned-driver inside, they will drag the pond on Monday looking for the body. When they do not find it, they will pay closer attention to the cut seat belts, the punctured airbags and the destroyed driver's window. Then they will find the hunting knife and the hammer and conclude that the driver made a miraculous escape. So, it will probably be Tuesday before they truly begin to search for me. However, unless I warn Gloria, she will most likely report me missing tomorrow. Then my colleagues at B, H, & G will reasonably do the same thing on Monday. But, right now, I need a secure place to sleep and a quiet place to do some planning.*

Eventually, he reached the cluster of motels around the entrance to the Interstate. He chose the cheapest of the lot, figuring that they would ask the fewest questions about his disheveled appearance. This motel would easily qualify as a flea bag. He suspected that more of their rooms rented by the hour than by the night. The night clerk, in his haste to return to his Internet porn, did not give him a second look. He registered using his Master Card for payment. It was still safe to use it for it would be at least Monday before anyone tried to trace him through his credit charges. He picked up a day-old newspaper from the table in the lobby.

Once in his room, he locked the deadbolt, put the security chain in place, and, for good measure, moved a stiff-backed chair over to the door, angling it so that the top of the back was wedged under the door handle. He was not in the mood for visitors. He drew the drapes, noting that, no matter how hard he tried, it was impossible to get them to close completely. In his travels, he had never found a hotel or motel where they closed properly. He lit the desk lamp.

He stank of the retention pond, rotting vegetation, perspiration, and naked fear. He stripped off his damp clothes, took a hot shower, and shampooed his hair. Next, he emptied the contents of his pockets onto the desk. Then he hung the clothes on hangers, put them in the bathroom, turned on the overhead infrared heater, and closed the door. His shoes he stuffed with the newspaper. Among his items on the desk was the thin leather folder that had been in his inside jacket pocket. He opened it and removed the contents, spreading them on the desk blotter to dry. There were five Benjamins, one William, and one Grover — two thousand dollars, his entire personal emergency fund. He never travelled without it. This money made the pittance he carried in his pants pockets seem trivial. Once it became unsafe to use his credit card, this would be all he had. From habit, he covered his stash with a dry hand towel from the bathroom. It was his practice never to leave substantial amounts of money lying around for others to see and be tempted. Never mind that he was not going to admit anyone to his room. Further, even if his attackers found his room and gained entry, they would be more interested in taking his life rather than his money.

The motel room provided only the bare necessities beyond cover and concealment. He missed the amenities of home. No night-cap to calm his nerves, no clean pajamas, no silk sheets, and no warm wife to cozy up next to. Naked, he crawled into bed under the two rough woolen blankets. Exhausted though his body was, his mind was wired and would not let go and relax. It insisted on reviewing the major events of his day. When the scene of his escape from the sinking car played out again on the inside of his eyelids, he realized just how very lucky he had been. But, it had not been all luck. He remembered a time, just before he bought the Lincoln, when he had spent a Saturday afternoon in an automobile junkyard, testing a variety of hammers on car windows to find which one was the most effective demolition tool. His friends thought him unhinged and more than a bit paranoid. However, he was just being thorough, preparing for the worst while hoping that it never arrived. *A little paranoia can go a long way to prolonging one 's life.*

   With that thought, he smiled and, exhausted, fell into a deep, but troubled, sleep.

Chapter 2

Boyd, Hunter, & Gould - I

T he founder and patriarch of the firm of Boyd, Hunter, and Gould, is Harold M. Boyd. He was born 8 March 1933 in Lincoln, Nebraska. He majored in Economics at the University of Nebraska and earned his B.S. in 1951. His Law Degree was from Columbia University in 1954. His initial professional employment was with the firm of George Graham Investment Advisors. The choice was an unfortunate one. Mr. Graham was already at an advanced age. A few years after Harold joined the firm, Graham decided to retire and, rather than turn his business over to his colleagues, he chose, instead, to liquidate the firm. Harold had learned a great deal during his time with Graham, yet it seemed like a failure when he had to begin all over again. He resolved that, when he had a firm of his own, he would take better care of his associates.

In 1955, Harold married Susan Andrews. Unfortunately, they never had any children. When both his father and his father-in-law died early, he and Susan took in both widows. There were two wings off the main house, one north and one south. Harold converted one into a suite for his mother; the other into a suite for his mother-in-law. Shrewdly, he kept the two ladies as far apart as possible, although the family often ate dinner together.

Harold was born a Presbyterian, spent time as an agnostic, and ultimately became a born-again Christian. He practiced his faith in his business, in his marriage, and in his family life. He was not ostentatious about it. He simply tried to live his faith. To an outside observer, he could be a study in contradictions. He became a very wealthy man, yet personally he remained quite frugal. He considered himself to be a good, practicing Christian, yet he could be unbending and unforgiving toward the wayward.

In his maturity, he had many opportunities to reflect on his early treatment at the hands of George Graham. With the passage of time, he mellowed, and his view softened. Being put out into the harsh atmosphere of the financial world had forced him to become more self-reliant. The lessons learned with Graham served him well and, in time, he formed his own firm. Ultimately, he came to realize that Graham had actually done him a favor. It was tough love, but it worked. He did not believe so at the time but being forced to fend for himself was the best thing that could have happened to him. He resolved that, when the time came, he would pass this favor onto his associates.

Despite his advanced years and a bout with prostate cancer, he still puts in a full work week. He might be slow of foot, but his mind is still quick and agile. His senior partners are more than ready for him to retire from the scene. However, there is no sign that this will be happening any time soon. There was much left to teach them, and he was still having too much fun.

The senior partners were two in number: Stephen Hunter and Jeffrey Gould. Harold had hand-picked them, and without advertising it, he had personally guided their advanced education.

They were his surrogate sons and he was preparing them for their independent careers, when he would no longer be there to prop them up.

Stephen Hunter was born 10 January 1958 in Seattle, Washington. His undergraduate degree in Economics was from Gonzaga University. He earned the Ph.D. in Finance from the University of Washington. Harold recruited him fresh out of graduate school. Stephen began working as a market analyst and then advanced to portfolio advisor, junior account executive, and then senior partner. While he appreciated everything that Harold had done for him, he was chaffing at the bit. He knew that he was ready to lead the firm. It was what he was born to do.

By nature, Stephen is an aggressive competitor who is extremely protective of his possessions, and that includes his family. Under pressure, he can appear distant and withdrawn. However, adversaries would be well-advised not to underestimate his focus and concentration. He likes winning and he has grown quite used to it, to the point that he expects it to happen every time.

He married Jennifer Allen in 1991. They have three children: Susan Adele (1993), John Howard (1996), and Andrew Peter (1999). Now that the children are adults, Jennifer has filed for divorce. The reason specified was the generic "Irreconcilable Differences". There are early signs that the proceedings will be contentious.

The other senior partner is Jeffrey Gould. He was born on 5 August 1955, in Bridgetown, on Barbados in the West Indies. He studied Economics and Finance at the Cave Hill Campus of the University of the West Indies. Then he went to Great Britain to study at the London School of Economics. It was there that Harold discovered him and persuaded him to emigrate to the United States and to

Harrison. Jeffrey became a Certified Financial Planner and rose through the ranks to his present position.

Jeffrey married early and impetuously. Different people marry for different reasons. The reasons are many, the spectrum is wide. With some, the driving force is lust. For others, it may be to produce an heir, for financial security, companionship, social status, power, protection, relief from an untenable situation, tradition, and even, in some cases, for love. Both Jeffrey and his first wife were immature, and the union did not last. In time, they had it officially annulled. His second marriage was to Eve Verona and this shows every sign of being permanent, and, for that, their six children are truly grateful.

Whereas Stephen is the more combative, Jeffrey is the more cerebral. He has initiative and imagination. Many of the new programs at B, H, and G were his creations. He championed the simple and commonsense approaches to investing that have become the firm's hallmark. Together, the two balance each other and, watching on the sidelines, Harold congratulates himself on his inspired choices.

It was Harold, himself, who had drawn up the partnership agreements. There were heavy emphases on company loyalty, high moral standards, and the ethical treatment of clients. However, buried in the mind-numbing pages of fine print and footnotes, there was a provision that said, in effect, that there was a limit to the partnership. Specifically, the firm remained the exclusive property of the founding partner and was forever his to do with as he pleased. Hunter and Gould had been so pleased with being named partners that they did not bother to read the fine print. When they find out, if they ever do, it will be too late.

Harold was always on the lookout for new talent. It was time for him to mentor another generation of surrogate sons. When Arnie P. King walked through the front door, looking for a job, Harold couldn't believe his good fortune.

King was born in Wampum, Pennsylvania, on 21 Jun 1973, he was the only child of William and Stella King. He received his B.S. degree in Finance from LaFayette College in Easton, Pennsylvania. His MBA was earned at The Wharton School. In 1998, he joined Boyd, Hunter, and Gould and rose through the ranks to become a junior account executive in record time. His performance reviews have all been excellent. With such early success, he was anointed as God's gift to Finance. It was predicted that he was on fast track to become a senior account executive. Many expect that, in a short time, he will join Hunter and Gould as a named partner in the firm. While some bystanders applaud such success, there are others for whom it breeds jealousy and resentment.

In 1997, Arnie married the former Gloria Hearney. They have two sons, Kurt (1999) and Bradley (2004). While the marriage appears to be a stable one, there was a rough patch in 2002. There was professional counseling, both individual and as a couple, and a trial separation of almost a year. The Kings appear to have weathered the storm and the marital waters now seem to be calm.

Personally, Arnie is an acquired taste. Some regard his risk adversity as tantamount to paranoia. Some are put off by his almost encyclopedic knowledge of his world of Finance, and his tendency to flaunt it with little provocation. Some claim, mistakenly, that he has no sense of humor. In fact, he does possess one, but it is well-hidden, quirky, and shared by only a few others. When he is deficient in social graces, his wife usually manages to step in and cover for him smoothly.

Shortly after King was promoted to junior account executive, Hunter met with Gould in the latter's office.

"Jeff, how did your meeting with Uncle Harold go?" In private, Hunter amused himself by referring to Boyd as if he was a member of the family. He was careful not to do it to his face. "Any luck in persuading him that he ought to do the honorable thing and put in his retirement papers?"

Gould gave a snort. "Dream on, my friend! He won't even consider it. He says that golf, tennis, and shuffleboard would drive him crazy. He's having too much fun doing what he's doing. I 'm beginning to believe that, deep down, he's afraid that this place wouldn't survive without him."

"It's hubris, pure and simple. We'll have to work around him. Have you heard anything further from Merrill Lynch about our merger proposal?" Hunter kept his voice low. Uncle Harold did not know what they were up to, and they wanted to keep it that way for as long as possible.

"Not a word," Gould replied. "One possibility is that their decision-making process is more cumbersome that I believed. Another is that they want us to sweat so that we will make some further concessions, sweeten the pot as it were."

"No more concessions. The three of us go in as full partners and then Uncle Harold is made Chairman emeritus and pensioned off. Take it or leave it. There are other investment firms out there who'd be happy to have us."

Gould was still troubled. "What about our young golden boy? Does King get to be a full partner also?" He knew the likely answer, but he enjoyed provoking his colleague every now and then.

"Hell no!" was Hunter's immediate response. "That guy's a weirdo and still wet behind the ears. If, and when, he grows up, he might be partner-material in some firm but, please God, not mine. He is one strange dude. He creeps me out. I wish that there was a delete button I could push that would make him disappear permanently."

Gould smiled. He, too, found King a bit eccentric but he didn't feel as strongly about it as Hunter did. Since Boyd fancied himself as the father figure, perhaps this was what sibling rivalry looked like. It made him thankful that he had been an only child.

Chapter 3

King's Confidante

The sun streaming through the gap in the drapes woke King the following morning. Momentarily, his strange surroundings confused him. Then the events of yesterday came flooding back into his consciousness. So, it had not been just a bad dream after all. What a pity!

He took care of the morning call of nature and examined his clothes from yesterday. Not only were they dirty but they were cut and torn beyond repair. The shoes had stiffened considerably and would be uncomfortable. Nevertheless, these clothes were all he had, so he put them on. Their date with the landfill would have to wait yet awhile.

The leather folder with his emergency funds went back into the zippered pocket in his jacket. The petty cash and credit cards went back into his pants' pockets. He left the room and stood for a moment just in front of the door while he surveyed closely his surroundings. He would not have recognized his assailants even if they were right in front of him. But, he saw no one paying any special attention to him. He locked the door, even though there was nothing left in the room worth stealing. He was a creature of habit.

He had not eaten since mid-day yesterday and he was hungry. In the next block was Al and Jim's diner. It looked unpromising, but it was handy and would meet his basic needs. The structure was in good repair and was not showing its age. Inside, it was scrupulously clean. The aromas wafting from the grill were seductive and got his gastric juices flowing. Frying pork fat has a perfume all its own. Slipping into a booth, he ordered juice, scrambled eggs with link sausage, a side-order of buttermilk pancakes, and coffee.

While he was waiting for his order to come up, he used the telephone in the rear to call Gloria. His cell phone had gone down with the car and was still there, completely useless unless the fish were more technologically advanced than they were given credit for. Gloria answered on the second ring. *She must have been waiting by the phone.* He gave her the executive summary, that he had been in an automobile accident and that the car was a total loss. He assured her that he was unharmed. She was overflowing with questions but, he cut her off and ordered her to be quiet and just listen. Then he told her that it was dangerous for her to stay where she was, and that time was critical. It was a matter of life and death. She was to take the children and go immediately to visit her mother. She was to tell no one about the trip. He would join her in a few days and then he would explain everything. She started to argue, as he knew she would, so he hung up and went back to his table.

Breakfast was very satisfying. He left not a scrap. The diner was a pleasant surprise. The food was good and the coffee even better. His opinion of diners went up several notches. Lingering over coffee, he examined his immediate needs. First, I must replace these clothes. *Next, I need to find someone who can help me with my problem. Then, I will need to arrange for transportation.* He returned to the telephone where he discovered a telephone book. This was more shock than surprise. He would have bet that these things had disappeared into the rubbish heap of History along with spats, doctors who made house calls, wrist watches that you wound every day, and automobile running boards. In the book, he found what he was looking for, a Goodwill retail outlet in Boulder Creek. There he should be able to upgrade his wardrobe without attracting undue attention or draining his cash reserve.

He paid his tab and added an above average tip. There was a city bus route that ran close to the retail store and he took it. He might have summoned a taxi, but he reasoned that this would burn up his petty cash too fast. There was no way to tell how long he would have to make it last. The other problem with the taxi was that it would involve adding another person to the equation, someone who, if questioned later, might remember him.

At the thrift store, he bought a pair of hiking boots, two pairs of sweat socks, a pair of jeans, a sweat shirt, and two sets of underwear. After he put on his new duds and transferred his possession from the pockets of the ruined suit, he consigned his old clothes to the garbage with a pang of remorse. They had been expensive, comfortable, and were symbolic of his former life, a life that he felt slipping from his grasp and one that he might never recover.

He returned to the diner, which had become his temporary headquarters. Over more coffee, he worked on his second problem. *I need someone who is above reproach, someone who will treat my problem with complete discretion, someone who is legally astute, and someone who will take my strange story seriously.* He ran down his list of friends, relatives, and associates disqualifying each on at least one, and some on several, of the criteria. Then he came to Carleton Dunn. Dunn was a lawyer, a partner in the firm of Gray, Arnold, and Young. King and Dunn belonged to the same country club. They had become frequent golfing partners, found that they had similar interests, and started to build a friendship. *This being Saturday, Carl is probably at the club. By now, he has finished his morning round of golf, and is relaxing in the grill.*

As often as he had telephoned the club, he knew the number by heart. The front desk put him through to the grill and soon he was talking with Carl. He told the lawyer that he found himself in a serious bind and wanted to hire Dunn to represent him. He refused to go into details over the telephone and, since he was without a car, he asked Dunn to pick him up. He provided the location.

Dunn didn't need another client. He was already quite busy, preparing to argue a case before the State Supreme Court. But he liked King and was intrigued by the little he had heard. He told Arnie that he would meet him at two that afternoon.

With problem two a work in progress, Arnie moved on to the third one. *I could rent a car. I still have my driver's license, although it is a little soggy. However, that transaction would leave a credit card footprint, something I am trying to avoid. While public transportation works, it doesn't go everywhere that I may need to go. Besides, their schedule may not always match mine. I could try to borrow a car from one of my friends but, once again, this widens the circle of those who know that I survived the retention pond. Such knowledge could put them at risk. I can't allow that.*

When no solution was forthcoming, he ordered a piece of peach pie and another refill on his coffee. It was said that some people did their best thinking while in the shower, or while shaving. With Arnie, his best ideas came while he was eating. Unfortunately, today even that approach was not working.

Just before two, Dunn came through the diner's doors. Arnie flagged him down and got up to greet him. The lawyer was still dressed for a casual day of golf. Arnie resumed his seat and gestured for his friend to sit across from him in the booth.

"Would you like something to eat? The pie is actually quite good, and the coffee is even better." He wondered what circumstances prompted Carl's best ideas.

Carl had not set foot in a diner since his freshman year in high school. That experience had been memorable but not in a positive sense. Food poisoning rarely is. The encounter still lurked in a dark corner of his memory. "Thanks, but no! I had lunch at the club. Now what's this all about? What couldn't you tell me on the telephone?"

Arnie sighed and began the full account, leaving nothing out. He started with a description of his responsibilities at Boyd, Hunter, and Gould. Then he reported his discovery that significant funds had disappeared from each of the portfolios that he managed. The withdrawals were unauthorized. An attempt to trace the missing money, revealed that it had disappeared into a collection of off-shore banks and holding companies.

At this point, Dunn interrupted him. "Just how much money has gone missing?" It was a fair question. He was not going to become involved over chump change. There were many other lawyers in town who could handle that.

"In all, it was eight million dollars, spread over a dozen accounts." Arnie was mortified at the amount almost as much as he was that it had happened on his watch.

That is not chump change by anybody's definition. "Impressive! Now, I mean no disrespect, but my profession obliges me to ask. Did you take the money?" With some clients, you don't want to know if they are guilty or innocent. With others, such as the present situation, it was well to find out at the beginning if you could. Even so, he had learned early on that not all clients gave truthful answers, even to their lawyers. Consequently, he had developed his own bull-shit meter.

Arnie placed his left hand on the menu and raised his right hand. "Carl, I swear to God that I didn't take that money. Neither was I complicit in its disappearance." He put on the most honest expression he could muster.

This left Carl with the question: could he believe Arnie when he was swearing to God on a menu in a diner? In the time that they had known each other, Carl had found Arnie to be scrupulously honest. He wouldn't even cheat at golf. *Very few of my playing partners could truthfully make that claim.*

"I believe you!" Carl replied. "Who else had access to these accounts?"

"They're stored on the firm's server. They're encrypted, and each account has its own password, one that changes every week. These passwords and my login ID are known in-house only to myself my supervisor, Nick Gestas, and the three named partners: Jeff Gould, Steve Hunter, and Harold Boyd. I doubt seriously that an outside hacker could get into our system. But if someone did, I don't know how we could determine the level of penetration." Arnie was getting indigestion just recounting what had happened.

Carl did nothing to ease Arnie's discomfort. "My experience tells me that hackers are getting more skillful every day. I wouldn't dismiss that possibility out of hand." The aroma from Arnie's coffee was beginning to get to him. Perhaps he would risk it. He signaled the waitress to bring him a cup. "What I don't understand is this: why would someone go to all the trouble to break into your accounts and then only take a small fraction of the money available? Why not drain them completely? It's what I would have done." One of his operating principles was: Never steal anything small.

"Perhaps the money was not the purpose of the attack." It was a possibility that Arnie had been picking at, like a scab on a healing wound. "Suppose it was somebody out to ruin me."

"Now, don't you go getting all paranoid on me! This could merely be a crime of opportunity and nothing personal." Carl knew that he had to keep Arnie focused if he was going to be of any use as a resource. "Have you reported this loss to your supervisor, Gestas?"

Arnie shook his head. "Not yet! But I can predict what'll happen when I do. He'll fire me on the spot, call the police to arrest me, and then sue me for the missing money. Even though the accounts are insured, Nick isn't the forgiving type. He'd make an example of me to discourage anyone else who might have similar ideas. I need to find that money and whoever took it. Will you help me?"

"I'll do what I can. I've a couple of very talented young associates who're specialists in cybercrime. They may be of some help." He tasted his coffee. It passed muster. "As for me, I can't take you on as a client. My plate is full. I'm going to be tied up with a major case down in the capitol. If you like, I can check with my associates and have one of them contact you." He drained his coffee. It was obvious that he was preparing to take his leave.

Arnie saw his only source of help getting ready to desert him. He was on the verge of a panic attack. "But, you can't leave yet. You've only heard half of the story." His voice was plaintive, almost begging.

The lawyer fixed him with a skeptical look. "There's another half? What've you been holding back?" He considered the possibility that this was just a ploy to keep him from leaving. *Was Arnie that hard up for male companionship?* Yet he recognized that there were other unanswered questions. *What is Arnie doing in this seedy neighborhood on a Saturday afternoon? Why is he unshaven and disheveled? Why the garb? He looks like a vagrant-in-training.* He sat back down and signaled for a refill on the coffee.

"I worked late last night trying to track the missing money. It was after midnight when I headed the car for home. I never made it. As I was approaching that retention pond about a mile west of here, two cars came out of nowhere and boxed me in. Then a Ford F-150 truck overtook me and deliberately ran me off the road. My car went over the guardrail and into the pond. It took on water and began to sink. I was able to extricate myself from the airbags and the shoulder harness. I broke the driver's-side window and managed to get out of the car. When I reached the surface, I swam to the opposite side of the pond. From that vantage point, I watched as the three vehicles returned and the three men began to search for me. When they were unsuccessful, after a few minutes, they left. Then, I walked back and checked into a flea-bag motel not far from here. This morning, I visited a Goodwill store and bought these duds. Yesterday's clothes were unsalvageable and went into the trash."

Carl sat there in stunned disbelief. "An F-150? Really?"

"God's honest truth! They were trying to kill me. Damn near succeeded, too."

"Your story is so incredible, that it has to be true. Nobody could invent anything so bizarre. That being so, you have every right to be paranoid. Have you made a police report?"

"No, and I'm in no hurry to do so. At this moment, whoever it is who wants me dead is uncertain whether they were successful. I like it that way. It's one of the few advantages I have. When the police drag the pond on Monday and don't find my body, my attackers will know that they failed. Then they'll search for me, intent on making a second try. I may not be so lucky next time."

Carl nodded in agreement. "So, you think that the theft and the attempt on your life are related?" He was not above asking seemingly dumb questions. Sometimes you can learn a great deal from the responses.

"Don't you? What a long coincidence it would be for those two things to occur in the same week and be unrelated! And, I don't believe in coincidence. So, yes, I'm convinced that somebody is trying to paint me as an embezzler, while at the same time attempting to kill me, making it look like an accident. Will you help me?" His plea was approaching pathos.

Since Arnie had not yet been charged with a crime, there is no risk for me in helping him. True, he did leave the scene of an accident and has not yet made a police report. However, the incident he described to me would be traumatic and could easily induce temporary amnesia. What Arnie needed right now was someone who would watch over him and keep him alive. "Yes, I will help you. What is it you want me to do?"

"My highest priority is for a safe place to stay while I figure out who is behind this attack. My present accommodations leave much to be desired. Then, I will want a set of wheels. The bus service limits me and walking slows me down."

Dunn realized that he needed to come up with a Lifeguard and fast. Immediately, he ruled out his legal colleagues, as well as his own staff. The former only thought in terms of billable hours while the latter were already seriously overworked. Then, he had an epiphany. Who better than an inoffensive History professor at the local university? They had both been members of a small, secret, civic organization, The Tribunes of Harrison. When Carl became a partner in his firm, his public profile became sufficiently large that he couldn't continue as an active member of the Tribunes. But, he remained in touch and, on occasion, when he could do so unobtrusively, he did them small favors.

Carl fished out his cell phone and punched in the numbers. Arnie fought down a surge of jealousy. He had become quite addicted to his own cell phone, and without it, he was experiencing withdrawal symptoms. Carl's call was answered on the fourth ring.

"Oscar, its Carl. I need you to undertake a corporal work of mercy. What's your schedule like?

The response must have been favorable for Carl continued, "I don't feel comfortable explaining the matter on the telephone. Are you at home? Can my friend and I come over right now?"

Again, there was a pause while Oscar answered the questions. "Good! We'll see you in about thirty minutes."

Carl tucked a five-dollar bill under his saucer. Then he slid out of the booth and stood up. Looking down at Arnie, he said, "C'mon, let's take a ride!"

As Arnie got up from his seat, Carl's choice of words made him smile. *It is truly a rare occasion indeed when a lawyer announces in advance to his client that he is going to take him for a ride.*

Chapter 4

The Banned

Barry Marsh had been a top tier Formula One professional race car driver until a catastrophic pile-up ended his career. In fifteen seconds, thirteen finely-tuned cars were transformed into a pile of twisted steel and burning tires. Marsh was dragged from the carnage still alive but with life-threatening injuries. Several of his colleagues were not so fortunate. In time, he recovered from his injuries but not to the point where he would ever be able to pass the physical for serious racing. The major problem was that, at odd intervals, with little warning, he would black out. If it happened while he was at home sitting in his easy chair, watching television, no harm was done. But the possibility that it might happen while he was on the track, in a tightly-bunched group of racers, all travelling inches apart at 190 mph, was unacceptable to the insurers.

He had made no provision for a life after racing. Driving was his one marketable skill. And, he missed the smell of burning fuel, the sound of the crowd, the camaraderie of his fellow drivers, and especially the adrenalin high of high speed racing. Moreover, the loss of his livelihood left him in a financial bind. He had a wife, two ex-wives, three mistresses, and a serious gambling habit to support. His bookie, Guido, was not noted for an abundance of patience or Christian charity. Marsh needed a new source of income and quickly.

Curiously, it was Guido who showed him a way out of his dilemma. In certain circles, there was always a need for a good wheel man, someone who did not have a scrupulous conscience about who his employer was and what he had to do to earn his money. At that moment, Marsh could not afford a conscience, scrupulous or otherwise. Guido provided introductions and soon Barry was driving for Doctor Rosario, one of the local consiglieri. Not only did this put a little more money in his pocket but also it persuaded Guido to ease up on the pressure.

In his new position, Marsh was privy to information that more law-abiding civilians never hear. Through this grapevine, he learned that an anonymous figure, known only as the Moneyman, had a job available that required a skillful driver.

The stipend was substantial, and Barry applied for the job. Given his credentials, he was hired. This opportunity for moonlighting had the Doctor's blessing. In fact, Rosario contacted the Moneyman and told him that, by allowing Marsh to freelance, he was doing him a favor. This favor was an investment and not without strings. The Moneyman was made to understand that a favor granted is a debt incurred. At some future date, a return favor would be demanded. Failure to repay such a debt was not conducive to a long and healthy life.

Barry and the Moneyman never met face-to-face. Communication was by telephone, a burner phone that was provided. The job was to intercept a certain Lincoln town car on a given night, west of Boulder Creek, and force the vehicle off the road and into a pond. Made explicit was that the intent of this contrived accident was to drown the driver of the Lincoln. The stipend for this job was ten thousand dollars. The choreography of this "accident" was well within Marsh's skill set. However, to do it properly, he would need two assistants.

Thus, it was that Marsh found himself in The Checkered Flag, a bar just a few blocks from the local raceway. As he knew he would, there he found two racing groupies who were down on their luck and were trying to drown their sorrows.

One was Hyrum Cassidy. He was a former Assistant Professor of Ethics at Harrison Community College. Hyrum's academic career was abruptly cut short when it was discovered, and publicized, that he had a penchant for underage young men. While the College declined to prosecute because of the unfavorable publicity it would generate, they held closed hearings and then dismissed him from the faculty. Further, they made it abundantly clear that they would do everything in their power to make certain that he never again held an academic appointment anywhere, at any level. Hyrum's next employment was as a truck driver, delivering baked goods for a national chain to the local supermarkets. In his free time, he volunteered as a cub scout leader.

The other was Enoch Harris. Enoch once had a promising career as a baseball shortstop. He had worked his way up to triple A and was a prime candidate to be added to the major-league roster of the Harrison Harlequins. That promise crumbled to dust when it was discovered that he had a gambling addiction. This was regarded as a serious behavioral problem. It was made worse when it was revealed that he bet on baseball games. Then it was disclosed that he bet on his own team's games. The final blow was that most of his bets were against his team. He was dismissed from the team and barred from any future involvement with organized baseball. Management knew that it should have detected and dealt with the problem much sooner. To save themselves further embarrassment, they resolved the problem privately and quietly. Enoch received a lump sum buy-out in exchange for agreeing not to contest the termination and never to talk on record about the circumstances. Coincidently, the amount of the buy-out was equal to the amount that was needed to pay off in full his gambling debts. When sportswriters enquired about Enoch's disappearance, it was suggested that he had blown out both of his knees thus tragically ending his promising athletic career. In need of new employment, Harris acted on the suggestion of his brother-in-law and enrolled in a training program that Sutton Security Systems conducted for prospective drivers.

During several rounds of drinks, they brought each other up to date on recent activities. It was Hyrum who observed that they now had in common life-time sentences exiling them from their former careers. He suggested that since they were now all in the same boat, they should organize themselves into a mutual support group. "We're now all charter members of The Banned."

Barry then proposed the first official activity of the group. He explained the nature of the commission. He promised them each a thousand dollars for their participation. No one objected to the destruction of a Lincoln Town Car. There were many more where that one came from. Barry choreographed the action for them so that they each knew their role. Then, he took them out to Boulder Creek and the retention pond so that they could familiarize themselves with the venue. Hyrum and Enoch each got to practice their segment of the action with unsuspecting passing traffic.

Originally, Barry intended to use a stolen Hummer for his vehicle. But then, Enoch pointed out that his night supervisor drove a Ford F-150 and parked it in the back lot. It would be easy enough for Barry to borrow it for the evening. Barry liked the idea of the extra weight. It would make his work that much easier.

On the designated Friday night, they executed the plan flawlessly. However, when the Lincoln was retrieved, and the pond searched the following Monday and Tuesday, no body was found. The mission had failed. The Moneyman did not reward failure. To be paid, The Banned would have to locate the driver and complete the assignment. The Moneyman provided a picture of King and some of his personal information.

With what they knew, they located King's house and staked it out. The house was empty. King never showed. But then, they were several days late in starting their search. They split up and started canvassing the neighbors, looking for their old friends, the Kings. All they learned was that, the previous Saturday morning, Mrs. King had packed the two boys into the car and departed in some haste. No one knew her destination.

Hyrum stayed with the house in Nailor in case Mrs. King's flight was a clever diversion to cover King's return. Barry and

Enoch went back to Boulder Creek and began visiting the local motels, looking for King's trail. In time, they found the motel where King had stayed but it had only been for one night. He was long gone. They checked with nearby businesses and eventually reached Al & Jim's Diner. The staff had a vague recollection of a seedy-looking derelict who had camped out in their diner for an entire Saturday morning and the early part of the afternoon. They remembered that another man, dressed like a golfer, had come to meet with the derelict. They left together, never to return. Nobody had bothered to check what kind of car the golfer was driving.

There the trail ended. Barry made his progress report to the Moneyman and had to admit failure. With no corpse, there was no payday. Barry was not satisfied with this outcome. He protested that he, and his associates, had done their part, and done it well. They deserved to be compensated. It was not their fault that the Moneyman had underestimated King's resourcefulness. Given that there was some merit to this argument, the Moneyman made a counter offer. When King was finally located, Barry would be given the opportunity to complete the original assignment, being careful to make it appear to be just another tragic accident.

Barry resumed his regular duties with the consigliere who was the only one to come out ahead on this deal. The Moneyman now owed him a favor.

However, Barry was a man of action and waiting was not something he did well. He noted the return of the King family from their impromptu vacation. There was still no sign of the head of the household. Then, in his free time, Barry began to shadow Gloria King to learn the pattern of her routine activities. Gradually, he assembled a remarkably detailed profile. He was looking for a plausible way to approach her and make her acquaintance. His plan was to insinuate himself into her life so that, when Mr. King reappeared, Barry Marsh would be on hand to welcome him, complete the mission, and collect his stipend.

He decided that Church would be the best venue. Gloria was a regular at St. Tibor Catholic Church in Nailor. She favored the 10:00 am Mass on Sunday. Now, he did too. As often as possible, he arranged to sit in the pew in front of her, or the one immediately behind. They regularly shook hands in response to the prompt to share the peace of Christ. He became a repetitive and familiar figure. Then, one Sunday, he purposely fumbled the exchange with her of the collection basket. Bills, coins, and envelopes cascaded to the pew and then to the floor. They both were embarrassed and made haste to gather up the offerings and return them to the basket.

Gloria whispered an apology. "I'm so sorry. It was clumsy of me. Please forgive me."

He whispered his reply. "No. It was my fault entirely. Besides, forgiveness is not mine to grant." He nodded his head toward the altar.

"You're being too gallant. I'm such a klutz. It's embarrassing." She was still whispering while she madly tried to rescue the last of the collection.

"They say that the best cure for embarrassment is a cup of strong coffee. Shall we test this in the church social hall after the service? It's the least I can do." He favored her with his most sincere boyish smile.

He does have a nice smile and he seems harmless enough. Besides, I haven't had an intelligent adult to talk to since Arnie left. And the church social hall should be a safe place. With the usher bearing down on them, she did not get a chance to reply.

They were both clutching the refilled collection basket when the usher arrived to relieve them of it. The look he gave them was one usually reserved for child molesters and mass murderers. Without a word, he snatched the basket from their grasp, wheeled on his heel, and headed for the center aisle at flank speed.

At the exchange of the peace of Christ, Gloria and Barry shook hands and their eyes met. She whispered just one additional word, "Yes!"

Later, in the social hall, over coffee and Danish, they shared life stories. Barry had to edit his account considerably to avoid spooking his new-found friend, who was obviously lonely. Before they parted company, they agreed to get together again the following Wednesday night for St. Tibor's Bingo Games.

Chapter 5

King's Lifeguard

Arnie and Carl exited the diner and crossed the street to Dunn's car. Arnie was disappointed to see that the car was a black, 2016 BMW 740i sedan.

"What? No Shark? I was looking forward to getting a ride in it." He voiced his displeasure. One of Carl's most prized possessions was an exact replica of the 1962 Shark Roadster Convertible that he had commissioned to be built.

Carl gave him a wry grin. "I only bring it out on special occasions. Forgive me for saying it but saving your ass doesn't qualify as one of those. Moreover, I wouldn't bring it into a seamy neighborhood like this even for the Pope himself."

They got on the Interstate and headed east toward Harrison. They passed on the northern edge of the city, crossed the Folsom Bridge over William's Bay, and approached the eastern suburbs. When the Interstate divided, they took the southern fork and exited at Haddam Road. They followed Haddam to Chancellor and then turned west.

During the trip, Arnie quizzed Carl about Oscar. "Who is this guy?"

"To begin with, Oscar is not his real name. Legally, he is Fingal O'Flahertie. A few close, personal friends call him Oscar. I suggest that you don't call him that until you get to know him well. Oscar is a tenured Professor in the History Department at Thornton University. He and I go back a long way. We have worked together successfully on numerous civic projects." He was understandably reluctant to go into detail on any of these projects. The Tribunes worked in secret, sometimes walking the fine line between what is legal and what is not. There was no need for Arnie to know any of this.

"Can he be trusted?"

Carl answered with an ironic laugh. It was late in the game, but Arnie was finally beginning to ask the questions that he should have asked years before. "Put your mind at ease. I trust him with my life. In time, you may learn to do the same." Arnie was not yet convinced. "What is it that you expect he will be able to do for me?"

"In the short term, you are looking for sanctuary and the loan of a set of wheels. Oscar will be able to provide both." Oscar had not yet been consulted but Carl was depending on what he knew of the man's skill at improvising. "Longer term, you'll need a network of collaborators. Oscar can be a valuable resource."

Arnie became quiet and pensive. *I'm a little long in tooth for blind dates, but I really don't have a choice.* He busied himself with monitoring the passing traffic. He was on the look-out for any sign of an F-150. There had been none thus far, a fact that cheered him a little bit.

They were approaching Thornton University when Carl turned left into Alethian Heights. Two short streets later, he made another left and pulled into the driveway of an attractive two-story Georgian-style home. The house was only a quarter of a mile from the edge of campus, within easy walking distance. Before he had married, Oscar had lived even closer to his workplace.

Oscar met them at the door and asked them in. He introduced his guests to his wife, Connie. He saw no reason to reveal that Constance was formerly Sister Mary Margarethe, S.S.S. Then he invited his guests to join in the happy hour already in progress. He poured Prosecco for everyone and passed around the cheese tray.

Taking note of Carl's garb, Oscar asked him, "Councilor, how goes your golf game?" For years, Carl had been a scratch golfer. But now, with age had come several frustrating physical problems, tendonitis in his right shoulder and a deteriorating rotator cuff in the left. His scores were trending upward, and it did not sit well with him.

"Don't ask!" was the brusque advice.

Oscar took a sadistic delight in playfully needling Dunn. "Is it so bad that you take your swing coach with you wherever you go?" He gestured at Arnie.

The needle had the desired effect. "Don't play the fool with me, Oscar. I know you too well. Arnie is the reason for this visit. He needs our help."

"Ah, the corporal works of mercy." Oscar pretended to be confused. "I have fed the hungry and given drink to the thirsty. What more do you expect of me?" "First listen to his story. Then you can tell us what you can do." Carl was betting that Oscar would be drawn into the narrative.

Thus prompted, Arnie told his tale once more. His account of uncovering the theft from B, H, & G, and his near-death experience in the retention pond, was presented without omission or embellishment. His audience hung on his every word, even Carl, for whom it was repetition.

When he had finished, Connie was the first to comment. "You've been through a life-altering experience, one that most of us are spared. Since there are still people who are intent on killing you, it isn't over yet. We will help you. Won't we, dear." Without waiting for Oscar's agreement, she continued, "We have a guest bedroom and you are welcome to stay the night with us. Tomorrow, we shall work out something more long range."

Oscar nodded his agreement. "Tomorrow, we'll check you in at the Thornton Memorial Union. One wing of the Union is set up as the Union Club

Hotel. Routinely, the History Department has a few rooms reserved for putting up visiting speakers and candidates who are interviewing for a job. What better place to hide than in plain sight, in a crowd of twenty thousand students, faculty, and staff? You'll be our purloined letter. And no one will be looking for you on this side of town, particularly in an academic setting."

With Arnie's problems taken care of, at least for the moment, the conversation turned to other dilemmas: local, regional, and national politics and the local athletic teams both collegiate and professional. At some point, Arnie and Carl were told that they were expected to stay for dinner. It was not so much an invitation as a statement of a *fait accompli.*

Dinner began with a roasted garlic soup. The main course was a seafood fettuccine with scallops, mussels, and shrimp. A simple garden salad of mixed greens was the accompaniment. There was a seemingly endless supply of crusty Italian bread. With a 2008 Vigneti del Sole Pinot Grigio, it was a meal both simple and superb. Everyone toasted Connie's skill. She blushed modestly.

After dinner, Carl took his leave. Home was a long drive away. He reassured Arnie that he was leaving him in good hands. He promised that, in the morning, he would get a team of his cyber-crime people on the trail of the missing money. He promised that he would stay in touch, as much as his time permitted.

Oscar excused himself and retired to his study to make a few telephone calls.

Arnie and Connie watched some television, mainly reruns of episodes of "As Time Goes By" and "The Vicar of Dibley" on the public channel. *Why is it that the British can create such light comedy seemingly effortlessly?*

Connie could appreciate the humor in the Vicar somewhat more than Arnie did. She was quite familiar with the problems of female clergy. For twenty-five years, she had been a professed Catholic nun in the Order of St. Stephen, Stoned. When she realized that she and her Order were growing in opposite directions, she decided that, for the next twenty-five years, she wanted to do something different. She petitioned Rome and eventually was released from her vows. Oscar was a great help in easing her transition back into the secular life.

Oscar telephoned a contact that he had in the Sheriff's Department in Boulder Creek. He asked whether anyone had yet reported an accident at the retention pond, specifically a car going into the water. The answer was negative. He made it clear that he was not making such a report, but he expected that, before long, someone else would. He asked for, and got, the name and telephone number of the towing company that the Department used routinely for recovery work. Finally, he asked his contact for a favor. When the car was back on solid ground, have someone take a color picture of the outside of the car on the driver's side and send it to his smart phone. He was looking for paint transfer from the collision. It was not that he disbelieved Arnie's story. It was just strange enough to be true. But, it did no harm to verify. Moreover, this evidence could be useful in tracing the Ford F-150.

His work done, Oscar fixed himself a drink, a double shot of Jameson Black Barrel Irish whiskey, on the rocks. He sat at his desk and meditated on the strange events of the day: Carl's call and Arnie's story. He wondered momentarily if he and his wife might be guilty of harboring a fugitive. However, as far as they knew, Arnie had not yet been charged with a crime, so technically he was not a fugitive.

That thought opened some very old chapters in Oscar's memory, chapters that he would rather remain closed. Oscar was, himself, a fugitive. Under his birth name of Aristotle Tipper, bench warrants for his arrest still existed in the Northern Territory of Australia. As a wild youth, he had operated an illegal and highly lucrative marijuana business.

When the government closed his operation, he fled the country, never to return. Under the alias of Fingal O'Flahertie, he became a naturalized citizen of this country and an upstanding citizen. He earned advanced degrees and joined the professoriate. His youthful indiscretions were buried in a very deep hole. He was not proud of them and was careful to share the information with no one. Yet, his visitors had managed, however unwittingly, to summon these ghosts. Carl and Arnie could not have known. Although lawyers were known sometimes to uncover information that they were not intended to have.

And he savored the delicious confluence of events, he had to admit that one would not find a better tutor for a person about to become a fugitive than someone who had been a successful one for thirty-five years. Whoever were the gods who were directing this piece of theatre, they must be laughing their asses off.

As he drained the last of his drink, he reminded himself that if he was running the marijuana business today, it would be perfectly legal. His problem was that he had been years ahead of his time. He smiled as he rinsed the glass and put it in the drain tray. Then, he went up to bed.

When Arnie turned in that night, he felt comfortable and, for the moment, safe. He did not even wedge a chair back under the bedroom door handle. He went to sleep still wrestling with the problem of how he was going to prove that he had not taken the money.

Chapter 6

Boyd, Hunter, & Gould – II

It was Wednesday in the week following King's impromptu swim in the retention pond. As was traditional at B, H & G, every Wednesday morning, promptly at 9:00 am, there was a general staff meeting to assess developments, evaluate opportunities, analyze problems, and chart the firm's path. The Managing Partner, Harold Boyd, chaired the meeting. Stephen Hunter sat at his right hand and Jeffrey Gould on his left. They were Boyd's lieutenants. Nick Gestas sat further down the table and was eaten away by envy.

Staff attendance was compulsory. Missing one of these meetings without a pre-approved excuse was a sin that cried out to heaven for summary dismissal. From such dismissal, there was no appeal. In the early history of the firm there had been two instances of these dismissals. Word spread quickly that "compulsory" really did mean that you damned well better be there. After that, perfect attendance was the norm.

Precisely at the appointed hour, Boyd gaveled the meeting to order. The cursory attendance check revealed that King was absent. Boyd knew that King had not been at work either of the previous two days. It was Boyd's policy to cut his most productive managers a little slack on their work schedules. They did not have to punch a time clock. But, missing this meeting was going too far.

"Does anyone know where Mr. King is?" It was a question Boyd addressed to the whole group, rather than to any individual.

The assembled staff, well-aware that King had been absent for two days, answered with a deafening silence. The question made them uncomfortable and they fidgeted in their seats. Everyone avoided making eye-contact with the Chair.

"Very well then. Mr. Hunter, you'll check each of his accounts to make certain that they are in order. Mr. Gould, you'll contact his family, friends, and neighbors to try to find out what has become of our Mr. King. Both of you will report your results to me, personally, first thing tomorrow morning." Boyd was not one to allow this glitch to derail his meeting. "Moving on then, let's have the reports on the market trends and then the portfolio balances."

The meeting returned to its usual pattern. The further they got from the subject of Arnie King, the more relaxed people became. The elephant was still in the room, but it was getting progressively smaller by the minute.

After the meeting, as was their custom, Stephen and Jeff had lunch together at the Main Bar Sandwich Shop. Their assignments could wait until the afternoon. They were creatures of habit and each ordered a cup of split-pea soup and their favorite sandwich. For Stephen, it was the Balkan Express (Ham, turkey, swiss cheese, tomato, and shredded lettuce, with Thousand Island dressing on pumpernickel). For Jeff, it was the Aztec (rare roast beef, provolone cheese, tomato, and shredded lettuce, on a soft Kaiser roll with a creamy jalapeno sauce on the side). The sandwiches were piled high. Two draft Stellas completed the order.

"What do you think has happened to King?" Jeff asked. He knew that his colleague was always tuned in to all the latest news/gossip.

"I haven't a clue. But just this morning, one of the secretaries pontificated that jihadists had kidnapped him and were holding him for ransom. However, since there has been no ransom demand yet, it looks like these jihadists do not understand how the game is played." Stephen refused to take the issue seriously. "Since he's still quite immature, perhaps Arnie has run off to join the circus."

"Why is everything a joke with you? What if he has had a serious accident or experienced some medical emergency?" Jeff was more generous with gravitas.

"We have enough real things to worry about, without you inventing imaginary ones. If some misfortune had befallen him, we would've heard by now. Even if he has died, it would be a small loss to all except Uncle Harold, who dotes on him."

"Stephen, you have made no secret of your disdain for King. I must ask, did you have anything to do with his absence?"

"What? Are you out of your mind? Why would I do something like that?" Hunter was starting down the road toward righteous indignation.

Gould was persistent. "You still haven't answered the question."

"You're unbelievable. Of course, I had nothing to do with it. Shall we find a Bible for me to swear on?" Stephen was beginning to see, and exploit, the humor in the exchange.

After lunch, they wasted no time getting back to the office. Their assignments would keep them busy for the rest of the day. At nine o'clock the following morning, they were seated together in Boyd's office.

Hunter reported first. "I did a thorough audit on King's accounts. There are eight million dollars missing. Each of his accounts is light by about two-thirds of a million. Curiously, none of the accounts was drained. To prevent the thief from returning for a second-helping, I took the initiative of changing the account passwords. I tracked the missing money to a cluster of Caribbean banks. There the trail disappears. I think we have a problem."

Boyd's blood pressure was rising, approaching dangerous levels. "You think? There is no thinking about it. We DO have a very large problem. Jeff, have you located our Mr. King?"

Gould consulted his notebook. "At the King residence in Nailor, the phone goes directly to voice mail no matter how often, or at what time, I call. The neighbors report that Gloria and the two boys packed the car and left in a hurry last Saturday morning. No one I talked with knew their destination. I worked systematically through the list of Kings' relatives. Finally, I found that Gloria and the children were out-of-state, visiting her mother. Gloria claimed that Arnie was not with them and that she had not heard from him since the previous Friday evening, when he called her to say that he would be working late. It was my sense that she was not being entirely forthcoming. Finally, I checked with the local hospitals. For several days now, no one fitting Arnie's description has been brought in as a patient. It appears that our boy is in the wind."

Hunter volunteered his opinion. "The obvious explanation is that "our boy" is a thief and that he's on the run."

Gould chided him. "Sometimes the obvious turns out not to be true. I think that it's premature to convict and sentence him before we have heard his side of the story."

Boyd sensed that this was the start of another volley. He put a stop to it quickly. "Enough, you two!" *He, himself, was greatly conflicted. I treated him like my son. How could he do this to me? I hand-picked him. How is it that I didn't see his dark side? Am I getting too old for this game? Perhaps I should consider retiring. But, why would he do this? I pay him very well. If he needed money, he could have come to me. Could someone else have taken the money? There is always the possibility of an outside hacker. But, our firewalls are strong. Looking in-house, there are only five of us who have access to the passwords: King, myself, Hunter, Gould, and Gestas. I find it unbelievable that any of my colleagues would stoop this low.* "What action do you recommend?"

Gould spoke first. "The logical thing to do is to inform the police, the FBI, and the SEC that we have been robbed. We should find out how much of our losses are covered by insurance. Then, the authorities should issue a fugitive warrant for King. They are better equipped to find him than we are."

Hunter objected. "I disagree. Part of what we offer our clients is security. They know that their money is safe with us. They trust us. To go public with the news of this theft could ruin us. There would be a panic with people rushing to pull out their money and invest it somewhere else. We need to put a lid on this, keep it in-house."

Boyd rubbed his right index finger across the bridge of his nose. It was a mannerism that surfaced anytime he had a difficult decision to make. "Jeff, I must agree with Stephen on this. To make our problem public would likely ruin us. We can't afford to do that. I will not allow it. I have spent most of my life building this firm and I will not give it up without a fight. So, what must we do to keep a lid on this issue?"

"First, we need to invent a plausible story to explain King's absence. It's now common knowledge that he's not here. But, where is he?" Hunter fervently hoped that King was rotting in Hell, but he lacked the power to make this happen. "Could we say that he is on an extended leave?"

"We could, but someone is bound to ask why or where. We need to flesh it out." Boyd was getting into the spirit of the conspiracy. "We could say that he's on a confidential assignment."

"That just begs further questions. Suppose that we say that he's on loan to the government of Kyrgyzstan to assist them in solving their continuing financial problems." It was Gould at his most inventive. "Few people can pronounce Kyrgyzstan and fewer still would be able to locate it on a map. The beauty part is that, the last time I checked, Kyrgyzstan doesn't have an extradition treaty with the United States."

For the first time that morning, Boyd was actually smiling. "I like it! What's next?"

Hunter answered him. "Without raising the alarm, we must find King. He is the only one who knows where the money has gotten to. We find him and squeeze him until he returns every bloody dollar." There was passion in his voice. One might think that the money had come out of his own wallet.

"And, how do you suggest that we go about this?" Boyd was a detail man who would not settle for a broad outline.

"There is a private investigator in town by the name of Marq Morgan. Nick Gestas swears by him. He has used him in all three of his divorces. Nick claims that he is honest, thorough, imaginative, and discrete. Why not have Nick contact him and see if he'll take the case? He'll have expertise and resources that are unavailable to us." Gould was pulling his weight and doing his best to balance out Hunter's extreme rhetoric.

"Good! Jeff, make it happen. What's next?"

Gould decided to build on his recent success. "In the interest of thoroughness, we still need to determine if the theft was the work of some very clever hacker. I suggest that we put a cyber research team on this to determine if that is what happened. Are our firewalls as impenetrable as we think they are?" Unspoken was the other question: have we jumped the gun by convicting King of the crime? Hunter weighed in with the opposing view. "That would be a waste of resources and time. The identity of the culprit is obvious. We need to hunt him down like the disloyal dog he is."

Boyd rubbed the bridge of his nose again. "Stephen, this time, I'm going to have to go with Jeff. We must be certain that our firewalls haven't been breached."

The meeting ended, and Gould went off to find Gestas and tell him about his assignment.

Gestas received the news with mixed emotions. He was pissed off that he hadn't been included in the partners' meeting. Yet, he was quietly pleased that he was being given a role in the ongoing investigation. Perhaps his abilities were finally being recognized and his value appreciated.

When he called Marq Morgan, he found that the investigator was booked solid for the next several months. Nothing would persuade him to make room for a new investigation, not even a lucrative gig with a prestige firm. Stymied, Gestas had to resort to plan B.

Chapter 7

Gestas and Greenfield

It had been ten days since Arnie discovered the theft from the accounts he managed. That date marked the beginning of his personal Odyssey.

In Atlanta, in the twentieth-floor offices of the wealth management firm of Greenfield and Associates, Maxwell Greenfield was working on his second cup of coffee of the day. Through the glass window wall, past the patio railing, the rising sun was playing an ever-changing game of light and shadow with the city' s skyline. The scene was different every time he witnessed it and it fascinated him. It also served to remind him that he was one very lucky son of a bitch.

Max had led a colorful life. In his youth, he had been rudderless. That all changed when he came of age and enlisted in the United States Marine Corp. The Corp taught him the virtues of organization and discipline. It gave him purpose and a family that cared about him, all things that he had not found in civilian life. He worked his way up through the ranks to gunnery sergeant. It was there that he fully expected to finish his career. The Iraq war and a battlefield commission changed all that. He advanced to the ranks of Captain and finally Major. He was reassigned to Special Forces and given command of an elite clandestine unit, Scorpion 8. In an operation in the "smuggler's triangle" region of Afghanistan, the unit had early success. However, one of their "successes" ruined a clandestine CIA operation. The brass in the pentagon viewed this as a muck-up, rather than a success. Max was forced into early retirement. He had learned another valuable lesson. In bureaucracies, loyalty is a one-way street. While there may be an occasional exception, in general this rule holds.

It was then that he and a few colleagues established the wealth management firm. It has been successful beyond his wildest dreams. He had a loving wife who was listed on the Social Register, and a comfortable home in a gated community in an upscale suburb. His suits were silk, fashioned by expert tailors in Hong Kong. Creature comforts he had in abundance.

However, some habits acquired in The Corp are difficult to lose. Every day, he arose in the predawn hours and swam a half-mile in his lap pool. He watched his weight and managed to keep it within a pound of what it was when he became a civilian again. He was careful about what he ate and drank, never allowing the occasional indulgence to become a bad habit. His chauffeur drove him to the office. During his commute, he enjoyed his first cup of coffee and worked his way through the New York Times. As he had for many years, he completed the crossword puzzle in ink.

When the sun moved on to other pursuits, he spun his chair 180 degrees and put his empty coffee cup on a corner of the desk. The surface was otherwise remarkably clear except for a leather correspondence folder, a silver fountain pen, a telephone, and a computer monitor. Against the right-hand wall were electronic screens showing the status of the major markets around the globe. On the far wall, directly across from his desk was a scaled-down reproduction of Dale Chihuly's Cranberry Red Persian Wall. Max had commissioned it from the artist. He prized it almost as much as he did his wife.

The phone rang. His secretary reported that a Mr. Gestas of Boyd, Hunter, and Gould, in Harrison, was on line two. Max did a quick search of his mental files and remembered that Nick Gestas was a client, and a rather unusual one. He and Gestas were in the same business but Gestas, instead of managing his own portfolio, had turned over these duties to Max and his people. The explanation offered at the time was that Gestas was seeking to avoid any appearance of a conflict of interest. So, his holdings were put into what was essentially a blind trust.

"Put him through, Ani." He couldn't imagine the purpose of the call. The Gestas holdings were doing very well and the quarterly report was not due out for another six weeks.

"Max, you old dog! How are things in Atlanta?" The voice coming across the wire seemed to be straining to sound jovial and upbeat.

"Sunny and warm, with a high of 84 and an overnight low of 72. The skies are clear and blue and there's no rain predicted for the next seven days. But, Nick, you didn't call me to get the weather report. What's on your mind?"

"You never were much of a one for small talk. You need to work on that. The reason I'm calling is to tell you that The Metropolitan Opera is putting on a special benefit performance this coming Saturday. They will be presenting Puccini's Tosca with Patricia Racette as Tosca, Roberto Alagna as Cavaradossi, and George Gagnidize as Scarpia. I've a ticket for you if you want it. I remember how fond you are of Puccini."

Only one ticket and no mention of the wives! Nick has something else on his mind. The opera is simply bait. "I surmise that you also have some business you wish to discuss, something that you are not comfortable sharing on the telephone."

"Quite true! The benefit is a matinee, so you can fly into New York that morning. I will leave your ticket at the box office. We'll have dinner afterward and then talk. I presume that you will be staying at The Pierre as usual. You can fly back on Sunday." Gestas sped through the arrangements almost as if he feared that, if he gave Max a chance to speak, there would be no deal.

For his part, Max was torn. He did like opera, particularly Puccini. What he didn't like was having the whole trip planned for him without being consulted. "You do presume an awful lot! I haven't yet even agreed to make the trip. For all you know, I could have a schedule conflict."

"Sorry to tread on your toes, old boy!" He was trying to sound truly contrite, but he could not bring it off. "But, I do hope that you will come. I need you!" Here the sincerity was genuine.

"Why don't you come down here? It's been awhile since you were last in Atlanta." Max was probing for more information.

"No can do, my friend." There was a trace of genuine regret in his voice. "This is a matter of considerable delicacy. I would rather that no one else learned of our meeting. Thus, the neutral venue."

While they were talking, Max checked his calendar. Next weekend was clear. He decided that he would go, not so much because of the pleading but because his curiosity had been piqued. *What is so damned important that we had to have a face-to-face meeting in New York City on very short notice? He liked a good mystery as much as he liked a good opera.* "I'll be there on Saturday, but this had better be worth the trip. By the way, since this is a business trip, naturally we'll be billing you for my time, travel, and miscellaneous expenses. Are you on board with that?"

"You drive a hard bargain. But, yes, bill me. I'll find some way to expense it that won't raise any questions. Max, thanks for being so agreeable. You won't regret it." Gestas broke the connection.

Max hated it when people made predictions like that. Deep in his gut he always got this sour feeling that, when the dust finally settled, he would have more than his share of regrets.

He called up the file on the Gestas' trust and went through it carefully. It was still out-performing the market indices. There were no red flags. Next, he searched the financial news for any recent mention of the firm of Boyd, Hunter, and Gould. All reports were favorable. There were no indications of any business problems. He did come across one piece of possible good news for the firm. This was in the form of a report of a rumor — financial reporting at its best — that the firm was being considered favorably as an acquisition target in a merger with one of the big three. Then, he searched under the heading,

Nicholas Gestas, looking for accident reports, criminal and civil lawsuits, police arrests or any other negative news. There was nothing. He finally gave up the search, admitting that he had no clue as to what was really on Nick Gestas' mind.

It was now approaching ten o'clock, the time for his daily briefing to the staff. Before he left, he asked his secretary, Ms Ani Mamea, to reserve the corporate jet for his trip to New York early on Saturday morning next, with return late on Sunday. Also, book a suite at the Pierre, for Saturday night only. The expenses were to be charged to Mr. Nicholas Gestas' account. That being done, he moved the Gestas matter to a side shelf in his mind.

Chapter 8

The Lure of Tosca

Max's flight lifted off from the DeKalb-Peachtree Airport at 8:00 am. Two hours later, the Gulfstream G550 touched down at La Guardia airport in New York. The flight had been uneventful, and Max used the time to try to catch up on his annual report reading. This was a never-ending struggle.

He caught a taxi into Manhattan, to the Hotel Pierre, on 5th Avenue at East 61st Street, facing Central Park. After checking in, he had lunch at the hotel's Perrine Restaurant. He had a Maine Lobster Salad with a glass of Viognier Blend, mas de Daumas Gassac Languedoc. Since time was short, he dared not linger no matter how much he wanted to. He changed into his tuxedo and had the doorman hail him a cab. He appreciated the fact that the benefit was scheduled for 2:00 pm instead of the usual 1:00 pm start. Thank God, the Met was not doing a piece of Wagner's ring cycle! Then, the starting time might have been noon, necessitating his arrival the night before.

The taxi dropped him at Lincoln Center fifteen minutes before curtain time. His ticket was waiting for him at the box office. Then he joined Nicholas Gestas in a box, balcony level, to the left of the stage as viewed by the audience. They barely had time to shake hands and exchange greetings before the house lights were dimmed and, with no overture, the first act began.

As he settled into his seat, he remembered his introduction to this opera. It was on a now-historic EMI recording featuring Maria Callas in the title role. She was paired with di Stefano, Gobbi, and the La Scala Chorus and Orchestra under the baton of de Sabata. Later, he added to his record collection an RCA Victor stereo performance with Milanov, Bjoerling, and Warren in the principal roles, accompanied by the Rome Opera Chorus and Orchestra conducted by Leinsdorf.

He enjoyed today's performance. The music was glorious and moved him in a way that little else did. The counterpoint of lechery and lust on the one hand with deceit and murder on the other, although a bit melodramatic, was overall well done. Even in 1900, sex and violence sold, as they still do today. They probably always will.

After the performance, they took a taxi to BluOnPark, arguably New York City's finest Steak House, for dinner. Such status is too often self-conferred. A dozen other steak houses probably claimed the same distinction. The sin is not restricted to steak houses. There is a professional football team that appropriated the title of America's Team without even a popular vote or an act of Congress.

Once seated, Gestas ordered the cocktails: Ardbeg Uigeadail Scotch, on the rocks. Max had never tasted it before, but he was always open to a new Scotch selection. The smoky bite did not disappoint. Thus far, there had been no discussion of the business that had prompted this trip. Not in the opera intermissions, nor in the ride to the restaurant. Max thought about broaching the subject but demurred. Gestas has asked for the meeting. He would bring it up when he was ready. They ordered dinner. Max, conscious of his weight, began with a roasted vegetable salad, then the filet mignon, medium rare, and the potato latkes. He washed it down with a Brooklyn Pilsner. With no swimming that morning, or the next, he would need to extend his pool time next week. Either that or begin a fast.

Gestas, who obviously never gave a thought to his weight, began with a dozen oysters. Max thought *This is probably the same tuxedo he wore when he first got married, a dozen years ago, and it still fits!* The main course was the Ribeye, medium well, with a side of roasted mushrooms. He passed on beer, preferring another round of the Scotch. Both steaks were perfectly aged and prepared and needed neither side-dishes nor conversation for support.

After the plates were cleared, the waiter enquired about dessert. For a fleeting moment, Max thought about the Tiramisu but then declined, settling for black coffee. Gestas did no such soul-searching. He ordered the sour cream cheesecake and black coffee. Max marveled at the man's metabolism. How else can one eat like that and show not the slightest sign of being overweight? In doling out genes, Nature just did not play fair.

They split the bill down the middle, adding a generous tip. It really didn't matter how they handled the bill; one way or another, Gestas would be paying for it. Then Max suggested, "Why don't we walk back to the Pierre? It's only a few blocks from here. We can use my suite for our business discussion."

Gestas made a sour face and shook his head. "I'd be more comfortable if we went back to my rooms at the Plaza. As I told you, this is a very delicate matter."

My God! He is concerned that I may secretly tape our conversation. His paranoia is running rampant. "Fine! Your place it is." *If he insists on a strip search to see if I am wearing a wire, I may have to punch him in the nose. That would certainly cost us a client, but it might almost be worth it.*

Once they had settled into comfortable easy chairs in Gestas' suite, he began to tell his story. At Boyd, Hunter, and Gould, one of their junior asset managers had gone missing. The authorities had pulled his car out of a retention pond, a few miles from his home. No body was recovered, even after divers searched and dragged the pond. In the car, the driver's shoulder harness had been cut and the window on the driver's side had been broken from the inside. The present theory was that the driver had survived the crash and escaped from the car. They checked his home. He was not there, and neither were his wife and children. None of the neighbors or business associates had any knowledge of what had become of the King family.

With such bizarre circumstances, suspicious minds turned to the accounts that Arnie managed. A hastily organized audit revealed a shortage of about eight million dollars. It did not take much imagination to jump to the conclusion that Arnie had absconded with the money and was now in the wind.

To this point, Max had listened in silence, but now he began to ask questions. "Have the police and the Feds been informed?"

Gestas shook his head violently. "No, and for a very good reason! B, H, & G, has built its reputation on integrity and security. News of this embezzlement must never leak out. In time, we can replace the money, but we could never rebuild our reputation. And all of this is happening at a most inopportune time. The firm is in the middle of some very delicate negotiations for a merger with one of the big three financial organizations. If word of King's actions becomes public knowledge, we can kiss the merger goodbye. We stand to lose many times the amount that King stole. It would ruin us."

"I'm sure that you are insured against loss. However, you can't make a claim without revealing what has happened."

"Precisely!" was Gestas' reply.

"Is this merger the one with Merrill Lynch that I've been hearing about?"

"I can neither confirm nor deny that rumor. With negotiations in progress, I'm sworn to silence." Gestas tried not to show how disconcerted he was by the accuracy of the question.

"Surely, you've dispatched private detectives to bring back Mr. King. What luck have you had?" Max was approaching the problem with an eye toward what he would have done. He did not yet realize that he and Gestas were not on the same page, or even working from the same script.

"Max, you misunderstand me. We don't want Arnie back, not now, not ever. If he's apprehended, old man Boyd will do three things by reflex, without even thinking. First, he'll fire King's sorry ass. Next, he'll turn him over to the authorities and insist that they prosecute him to the full extent of the law. Finally, he'll go to civil court and sue Arnie and his entire family for every missing cent. Harold Boyd is an old-school man of principle, and one of these principles is to give no quarter. Mercy and forgiveness aren't in his lexicon. If faced with the choice of doing what is right versus doing what is financially expedient, he'll choose the former every time. The Press would love this, and they would be all over it. As for the rest of us: Goodbye merger; goodbye firm; hello breadline."

Max was beginning to get the picture and he shook his head in disbelief. "So, you're just going to pretend that nothing has happened and hope that Arnie remains among the missing. Good luck with that! I don't see why you need me or my firm." That was, strictly speaking, not true. Deep down in his gut, he was beginning to get a sick feeling that he knew where Gestas was heading with this presentation and he really didn't like it at all.

Nick Gestas was quietly pleased. He had safely maneuvered the discussion to his intended destination. "I want to open an account with your firm in the E.P. fund." He sat back satisfied and more than a little smug.

Max's suspicions were being confirmed. Yet, he had to play out his hand. "The Extraordinarily Profitable Fund is presently closed to new investors. Even when it is open, the amount of the initial investment is quite high to discourage all but the high rollers it was designed for. I'm not sure that you would qualify." He seasoned the last statement with a dash of genuine regret.

Nick was not buying it. "My source tells me that E.P. stands for Extreme Prejudice and that you, as Chairman can reopen the fund whenever a suitable opportunity presents itself. I'm arguing that this is a special case and a deserving one. "

Clearly, one of our special clients has been telling tales out of school. When I find out which one, I'm going to cut him off from doing any further business with our firm. The more the people who know what we do, the more dangerous it becomes for everyone. We don't need a blabbermouth. "What is it that you wish to accomplish? What are your investment goals?"

"I want assurance that Arnie King won't suddenly reappear and foul up all of our plans. It should be done without fanfare, a case of "dry cleaning" as I am told you call it."

He has clearly mastered the euphemisms. He wants us to dispose of Arnie, making it appear to be nothing more than a tragic accident. Ideally, he would simply be made to disappear permanently, without so much as making a ripple in the Minkowski space- time continuum. "What you suggest is possible. But first, we would need to study the matter to see if it qualifies under our business model. Even if it does, it'd still be seriously expensive. You may want to reconsider if there is some other way to accomplish your goals." He made his reluctance palpable and it was obvious that he was uncomfortable with the topic.

For his part, Nick was finding pleasure in Max's discomfort. It was his *schadenfreude* moment. "We'd prefer that you and your people handle it. Let me know what you decide. But understand that there is some urgency. If Arnie should surface on his own, and Boyd and the Press find out, then all bets are off. Do we have a deal?"

Max acquiesced, and they shook hands. Lost in thought, he left and walked back to the Pierre, being careful to avoid the park, a place into which one never ventured after dark unless accompanied by a personal SWAT team. Of course, trained as he was in hand-to-hand combat, he had little to fear from the park. But, tonight he had other things on his mind and, besides, he was not properly dressed for combat. *Nick's logic is seriously flawed. His major premise is that King embezzled the money. Then, the other known facts fall neatly into place. King has disappeared and so has his entire family. Only the guilty run. Thus, leading to the inescapable conclusion that King is a thief This is a classic case of circular logic. Was there any hard evidence that King was guilty? The car in the pond and the convenient disappearances are all circumstantial. Other explanations are imaginable. I have seen enough situations, where the obvious is not what actually happened. I am skeptical. I will put a research team on it. King may, in fact, be guilty, but I will want proof that he is, not some circular argument from a third party with his own agenda, before we become involved.*

Of course, if we decide to take the commission, I'll need someone to take charge of the disposal phase. There are several of our people who come to mind, and they are all between assignments at present. They each have their individual strengths and it will be a challenge to find the right match

But why would Nick try this lame circular-logic ruse on me? He's smart enough to recognize it for what it is. Did he think that I am so stupid as to fall for it? There is more to this than meets the eye. What is it that he isn't telling me? And what would be his purpose in withholding information? There is a chess game going on and I'm being kept in the dark. Why? What is Nick up to? Clearly, he wants King gone. But is this for his own reasons? Or does he represent a third party? It's a most intriguing puzzle. I'm fond of puzzles. And, if I do say so myself, I'm rather good at them.

The trip from the Plaza to the Pierre was uneventful. He set a brisk pace and the exercise felt good after so much sitting. It may even have burned off some of the calories from dinner. Once back in his suite, he took a hot shower and then retired for a night of untroubled sleep.

Max awoke before dawn as he usually did, feeling completely refreshed. He worked on his backlog of reports and then, when it was time for the dining room to open, went down to breakfast. After breakfast, with the sun fully up, he went for a walk in Central Park.

Previously, on many occasions, he had visited New York City, and sampled her wonders, both the obvious and the hidden. Just when he was about to conclude that the City held no more surprises for him, she proved him wrong. Only very recently he had stumbled across some pictures on the Internet of the Bethesda Terrace and the Arcade lying underneath. That was his destination this morning.

The fountain and the mall were somewhat familiar, as was the terrace. However, the arcade underneath the terrace was a new experience. He was at a loss to explain how he had missed it on previous visits. The unique Minton Tile ceiling, dating back to 1869 and recently restored, mesmerized him. There were 49 panels each comprised of over 350 Moorish-patterned encaustic tiles. He could have spent the entire day just standing there and drinking it all in. He wondered how many native New Yorkers were even aware of the existence of this treasure. Reluctantly, he tore himself away in time to catch his flight back to Atlanta. Wheels were up at 2:30 pm.

He was home in time to have dinner with his wife.

Chapter 9

The Search for King

After the Monday morning staff briefing, Max gave his research department new marching orders. First, they were to verify, if possible, each of the claims that Gestas had made. Did money recently go missing at Boyd, Hunter, and Gould? If so, how much? What evidence was there that Arnie King was the one who had taken it? Who else had the opportunity to do it? Beyond greed, what other possible motivations were in play? What were the circumstances surrounding the dive of King's car into the retention pond? Was King dead or was he on the run? What had become of King's family? If, in fact, King was on the run, who were the relatives, friends, and associates to whom he might reach out for help? The researchers had, as their primary objective, locating King if he was still alive. King's fate after that would be in Max's hands.

Max's research people were a very talented group and, when they did an analysis, it was in-depth and thorough. The easy results came quickly. Yes, B, H, & G had suffered a loss of eight million dollars. The company was taking steps to cover the loses but that would take time. Thus far, news of the loss had not leaked, and the firm's financial reputation remained unmarred. But, how long can one keep such news quiet?

Whether Arnie had taken the money was yet to be proven. While he was the one who had the best opportunity, and was thus the front-running candidate, there were at least four others: Boyd, Gestas, Gould, and Hunter, all of whom had the means and the opportunity. Outsiders, while deemed unlikely, were not dismissed out-of-hand, but instead given a very low priority. Long ago, the research team had learned not to fixate on the obvious suspect to the virtual exclusion of all others. As was their practice, they would be constructing detailed profiles of all five. However, this, too, would take some time.

Arnie's car had been recovered from the retention pond on the Monday following the incident. It did show paint transfer on the driver's side. The transfer was fresh, but the type of paint was generic and of little probative value. The punctured airbags, the severed shoulder harness, and the broken side window all supported the premise that the driver had escaped the car. The absence of a body on dragging the pond argued that the driver had survived the incident and left the scene.

After a search of several days, King's immediate family was found in an adjacent state, visiting his mother-in-law. On questioning, they all swore that they had no knowledge of Arnie's whereabouts. A short time later, they filed an official missing person's report.

Among the rest of his family, his friends, and associates, the responses were consistent. Everyone denied having any recent contact with Arnie King. The firm of B, H, and G, instead of filing a missing person's report, covered its ass by listing King as on unspecified, indefinite leave. When pressed for details, they claimed that he was in Kyrgyzstan, advising that government on financial matters. Arnie could not have disappeared more thoroughly had he been abducted by aliens and spirited away in a flying saucer.

Undaunted, the searchers dug deeper. They went through the telephone records for the King home on the days following the incident at the pond. Thus, they found an incoming call to the King residence placed just before 9:00 am on that Saturday from Al & Jim's diner in Boulder Creek. The King family denied ever receiving such a call and all knowledge of the diner. Someone was covering up a contact. A visit to the diner and circulation of a photograph of Arnie produced no recognition. For the Saturday in question, they did remember a scruffy-looking vagrant who had used the telephone several times. But, they were certain that he was not the man in the photograph.

In this age of perpetual electronic connection, when everyone owns at least one personal cell phone, a public telephone does not get that much traffic. A search of the calls made from the diner's public telephone turned up only one rather incongruous call. It was made at 11:30 am to the Nailor Country Club. The clientele at the diner hardly seemed the country club type. Could this have been Arnie reaching out for help? A team of investigators was dispatched to the Country Club. The staff all identified Arnie as a member, but no one admitted fielding a telephone call from him on the Saturday in question. The quest had reached yet another dead end.

The searchers followed their standard protocol. Logically, Arnie would soon need either cash or credit. They circulated

Arnie's driver's license number, his social security number, his major credit card numbers, and his bank account numbers, along with a recent picture. If Arnie used any of these, Max's people would be notified, and they would have him. It is said that no one can stay hidden forever. If you doubt that, ask Whitey Bolger. However, if one could contact Jimmy Hoffa, one might get an entirely different answer.

While they waited for a hit, they turned their attention to the profiles.

For Max's research group, the activity summaries are only a good start. For each of the persons of interest at B, H, and G, there was now an open file, updated frequently as new information became available. The researchers mined records both public and private. Their methods sometimes strayed beyond the boundaries of what is legal, but they were careful and rarely got caught. Before the case was finally closed, each file had grown into a detailed picture that would have been the envy of federal profilers.

Chapter 10

Maxwell Greenfield and
Bergen Sawyer

Max had been a career military man until he ran afoul of the civilian bureaucracy and was forced to retire before he had planned. The military had made him a man of decisive action. He always seemed to know the appropriate thing to do and there was never any hesitation in doing it. He knew all too well that doubt, and its sibling, hesitation, had claimed the lives of many good men. Yet now, Max was facing terra incognito and he was unsure of the way forward.

Gestas had commissioned Max to make Arnie King disappear permanently, arranging, if necessary, some unspecified "tragic accident". However, Max was troubled by many questions; not the least of which were about Gestas' motivation. There was much that had been left unsaid. Where was the evidence that King was guilty of the crime he was being accused of? And, even if he was guilty, did this crime warrant a death sentence? The bottom-line was that Max simply did not trust Gestas. He would reserve action until he was convinced that he had the full story.

While Max had faith in his research group, another pair of eyes might be helpful. His thoughts turned immediately to Bergen Sawyer, one of his assets who now lived in Harrison. Max's association with Bergen went back a long way, to the time when Bergen was just finishing grammar school and Max was a gunnery sergeant. Bergen's father, Roscoe, and Max were comrades-in-arms and friends.

During a tense period, Roscoe had asked Max to act as a bodyguard for his son. This marked the start of a mutually beneficial friendship that continues to this day. Max invited Bergen along when he settled the score with the gang that had assassinated Roscoe and his wife, Rebecca. Years later, when Max was commanding a Scorpion unit in the smuggler's triangle area of Afghanistan, and Bergen was fulfilling his military obligation, Bergen was assigned to Max's unit. Still later, when they were both civilians again, with Max heading a wealth management firm in Atlanta, and Bergen a faculty member in the Sociology Department at Thornton University in Harrison, Max recruited Bergen to be a resource person for his E.P. unit. Bergen's research area was hazardous waste disposal and his association with Max provided him with considerable professional practice that was not easily available elsewhere. The association proved remarkably successful as well as lucrative.

Max telephoned Bergen at the University.

"Bergen? Max here. How are things in Harrison?" Max kept his greeting upbeat.

"Everything is wonderful! Moira is well, and the children are growing up much too fast. But that's not why you called.

What's on your mind, my friend?" Bergen was aware that Max was not one to waste valuable time on social pleasantries.

"Two days from now, on Wednesday, I'm going to be in Harrison. I've a matter that I'd like to discuss with you. Can we get together?" He was not going to get into details over the telephone. He knew enough about electronic eavesdropping that he never trusted that his telephone line was a secure one.

"Certainly! It'll be good to see you again. I presume that you'll be using the corporate jet and landing at Morton International. Send me your schedule and I'll pick you up at the airport. You're invited for dinner. Moira will accept no excuses. Your room will be ready, and we hope that you can stay the night. That'll give us ample time to talk." He was speaking for Moira even though he had not yet consulted her. But he was on safe ground. Max was essentially another member of the family and his visits were too few and too short.

"Very good! Once we're airborne, I'll send you our estimated time of arrival. Your hospitality is appreciated. Stay well!" Ever since Bergen's parents had been ambushed, Max was reluctant to provide flight details to anyone before he was in transit. In some respects, he was not very different from Arnie King.

Bergen called Moira and informed her that they were going to have a house guest. The news made her day.

On Wednesday, at four in the afternoon, Bergen welcomed Max at the arrival gate at Morton. Bergen took charge of Max's overnight bag and hustled him to the car. Max kept his briefcase. Bergen wanted to stay ahead of the rush hour traffic. As he drove across the Folsom Bridge and into Mohawk County, they caught each other up on recent activities, only personal, no business.

The Sawyers lived out in the countryside, east of the University. It was only there that they could find a five-acre parcel at a reasonable price. The house was a sprawling ranch with five bedrooms, two of which were presently serving as his and her home offices.

Dinner was sauerbraten, with potato pancakes, sour red cabbage, and spiced apple sauce, all accompanied by steins of Wurzberger. Nobody left the table hungry. After the children were put to bed, Bergen and Max retired to Bergen's office for a little schnapps and a lot of serious talk.

Max's opening statement had all the drama of dropping a live grenade in the middle of the floor. "My problem involves Arnie P. King." He paused for effect.

"Good God Max! You do know that he's married to Moira's sister, Gloria? Personally, I've had no use for the cad ever since he made Gloria sign a prenuptial agreement. What's the bastard done this time?" Any mention of Arnie was bound to get a rise out of Bergen.

"Truthfully, I'm not at all certain. Let me catch you up on as much of the story as we know at present." Max began with the embezzlement, the drowning of Arnie's car, and the driver's disappearance. Then he moved on to his own meeting with Nicholas Gestas and the resulting commission to eliminate Arnie King. He finished by summarizing his misgivings.

Bergen listened thoughtfully. Then he shook his head. "Max, surely you aren't here to ask me to dispose of my wife's brother-in-law? You remember that I've rules. I don't work in Harrison. I don't work on my own campus. To that I would add that I don't do family, no matter how sorely I am sometimes tempted." However, they both knew that Bergen had, for a very persuasive reason, made an exception to the jurisdictional impediment in the case of Wilson Lustig.

"Don't get your knickers in a knot, my son. You misunderstand me. I'm not asking you to eliminate Mr. King, at least not just yet. What I'm suggesting are two things. First, I need your help in finding King. He's gone to ground and done a first-class job of disappearing. Either he's a very resourceful individual or he's had some expert assistance. I suspect the latter. Then, once you have found him, I want to sit him down and find out his side of the story. Only then will I know what action to authorize." Max paused and sipped his schnapps.

"I see. But, why me? You have a lot of talented people in your organization who could handle this assignment." Max had trained Bergen always to be on the lookout for a hidden agenda.

Max had expected such a response. "There are multiple reasons." He began to tick them off on his fingers. "First, you have had contact with Arnie. You know what he looks like. You know how his mind works. You know his idiosyncrasies. Second, you know Harrison, with its various ethnic neighborhoods. You'll be able to find hiding places that no one else can. Third, you've a deliciously devious mind. You've the skill of putting yourself in the head of the fugitive and predicting what he is going to do before he does it. Finally, while I do have other operatives, you're the best of the lot, and this job calls for my best." He accepted a refill on the schnapps.

Bergen replied modestly. "You give me too much credit. From what you've told me, I suspect that Arnie's car did not go into that retention pond simply by accident. I think that he was targeted; someone was out to get Arnie. It may be people that Gestas dispatched or someone else who had sufficient provocation. Either way, Arnie would be scared shitless. In that condition, he'd never have been able to engineer a successful disappearance. So, I think that he must've had help. If I'm right, then we aren't the only ones who are searching for Arnie. This makes the job more difficult. We must find him first and then protect him from these other people who are intent on killing him."

"You set me thinking," Max responded. "If Gestas was behind the failed hit, and then his crew were unable to find any trace of Arnie, it'd make sense that he'd be in the market for more skillful trackers. Logically, it hangs together, but it's hardly proof. Will you take the job?"

Max got the answer he expected. "Let me sleep on it. I'll talk to you again in the morning." Bergen saw Max off to bed and then returned to his study. He poured himself another drink and sat at his desk for several hours, turning the problem over in his mind.

Max arose fully rested at his usual time the following day. Lacking a pool for his morning routine, he showered, dressed, and went to the kitchen and made himself a pot of coffee. He read the suburban edition of the Harrison Herald and was on hand to welcome first Moira and then the children when they appeared for breakfast. They chatted about what was going on at the children's school and the fortunes of the local sports teams. Bergen was the last to arrive, just in time to see the children off for school. The adults stayed at the table and finished off a second pot of coffee. The conversation shifted to Moira's work at the law firm. Noticeably absent was any mention of Arnie King and the assignment that Max had offered to Bergen.

They left the house together just before nine, Moira to court and Max and Bergen to Morton International. Only when they were alone again in the car did Bergen bring up the question of the assignment.

"Max, thanks for not bringing up Arnie King when Moira was present. I haven't yet told her about your problem. Depending on how things turn out, I may never discuss it with her." Bergen was not in the habit of keeping secrets from his wife. Yet, sometimes there were things that a person was better off not knowing.

Max nodded agreement. "Have you come to any decision?"

"I have! I'll do it, with the understanding that all I'm committing to is finding Arnie, bringing him in for a serious talk, while keeping him alive long enough to have that talk. If you want me to do anything after that, we'll need to have a serious talk of our own. Is it a deal?"

"It's a deal! I'll tell my research people to share with you all information they collect as soon as they get it. You'll have full access to our resources." At this point, he opened his briefcase and extracted a large brown envelope. Tapping the envelope, he said "In here is the detailed report from my research committee. It's everything we found out up until yesterday noon. There's also a recent picture of Mr. King for whatever it may be worth. Lastly, there's a burner phone. My Research Department will be sending you daily updates. I'll leave the envelope on the seat when you drop me off. Anything else you need, just ask. One more thing. Be careful! If you are correct that there's another crew looking for King, then they'll not take kindly to the competition, and they've shown themselves to be ruthless."

Bergen shook his head. "Max, you were pretty damn sure that I'd accept the assignment. One of these days I'm going to surprise you."

Max smiled. He doubted that he would live long enough to see that day. He believed that he knew Bergen better than Bergen knew Bergen. "I've already put you on the payroll as a consultant at your usual rate."

They pulled into the departure lane at the airport. Since Bergen was driving, they skipped the ceremonial handshake. "Don't worry, Max, I am not about to get injured or killed to protect a jackass like my wife's brother-in-law."

Max's plane had wheels up at ten and Bergen got to Thornton in time for his eleven o'clock class. Max was back in Atlanta in time for a late lunch.

Bergen took his usual seat with his colleagues in the Faculty Dining Room. The group was a mixed one, with representatives of at least six different academic departments. The regulars had in common an appreciation of a good story or a joke, well told, palatable meals often accompanied by an adult beverage, friendly banter that, at times, cut close to the bone, and a willingness to share the latest news or rumors about what was going on at Thornton. Some observers had christened the gathering as The Philosophers' Table. Others who were not quite so favorably impressed referred to it as The Table from Hell.

Chapter 11

Oscar and Arnie P. King

O scar had gotten Arnie settled into a guest room at the Student Union Building on the Thornton campus. It was one of several rooms that the History Department keeps on standing reserve to accommodate seminar speakers and visiting faculty. There is no charge for these rooms. They are awarded to the History Department in recognition of the number of income-producing rooms that are occupied every July during the third week when the Department hosts an annual conference of four thousand Medieval Historians. The previous week, the Union is host to five thousand regional new car dealers. The week following, it is six thousand Future Farmers of America. The union staff has honed its logistical skills so that now there is no chance of a repetition of the disaster of several years past. Many of the locals still remember fondly the bacchanal that ensued when five thousand Presbyterian men mistakenly descended on the campus in the same week as five thousand Methodist women. Neither group has been back since. Some wounds even time will not heal.

In the first few weeks, Arnie occupied his time by learning to navigate the campus. He discovered the Library and the Union's Music Room. The latter was in a large corner room on the second floor and was decorated with comfortable furniture.

It featured an outstanding collection of classical compact discs and a state of the art player. He was partial to the tone poems of Richard Strauss and the orchestral music of Richard Wagner. None of his colleagues and very few of his friends had ever seen this side of Arnie P. King.

He shaved his head, and began to cultivate a full beard, one that was now coming in strongly. With a pair of horn-rimmed glasses, he would soon be unrecognizable even to his own mother. Some of his meals, he took in the Union Cafeteria. Others were in the Home Economics Cafeteria, where the food is decidedly better. He followed Oscar's advice and, to the extent possible, he avoided personal interactions by keeping his nose buried in a book. But, the isolation and the contemplative life were beginning to wear on him. Thus, an invitation from Oscar for lunch the next day in the Home Economics Cafeteria was particularly welcome.

They met at 1 pm as the lunch crowd was thinning, some going to class, others back to their offices or laboratories, and not a few to a quiet place for a siesta. Oscar and Arnie sat at a table for two off in a comer.

Oscar appraised Arnie's new look. He approved. His suggestion for a gold ring hanging from Arnie's left ear had been vetoed. Now, he had to agree that it would have been overkill.

"Thank God, you called this meeting," Arnie exclaimed. "I was beginning to go stir crazy. When will I be able to talk to my wife?"

Oscar shook his head. "Sadly, not for a while yet. It's too dangerous, not just for you, but for her as well. I expect that your adversaries have her phone line tapped and, when your wife leaves the house, someone will be following her. We've worked very diligently to make you disappear. Don't spoil it now."

Clearly, Arnie was disappointed. He had expected better news. "What progress have your people made on my new identity?"

"That's why I called this meeting. I have several things for you." He opened his briefcase and began to deal out, one-by-one, his largess. "First is your passport identifying you as Artemus C. Scott."

Arnie studied the passport closely. "What does the C. stand for?"

"Clifton! Notice that we've taken the liberty of aging your beard by several months. But then, no reasonable person expects the passport picture to be a good likeness."

"Why is my country of origin listed as India?"

Oscar smiled. "I was hoping that you'd ask. Your parents were British administrators before Indian independence. After, the family stayed on. You're a Dean at the Indira Gandhi National Open University (IGNOU). Here is your faculty identification card. After twenty years in administration, you're being replaced as Dean and sent back to the classroom to teach History. Naturally you need some refresher work and you've been granted leave for a year to retool here at Thornton."

"But, I don't speak any of the Indian dialects. What do I do if someone wants to converse in their native language?"

"Artemus, relax! It's unlikely to happen. If it does, insist on English, the language of your host country. If that doesn't work, shut them down. Tell them that you've more important things to do." Arnie looked unconvinced, but Oscar plowed ahead. "Now, here's a card identifying you as a Visiting Faculty member at Thornton. It'll let you take advantage of the assets of the Recreation Complex, provide admission to all athletic events, and give you Library privileges.

Also, you now have a meal ticket that you can use at either the Union or the Home Ec. facility. When that runs out, let me know and I'll get you another." Piece by piece, he was fleshing out the identity of Artemus C. Scott, Visiting Faculty Member. "Finally, I have for you my crowning achievements, a driver's license and a Chase Visa card, both in the name of Artemus C. Scott. Both are forgeries, but they'll stand up to close inspection. However, you don't want them checked against the records of the issuing agency."

Arnie gather up the gifts and divided them among his pockets. "What about the use of a car?" Oscar suspected that he wanted a car to go and see his wife. He believed that this was a very bad idea. In truth, Arnie was devising a contingency plan in case he had to beat it out of town to escape a death squad.

Oscar deflected the question. "I'm working on it, but it's going to take some time. Besides, right now, I don't see the need for one."

Once again, Arnie registered disappointment. "Without mobility, I feel so vulnerable. I'm a sitting duck. If those guys ever find me, I'll be a dead duck."

"First, they have to find you. This is most unlikely and, if they do, my friend, I've got your back. To get to you, they're going to have to come through me. Try to relax."

This discussion of Artie's pursuers provided a natural segue into another topic that Oscar had on his agenda. "When we took over your security, we confiscated your collection of credit cards. We did this because any use of them would have left an obvious trail back to your hiding place. The people who are after you are smart enough that they would have discovered this. We're continually monitoring your backtrail for any sign of pursuit. My question is: if we detect someone closing in, what action do we take?"

"If it was up to me," Arnie responded "I'd kill them all."

Oscar smiled to himself. *When one becomes a target, live and let live flies out the window.* He baited Arnie "And how would you go about it?"

"I would herd the group of them into an armored truck." Arnie was clearly warming to his task. "Then I would lock the door and drive the truck into a deep retention pond." His enthusiasm was fierce and frightening.

Oscar clapped his hands. "Totally appropriate! However, completely impractical as well as illegal! Much as we may both wish otherwise, it's never going to happen."

"Well, what would you do?" The tone made it clear that Arnie was issuing a challenge.

"Given that our principal responsibility is protecting you, I'd try to mislead the pursuers." Oscar was quite a decent chess player.

"And just how would you go about that?" The tone had not changed.

"With your permission, I'd lay a false trail leading away from you. I'd have them chasing a will-o'-the-wisp." He paused for effect and then said "They're about to close the serving line. Why don't we go and get dessert before it's too late?"

They just beat the closure and got the last two pieces of cherry pie. This pie was one of the best things that the kitchen turned out. The cherries were plump and satisfyingly sour. The thickening agent had been used sparingly. The bottom crust was flakey with no trace of sogginess. The top crust was a lattice network. the servings were generous. Even though these were the last two pieces, they were still warm. Oscar thought for a moment about adding a crowning scoop of vanilla ice cream. Then, he remembered the admonition about not trying to gild the lily.

After they finished the pie, Arnie had another question. "Have Carl's cybercrime specialists made any progress in tracking the money missing from B, H, and G?"

Oscar had to disappoint him one more time. "The simple answer is not yet. It's a trail of Byzantine complexity. The going is slow. But, they're pressing on. As soon as I hear something, I'll let you know." He stared out the window at the migration of the students between classes. He was searching for something he might do to speed up the process. "Artemus, since you brought it up, let me ask you. You've had time to meditate on your situation. Do you have any insights into who may be behind this and/or why they did it?"

Arnie regretted that he could not contribute some good news. "Nope! I've gone over the whole problem, backwards and forwards. I've turned it inside out and given it a good shake. I go to bed thinking about it and it's the first thing in my mind the next morning. I'm embarrassed to admit that I'm no closer to a solution today than I was on that Friday night when I last left the office."

"Well, don't beat yourself up. The people who did this are very clever and, thus far, they've been careful and lucky. But, their luck cannot hold forever. We've some very clever people in our camp as well, and we're going to nail these bastards." Oscar looked at his watch. "I've to get back for a meeting. We'll talk again soon. Meanwhile, you should keep a low profile and continue to think about our problem. We're going to win this one."

On that encouraging note, Oscar left and, a few minutes later, Arnie headed for the Music Room.

Chapter 12

Bergen Sawyer

When Bergen was stalking his prey, whether of the two- or four-legged varieties, he was patient, methodical, and thorough. On occasion, he would play hunches. However, when he did so, they were built on a foundation of solid facts. His success rate was one of the reasons that Max had chosen him for his present assignment, finding the missing financial manager, Arnold P. King.

Thus, it was that, at eleven o'clock on the Friday night following Max's visit, Bergen was sitting in his black 2017 Mercedes-Benz S-Class Sedan outside the downtown high-rise office building that housed the offices of B, H, and G, financial advisors. His notes told him that, exactly four weeks earlier, at 12:12 pm., Mr. King had been clocked out of the building's underground parking garage. Precisely at 12:12, Bergen started the engine and merged into the traffic headed for the Interstate. He drove at the speed limit and religiously obeyed the traffic rules.

Westbound on the Interstate, traffic was moderate, thinning the further west he went. Exiting at Boulder Creek, he noted the cluster of motels as well as Al and Jim's Diner. Elapsed time: forty-five minutes. He followed the state road heading southwest toward Airely and Nailor. There was very little traffic on the state road, much as it probably had been on King's fateful night.

When he reached the retention pond, he put on his emergency flasher and pulled off onto the berm next to a stretch of bright, newly installed guardrail. *This is likely the spot where the car went into the pond.* He sat there quietly trying to imagine the various scenarios. *King could have dunked the car on his own volition. But it isn't that easy to roll a car over the guardrail. Besides, it would be a ballsy thing to do and I don't believe that a wimp like Arnie has what it takes. Then again, he could have fallen asleep at the wheel. After all, it had been a difficult week for him and the hour was quite late However, the damage to the driver 's side of the car as well as the paint transfer argue that there was a second vehicle involved. So, an attempt on Arnie's life, while not proven, is a plausible hypothesis.*

Bergen had trouble picturing Arnie escaping from a submerged car. *Perhaps I have underestimated his resourcefulness.* He tried to put himself in Arnie's place when he pulled his body out of the pond. *I have survived a near death experience and I am scared shitless. What if my assailants come back to make sure that I am dead? The water was filthy, and I am soaked to the skin; I am cold; and I am defenseless. I must hide and wait until I think it's safe. But then, where do I go? I can't go home. Surely my adversaries will be monitoring my house. God help me! I am on my own.* Bergen felt a momentary chill and turned on the heater in his car.

I need cover and concealment. The closest prospects are back in Boulder Creek. Since it is possible that those people will still looking for me, I don't dare hitchhike. So, I must walk.

Bergen drove back to the entrance to the interstate, a distance of 1.2 miles. He estimated that it would take an old, out-of-shape Financial Planner about an hour to cover this distance on foot. Working on the time-line, he allowed Arnie two minutes to drive from the Interstate exit to the pond. Dunking the car, perhaps another five minutes. For the miraculous escape from the car and a reasonable period to watch, he estimated fifteen minutes. An hour's walk back to motel row would put him there at about 2:15-2:20 am. This agreed reasonably with the results from Max's researchers. Arnie's Master Card was swiped at 2:30 am on that Saturday morning. *All of which supports the idea that Arnie didn't have an accomplice. Surely if he had, he'd have gotten a ride back to the motels and arrived much sooner.* The diner was closed at this hour. However, he didn't expect to learn anything new there just now. Bergen headed for home.

The next day, he visited the Nailor Country Club where King was a member. Unlike Max's investigators, he did not want to interview personnel from the front desk or the grille. Instead, he sought out the Golf Pro, the fellow who handled the golf cart rentals, and the regular cadre of caddies.

The Club Pro had spent a dozen years on the PGA tour. He is credited with three career tournament victories and he managed to make enough money to survive. However, after a time, the tour, with its gypsy life-style, began to wear on him. The rising cohort of youngsters, who could consistently outdrive him by twenty yards, that were joining the tour, made his decision easier. He traded the glamor and the prestige of the tour for the stability and regular paycheck of a Club Pro.

Bergen's basic premise was that, if you belonged to the Country Club, then you played golf. You may not play well, but you did play. As he knew it would, a few rounds of drinks made the staff rather voluble. He spent Max's money very freely. His cover story was that he had recently moved into the area and was considering joining the club. Bergen could be a very convincing liar. Among other things, he learned that his wife's brother-in-law was only a fair golfer and would never win the Club Tournament. Arnie's regular playing partner was a big-shot Harrison lawyer, Carleton Dunn. The two usually played thirty-six holes every Saturday. However, four weeks ago, Dunn only played the morning round and King was a no show. King had not played since. Dunn also had been absent. He was said to be spending a lot of time down in the state capitol, involved in a high-profile trial.

What a coincidence that Arnie 's hiatus from the country club dates to the weekend of his car incident! Except that I don't believe in coincidence. And why did Dunn only play the morning round? Did Arnie call him for help? I need to find out more about Dunn and, since I have an in-house lawyer, I know where to start.

After Bergen's visit, the club Pro thought about Dunn. At one time, the lawyer was having trouble with his swing. He was developing a very nasty slice. The Pro gave Dunn a series of lessons and solved the problem. When Dunn paid him, he included a most generous tip. That is something not easily forgotten. The Pro telephoned Dunn at his home and told him about Bergen's visit. "He said that his name was Bergen Sawyer.

He seemed to be more than casually interested in you and Mr. King. It may be nothing, but I thought that you should know."

Dunn thanked him, rang off, and then sat quietly for a few moments staring at the telephone. *So, someone is sniffing around King's trail. I expected it but not quite this soon. I need to alert Oscar. And, we must take some measures to slow Mr. Sawyer down.*

He telephoned Oscar and shared the disquieting news. Oscar told him that he understood and had a counter-measure in mind. Next Dunn telephoned Alf Whitman, the youngest of his crew of associates. Whitman was a bachelor and a lady's man, known to be heavily into the dating scene, looking for a suitable wife.

Dunn invited Whitman to come 'round the house for a drink. He added that he had something important to discuss with him.

When you are a young associate, at the bottom of the seniority ladder, and the boss summons you, you go without question. Later, when they were seated in Dunn's study with libations in hand, Dunn got right down to business. "I need you to do a little play acting for me. In a few days, a fellow by the name of Bergen Sawyer may come to ask you some questions about where you were and what you were doing four weeks ago, today. You'll tell him that you were dating a leggy blonde from Kappa Kappa Gamma Sorority over at Thornton University. I loaned you my black, 2016 BMW 740 sedan so that you could impress her. You had the car all day. When pressed, you will refuse to reveal the young lady's name to protect her privacy and her reputation."

"You're asking me to lie for you." Dunn winced at the word "lie". "Why are you doing this? Where you in an accident that day? Did you kill someone?" There was a limit to how far Whitman was willing to go to butter-up his boss.

"Relax, son! Rein in your imagination! Let me reassure you. I committed no crimes that day. I played golf that morning. In the afternoon and evening, I was with a new client. It's a very sensitive matter and it's better if it does not become common knowledge. My story is that I was here for the rest of the day preparing for a trial. But, no one else was home, so I cannot prove that I was here. You'll merely be supporting my story." Dunn was trying his damnedest to close the deal, but Whitman needed more convincing.

"Where was the car that day? Who was driving it?" They were both reasonable and intelligent questions. However, Dunn was having no part of them.

"Surely, in Law School they taught you that there are some questions you never ask because the answers could compromise your plausible deniability."

Whitman was still skeptical.

Dunn relented. "I was driving, and we were on the east side, near Thornton, but that information must never come out. Do I make myself clear? You have your story. Memorize it and stick to it."

Whitman was no fool. He knew where his paycheck was coming from. "Certainly! You can count on me, sir."

"Good! Your service will be remembered when it is time for our annual performance evaluations."

They finished their drinks and then Whitman suddenly remembered that he had someplace else to be.

Carleton had another drink and sat and reexamined the story. *Aside from King, Oscar, and Oscar's wife, Constance, nobody had seen him on the east side of town that day. However, the car probably appeared on numerous traffic cameras. But now, the car had an alibi. People might not want to believe it, but they would have no evidence to discredit it. Take that Mr. Sawyer, whoever you are.*

Chapter 13

Oscar and Gloria King

O scar thought long and hard about one aspect of King's discontent. Clearly, he missed Gloria, his wife. If Oscar gave Arnie a cell phone, it was a foregone conclusion that he would call her. If he gave him access to an automobile, he would certainly go and visit her. Either of these actions would blow the cover that Oscar had worked so assiduously to establish. And that would put both Arnie and Gloria's lives in peril. Oscar would not allow that. But, there were some things he might do. Quietly, he could visit Gloria and reassure her that Arnie was safe and missed her desperately. However, even such indirect communication had its risks.

He discussed the plan with Arnie, and managed to persuade him that, under the present circumstances, it was the best they could do. Oscar did not want any written communication, so he memorized Arnie's message. Then he drove out to the King home in the western suburb of Nailor. His ride was a lovingly preserved 1978 GT Gremlin, bilious green in color. It was fitted with a 401 cubic inch (6.6L) replacement engine. To improve the performance, he had made several other modifications.

The King home sat on a three-acre parcel of land, partly in woods and partly in well-manicured lawn. The house itself was two-stories, mainly stone and glass.

It virtually screamed "Money!" to everyone who passed by. As Oscar pulled into the King circular driveway, he looked around for any evidence of a surveillance team. He saw none.

When he rang the doorbell, the maid answered. Responding to her quizzical look, he introduced himself using one of his favorite aliases. "Good afternoon, Ma'am. I'm Inspector Grimshaw." He didn't bother to flash his identification. Most of the time, his name and title were enough to convince the help that he was legitimate. "I'm here to talk to Mrs. King about her husband." The maid invited him in and showed him through the house to the solarium.

There he found Gloria and her two other guests. He introduced himself again and, this time, he flashed a thin leather folder that would have held his credentials had he any. The folder was flicked open and closed with a speed that would have been the envy of a bolt of summer lightening. He had practiced the flash until it was perfect. Nobody ever saw what was inside the folder.

In turn, Gloria introduced her guests. "This is Nicholas Gestas, one of my husband's business partners. And this is Barry Marsh, a friend from church."

Hands were shaken all around. Gestas starred at him suspiciously. "Inspector, what organization did you say you represented?"

Oscar was prepared. "I didn't say. That information is classified. If I told you that I was with the National Security Agency, you would never be able to share this information with anyone. If you did tell someone, I'd be forced to deny it. Then, any number of unpleasant things might befall you. It's better that we speak no more of my organization."

It was clear to Oscar that he had interrupted a cocktail hour. Gloria, ever the gracious hostess, didn't miss a beat. "Can I get you something to drink?"

They were drinking mojitos and he was tempted. However, Oscar stayed in character. "Thanks, ma'am, but I'm on duty." *How I suffer for my art!* "As I told your maid at the door, your husband is the purpose for my visit. Have you heard from him since that evening when his car went into the retention pond?"

Gloria was somewhat miffed by the question. "No! Of course, not. What an insensitive question!" She was almost believable. But she was lying. Clearly, she needed more practice, or a better teacher.

Oscar let the lie pass. He turned to the others. "What about you, two?" They both denied any communication. Oscar pressed on, "Do any of you know where Mr. King is at this moment?"

"If I knew where he was, I wouldn't have filed that missing person's report, would I?" Gloria's logic was letter perfect.

Gestas volunteered that ". . .our senior partners at Boyd, Hunter, & Gould have told me that Mr. King is out of the country on special assignment. He's said to be in Kyrgyzstan, advising that government on its financial problems. I've no direct knowledge of this, but why would our senior partners lie?"

Oscar could think of any number of reasons, but there was nothing to be gained by articulating them. He turned to Barry Marsh and said, "What about you?"

Marsh flashed a killer smile, shrugged his shoulders, and said, "I wish I knew."

For that question, all three would have easily passed a polygraph test.

"I see," said the Inspector, setting his jaw. Given the thickness of his glasses and the way he peered through them, his audience had good reason to doubt this assertion. "I need to talk privately with Mrs. King. Will you two gentlemen please excuse us?"

Gestas took the hint. "I should be getting back to the office. I just stopped by to see that you were all right, Gloria. If you need anything just call me. If you don't mind, I will check back with you from time to time." He put down his drink and headed for the door.

Marsh, too, had found a way to make a graceful retreat. "Inspector, is that your Gremlin parked out in the driveway? I haven't seen one of those in ages. Do you mind if I go have a look?"

"Go ahead," Oscar replied. "Look, but don't touch! My baby is very sensitive."

Outside on the driveway, Gestas was waiting, and challenged Marsh. "What the Hell are you doing here?"

Marsh thought that there was something familiar about Gestas' voice, but his subconscious would not complete the identification. "The same thing you are." Marsh was not about to let Gestas intimidate him. "We are both betting that, eventually, Arnie will contact his wife. When he does, his days as a fugitive will be over. However, I was here first, and you should take a hike."

Gestas pulled himself up to his full height and looked down his nose at Marsh. "I don't take orders from you. I give them." Then abruptly, he changed the subject. "What do you make of the Inspector?"

"He's a buffoon. He makes Inspector Clouseau look like a candidate for Mensa. I doubt that any serious law enforcement organization would put him on the payroll."

"I agree." Gestas contributed. "But who is he? And what is he doing here? Could he be a messenger from King to his wife? Why don't you follow him when he leaves and find out who he really is?" With that, Gestas got into his car and drove away.

Marsh then busied himself with examining the Gremlin. Once you got past the color, it was a thing of beauty. Marsh noted the license plate alphanumeric, as well as the window sticker that proclaimed that the owner was a member of the Harrison Classic Car Club. Then he retreated to his own car, left the property, and took up a position several hundred yards west, where he could watch the exit, waiting for the Inspector to leave.

Back in the solarium, Gloria led Oscar into Arnie's home office. "For some reason, I always feel closer to Arnie in this room. We can talk in here with no fear of being overheard or interrupted."

They sat in stuffed armchairs facing each other. Oscar led off the dialog. "I have a message for you from Arnie. "

"Pardon me Inspector," she cut him short. "No offense intended, but I don't know you. How can I be sure that this message actually comes from my husband?"

Oscar smiled broadly. "You do well to be suspicious. Arnie said that you would be. So, he gave me some information that no one else was likely to know, He told me that, the first time the two of you went out, it was a blind date and that you went to see a student production "Death of a Salesman" by Arthur Miller".

Gloria wiped away a tear. "Inspector, forgive me for doubting you. How is my husband?"

"He is alive and well, but he misses you terribly." Oscar led off with the good news. "However, that incident at the pond was no accident. It was a deliberate attempt to murder him. There are people out there who are still trying to kill him. My associates and I are trying to identify these people and, in the meantime, to keep Arnie safe."

"Where is he? When can I see him?" Gloria was pleading.

"We have him hidden away and I will not tell you where. The more people who know the location, the more vulnerable he is. And, if anyone even suspected that you knew the location then you, too, could be at risk." Oscar had often been the bearer of bad news and, no matter how many times he relayed it, it never got any easier. "I can assure you, though, that he is not in Kyrgyzstan."

"Very well then, what does he want me to do?" There was a note of fatalism in her voice.

Oscar replied. "There are several things. First, forget the news that I just brought you. If anyone asks you about my visit, just tell them that you concluded that I was just a smooth-talking con man and sent me packing. Second, you haven't heard from your husband. You haven't the slightest idea where he is. Third, go on with your daily life as you have been. We need time to identify the villains and deal with them. Finally, I promise that we'll get your husband back to you just as soon as it's safe to do so. You have my word."

It was not what Gloria wanted to hear but she had to accept it as the new reality, and hope that it was only temporary. "Thank you!"

"You're welcome. I'm sorry that it could not be better news. I'll find my way out."

When Oscar drove off, Marsh gave him a generous head start before he followed. With a car that distinctive, tailing him would be easy. Marsh tried to keep several cars, and the occasional truck, between them. The route led back to the Interstate, then through Harrison, across the Folsom Bridge, to the eastern suburbs. Where the Interstate forked, they took the southern arm. They exited at Haddam Road and continued south, passing the Basile Medical Center, to Chancellor Boulevard.

It was at this point that Marsh began to get a familiar, but unwelcome, feeling.

His hands and feet started to tingle. This was usually the first warning sign that a blackout was imminent. Knowing that the time was short, he looked for a place to get off the road. He turned into the parking lot for the Synagogue of Tikvah Congregation Shaarey in the suburb of Arbordale. He felt as if all his body fluids were being drained from his body. *God damn it, not now!* There were only a few cars in the lot and they were clustered near the Temple. Taking the first available parking space, he braked the car, killed the engine, and passed out, slumping down on his right side.

Three hours later he regained consciousness. He was momentarily disorientated. Evening had arrived and, with it, darkness. The only light was from the security lights around the Temple and the distant streetlights. He rested his head on the steering wheel, closed his eyes again, and tried to regroup his thoughts. It took a few minutes, but he finally remembered tailing a bilious green Gremlin hoping to find out the real identity of the clown who had introduced himself as Inspector Grimshaw. Unfortunately, his blackout had put an end to that approach.

However, the effort had not been completely unproductive. It was likely that the Inspector's home base was somewhere here in the eastern suburbs, in the general vicinity of Thornton University.

I will have to fall back to Plan B. How many 1978 bilious green GT Gremlins can there be in these eastern suburbs? Moreover, I have the license plate alphanumeric and I know that the owner belongs to the Harrison Classic Car Club. I have many acquaintances in the automotive community and more than a few owe me favors. It shouldn't be that difficult to identify Grimshaw.

Pleased with himself, he started the engine and headed for home.

Chapter 14

Oscar's Honor Students

When Oscar got Carleton Dunn's telephone call, his reaction was neither surprise nor panic. He had expected it but not quite this soon. Nevertheless, he was prepared. He summoned three of the brightest students in his Honors Class. Much as it went contrary to his convictions, he chose only males. But then, this project required males.

Parker Birchwood, Wesley Colby, and Baxter Gilbert gathered in Oscar's office at 5:00 pm on the Monday after Dunn's phone call. Oscar provided refreshments signaling that none of them was in trouble. The three avoided the side chairs and sat together on the more comfortable couch.

"I invited you here to offer each of you an extra-credit assignment. It's completely voluntary. You need not accept it. There'll be no penalty for refusing now or backing out later down the road." Oscar locked eyes with each of them in turn. Nobody blinked. They were all on board.

"Good! The first assignment goes to Parker. On Saturday, next, I want you to drive to Fort Wayne, Indiana. There you are to visit Newman Outfitters and purchase a collection of outdoor gear: a sturdy tent, a comfortable sleeping bag, a complete set of top-of-the-line cooking gear, an ice chest, two canteens, three sets of thermal socks, and an emergency medical kit. You're to create the impression that you're planning an extended camping trip. If you see anything else that would play into this scenario, add it to the list. You'll take your purchases with you when you leave and bring them back here. Now, for the most important point. You'll charge these purchases with this Master Card." He held it up for all to see. "It's made out in the name of Arnold P. King and that's the way you should sign the charge sheet, although I wouldn't waste any time on trying to make the signature legible. I'm also providing you with a driver's license in King's name in case the clerk asks for identification."

At this point, Wesley, Student Number Two, interrupted Oscar. "But, Doc, isn't that credit fraud. They'll catch Parker and lock him up in the slammer. With that on his record, goodbye Medical School."

"Wes, you sure have a lurid mind. You've been watching too much bad television. Go back to "House of Cards" and "Suits". Nobody's going to get locked up. Mr. King has loaned me his credit card and has, in writing, authorized me to use it as I see fit".

"Now, Parker, there's one more important point. You aren't to use this credit card anyplace other than Newman Outfitters. Record all your other expenses: lodging, meals, gasoline, etc., keep your receipts, and I'll reimburse you on your return. One last thing. To the extent possible, without being obvious about it, try to avoid as many of the security cameras as you can. Do you have any questions?"

"Just one. Why are we doing all this?" The question was a perceptive one and one that Oscar had anticipated.

"It's very simple," Oscar replied. "It's an experiment. We're laying a false trail for someone to follow. Your challenge is to make it convincing."

Wesley was beginning to warm up to the game. "And what do you have for me?"

"All of the assignments are different," Oscar answered. "Some are simple, others elaborate. Some can be completed quickly, others require an investment of time. Wes, I think you'll like what I've chosen for you. It's to be accomplished on a Saturday, one week after Parker has completed his buying spree. You're to be in Indianapolis, Indiana. I don't care whether you drive or fly. You're to make a reservation, and have dinner, at King Cole's restaurant. It's on Monument Circle, one floor below a shoe store. Don't let the location mislead you. It is a posh operation. Eat and drink what you will and then pay with the King Master Card. This is the only occasion on which you may use it. Once again, as much as you can, you should avoid the surveillance cameras. Keep your receipts and I'll reimburse you for your other expenses. The meal, however, is on Mr. King. Do you have any questions?"

"Just one. I know this young lady who is a student at the Purdue-Indiana University branch campus in Indianapolis. Can I take her along for this dinner?" This was a question that Oscar hadn't prepared for. Mentally, he kicked himself. He should've known better. Wesley was reputed to lead a very active social life and, if he was to be believed, he had at least one girl friend on every college campus east of the Mississippi.

"Nice try, Wes, but the answer is no. Mr. King is happily married and we cannot have you raising any doubts about that. It's necessary that you dine alone. But don't let that stand in the way of enjoying yourself."

Wesley pretended to be crushed with disappointment. He couldn't do it convincingly.

"All of which brings us to you, Baxter." Baxter was barely able to contain his excitement. "If I remember correctly, last year your family rented an RV to travel to the home-coming football game at the University of Nebraska. Your father is a long-time member of "Husker Nation". I understand that you did a fair amount of the driving and became quite proficient in steering that big monster."

"You remember correctly. Driving something that big was scary at first, but after a while, it became comfortable and easy. You must remember that you need to leave much more lead time for any maneuver. Also, you never want to take any chances. Things you might get away with in a car, can be a disaster in an RV." He had enjoyed being one of the biggest vehicles on the road. The ego boost was unbelievable. In its own way, it was a narcotic.

"Good! You get the third Saturday in our sequence. I want you to fly into Indianapolis and go to Touchdown RV rentals. They are northwest of the city, just off 1-465. There, you will rent an RV, the biggest one that you think you can handle solo. You cannot use the King credit card for this rental. I want you to take the RV on the Interstate and pick up 1-70 heading west toward Terre Haute. Stay on 1-70, bypassing the city, and cross over into

Illinois. When your gas gets low, pull off at the next interchange and fill the tanks. There, you will use the King credit card. Once again, avoid the cameras as much as you can. Then, get back on the Interstate and drive back to Indianapolis where you will return the RV. All that remains is for you to fly home and see me about collecting for your expenses. Do you have any questions?"

"It seems like a rather meaningless trip. What's the point to all of this?" Baxter had not put the pieces together. For an Honors Student, he could, at times, be incredibly dense.

It was Parker who enlightened him "Get with it Bax, Doc has us laying down a trail of breadcrumbs to misdirect anyone trying to track Mr. King. This trail leads away from Harrison, so my guess is that King is still somewhere in the neighborhood. Or, maybe he went in the opposite direction. How am I doing, Doc?"

"Your analysis rates an A. I'm betting that whoever is chasing King has access to credit card information and will detect this usage. I've no delusions that our actions will put a stop to the pursuit. However, I hope that it will slow it down and provide us with some valuable time." Oscar was already evaluating various scenarios that could come into play when the pursuers got close.

Wesley was not content to let matters rest where they were. "Will you tell us what Mr. King has done to be pursued like this? Is he some sort of criminal? Is he a serial killer? Or a politician who has been found with his hands in the till? Are we at risk of being accessories after the fact?" Wesley was headed for Law School and was already developing the critical thinking skills that would make him a success.

"I cannot tell you everything. However, I'll tell you this much. Mr. King has been accused of grand theft. But, there's no evidence to support this accusation. Also, there are reasons to question the accuser's motives. There has already been one attempt on Mr. King's life. Someone doesn't want him to have his day in court. I have been tasked with the responsibility of protecting him so that he will live to see that day. You are assisting in a worthy cause. There's still time for you to back out. How say you?"

Nobody went for the bait. Instead, they took their leave and headed out for dinner. Oscar was encouraged. His plan was in motion and, for the moment, there was nothing else he could think to do. He was still uneasy that he had no workable action plan for that time when the pursuers finally did catch up.

Chapter 15

The Banned – II

ontinuous, heavy rain had washed out the card of races at The Harrison Speedway. Many of the unhappy fans took refuge at The Checkered Flag, and, appropriately, were trying to drown their disappointment, not in water but in alcohol. They mixed in with the regulars who were chagrined to find themselves crowded by so many noisy, amateur drinkers. The serious drinkers made no secret of their disdain for the newcomers. Outbreaks of fighting were the order of the day. The bartender retrieved his blackjack from its perch on a shelf beneath the bar and he was prepared to defend his stock and the cash register. The official bouncer tried for a level of containment that would avoid an appeal to the local police precinct.

Barry Marsh, Hyrum Cassidy, and Enoch Harris shared a table in a corner just beyond the bar. They were on their second pitcher of Miller's Light. Marsh was describing the details of his recent encounter with the so-called "Inspector Grimshaw", including his failed attempt to track the Inspector home to his lair. Then, he redeemed himself by recounting his implementation of Plan B. An acquaintance at The Harrison Classic Car Club, had no trouble identifying the owner of the 1978 Gremlin GT as Professor Fingal O'Flahertie, a faculty member in the History Department at Thornton University. Immediately, O'Flahertie replaced Grimshaw as the person of interest. The suspicion was that he probably knew where King was hiding.

Marsh shared with his colleagues what little information he had been able to garner on O'Flahertie. He had a Ph.D. in History and had been on the Thornton faculty for about ten years. He was tenured and held the rank of Associate Professor. He was highly-regarded by both his faculty colleagues and the administration. He was married, with no children, and appeared to be well connected in the Harrison community. The only flaws that had surfaced were his penchant for impersonating authority figures, his ability to lie outrageously with a perfectly straight face, his fondness for classic cars, and his tolerance for nauseating colors.

But, Marsh wanted to know much more about O'Flahertie. He proposed a plan based on the assumption that, O'Flahertie knew where King was, and eventually he would lead them to King. The plan would begin with saturation surveillance, shadowing the Professor for every one of his waking hours to establish his routine and to determine when they needed to watch him and when they could ignore him. After that, they would divide the non-routine hours so that he would never be out of their sight. Since O'Flahertie already knew Marsh by sight, there were certain segments of the surveillance where, unfortunately, Marsh would not be able to participate. It was going to be a time-consuming process, but the organizers deemed it worthwhile.

Hyrum Cassidy suggested an alternative plan. "Why don't we simply snatch Professor O'Flahertie, take him to a nice quiet place, and persuade him to tell us where King is hiding?

It would save us time and effort as well as being much more fun." Cassidy betrayed a thinly disguised sadistic streak.

"While it might be more fun," Marsh countered "there are several problems with that approach. First, two missing persons rather than one broadens the scope of our job beyond what was authorized. We will only be paid for one. Also, it would draw more attention. That we don't want. Second, information obtained by torture is notoriously unreliable. People who are being hurt will tell you what they think you want to hear just to make the pain stop."

"Presuming that O'Flahertie does lead us to our target, how are we going to dispose of King?" Harris was thinking ahead.

Marsh admired the thought process. "It is going to depend on the location and the circumstances. First, we must separate King from the Professor. Then we must make King's demise look like an accident. He should never have escaped from the retention pond. The fact that he did says that either he is quite resourceful, or he is one damn lucky financial analyst. This next time, we must leave nothing to chance."

They had to pause the conversation momentarily when one of the brawlers was knocked backwards and came sliding across their table. Only quick action by Harris saved the pitcher of beer and two of the three glasses.

"Good reflexes!" observed Cassidy. They righted their chairs and Cassidy went and got himself a new glass. Then he settled into his chair, poured himself another beer, and took a long swig. "Barry, what are you going to be doing while Enoch and I are chasing around after the Professor?" The question was not delivered as a challenge, but as a thoughtful request for information.

Marsh approached the answer in a roundabout way. "When I met Inspector Grimshaw at King's house, another fellow, Nick Gestas was present. He was introduced as a business associate of King at B, H & G. Now we know that Grimshaw was really O'Flahertie. But is Gestas really someone else? I intend to find out."

"Understood," replied Harris. "So, who do you think he is?"

Marsh gave an eloquent shrug. "He could be a King accomplice. He might be our Broker or even the Banker. He might be an opportunistic lothario trying to move in on Gloria while Arnie is away. He could be someone who has a score to settle with King. If he's a player in our little game, I need to find out his angle. Otherwise, we could get blindsided."

But, Harris was not finished. "We know that the Banker wants King dead and he's willing to pay for it. But, do we know why he wants King dead? It's a missing piece to the puzzle."

This was a question that Marsh didn't want to deal with. He had hoped that it would never come up. But, now it had. "The Broker never said, and I didn't ask. However, there have been rumors that a large sum of money disappeared from B, H & G about the same time that King did.

Harris' eyes lit up and a second later so did Cassidy's. They sensed that there might be an even bigger payoff down the road if they played their cards right. Nobody said anything more, but the mental wheels were turning. Arnie King had just become potentially a much more valuable prize.

Chapter 16

Bergen Sawyer – II

When Bergen's investigations led him to Carleton Dunn, he believed that he had a substantive lead. He was determined to find out as much as he could about Dunn. His research started at the most obvious source. His wife, Moira, was a lawyer practicing in Harrison. She was likely to have information about Dunn that would not be available to mere civilians.

The morning after Bergen had interviewed the Club Pro, the Sawyer family attended Mass at the church of Saint Lanfranc. Then, at home, they had a large breakfast. When the children went off to play soccer, Bergen and Moira lingered over a fresh pot of coffee. Sunday mornings were one of the few times during the week when the two of them had quiet time for extended, serious talk.

Bergen was not one to approach a topic obliquely. "Moira, what can you tell me about a lawyer named Carleton Dunn?" He didn't elaborate on his reasons for asking.

Moira smiled. She was quite accustomed to deconstructing dialog. She understood that his question left a great deal unspoken. "To begin, you need to remember that I am a corporate lawyer. Dunn's specialty is criminal law. It is unlikely that we are ever going to oppose each other in court. I know him only by sight and reputation. He is top notch in his field. He is formidable. If, God forbid, you were ever charged with murder, Dunn is the person you would want managing your defense."

Just for a moment, Bergen wondered if Moira had found out about his avocation, handling waste disposal problems for Max. He shook it off. Long ago, she had decided that she didn't want to know what sort of "consulting" he did for Max. It was agreed that this was something that they wouldn't talk about. "What else do you know?"

"Recently, he was promoted to be a partner in his firm, Gray, Arnold, and Young. He has a stable of bright, eager young associates. He's very good at what he does. He's tenacious and hates losing. In his closing statements, he's articulate and eloquent, with occasional flashes of brilliance. His winning percentage is almost off the charts. In a legal dispute, I would want him on my side." Moira was not one to dole out such praise casually. Bergen was duly impressed.

"No offense, but I have to ask. Do you think that he's honest?"

"None taken. A man in his position cannot afford to be anything else."

"So, it'd be a serious blunder to underestimate Dunn?" Bergen was making his own closing statement.

"Damn right," Moira responded. "And serious blunder doesn't really come close to describing such a situation. It could be a fatal mistake. So, whatever you and Max are up to, please be careful."

Bergen thanked her, and the two went their separate ways, she to her study to work on some briefs, he to his office to call

Max. He reached Max at home. "Sorry to bother you on Sunday, but I think that I may have a lead and some help from your research department would be useful."

"Not a problem. Tell me what you want." Max understood that with a cold trail such as they had with King, there was no time to be wasted.

"Here in Harrison, there is a criminal lawyer by the name of Carleton Dunn. He is a partner at Gray, Arnold, and Young, he lives in the western suburbs out beyond Boulder Creek, and he is a member of the Nailor County Club. I would like an in-depth profile of the man, the same sort of treatment that your people did for Harold Boyd, Nicholas Gestas, Jeffrey Gould, Stephen Hunter, and Arnold King." Bergen didn't think that there could be more than one Carleton Dunn but believed that Max's team should have sufficient information to be certain.

"No problem! What else can we do for you?"

"See if you can find me a recent photograph of Dunn, preferably in his golfing togs. I suppose that I could get my camera and go stalk him myself. But, I'd rather keep my distance for the time being. I don't want to spook him."

"Anything else?" He suspected that there was more to come.

"Find out what kind of car he drives. Then search the traffic cameras for the area around Al & Jim's diner in Boulder Creek on the Saturday afternoon following King's incident. If his car shows up, track it and let me know where it goes."

"Also, can you have your people find a recent picture of Mr. King and photoshop it? What I have in mind is to change his appearance from corporate financial wizard to street vagrant.

Give him several days of stubble, hollowed out the eyes from lack of sleep, and dress him in clothing suggesting a dumpster diver." Then he had another idea. "While they are doing that, why not have them mock up a picture of King with a shaven head and another of him with a beard. After all, it's been what, four weeks, since anybody has seen him? God only knows what he looks like now, and She isn't talking."

"I'll get my people working on it right away. Give my regards to Moira and the kids. And, I know that I don't have to tell you to be careful. Talk to you later."

That was all the "consulting" he could do for the moment. Ferreting out Arnie King's hiding place would have to wait for some other day. He turned his attention to preparing an examination to be given to the students in his Urban Planning class the following Tuesday.

* * * *

When Arnold King, in the person of Parker Birchwood, visited Newman Outfitters in Fort Wayne, Indiana, he wore a hoodie in case there were security cameras that he had not detected. It was a simple disguise but not a bad one. It masked his face considerably. He purchased a long list of camping equipment, charging it to Arnold King's Master Card. The salesman was too busy deciding how he was going to spend his commission to ask for identification, so King's driver's license never came into play. The salesman even assisted in loading the purchases in the waiting SUV. Later, he remembered the vehicle because it was a BMW, a ride that he hoped one day he would be able to afford. The out-of-state plates bore the alphanumeric TU 1995 and that stuck in his mind because his wife's maiden name was Trudy Uhler, and 1995 was the year he started working at Newman Outfitters. Nobody had told Parker that it was a bad idea to borrow his father's car for his part in this caper. Even Honors Students can sometimes come up short in practical smarts.

Several days later, Max's contact at Master Card passed along word that Arnie King's card had been used in Fort Wayne. This was the first use since the weekend of King's disappearance. It got the attention of the research team. They dispatched a man to Fort Wayne. He began by looking for camera footage and was disappointed to find only a few that showed anything relevant and those were ill defined pictures of a man wearing a hoodie. However, when the investigator chatted up the clerk. He found that the fellow was all too willing to talk about the best sales' day he had all year. Getting the make and model of the vehicle and the plate number was easy. Once again it was demonstrated that personal contact can make a big difference.

The following Saturday afternoon, Wesley Colby flew into Indianapolis on Pegasus Airlines. He took a cab from the airport to Monument Circle where he spent some time studying the monument, reading the inscription, and admiring the passing parade of sweet young females.

Previously, Arnold King, in the person of Wesley Colby, had phoned in a dinner reservation at King Cole for 6:00 pm. He was punctual and bemused by the subterranean location. *Why would anyone hide a first-class restaurant underneath a shoe store? The only reason I can think of is that by so doing the rent might be more affordable.* The décor was first class and it whispered "expensive". Professor O'Flahertie had cautioned him that there was a dress code and he had heeded the advice by wearing a tie and a suit jacket. When he first walked in, he experienced a moment of panic. *Can I afford to eat here and leave without having to wash dishes? From the looks of it, it would bust my budget.* Then, he reminded himself that Arnie King would be paying with his credit card, and he relaxed and prepared to enjoy his evening.

He spotted the surveillance cameras right away. They covered the entrance, the Maitre d's station, the backbar area, the servers' staging area, and, of course, the cashier. It was going to be impossible to avoid showing up on one or another of the cameras. Earlier, he had considered wearing a patch over his left eye as a disguise. While it did give him a rakish look that he rather admired, he dismissed the idea when he found that it threw off his depth perception enough to make eating a challenge. That disguise was not yet ready for prime time.

To start things off, he ordered a Russian Mule. It arrived in a copper mug garnished with muddled mint. The Vodka was top-of-the-line. The ginger beer imparted a peppery burn, mitigated slightly by the lime. The drink had a kick appropriate to its name. Quickly, it convinced him that one was his limit, especially on an empty stomach. He had skipped lunch, anticipating that, for dinner, he was going to be eating like a Cossack.

For an appetizer, he ordered the shrimp cocktail. Next came a brace of Manicotti covered with a blanket of savory meat sauce. It was so wonderful that he wanted to lick the plate when the pasta was gone. Fortunately, his parents had taught him proper manners. The third course was a hearty minestrone soup, raised from the ordinary to the truly memorable by the addition of a generous amount of Yellow Tail Shiraz in the last stage of preparation. Wesley didn't know when, if ever, he would have another meal as fine as this one. He paced himself, allowing time between courses for clearing his palate. His main course was rack of lamb, a house specialty at King Cole. It was presented at the table attended by oven-roasted potatoes, yellow onions, and carrots, all browned in the drippings from the meat. He paired the lamb with a glass of 2005 Beringer's Cabernet Sauvignon. When he had finished the lamb, there was nothing left but a pole of eight very clean bones. He indicated to the waiter that they were the remains of a great warrior who had perished in a worthy cause and that they should be buried with full military honors.

After a taste of raspberry sorbet to clean his palate, he moved on to dessert. He returned to the Italian theme by ordering Tiramisu and coffee, high test and black. He was enjoying his moment on stage and he was in no rush to finish. As the tables began to fill, he studied the gentry of Indianapolis. *Not much different from those of Harrison.* In time, he called for the bill. When he saw the total, he blanched. Then he reminded himself that it was Arnold King who would be paying. *It must be nice to be able to live like this.* After adding in a twenty-five percent gratuity, he paid with the credit card. The waiter did ask for identification and Wesley produced the King driver's license. He held his breath expecting questioning about the picture.

However, the waiter ignored the picture. He was only concerned with recording the license number and the home address.

Once he had regained the street, he realized that he was full of nervous energy and far too much rich food. Walking for several miles at a brisk pace made him feel more comfortable. Then he hailed a taxi for the ride back to the Indianapolis International Airport. *It does seem like a great amount of energy and money to expend just to add one more breadcrumb to a false trail. However, I wouldn't have missed it for the world.*

The following Saturday, Baxter Gilbert flew to Indianapolis on Pegasus Airlines. He took a taxi to Touchdown RV Rentals and presented himself as Arnold King. A thirty-four-foot Class A, Fleetwood Bounder had been reserved by e-mail for three days and prepaid by cashier's check. The agent on duty accepted his driver's license and proof of insurance without question. The make and model of the RV were the same as Baxter had driven the previous summer so there was no learning curve.

He got on 1-70 and headed for Terre Haute. After he crossed into Illinois, he exited at Marshall where he stocked up on groceries. Then, he proceeded to the Lincoln Trail Camp Grounds. For payment at both locations, he used the King credit card. He had a term paper due at the end of the following week, so he put the peace and quiet of the location to good use on Sunday. On Monday, he filled the gas tank thankful that he did not have to pay the bill. The drive back to Indianapolis was uneventful. He checked the vehicle back in to Touchdown and caught a cab to the airport. Pegasus Airlines returned Baxter to Harrison where he resumed his academic schedule on Tuesday.

Once they were posted, these additional uses of the credit card were reported to Max's research team. Being thorough, they dispatched their investigator to Indianapolis and then to Marshall. The results were shared with Bergen as they came in.

Chapter 17

Tracking King

When the new pictures of Dunn arrived, Bergen was impressed. The fellow in formal wear, posing for a vanity shot suitable for publication in Gentleman's Quarterly, looked nothing like Carleton Dunn in his Saturday golfing regalia. Similarly, the dressed down picture of Arnold King added credence to the aphorism that clothes really do make the man.

Armed with these new exhibits, Bergen paid a return visit to Al and Jim's diner. This time there was general agreement among the staff that the picture of King did look "something" like the vagrant who had spent half of a Saturday hanging out in the diner some weeks ago. The agreement was much better with the picture of Dunn, the golfer. That was the fellow who had met with the vagrant. Those two had left together that day. The diner staff had not seen either of them since. Of that, they were certain.

This made the tracking of Dunn's car critical. Max's research staff had identified Dunn's standard ride as a black, 2016 BMW 740i sedan with vanity plates DUNN RIGHT. Using footage from traffic cameras, they picked it up near the diner at about 3:00 pm on that Saturday afternoon. They traced it sporadically across Harrison to the vicinity of Thornton University. There the trail ended until late that night when the car was spotted going back to the west side. That trip ended at Dunn's home.

Bergen was pleased. No longer was Dunn simply a person of interest. The evidence suggested that he was a key player in King's disappearance. The next step would be to confront Dunn and persuade him to reveal King's present whereabouts. When he called Dunn's office, he had to deal first with Dunn's secretary who was the designated gate-keeper. She screened all of Dunn's calls and blocked those that were trivial or distractions. After all, the Great Man's time was valuable and not something to be squandered.

"Who is calling?" the gate-keeper demanded.

"A potential new client," Bergen responded.

"What is the nature of your business?" She needed more information to decide if the call was trivial or a distraction. She was experienced at this and could keep asking questions all day.

"It's sensitive and confidential." Bergen was no stranger to inquisitions.

"You'll have to be more specific than that." Her time was valuable, too, and her patience was wearing thin.

"Tell your boss that Mr. Sawyer is calling, and he wants to meet to discuss King." *That should cut to the chase.*

There was a lengthy pause and then the secretary came back on the line. "Mr. Dunn suggests that you come to his office next Monday at 4:30 pm. Does that fit your schedule, Mr. Sawyer?"

"Not really," Bergen answered. *Dunn is stalling.* "Tell him that I will meet with him at "The Beekman Bar" at 4:30 tomorrow afternoon." The Beekman was a favorite watering hole for jurists and lawyers only a few blocks away from the Federal Courthouse. Bergen broke the connection without waiting for a reply. *I've attached the appropriate lure and cast the line. Now we'll see if Dunn is inquisitive enough to rise to the bait.*

Bergen arrived at the Beekman at 4:15. He took a seat in a booth that provided a clear view of the front door. At 4:35, Dunn walked through the door and looked around quizzically. Bergen, his face arranged in a broad smile, waved at him. He rose to greet the lawyer.

Extending his hand, Bergen greeted his guest. "Mr. Dunn, thank you for coming. "

Dunn shook Bergen's hand and settled into the booth across from him. "Mr. Sawyer, I presume. Now tell me what the Hell is this all about." There was just the right note of exasperation in his voice.

"Counselor, we're here to discuss Mr. King. If you didn't know him, you wouldn't be here." Bergen knew that there was nothing like logic to irritate a lawyer.

"I know several people named King. When I was a youngster, Donald King lived up the block from me. George, Gordon, John, and Martin King were among my classmates in high school. In scripture studies, I learned about the Magi. The three kings were Melchior, Caspar, and Balthazar. Then, last Friday evening, in my weekly poker game, I won a big pot with three kings: David, Charles, and Caesar. Only Alexander was missing. You're going to have to be more specific." The lawyer's tone was pitch perfect.

Bergen smiled. He appreciated a good performance. "Cute, but unhelpful! I am referring to Mr. Arnold P. King, an associate in the investment firm of Boyd, Hunter, & Gould. Is that specific enough for you?"

Dunn chose to go with a simple denial. "Never heard of the fellow!" It was his first lie of the interview and he presented it as if it was dogma. "What kind of scam are you trying to run?"

At this point, the waitress arrived to take their orders. They both ordered Jameson Black Barrel on the rocks. Then, they each chose an appetizer: Marinated herring in cream sauce for Bergen and Irish smoked salmon for Dunn. The fact that Dunn had placed an order strongly suggested to Bergen that this dialog duel was far from over.

After the waitress withdrew, Bergen responded. "As a professional courtesy, I would never try to scam a lawyer." He, too, could lie easily and convincingly. "Let me refresh your memory for you. Five weeks ago, on a Saturday morning, Arnie King failed to show up at the Nailor Country Club for your scheduled golfing outing. You played alone that morning and then had lunch in the club Grille. There you received a telephone call from Arnie asking you to meet him. You left the club and drove to Al and Jim's diner in Boulder Creek where you picked up Arnie and drove him to the east side of Harrison. How am I doing so far?"

Dunn was impressed with the thoroughness of Sawyer's investigation. "You do have a gift for fiction. But, you left out my score from that morning and what I ate for lunch." He was trying to make light of the situation, hoping that it would go away.

Bergen was not going to be put off so easily. "You shot 84, a commendable score for a man of your age. For lunch, you had the burger, rare, with grilled mushrooms and onions, and sour cream on the side. You washed it all down with a draft Stella Artois. Your cardiologist probably wouldn't approve."

The lawyer was irate, and this was not an act. "Let's leave my golf score and my health out of this. Who gave you permission to go digging around in my personal life? You have one Hell of a nerve invading my privacy."

Bergen spread his hands indicating that he was not going to contest that charge. "So, sue me! Like it or not Counselor, we both know that privacy is not what it used to be. Yesterday, it was a right. Today, thanks to the instant, electronic communication of information, privacy is a privilege that is on the endangered species list. Tomorrow, it will be as extinct as the Dodo and the Passenger Pidgeon. As a public figure, you, more than others, should know just how difficult it is to keep anything secret. I'll make it easy for you. Just tell me where you have squirreled away Arnie King and you will be rid of me."

They paused when their drinks and appetizers arrived. Small rounds of rye and pumpernickel bread accompanied the herring and salmon. In a spirit of camaraderie, they agreed to share the appetizers. They raised a toast to law and order.

"Why are you so intent on finding this King character?" It was a sincere question and one that had been bothering Dunn. *What are Sawyer's motives?*

Bergen frowned at the question. He was in the process of rescuing a piece of herring that was in danger of drowning in the sour cream and installing it safely on a raft of pumpernickel. "Mr. King has been accused of grand theft and flight to escape prosecution. There's also some indication that an attempt was made on his life. I have been retained to find him. We've only heard one side of this story and we really want to hear his side. So, why not save us all a lot of trouble and tell me where you have him?" He downed the raft and its passenger. *That's the best herring I've tasted in a very long time.*

Dunn paused in his assault on the salmon. "Who retained you? Who do you represent?" He was seizing on a line of questioning that Sawyer had, in an unguarded moment, opened.

"That is confidential and not germane to the present discussion." Bergen realized that he had made a tactical error. "What do you have to lose in letting me talk with Mr. King? You can pick the location for the meeting so that his hiding place will not be compromised. I personally vouch for Mr. King's safety when we get together. We could even meet in this very booth. What do you say?"

Dunn drained his drink and gestured to the waitress for a refill. "I say that you have your facts terribly confused. I neither met with, nor drove Arnie King anywhere, on the Saturday in question." He lied smoothly, injecting as much sincerity into his speech as he could muster. "After lunch, I went home and spent the balance of the day, and most of the evening, preparing for a court appearance down in the capitol the following Monday."

Not for a moment did Bergen believe any of this. He had the identification by the staff at the diner, as well as the traffic surveillance. "Au contraire, M'Lord! We have footage from traffic cameras putting your car in Boulder Creek that afternoon. Later it was spotted near Thornton University."

The lawyer's smile exuded confidence. It was a sight very familiar to opposing counsels when they were about to lose to Mr. Dunn. "Mr. Sawyer, you may have found my car, but I was not in it. On the day in question, I loaned it to Alf Whitman, one of the young associates at my firm. He is single and leads a very active social life. At present, he is wooing a coed at Thornton University. To help him impress her, I loaned him my car. Check with him yourself. Here is his phone number." With that, he slipped an index card containing the contact information across the table.

Way too slick! He prepared that card in advance and had it in his inside pocket. He knew what was coming and had arranged an alibi. Moira was right. This is one clever shark. "Mr. Dunn, no offense intended, but this is all bull shit and I don't believe any of it. I won't waste my time talking to Mr. Whitman. I'm sure that he'll tell me exactly what you told him to say. Eventually, I'm going to find Arnie King and get my questions answered. Why not save me some time and tell me what I want to know?"

"Mr. Sawyer, I swear to you that I don't know where Arnie King is." He raised his right hand in the Boy Scout salute. His statement was technically true, but it was not the whole truth. *While I don't know where Arnie is, I do know someone who does, and I can easily find out what you want to know. But, even if I knew where he was, I wouldn't tell you.* "I'm glad we had this meeting. I think that we understand each other." With that, he drained his drink, left two twenties on the table, and made for the door.

Bergen watched him go. *Moira was right. If I ever need a criminal defense attorney, Dunn is the go to person.* He signaled for a refill on his drink and turned his attention to the residue of the appetizers, as he replayed the meeting in his mind.

Chapter 18

Search for the Commonality

T he use of the King charge card triggered reports that soon arrived at Max's offices. Max's research team also obtained copies of the pictures taken by the nearby surveillance cameras. On receipt, copies were forwarded immediately to Bergen.

The purchase of the camping gear in Ft. Wayne provided a wealth of information. True, the photographs of the buyer were not particularly helpful. One never got a good look at the customer's face. He was probably male, but he looked to be a mismatch for King in age, height, and weight. Bergen's first theory was that King had paid some youngster to make the purchases and use the card. It was something a careful and clever fugitive might do.

As the gear was being loaded into the car, a camera unexpectedly struck gold. It recorded the alphanumeric on the license plate of the car. It was then a simple matter to trace the plate to the owner, Mr. Sinclair Birchwood of Harrison. But Mr. Birchwood's age, height, and weight were not a match for the figure in the pictures. However, Sinclair did have a son, Parker, who was about the right age. But, the son was a student at Thornton University and had no obvious reason for being in Ft. Wayne and purchasing camping gear on a Saturday morning.

Bergen wondered if the car had been stolen. He checked and found no police report of such a theft.

There the matter rested until the second report of the use of the King credit card arrived. Indianapolis was several hours drive south and west of Fort Wayne. The location suggested that King was moving in that direction. *But why had it taken him a full week to cover so short a distance? Being hunted by people who wanted you dead should induce some urgency.* At the King Cole restaurant, there was no escaping the cameras, although the patron did try. Once again, the subject was a male and no match for Arnie King. But, neither was he a match for the fellow in Ft. Wayne. *Was King employing a string of surrogates?*

Max's research crew had access to state-of-the-art facial recognition software. It took a few days but the fellow in the restaurant was finally identified as Wesley Colby, a pre-law student at Thornton University. Bergen began to smell a rat. *Two associations with Thornton University. Yet, there was the possibility that King had been mugged and robbed. A gang of young hoods milking a stolen credit card for as much as they can get before the card was cancelled could explain the known facts.* He really didn't believe this, but he was struggling to retain a measure of objectivity.

The third report came from Marshall, Illinois, a town just across the border from Terre Haute, Indiana. This information, if it was to be believed, made it appear that King was in a motor home on 1-70 heading for St. Louis. Again, Bergen was skeptical. *Why had it taken King a week to travel from Indianapolis to Marshall? For one on the run, he was certainly taking his sweet time.* The pictures from security cameras in Marshall were inconclusive. However, they did suggest a mismatch with King's age, height, and weight.

Pictures of the motor home were more helpful. The vehicle was a Class A, Fleetwood Bounder. The license plate led the trackers to Touchdown RV Rentals in Indianapolis. The driver's license and the proof of insurance led directly to Baxter Gilbert of Harrison. Now, it came as no surprise that he, too, was a student at Thornton University.

Next, Bergen sought a copy of the class schedules for these three students. In bygone days, that would have been child's play. In those gentler and more trusting times, all he had to do was to walk into the Registrar's office and show his faculty identification. He could have copies of whatever student records he asked for. But now, in this more enlightened age, when personal privacy is sacrosanct, this information was guarded as closely as the nuclear launch codes. *When had the Registrar's staff been recruited as national security officers?*

So, he went to plan B. Selena, although approaching retirement, still worked in the Registrar's Office. Ever since Montego O'Higgins introduced them many years ago, they had been good friends. Bergen called her and told her what he needed. She joined him for lunch in the Faculty Dining Room at 1:00 pm. By that hour, most of the regulars at the Philosopher's Table had left for classes or their offices. For even more security, they chose a table on the other side of the room, away from the Philosopher's Table. They swapped stories about their families, their vacations, and the latest campus gossip. After a most pleasant meal, Selena excused herself to go to the Ladies Room to freshen up. At her place at the table she left a set of three sheets of paper, folded into thirds. When she was out of sight, Bergen picked up the papers and, without reading them, put them into the inside pocket of his suit jacket.

On her return, Selena thanked him for lunch and took her leave. Her supervisor would not be happy if she lingered too long over lunch. Bergen, on the other hand, did not have another class until late that afternoon. He called for a refill on his coffee. Fifteen minutes later, he paid his tab and headed back to his office. For just a moment, he pictured himself as a character in a John Le Carre novel. Then, he returned to the real world.

Back in his office, Bergen left word with his secretary that he was not to be disturbed for anything short of an alien invasion. He sat at his desk and unfolded the three transcripts, placing them side by side: left-to-right Parker, Wesley, and Baxter; Fort Wayne, Indianapolis, and Marshall, Illinois; Camping gear, a very fine meal, and a motor home. He searched for commonalities. They were all seniors, but they had few classes in common. They all had above average grades, but almost half the student body at Thornton could claim that. Their majors were quite different. They lived in three different residence halls. They engaged in completely unrelated extracurricular activities. Their homes were in different parts of the state.

Their parents practiced different professions. *How did they know each other?* Bergen was convinced that the answer was here somewhere and, resolutely, he cycled back through the data.

Finally, the answer jumped off the page and punched him between the eyes. *How obvious! How stupid of me not to have seen it right away!* They were all in the Honors Program and they all were enrolled in a senior Honors Seminar taught by Professor Fingal O'Flahertie of the History Department. *At last, the commonality! I must find out all I can about O 'Flahertie. Then he and I are going to sit down someplace private and have a long heart-to-heart talk. I'm one step closer to finding Arnie King.*

Bergen mined the in-house resources at Thornton. He learned where and when O'Flahertie had earned his degrees, both undergraduate and graduate, the date that he had joined the faculty, and his progress in rank. He discovered O'Flahertie's research specialty and his publication record. He knew the courses that O'Flahertie had taught as well as the committees on which he had served. What was missing was any record of O'Flahertie's activities before he enrolled in college. It was an academic black hole. He called on Max's research staff for help.

A week passed before he had a response. Fingal O'Flahertie was a naturalized United States citizen. He had entered this country from Brazil, on a Brazilian passport. However, there the back-trail ended. There was no evidence that O'Flahertie had ever lived in Brazil. No record of birth, education, tax filings, voting, or transgressions, be they civil or criminal. It was as if he had not been born until the moment that he checked in for his flight to this county.

Bergen knew that such gaps in the historical record do not occur by chance. Someone had done an expert job of making the details of O'Flahertie's early life disappear. Further, one never went to that much trouble and expense without a very good reason. With that much effort invested, was Fingal O'Flahertie even his real name? *Our mysterious history professor gets more interesting by the moment!*

Historically, in Ireland, there had been a notable literary figure, Oscar Fingal O'Flahertie Wills Wilde. But, he had died in 1900 in France. It seemed highly unlikely that the two were related.

Bergen put in a call to Professor O'Flahertie but got no further than the Secretary.

"This is Professor Sawyer from Sociology. May I please speak with Professor O'Flahertie?"

"I'm sorry, Professor O'Flahertie is away for a few days. May I take a message?"

There flashed through Bergen's mind a picture of O'Flahertie speeding down Interstate 70 in an RV, heading toward St. Louis. He dismissed it quickly. "Yes. Please inform him that I've some business that I want to discuss with him. I suggest lunch at noon in the Home Economics Cafeteria on a day of his choosing."

"May I ask the nature of this business?"

Bergen was no stranger to secretaries who absolutely had to know everything. Information was their stock in trade. He rejected most of the rude answers that came to mind. He compromised with "Tell him that the subject matter is royalty."

"Royalty?" He could almost hear the confusion dripping from the word.

"That's correct. He will understand my meaning. Please call me when he chooses a date. Have a good day." With that he broke the connection, pleased with himself that he had not enriched the secretarial information pool.

Chapter 19

Professors Sawyer and O'Flahertie

everal days later, Bergen received a telephone message from Professor O'Flahertie's secretary. The Professor agreed to meet but he asked for a change in the venue from the Home Economics Cafeteria on campus to Jedidiah's Restaurant, off campus in a nearby shopping mall known as "The West Bank". He suggested the following Tuesday, but he wanted to change the time from noon to 12:30.

Bergen smiled. Changing the meeting site and the time were exactly what he would have done if he was in O'Flahertie's position. The History professor had a class that met on Tuesday and Thursday from 11:00 to 12:15, so the time change was logical. The off-campus site made sense if one did not want faculty colleagues to know of the meeting. Or, it could also be that O'Flahertie had a taste for kosher food. This was fine with Bergen for he shared this fondness. Jedidiah's was a long-time favorite. Making these arrangements through a third party was cumbersome but practical. Bergen returned the call and left a message that he approved of the day, time, and site.

On the agreed Tuesday, Bergen arrived at Jedidiah's Restaurant fifteen minutes early. The early bird not only gets the worm but also a tactical advantage. He managed to get seated in a booth with a clear view of the entrance. Jedidiah's was a place that he knew well.

When he was a young faculty member, he had been assigned to teach a class that met only once a week, from 6:00 to 10:00 pm on Friday evening. The course satisfied a requirement for evening college students. The peculiar schedule for this course was actual a student preference. Why make multiple trips to campus when killing one evening would get the job done? The only alternative was even more unappealing, 8:00 to 12:00 on Saturday morning. Unfortunately, Bergen also had another class that met from 1:00 to 5:00 on Friday. This actual class schedule meant that, on Friday, Bergen did not have time to go home for dinner with his wife. So, once a week, he brown-bagged dinner. After the evening class, he drove home, watched the eleven o'clock news with Moira, and then they both got in the car and headed for Jedidiah's. At that time, the Vatican's rules on Friday abstinence were still strict. However, by the time they got to the restaurant, were seated, placed their order, and welcomed the king-sized corn beef sandwiches, it was after midnight, and their activity was canonically legal. He remembered those as among the best corned beef sandwiches ever.

Bergen surveyed the room. Jedidiah's had not changed much. At each table, there was still the complimentary bucket of kosher dill pickles. He helped himself. They were as crisp and as sour as he remembered.

Since he and O'Flahertie had never met, Bergen had consulted the most recent yearbook and familiarized himself with the History professor's picture. It showed a man of short stature with a round head that was rapidly going bald. All that was left was a narrow strip of hair running around the back of the head from ear-to-ear. He was clean shaven and wore a pair of horned-rim glasses. He peered out through thick lenses and the look on his face was that of a mischievous owl who was extremely skeptical about everything that he was seeing.

When O'Flahertie arrived promptly at 12:30. He scanned the room and then made directly for Bergen's booth. He, too, had consulted the yearbook. He extended his hand, "Professor Sawyer, I presume! Don't get up." Oscar slid into the booth across the table from Bergen.

Bergen appraised the handshake. It was firm with no nonsense. "I find it incredible that we have been colleagues on the Thornton faculty for — what is it now? — almost ten years and we have never met. Our paths never crossed."

"Sometimes, blessings are bestowed," was the cryptic reply.

"For you? Or for me?" Bergen asked.

"Yes!" was the simple response.

Bergen made a mental note never again to ask O'Flahertie an either/or question. "So, we have a lot of catching up to do. Tell me, Professor, what was your childhood like?"

The historian stared off into the far distance, perhaps trying to look down the moldering corridors of time. "It was a long time ago, in another life." He refocused on the present. "What about you? How did your military service go?"

Touche! He has certainly done his homework. There are things that happened during my service that I've never even shared with Moira. I'm not about to parade *them in front of this stranger. Clearly, we each have some subjects that we would prefer to remain buried. But, it's most peculiar that an historian wants to keep the past buried. Perhaps someday, he'll explain it to me.*

"That was in another life and a long time ago. Obviously, there are certain topics that we're not going to discuss. Why don't we agree, up front, that these are off the table and proceed from there?"

"Mais Oui, mon Capitaine." The response was delivered with a mock salute.

* * * *

It was Enoch Harris' turn for the O'Flahertie surveillance detail. Harris followed him when he went to lunch. When the History Professor was being seated at Jedidah's, Harris lingered in the entranceway, pretending that he was waiting for a luncheon companion who hadn't arrived yet. Actually, there was a particular table at which he wanted to be seated. When the previous diners were getting up to leave, Enoch slipped the hostess a twenty and claimed the table, even though it had not yet been cleared. He was off to Bergen's left, but he had a clear diagonal view of Fingal O'Flahertie. As cover, he propped up on the table in front of him a copy of Stephen Mitchell's "The Epic of Gilgamesh", and pretended to be engrossed in it. He watched the History Professor over the top edge of the book. Putting his lipreading skills to work, he tapped into half of the conversation. It was not ideal, but it would have to do. He ordered a bowl of matzos ball soup to make it appear that he was only here for lunch.

* * * *

With the arrival of their waitress, the banter was put on hold. O'Flahertie ordered the corned beef tongue sandwich, king-sized, on rye, with a snifter of draft Mikkeller ("the beer of milk and honey" from the Alexander Brewery). For Bergen, it was the traditional king-sized corned beef sandwich on rye, with a tankard of Shapiro Jack's Winter Ale (a Belgian-style strong ale). He had tried the Mikkeller but found it too sweet for his taste.

After the waitress left to place their orders, conversation resumed although restricted to less sensitive topics. By mutual tacit consent, the reason for this meeting, and the only serious topic on their agenda, would have to wait until their lunch was finished. Why spoil a fine meal with contentious haggling?

Bergen tried a different line. "What do you think of our new Mayor?" The previous Mayor, Louis Scarfino, had been assassinated in his office by his Chief-of-Staff, Marcus Bryce. In turn, Bryce had been shot by Joyce Lakin, Bryce's would-be replacement, in a clear case of self-defense.

O'Flahertie frowned. "That whole story played out like bad soap opera. Had he lived, Scarfino would likely have been indicted on numerous federal counts, convicted, and sentenced to a long prison term. Then Charles Fairbanks, the odds-on-favorite to replace the mayor, decides that he doesn't want the job after all, and disappears into a Monastery. After that, no one wanted the job. It was as if the position was radioactive. Finally, Calvin

Payne, one of our U.S. Senators, agreed to spare the city further humiliation. He resigned his Senate seat and was elected Mayor."

"That move puzzled me. Why did he do it? Was it altruism or does he have some ulterior motive?" Bergen was not one to accept something blindly, at face value.

"I know the man fairly well. What you see is what you get. He had grown weary of the games played by the Washington bureaucracy and he saw a chance to help his community. He is quiet, low-key, and he is just what this town needs. There may still be political infighting, but now it will play out where it is supposed to, in back rooms and not in front of television cameras. We lucked out." Coming from a cynic like O'Flahertie, this was high praise indeed.

At this point, their lunches arrived. Bergen surveyed his sandwich. It was even taller than he remembered. Rather than risk dislocating his jaw, he rearranged each sandwich-half into two open-face sandwiches. He applied the spicy mustard liberally. The taste was sublime and made him nostalgic. The bite of the ale was perfect accompaniment.

He stole a look at his companion. The tongue sandwich was just as tall as Bergen's corned beef. The historian was attacking it directly. *How can he do that? Are his jaw's disarticulated? Is he a member of the snake family? Whatever, he certainly is enjoying his sandwich.*

O'Flahertie noticed Bergen staring. However, he misunderstood the attention. "Good cured beef tongue is so hard to find in restaurants these days. I'm afraid that when I have the opportunity, I forget my table manners and just pig out."

Not a morsel of either sandwich survived. The waitress came by to remove the plates and to enquire if anyone was interested in dessert. O'Flahertie opted for a piece of the sour cream cheese pie. Bergen passed. They both ordered black coffee, full strength.

Bergen watched the historian devour the cheesecake with a twinge of envy. It looked enticing, but he had to watch his weight.

After the last of the dessert disappeared, Bergen brought up the reason for this meeting. "I want to talk about the Monarch."

"It's a rather beautiful butterfly," said the historian with an enigmatic smile.

"Cute!" was Bergen's reply. "Did you learn that from Carleton Dunn? He also does cute. I don't do cute. I have no time for cute. Where is Arnie P. King?"

"What makes you think that I know anything about your Mr. King?" O'Flahertie blinked several times behind the glasses giving the impression that he was a perplexed owl.

"Is that really the way you want to play this hand? If you didn't know Mr.King and have no serious interest in his welfare, you wouldn't be here now." Bergen was at his most serious. "I don't have time for games and I suspect that Mr. King doesn't either. So, let's cut the crap. Why don't I start by telling you what I know and then you can do the same?"

"I'm listening," was O'Flahertie's guarded reply.

"Let me begin where King discovers that eight million dollars has vanished overnight from the accounts that he managed at Boyd, Hunter, and Gould. Later that same evening, King's car goes into the retention pond just west of Boulder Creek. King escapes the sinking car and makes his way back to Boulder Creek. He passes the night at a flea-bag motel and then spends part of the next day at Al & Jim's Diner. From there, he telephones his wife and advises her to leave town in haste. She obeys, taking the children for an impromptu visit to their grandmother. Later, he telephones Carleton Dunn at the Country Club and persuades Dunn to come and get him. Dunn picks King up at the diner and drives him to your house on the east side, near the University. You take charge of King and find him a safe place to hide." Most of this was factual either from the work of Max's crew, or from his own digging. Of course, some of the connective tissue was pure guess work, but plausible.

"Professor Sawyer, you certainly have a talent for fiction. Are you sure that you're in the right academic discipline?" Since the question was rhetorical, he did not pause for an answer. "Let's assume for a moment that there's some truth in your account. Why are you trying to find Mr. King?"

This was the delicate part of the dialog. How to provide enough information to be persuasive and yet not reveal too much. "I'm a consultant for a firm that was asked to locate Mr. King. However, the firm hasn't yet accepted this client because they have serious reservations about his motives. The firm has heard only one side of this story. It would like to learn the other side before it makes a decision. They have tasked me with finding these facts. In the interest of full disclosure, I must tell you that Arnie King is a cretin who just happens to be married to my wife's sister. It is a connection of which I am not particularly proud."

"What sort of facts are you concerned about?"

Bergen was encouraged that the historian appeared to be taking his proposal seriously. "First, did he take the money? If not, does he have any suspicions about the identity of the actual thief? Then, of course, there's the matter of the car in the pond. Did Mr. King do that deliberately, or was he victimized? Did someone try to kill him? If so, who? Does he have any other information that might persuade us to take his side?"

O'Flahertie was turning the problem over in his mind and he needed more time. "How did you find me?" It was a serious question. He had not yet figured it out.

Bergen smiled, pleased that the dialog was moving on to less sensitive topics. "You gave yourself away. It was the bread crumbs that you placed to throw off any pursuers. Fort Wayne, Indianapolis, and Marshall, Illinois. You wanted the hunters to think that it was King using the credit card. There are two basic flaws in this scenario. First, anyone on the run from determined killers is going to move a lot faster than that. Second, you didn't account for the prevalence of cameras these days. It soon became obvious that it was not King using the card. Instead, it was Parker, Wesley, and Baxter. Those three became my breadcrumbs leading me directly back to Thornton in search of a commonality. What they had in common was you, Professor."

"Done in by cheap labor!" O'Flahertie summarized.

"Don't be too hard on the lads," Bergen implored. "They are bright, but brilliance alone does not necessarily make for good undercover agents. They were inexperienced and trying to execute a flawed plan. I'd give them an A for effort, but an F for results."

O'Flahertie accepted this criticism without flinching. "Hypothetically, let us suppose that I can produce Mr. King for a meeting. How do I know that I can trust you?"

Bergen erupted in a boisterous laugh. "Trust me? Are you out of your mind? We only just met. You can no more trust me than I can trust you. In some ways, Trust is like a pearl. The pearl is built up by gradual accretions of hexagonal aragonite crystals of calcium carbonate around a nucleus. This process may take anywhere from one to twenty years. It doesn't happen overnight. Trust is similar. Its formation is a gradual development spread over many years. And, once trust is broken, it is almost impossible to rebuild. At this moment, the best that you and I can hope for is an uneasy mutual understanding and a common goal. This could one day grow into trust, but that day is a long way down the road." He rewarded himself with another mouthfull of coffee.

"Understood," the historian said. "But doesn't the pearl begin with the intrusion of an irritant into the oyster's innards? Are you that irritant?"

Bergen spread his hands indicating that he would not challenge this assertion. "The analogy is not perfect."

O'Flahertie accepted his point graciously. He was beginning to believe that he and Sawyer could work together. "What would you say to a meeting next Tuesday evening at 8:00 pm? The Natatorium at the Walton Gymnasium on the Thornton campus has a faculty swim session from 7:00 to 9:00 pm. I understand that you are a swimmer."

Any doubt that O'Flahertie had done his homework was now gone. "Not as much as I did when I was much younger."

"Why don't I bring Mr. King and meet with you at poolside?"

Bergen admired the cleverness of the proposal. The Natatorium was a public place. Probably there would be other people present, making it unlikely that Bergen would try to murder or abduct King. Moreover, there was no simple way to conceal a weapon in a bathing suit. While it wasn't fool proof, it was a reasonably safe arrangement for King.

Bergen agreed. "It's a date. I will mark it on my calendar." They shook hands, paid their tabs, left the restaurant, and went their separate ways, each pleased with the arrangements.

Enoch Harris followed them out. Faced with a decision of whom to follow, he kept with the original plan and trailed O'Flahertie back to his campus office.

Chapter 20

The Natatorium

B arry Marsh, Hyrum Cassidy, and Enoch Harris arrived at the Walton Gymnasium in the middle of Tuesday afternoon. Their cover story was that they were from the gas company, inspecting for leaks. Security at Thornton did not have a high priority. They had no trouble locating the electrical control boxes containing the circuit breakers. They choreographed the action for the evening's work and agreed on a timetable. After that came the most difficult part, the waiting.

Bergen arrived fifteen minutes before the appointed hour. In the locker room, he changed into his swim trunks and went upstairs to the poolside. He emerged near the shallow end of the pool, on the west side. Here, the pool apron was generous in size. Against the west wall, there were three tiers of stands for the spectators at the meets. In front of the stands, at middle distance were two tables for the judges and timekeepers. North and south of the tables, there were low benches for the athletes. Tonight, the stands, the tables, and the benches were unused and in shadow. Energy conservation was something Thornton took seriously. To the north, beyond the swimming pool, were two separate dive pools.

The air was heavy with humidity and pungent with chlorine. For Bergen, the smells dredged up long-suppressed memories. On the east side of the pool, the area of the apron was much smaller, giving way quickly to a concrete block wall that rose almost to the ceiling where it was ultimately interrupted by a horizontal row of narrow windows. Through one of these panes, a sliver of the new moon was keeping a watchful eye on the gathering.

In the pool, there were a few people, the serious swimmers, swimming laps. Others, the waders, just stood around, conversing in small groups. Then there were the dilettantes, sitting along the side of the pool, soaking their feet. Briefly, he considered jumping in and swimming a couple of laps. Quickly, he rejected the idea. Tonight, he was here to work, not to enjoy himself. On the pool apron, other groups of two or three were forming, dissolving, and drifting aimlessly, as if trying to mimic Brownian Motion. Bergen wandered toward the deep end and finally took up a position in the shadows at one of the judges' tables where he could watch the stairway coming up from the locker rooms.

At a few minutes past the hour, O'Flahertie and his guest came up the steps. Bergen drew in his breath sharply. For a moment, he didn't recognize the guest as his brother-in law. The polished bald head and the full beard combined for a superb disguise. He waited until the pair was directly in front of him and then, he stepped out of the shadows and greeted his in-law. "Hello, asshole! It's a fine mess you've gotten yourself into this time."

Arnie was used to Bergen's abuse. Where once it had disturbed him, now it simply rolled off. "And a cheery good evening to you, too, Brother-in-law! How are Moira and the kids?"

O'Flahertie watched the exchange with amusement, seasoned with a good measure of relief. It was clear that the two men knew each other, and that Sawyer was who he claimed to be. "Now, play nice you two! I suspect that we may have to work together. "

The three continued their walk toward the deep end of the pool. Arnie's head was in constant motion, as if he felt threatened and did not know from which direction the attack might come. In fact, he was noting the exits and making a short list of places that provided cover and/or concealment. If all Hell should break loose, he wanted to be prepared. Bergen did not answer Arnie's question, but posed one of his own. "Did you steal the eight million dollars?"

Artie smiled at Bergen. "What, no foreplay?" Then, he turned very serious, and his speech had the sharp edge of irritation. "Hell, no! I don't steal from my clients. What kind of a monster do you think I am?"

Before they reached the far end of the pool, the group stopped walking and stood facing each other. Bergen shrugged. "I had to ask. If it matters, I believe you. You never learned to lie convincingly. Now, the second question, who do you think took the money?"

It was Arnie's turn to shrug. "I've been wracking my brain trying to find a plausible answer to that question. So far, I've nothing. Those in-house who had opportunity make up a very short list: Harold Boyd, Stephen Hunter, Jeffrey Gould, Nicholas Gestas, and myself. But, these are my friends, my work-family. I cannot find a single persuasive motive for larceny in the whole lot. They are all financially well-off. None of them are hurting for money."

Bergen took that under advisement. *There are always some people who will never have enough money.* "What about outsiders? What about a hacker?"

"I considered that possibility and finally rejected it. Our firewalls are state of the art and our internal security is first rate. Even if someone managed to get in, there would be footprints. I looked for them and found none."

Bergen shifted his line of questioning. "I noticed that none of your accounts was drained dry. Why do you think that was?"

"Who knows? Perhaps the bastard ran out of time."

"Or, this whole game may be about something other than money. Think about it."

Hyrum Cassidy and Enoch Harris had noted the arrival of Professor O'Flahertie and his guest. They guessed correctly that the guest was the elusive Artie King. Cassidy and Harris came shuffling along the pool apron from the shallow end. Harris checked his wristwatch. It read 8:14 pm. As they approached O'Flahertie, King, and Sawyer, Cassidy and Harris began to playfully push each other. Then Harris pretended to slip on the wet tile surface. With arms flailing, he appeared about to take a nasty fall. At this moment, all the lights in the Natatorium went out, plunging the area into near total darkness.

One person screamed in panic. Another burst into a hysterical laugh. Others asked of no one in particular, "What the Hell is going on?" People in the pool quickly dragged themselves out of the water. Of those on the apron, most remained silent, frozen in time and space, like insects in amber, waiting to find out what was coming next.

Bergen shifted into protective action mode. He moved toward the place where he had last seen King. But King, himself on the move, was no longer there. Bergen stopped and called out tentatively, "Arnie?" At that moment, he was struck forcefully on his left shoulder by a pair of outstretched hands. The momentum drove him backward and, as he reached out for support, he grabbed for the body behind the hands and they tumbled into the pool together.

As they sank to the bottom, Bergen's first thought was that some poolside spectator had become disoriented in the dark and had accidently knocked him into the pool. He hoped that the poor soul knew how to swim, for he was not in the mood to rescue a flailing, panic-stricken neophyte.

But, from his partner, there was no panic, no flailing. Instead, Bergen felt hands closing around his throat, trying to cut off the blood flow in his carotid arteries. He reassessed his situation. *This was no accident. It had been a deliberate attack. But was I the intended victim, or was it Arnie? He pushed this question to the back of his mind. Now was not the time for debate. Desperate action was called for.* He brought a knee up sharply into his attacker's scrotum. The hold around his neck loosened somewhat. He reached out and his thumbs found his adversary's eye sockets. He gouged with all his strength. When this bizarre, aquatic *pas de deux* broke the surface, Bergen pulled his attacker's head sharply forward before abruptly ramming it back, smashing it into the tile on the side of the pool.

The aggressor's body went limp and Bergen hefted it onto the pool apron. As he, himself, climbed out of the pool, the lights came back on. He checked the body to confirm that it was still breathing. While thus bent over, he studied the man's face. *I've seen this guy recently, but I don't remember where.* At this point, O'Flahertie showed up at Bergen's side. "What happened?"

Bergen grinned at him. "The lights went out."

This was greeted with a scowl. "Don't play the fool. I know that the lights went out. And now, they're back on." He pointed at the body on the pool apron.

"He's bleeding from the head. What happened?"

Bergen gave an eloquent shrug. "Who knows? I suspect that he became disoriented in the dark and fell in, hitting his head as he did so. I pulled him out." He might have said more but the History Professor had already turned away.

Facing the gathering crowd, O'Flahertie called out. "This man has had an accident. Is there a doctor among you? If someone has a cell phone, please call 9-1-1."

On the edge of the shadows, Cassidy who had never learned to swim, took this all in. His role in tonight's play was to act as a spotter and, if things got out of hand, to act as reinforcement for Harris. But with Harris out cold on the pool deck and bleeding from the head, he concluded that any intervention on his part would be futile. He made for the stairs to rendezvous with Marsh and give his report.

A doctor emerged from the spectators and took charge. O'Flahertie and Bergen moved back toward the stands to give the doctor room to work. Finally, they turned toward each other and spoke simultaneously. "Where is Arnie?" In the excitement, they had lost track of the third member of their group, the person that they were supposed to be protecting.

They searched through the crowd and did not find him. They widened their search to the environs. Finally, they discovered him hiding under one of the tables. He was on his hands and knees, with his eyes tightly closed. He was shaking violently while clutching his stiletto in his right hand. If he was going to die, he was determined to go down fighting.

O'Flahertie bent over and tried to coax Arnie from his refuge. "The excitement is over Arnie. It's safe to come out now." They lifted Arnie to his feet. Bergen relieved him of the stiletto. "Where did you get this cute little pig sticker?" He tested the balance of the weapon and the sharpness of the blade.

"I bought it for protection at a local pawn shop." Arnie answered. "I sewed a sleeve for it inside the right thigh of my bathing suit. It makes me feel a little less helpless."

Bergen returned the blade. "Be careful with that. Don't hurt yourself." *Under similar circumstances, most people would have bought a gun. Not Arnie. He goes for a small knife. But, if it makes him feel safer, why not?* Then. Bergen focused on the matter in front of him. "Let's get out of here. We need a quiet place to talk."

Chapter 21

After Action Analysis

Taking no time for showers, Bergen, O'Flahertie, and King, dressed quickly and made for the exit. As they left, they passed the Emergency Rescue Squad, rushing to the aid of the accident victim. O'Flahertie suggested that they go to the Caruso Building, home of the History Department. Bergen vetoed the idea and pushed instead for the Sociology Department where he believed that they would be safer. At that hour, the department offices were a ghost town. They set up shop in the Sociology Conference Room. Bergen managed to find a bottle of Jameson's Irish Whiskey and some clean glasses. They would have to make do without ice.

Bergen took over directing the session. No one objected. "What do you think just happened?"

The history Professor chose the obvious answer. "There was a temporary electrical outage and this fellow at poolside became disoriented in the dark and stumbled into the pool, hitting his head in the process. It was quick thinking on your part, Bergen, to haul him out. Otherwise he might have drowned."

With nothing to contribute, King was silent. Bergen made eye contact with O'Flahertie. "That is a plausible theory but let me give you an alternative narrative. Just before the lights went out, I saw our accident victim, let us call him John Doe, check his watch. That blackout was scheduled, and he was expecting it!"

O'Flahertie objected. "Don't be silly! You can't possibly know what that poor fellow was thinking when he looked at his watch. The time check and the blackout were two unrelated events. "

Bergen smiled at his colleague. "You don't know the whole story. When the lights went out, I moved to the location where Arnie here had been standing. But, Arnie was gone. At that moment, strong hands pushed me backward toward the pool. Instinctively, seeking support, I reached out and grabbed this person. Together, we went into the water."

"Quite understandable! With people moving around in the dark, there were probably many collisions. I wouldn't read anything sinister into it." Oscar was playing devil's advocate.

Bergen shook his head sadly. "You still don't get it. As we sank to the bottom, he locked his hands around my throat and tried to pinch off my carotids. He was trying to kill me." O'Flahertie started to object and Bergen stopped him short. "I know what you're going to say. You think that this fellow feared that he was drowning and acted in panic. But, I tell you that his actions were deliberate and determined, not the work of someone in the middle of a panic attack. And while I do admit to having enemies, they're not so passionate that they would try to murder me in public. Furthermore, to my knowledge, none of them were poolside this evening. No, I wasn't the intended victim." He turned and faced Arnie, holding his gaze. "It was you John Doe was trying to kill. I just happened to be standing where he expected to find you. It was lucky for you that you moved."

Arnie started to shake uncontrollably. He was beginning to realize just how close he had come, for the second time, to a watery demise.

Bergen rubbed salt in the wound. "I suggest that from here on, you stay away from water. Try tequila instead."

O'Flahertie addressed Bergen. "But, not to belabor the obvious, John Doe didn't kill you."

"Obviously!" replied Bergen with a withering stare. "But it wasn't for a lack of effort and resolve. Whoever John Doe is, he is young, strong, and he was a man on a mission. I fought back. When we broke the surface again, I was getting leverage to gouge out his eyes. However, it wasn't until I bashed his head against the side of the pool that he loosened his hold on my throat. I got lucky."

"You could have killed him," O'Flahertie criticized. "Couldn't you have found a less violent way of dealing with him?"

Bergen shook his head sadly. "When someone is trying to kill you, that's not the time for reason or restraint. You do whatever you must. It was a clear-cut case of self-defense. Now, tell me Professor, did you recognize our John Doe?" The question took O'Flahertie by surprise. "No. I can't say that I ever saw him before."

"When I got a good look at him, there was something familiar about that face. But, I couldn't place him. I kept turning it over in my mind as we walked over here from the Natatorium. Finally, all the pieces snapped into place. When we had lunch at

Jedidiah's last week, this fellow arrived just after you did. He waited to be seated and got a table to my left. He pretended to be reading a copy of "The Epic of Gilgamesh", but he really was watching you closely. When we left the restaurant, he was close behind. I thought little of it at the time, but now, I think that he was following you." Bergen was leading his colleague down a path that would soon turn uncomfortable.

"That does sound suspicious. Who reads Gilgamesh for pleasure?" O'Flahertie still had not connected all the dots.

Bergen shook his head sadly. He tried to be as gentle as possible. "Oscar, if I'm right, he was following you, gambling that eventually you would lead him to Arnie." This was the first time that Bergen used the name reserved for the Historian's close friends.

The enormity of what he had done finally settled on O'Flahertie, like the weight of the world. He bowed his head. "I blew it."

Arnie stared at him in horror. The man he had been counting on for protection had inadvertently come perilously close to delivering him into the hands of his enemies.

"There is both good and bad news here," Bergen pronounced, reclaiming their attention. "The good news is that whoever wants Arnie dead have thus far been employing amateurs. It is only a matter of time before they abandon this approach and bring in a professional. When that happens, our job will become much more difficult. The other bad news is that Arnie's cover is blown, and we're going to have to relocate him. Given the circumstances, I suggest that you let me take charge of the security detail."

O'Flahertie was both contrite and reluctant. However, he realized that it was the right move. Arnie was suspicious and uncomfortable, but he, too, had no other choice.

* * * *

When Marsh heard Cassidy's report, he was livid. It took half an hour for Hyrum to calm him down. Much as he didn't want to, Marsh had to call the Broker and tell him what had happened. And, the Broker was certain to inform the Banker who would be furious. Marsh saw his payoff disappearing forever down the drain.

As expected, the Broker chewed Marsh out in most colorful language. For a finale, he told Marsh that the services of he and his band of rejects was no longer needed. They should cease and desist and get off the playing field.

The Broker's call to the Banker did not produce the expected response. No histrionics, just a long sigh of disappointment. Then, he gave the Broker his marching orders. "I have two assignments for you. First, amateur hour is over. You will clean up this mess you have made. Do this by tying off the loose ends. Otherwise they may come back to do us in. I cannot allow that. And the expense of this clean-up is on you."

"But... "

"No buts! If you don't take care of these loose ends, you run the risk of yourself becoming an additional loose end. I would hate for that to happen. I guarantee that you wouldn't like it either. Do you understand?"

The thinly veiled threat was not lost on the Broker. "I understand. I will see to it."

"Second, award the King contract to the best available assassin. Find a professional with an outstanding record. I've heard good things about this fellow who calls himself God's Judgment. See if you can get him."

"He will be expensive," the Broker cautioned.

The Banker's reply was direct "I don't give a Damn what it costs. I want to water the flowers growing on King's grave. Make it happen! You don't want to disappoint me again."

The Broker sat quietly, breathing deeply, and letting his blood pressure return to normal. Then he began to explore the channels through which he might get a message to God's Judgment (G.J.). *Perhaps, when I make contact, I can get him to take care of our loose ends.* That thought died an early death. G.J. was unlikely to agree to a package of four terminations. Then, even if he did agree, it would be prohibitively expensive. Moreover, the Banker would never allow it. He would have to find some other way to tie off the loose ends.

Next, he thought of his cousin, Vito Novelli, in Detroit. He was rumored to have handled the occasional termination for the mob. Vito would work much cheaper than G.J. and there was the possibility that Vito might give him the family discount. The Broker made a call and set the wheels in motion.

John Doe had been taken to the Basile Medical Center where an emergency physician stitched up his head wound. The injury was not life-threatening, and the prognosis was for a full recovery. Given the possibility that he might have a concussion, he was admitted for observation. He had been carrying no identification and no one had been able to find his street clothes in the Thornton locker room. Hospital security took his fingerprints and sent them off to the F.B.I. The hospital needed to identify him. How else would they know where to send the bill?

On the third night of his stay, a routine check found him dead. The autopsy revealed that he had been suffocated, likely with a pillow. The security cameras revealed only one anomaly. A tall, thin man in clerical garb and bearing a bouquet of flowers walked the corridor that led to John Doe's room. No one on staff could identify this priest. Further, he did a very good job of avoiding the cameras, either by turning his head, scratching his nose, or smelling the flowers. The deceased was eventually identified as Enoch Harris. What he had been doing at the Thornton Natatorium and who had smothered him remain a mystery.

A day and a half after Enoch departed for that great ballpark in the sky, Hyrum Cassidy was found dead in his closed garage. He was seated in his car which had been left running until it was out of gas. The official cause of his death was listed as accidental carbon monoxide poisoning. The consensus guess was that he had come home, driven into the garage, closed the overhead door, and then fallen asleep. Since Hyrum was a known pedophile, the police took the incident at face value and did not look more closely. Had they bothered to do so, they might have found the small injection mark behind his right ear.

Barry Marsh, while hardly a candidate for Mensa, read the signs very clearly. When two of your co-conspirators turn up dead within a forty-eight -hour period, you are likely to be next.

He went to ground and disappeared completely. There were occasional reports that he had been seen in Chile, in New Zealand, and in Canada. They were all discredited. Even Vito, with his considerable resources, could not find him although he searched diligently.

Part Two

THE
PROFESSIONALS

Chapter 22

Katie Carey

She was born Aphrodite Burke, the only child of Aureolus and Yolanda Burke. Aureolus was career military and spent more time posted overseas than he did stateside. Yolanda had complete artistic control in the raising of Aphrodite. This was unfortunate since the mother did not want a daughter and, if there must be one, she was determined to mold her into the ideal sociopath. This project had three phases. First, the daughter is made to hate the mother. Second, this hatred is turned inward so that the daughter comes to hate herself. Finally, this self-loathing is redirected outward against humanity at large. Yolanda's work began with her daughter's given name. Aphrodite despised it and she hated her mother for inflicting this burden on her. After that, the rest of the first phase was easy. At every opportunity, Yolanda added to the burden with relentless disparagement, denigration, and criticism, slowly, but surely, erasing her daughter's self-esteem.

After graduating from high school, Aphrodite found employment with a large, Harrison catering firm. She began as kitchen help. However, the firm recognized raw talent and systematically schooled her in the various components of the operation. For the first time in her life, Aphrodite found something that she was good at and that gave her satisfaction. This made Yolanda's work more difficult.

When she married Eric Carey, Aphrodite seized the opportunity and rebranded herself as Katie Carey. She liked the ring of it and, as a bonus, it put an end to her given name. During her long and colorful life, she answered to a great many names, but, of them all, Katie Carey was her favorite.

Eric was a policeman for the city of Harrison. It was honest work, but stressful. The black humor of the day was that an early coronary was an occupational hazard. But the pay was decent, and the benefits were first-class. Katie left the work force and bore him three children, two girls and a boy. Unfortunately, Yolanda had done her work well and Katie's parenting skills turned out to be abysmal. Eric was a countervailing influence but, sadly, he died of his first and only coronary at age thirty-eight.

As the children legally became adults, each quickly left the toxic environment of their childhood. They soon learned that their family was far from normal. They never looked back, but they spent many years and considerable money on therapy.

About six months after she buried Eric, Katie had an unexpected visit one evening from Uncle Byron, Eric's brother-in-law. She was alone in the house. Her two daughters were away at a sleep-over with girlfriends. The son was on a school trip to Washington, D.C. The children had learned to seize every opportunity to distance themselves from their mother.

She was nearing the end of a very difficult day. The job hunting was not going well. The cumulative rejection was depressing. Moreover, her emergency supply of cash was beginning to run low and the insurance company was dragging its feet in paying Eric's death benefits. She was one disaster away from a nervous breakdown.

Her visitor appeared just as she was about to fix herself dinner. She was planning bacon, scrambled eggs, toast, and a pot of coffee. It was an inexpensive meal, quickly prepared, and one she always enjoyed. One of her core beliefs was that breakfast was good any time of day.

Byron was not one of her favorite people. He was a bully, and, like many bullies, he was a coward. Furthermore, he was overly fond of the bottle, and when he crawled into it, he was a nasty drunk. At present, he was on the wagon because he had a job as chauffeur for a doctor. But, for Byron, sobriety was a transient condition, a brief respite between prolonged periods of inebriation.

"How's my favorite sister-in-law?" Byron was trying to ingratiate himself.

"Byron, I've had a bad day. Why not cut the crap and tell me what you want?"

"What's the matter, Chickie? Tell Uncle Byron your troubles."

"I miss Eric. Why did he have to go off and leave me all alone?" She didn't realize that, while true, this was exactly the wrong thing to say.

"You're not alone, Chickie. You've always got me." He advanced, grabbed her in a bear hug and began groping her.

She retreated but soon was trapped between Byron and the stove. "Let me go, you animal!" She struggled but Byron was a good eight inches taller and fifty pounds heavier than she was."

While he continued to grope, he began nuzzling her neck. "Just relax, Chickie! A roll in the hay will make you feel much better. I've got what you need, and I know that you want it."

Although her right arm was pinned in his embrace, her left arm was free. "Back off, you bastard!" With that, she drove her left fist into his solar plexus. The punch was short, compact, and delivered with all the strength she could muster.

He broke his hold and staggered a few steps backwards, struggling to catch his breath. When he did, a salacious grin appeared. "So, Chickie likes it rough! That's fine with me. It makes it more fun." Again, he started to advance toward her.

Still leaning against the stove, she reached behind her with her now-free right hand and found the handle of the cast iron frying pan. She brought the pan around in a side-arm swing. She powered it with a combination of all the grief, longing, frustration, fear, and loathing that she had kept pent up. The blow caught Byron on the left temple, fracturing his skull and driving the shards deep into his brain. He dropped like a sack of manure. Afterwards, what she remembered most was the sound of the impact of pan on skull. It reminded her of the sound of the gong used in the introduction to J. Arthur Rank movies.

She checked Byron for vital signs. He was not breathing; there was no pulse. She had killed him. Yet she felt nothing, neither elation nor remorse. Curiously, there was hardly any blood, save for what was leaking from his nose onto his shirt. She pulled the body out of her traffic pattern and resumed preparing her dinner as if the fatal encounter had never taken place.

After dinner, she did the dishes. Then, she emptied Byron's pockets and cut the labels from his clothes. In the linen closet, she found a frayed old khaki blanket that was never used any more. *Could it be that the blanket had been saved in anticipation of this occasion?* She shook off such weird thoughts and spread the blanket on the kitchen floor. Then, she rolled the body onto the blanket and wrapped it around Byron. She secured the package with pieces of clothes line from the attached garage.

She moved her car from the garage and parked it out on the street. Then, returning to the kitchen, she put on a pair of rubber gloves. Next, using Byron's keys, she backed his car into the garage, and popped the trunk lid. Returning to the kitchen, she picked up her shoulder bag and added to its contents her best carving knife, tin snips, several zip-lock plastic storage bags, and a small flash light. Dragging the body into the garage, down the steps, and into the car trunk took all her strength. But, perhaps it is true that, in desperate times, one can discover a reserve that one never knew existed.

After closing the garage behind her, she drove Byron's car out onto the Interstate. She was careful to keep the speed just below the limit and to abide by all the traffic rules. In downtown Harrison, she picked up the Interstate that led south to the state capitol. Forty-five miles south of the city was the first rest stop. The amenities were few, just bathrooms, a few picnic tables, and a cluster of vending machines. What activity existed was focused in this area. She drove to the back of the property, as far away from the highway and the rest area lights as she could get. For what she was about to do, she didn't want an audience.

She hefted the body from the trunk and dragged it into the woods, stopping only when she came to a wire fence marking the property boundary. Unwrapping the package, she pulled the blanket from underneath the body. After folding it neatly, she put it to one side. On the trip from home, she decided that she would take some souvenirs to mark the occasion. Briefly, she considered removing his privates. *Given that Uncle Byron was a sexual predator, it would be altogether appropriate.* Rather quickly, she concluded that this would be egregious. *Only a monster would do something like that. And, I am not a monster.* Working by flash light, she took her carving knife and amputated his lips and tongue. Then, using the tin snips, she cut off all ten of his fingers. These souvenirs went into separate plastic bags and then into the shoulder bag. She cleaned the knife on Byron's shirt before it, too, went into the shoulder bag. *If Byron's shade ever returns to this mortal coil, he will find himself at a considerable disadvantage.*

Making her way back to the car, she continued driving south until she came to an exit where she could cross over and head back north. Byron's house was only about a mile from her own. She parked the car in his driveway, left the keys in the ignition, and the doors unlocked. *With a little luck, someone will steal it.*

She started walking home. In the first trash barrel she came to, she deposited the blanket; in the next, the clothes line. The rubber gloves went into the third one. After so much driving, she found the walk to be refreshing. With more important things on her mind, she failed to notice the black car that was following her at a distance of several blocks. It was running dark and it did what it could to avoid the street lights. In fact, it had been following her ever since she set out from home in Byron's car.

When she reached her house, she deposited the plastic bags in the freezer and the carving knife in the dishwasher. Exhausted, she fell into bed without even getting undressed. A dreamless sleep overtook her immediately.

The black car parked up the street. The driver waited five minutes after the last house light went out before powering up and driving away.

Chapter 23

Carey and Franklin

T he day after disposing of Byron's body, Katie was back, pounding the pavement, looking for a job that would provide her with satisfaction, a decent wage, and a competitive package of fringe benefits. Unfortunately, her search was taking place in the middle of a brutal recession, where any job at all would be a Godsend. Times were tough. Opportunities were sparse. She had set the bar rather high. It might be necessary to settle for one out of her three requirements.

It was noon and time for a lunch break. She found herself in Xeuma Park, an oasis of calm in the middle of the pandemonium of Harrison's market place. She managed to snag one of the few unoccupied tables before the chess players commandeered it for their collection. From her shoulder bag, she retrieved a Tupperware container of mixed salad greens with a Vidalia onion dressing, a sandwich of bologna with mustard on store-bought white bread wrapped in wax paper, an orange, a pint bottle of mineral water, a plastic fork, and a copy of this morning's Harrison Herald, turned to the Help-Wanted Section. It was at times like this that she most missed the fringe benefits of the catering business.

She had nearly finished with her lunch and was peeling the orange when a man stopped at her table. "May I join you?"

She looked him up and down. He didn't appear to be one of the panhandlers who frequented the park, looking for handouts. She judged him to be in his mid- to late-sixties. He was neatly dressed and clean shaven. His wrinkled face was wearing a broad smile. "If you can spare the time, I would like to talk to you."

This put her on her guard. "If you're an agent for a Nigerian Prince who wants help getting his money out of his home country, I'm not interested. If you just found a purse full of money that you want me, for a fee, to mind for you while you go in search of the owner, I'm not interested. If you've a bridge that you would like to sell me at a bargain price, I'm not interested. Failing all of that, please, have a seat."

His grin got even broader. "You left out the one about the underwater property in Florida. Let me assure you that I'm not running a scam."

"If you're not a beggar, or a con man, or a chess player, what are you?"

He took the seat across from her and then answered her question seriously. "I'm a craftsman, a skilled artisan, working as an independent contractor. My clients are wealthy people who have problems that they either cannot, or choose not to, solve on their own."

"And why would you want to talk with me? I 've no such problems and, even if I did, I have no money to pay you. Have we met before?"

"No, we haven't. Had we, I am certain that I would remember. But, we do have an acquaintance in common. He goes by the name of Byron." He watched her closely for a reaction.

A chill ran up her spine. He had struck a nerve. However, with great effort she suppressed all outward indications. "I don't know any Byron. I think that you've got me confused with someone else."

"Good try, but you'll have to do much better than that to convince me. Let me anticipate your next question. I'm not the police and I'm not here to make any demands of you. Ms. Carey, you've nothing to fear from me."

"How is it that you know my name while I don't know yours?"

He was apologetic. "Please forgive my bad manners. I am Ed Franklin." He extended his hand across the table.

She gave it one disdainful look and then pointedly ignored it, folding her arms across her bosom. "Mr. Franklin, have you been stalking me?"

"Lord no! I'm very good at what I do. Had I been stalking you, you wouldn't have detected my presence until it was too late."

"I am curious. What's your interest in this Byron fellow? Tell me! Perhaps it will jog my memory."

"To begin with, Byron was a most unsavory character. My client, who wishes to remain anonymous, has a very attractive teenage daughter. When Byron first caught sight of her, he determined that he must have her. He kidnapped her, forced himself on her, and, when she resisted, he beat her within an inch of her life. It was the very definition of sexual assault. He left her for dead but, miraculously, she survived. Although her body finally healed, her mind is irremediably broken. She's confined to a sanitarium in an adjacent state. It is unlikely that she'll ever leave that facility."

She noted the use of the past tense when speaking about Byron, but she wasn't about to challenge him on it. "It sounds like the beginning of a plot for a dreadful soap opera. Have you tried pitching it to any television producers?" She did not expect an answer and did not wait for one. "I do have one question though: what is the service your client expects you to perform?"

"My client has a very good idea who attacked his daughter. However, there is insufficient evidence to produce even an indictment, much less a conviction. The victim is in no condition to testify and there were no other witnesses. So, I was hired to find Byron, extract a confession, and then deliver God's Judgment on him. I was making good progress until you, dear lady, accidently stumbled into the middle of this little melodrama." With that, he reached into the left inside pocket of his jacket and extracted a fat plain white envelope. He pushed it across the table to her.

She looked at it skeptically, as if it might suddenly grow fangs and attack her. "What's this?"

"Take it. It's yours. It won't bite. You earned it. Without either of us being aware of it, you worked as my sub-contractor. You performed well. You are entitled to be paid for your services. I'm many things, but I'm not a thief."

She was sorely tempted but she resisted touching the envelope. "What sort of service do you think that I performed?" She believed that she knew the answer but, a part of her was still hoping that she was wrong.

While it hardly seemed possible, his smile appeared to get wider. Instead of answering her question, he reached into the right inside pocket of his jacket and brought forth a smart phone.

He turned it on and thumbed his way his way through his archived pictures until he found the one he wanted. Then he handed her the phone.

The picture had been carefully framed and showed Byron laid out in the woods on his journey into the afterlife. She noted that the picture had been taken in full daylight.

"What is that small piece of paper on his chest?" It had not been there the last time she saw the body.

"I can explain that. Whenever I dispose of a body, I use a single straight pin to attach to the clothing a Post-It note bearing the letters GJ. Those aren't my initials, but it's the way I sign my work. It was presumptuous of me, but I took the liberty of using it here even though you did all the heavy lifting. After all, it was my contract. Besides, it will have the authorities looking for me and not you."

"GJ for God's judgment. I like it." Passing the phone back to Franklin, she pronounced the coda, "Byron got what he deserved! Darwin's Law in practice. How did you find his body?"

"I had been following his car, looking for an opportunity to take him. I trailed him to your house and observed the switching of drivers. After that, I stayed with the car until you finally parked it in his driveway. Then, I shadowed you as you walked home. You were so preoccupied that you never noticed me."

She picked up the envelope and checked the contents. It contained fifty, one-hundred-dollar bills. "Who knew that problem solving paid so well?"

The smile disappeared, and he became quite serious. "You have considerable talent. However, you are still an amateur. I find myself in need of an apprentice. Come work with me and I'll make you into a consummate professional. I don't expect an immediate answer. Think about it and give me a call next Tuesday. My cell phone number is written on the back of that envelope." With that, he stood up, gave her a small salute, and walked leisurely toward the park entrance.

She watched him go until he passed under the arch at the entrance, turned right, and disappeared. *Now that was surreal!* She put the white envelope in her shoulder bag, along with the Tupperware container and the plastic fork. Everything else – the waxed paper, the orange peel, the empty water bottle, and the newspaper – went into a nearby trash barrel. There would be no more job hunting today. She already had one job offer to consider. It was unlikely that she would get two in the same day. She walked to the Art Museum and spent the rest of the afternoon enjoying a retrospective of the works of Georgia O'Keefe.

Four days after she had dispatched Byron, his body was found by two children who were exploring the woods behind the rest stop. They were traveling with their parents, on the way to Florida, when the family made the unfortunate choice of this site for their picnic lunch. The discovery ruined lunch. The children required several years of psychiatric counselling.

The coroner had a hard time identifying the deceased. The corpse's pockets were empty. Ordinarily, the fallback position was fingerprints. However, without fingers, there were no prints. A casual observer might conclude that the local wild life had made off with the fingers. To the trained eye, that was not possible. The cuts were too clean. Also, the missing lips and tongue argued for human intervention. With no prints, the default position was DNA analysis but that could take weeks and would only work if the deceased was already in the system. In a press conference, the coroner asked for reports of missing persons who fit the general description of the deceased. Mention was made of the Post-It note, but the fact of the mutilation of the corpse was deliberately withheld from the reporters.

Mulling over Franklin's offer made for a very troubled weekend. But, the contents of the white envelope helped assuage the discomfort. She realized that the five thousand dollars was a windfall that might never come again. She hoarded it and spent sparingly. *But, how do I explain this windfall to the children.* Her first line of defense had always been to lie. She had done it so often that she had become rather proficient. She told them that the catering company had relented and given her a job. Also, since she was hurting financially, they agreed to advance her a month's salary.

The children were elated for two reasons. First, they were pleased to see her gain some traction in the business world. Anything that helped focus her mind on something other than ways to torture them was most welcome. Second, she would be spending less time at home and when she was home, she would likely be too tired to raise Hell with them. It was all good.

On Tuesday, she telephoned Ed Franklin and told him that she had decided to take him up on his offer. He was pleased. He gave her an address and told her to report at nine the following morning. The building proved to be a former warehouse on the south side of Harrison. It had been repurposed with ground floor boutiques, second floor gallery space, and third floor offices. Franklin had the entire fourth floor loft. He had subdivided it into living quarters, a suite of offices, and a work space.

For the first phase of her apprenticeship, she was to shadow him, watch what he did, and learn why he did these things the way he did. He would answer all her questions and he might ask some of his own. He explained in detail how his business was organized. All requests for his services were funneled through an agent who screened out the ridiculous, the trivial, and the bogus. There was never any personal contact between Franklin and his agent. All communication was electronic. Since the agent was not doing anything illegal, he was protected and well compensated. Moreover, no one could use the agent to discover Franklin's identity. Next, Franklin researched the remaining requests and discarded those that he felt did not require a person of his abilities. The few that survived, he researched meticulously. In his own way, he was like Bergen Sawyer, a man of principle and ethics. Franklin and the client never met face-to-face. His fees for service were deposited to a numbered account in a bank in Antigua, and then were promptly moved elsewhere.

After a few weeks, when she had a working understanding of his operation, Franklin moved on to phase two. Here, he entrusted her with a share of the research. Once she had absorbed that, he involved her in the planning of the actual operation. In phase three, she accompanied him, and they worked as a team when he fulfilled his contracts. Finally, when he judged that she was ready, he sent her out to do jobs solo. Even though he did not go with her, he followed her progress and graded her performance. Overall, he was quite pleased with the product he had fashioned. From her celestial gallery, Yolanda was watching and smiled her approval.

Two years into this collaboration, Franklin called Katie in for a serious conversation. He told her that his lung cancer, once thought to be in remission, had returned and that his doctors had estimated his remaining time as two months at best. He gave her detailed instructions for the disposal of his body. She was to load the body in his car and, late at night, drive it to The Vale of Lazarus cemetery. There she was to undress the body, douse it with gasoline, and set it ablaze. His clothes were to be neatly folded and piled on top of a nearby tombstone. His shirt should be on the top and it should bear a Post-It note, with the initials GJ, attached by a single straight pin.

All his earthly possessions, his car, the loft, the business, and his off-shore bank account, he was signing over to her. The torch had been passed. The work of the problem solver who signed himself GJ would continue unabated. And, the final delicious piece of irony was that everyone believed that GJ was male.

She followed his directions not because she wanted his possessions, but to honor his wishes. The charred remains were never identified. Thus, Katie Carey became Ed Franklin. She rationalized that the "Ed" might reasonably stand for Edwina.

This being the time of multiple transitions, she added one more. She needed a legitimate cover for her problem-solving activities. The job market had improved somewhat, and the Harrison Herald hired her as a fledgling reporter and assigned her to the Home and Garden section. There she languished until the day that the restaurant critic came down with a virulent case of ptomaine poisoning. Katie volunteered to fill in. Her catering background served her well – she knew food both good and bad. She wrote well, engagingly, with wit and style. Moreover, she wrote honestly, bestowing modest praise where it was earned and damning brutally when that was deserved. Her writing drew critical acclaim and her editors showed their appreciation. She was given her own column and byline. Thus "Dining to Die for" by "Aunt Marcy" was born. Papers around the country began to pick it up in syndication. Aunt Marcy started to review restaurants regionally and then nationally. Each month, she would spend one week in a different city, sampling the local fare, and then writing about it. No longer limited to Harrison, her reputation grew, as did the footprint of her problem-solving enterprise.

When the previous restaurant reviewer recovered sufficiently to return to work, she found that she had been replaced. You snooze, you lose!

Chapter 24

Bergen Takes Charge

O nce Bergen relieved Oscar of the duty of protecting King, he had to assume the responsibility of finding some place to conceal his charge. The on-campus cover was blown. He needed someplace convenient yet unconventional. This was not a comfortable assignment. Given their history, Bergen's first choice would have been to let the villains have Arnie. But, he had given his pledge and so that option was no longer on the table.

His first move was to make a phone call. "Max, it's Bergen. I finally caught up with Arnie and we've spoken at length. Much as I would prefer to believe otherwise, I've concluded that he is the victim here. Somebody has gone to a great deal of trouble to make it appear that Arnie committed grand larceny. Then, to prevent him from having a chance to clear his name, there've been two attempts to kill him. Both proved unsuccessful. The first one was when his car was forced off the road and into the retention pond. The second one was just last evening. It was an attempt to drown him in the pool at the Thornton Natatorium. I don't understand this obsession with a watery demise."

"It sounds like you've been rather busy." Max guessed that Bergen was calling to ask for assistance. "What can I do to help?"

"Arnie's sanctuary here at Thornton has been compromised. I need to move him to a safe house. Do we still have that place on the west side, up near the lake?"

Max answered with a touch of regret in his voice. "We do. However, it's presently unavailable. It's being used to protect that accountant who is testifying against his mob boss in the federal trial at the courthouse."

"Damn! I was afraid of that. Do you have anything else?"

"Not in Harrison. Why not bring him down here to Atlanta?" was Max's suggestion. "At the moment, we have a number of available sites. Furthermore, who would think of looking for him here?"

Bergen considered it and quickly dismissed that option. "Thanks, but no! We need him here to help us smoke out those responsible for the theft and the murder attempts. He's our best hope. Don't sweat it! I'll work something out."

"Good luck! Stay in touch!" With that Max broke the connection.

Then, Bergen placed the second phone call, this one to his long-time colleague and friend, Professor O'Higgins, in the Chemistry Department. "Montego! Bergen here! It's been too long since we last got together. How about lunch today, just the two of us, in the Home Economics Cafeteria, at 12:30? I've something to discuss with you."

Montego suspected that there had to be much more to this, some unspoken agenda. Ordinarily, he saw Bergen at lunch at noon in the Faculty Dining Room, at the Philosophers' Table. The time and the site for this proposed meeting suggested that Bergen wanted to exclude their usual luncheon companions. This piqued his curiosity. "Sure, I can do that. What is this all about?"

Instead of answering, Bergen added to the mystery. "I'll tell you when I see you."

They met on schedule and joined the lunch queue, relatively short at this hour. Picking up trays, cutlery, and napkins, they moved with the line. For a starter, they each chose the cream of tomato soup, arguably one of the best things the kitchen did. Bergen added a taco salad with extra jalapenos and salsa. Montego elected the tuna casserole. For dessert, Bergen had a dish of flan while Montego couldn't resist the tart cherry pie, another kitchen specialty. Both chose coffee, hot and black, for the beverage.

When they had finished eating, Bergen opened the dialog although not in the way that Montego expected. "So, my friend, how are things in the realm of ten thousand stenches, stinks, and malodorous compounds?"

"The next time you come by my office, remind me to show you my copy of "The Creed of a Chemist." It goes like this:

> *"The chymists are a strange class of mortals impelled by an almost insane impulse to seek their pleasure among smoke and vapour, soot and flame, poisons and poverty, yet among all these evils I seem to live so sweetly, that may I die if I would change places with the Persian King."*

Bergen wrinkled his nose. "But that doesn't answer my question."

"The discipline is the same, but the natives are getting increasingly restless. I'm beginning to believe that I should think seriously about retiring." For Montego, it was a subject that could induce indigestion.

"Say it ain't so, Joe." Bergen had lifted a legendary quote from the account of Baseball's Black Sox Scandal. "You can't retire. This place would fall apart without you. All your colleagues, myself included, would be turned out onto the street, and forced to look for honest employment. Do you really want that on your conscience?"

Montego ducked the question. "Well, I'm approaching the traditional retirement age. But, my mind and my body are still healthy, and I continue to enjoy both the teaching and the research. The problem is that, while I am not yet ready to retire, my young colleagues are impatient for me to be gone."

"What seems to be their problem? You hired bright young people from some of the best graduate schools, didn't you?"

"Of course, we did! But, while they are up on the latest developments in the field, there are several massive blind spots. For one, there is a prevailing attitude that nothing of any significance occurred in Chemistry before they set foot in graduate school. When they begin a research problem, they take their literature search back only to 1969, when Chemical Abstracts first appeared on line. They ignore a lot of interesting Chemistry done between 1910 and 1940. These people never see it. They run the risk of unnecessarily repeating research that was performed and reported seventy-five to one hundred years ago, and then publishing it, thinking it something brand new. My students, on the other hand, are instructed to take their searches back to 1840."

Bergen laughed. "But, in 1840, it was still unknown that a molecule of water contained two atoms of hydrogen, rather than one. Beyond that, one must deal with the antiquated terminology: things like muriatic acid, oil of vitriol, and fixed air. Give me a break!"

"I'll grant you that 1840 is a little extreme. But, they should at least go back to 1910 when Chemical Abstracts was first published." Montego was on the defensive. "However, the CA coverage was spotty until about 1929, so they should also search Chemische Berichte and Justus Liebig's Annalen der Chemie back to 1910, to be sure that they aren't missing anything."

"In what other ways does the younger generation disappoint you?"

"Well, they have no institutional memory and they're not terribly interested in acquiring it." Montego was warming to his subject. "When they propose a change in the way we do things, I'll tell them that we tried that twenty years ago and it failed miserably. Then I rehearse for them the reasons why it failed. This, of course, is something that they don't want to hear. They react as if I'm some subversive, standing in the way of progress. Yet, all I'm doing is trying to prevent them from making the same dumb mistakes we made back then."

Bergen had been content to let Montego rant. "And they don't appreciate your good intentions, do they?"

"Not one bit! It's as if, when they were awarded their doctoral degrees, they were given a guarantee that now they knew everything, that there was nothing left to learn."

Bergen shook his head sadly. "Montego, I'm sorry to be the one to break this news to you. It has always been like this. I expect that, when we began our academic careers, we, too, were full of ourselves, and mistreated our elders in much the same way as your junior colleagues are now doing to you. Fortunately, our elders tolerated us and taught us many things that we thought we already knew. Their revenge, if you can call it that, is that now our younger colleagues are doing to us what long ago we did to our elders. Payback is a bitch!"

Montego looked on as if stunned. He'd never thought of it in quite that way. He was uncharacteristically speechless.

"Tell me, how do you plan to spend your retirement?" Given an opening, Bergen was going after Montego with a missionary zeal. He was relentless.

"Well, I suppose that I'll just sit in my rocker on my front porch, with my feet up, and watch the passing parade." This answer was manufactured on the spur of the moment. The truth was that he had never given the matter any serious thought.

Bergen greeted this answer with a sour expression. "People who follow that path usually are dead within two years. Montego, you need to retire TO something. You need some activity that will energize you, get you out of bed in the morning, wind you up, and send you on your way. It might be writing your memoirs for your grandchildren, learning oil painting, volunteering at a local hospital or soup kitchen, getting involved in local politics, or becoming a youth counselor. If you have nothing to retire TO, then don't retire."

Montego smiled at him. "Thank you for that! I'll take it under advisement."

For the moment, Bergen had gotten so deeply involved in Montego's angst that he lost track of the reason he had asked for this meeting. Then, it came rushing back. *Now that I have solved your problem, it's time you helped me with mine.*

"Montego, I know that you and Syn have a home here in town, on Arthur Avenue, just off the edge of campus. But, I seem to remember that you once owned a farm out in the boonies east of here in Mohawk County. Do you still have that property?"

"Yes, we do! When there's nothing else scheduled, we try to get out there for quiet weekends. However, such opportunities seem to be getting more infrequent. Many times, I've thought about selling the property, but then, what would become of our kennel and of Mason who manages things for us? Why do you ask? Would you like to buy the property?"

"God, no!" was Bergen's immediate response. "Let me lay out for you the background to my problem. I've been assigned to host a visiting scholar who is trying to finish a difficult research problem. Looming is a serious deadline. Temporarily, he's living with us. But, with the kids at home, and with both Moira and I working insane schedules, our place is a zoo. Some people can manage working in a zoo, but not this fellow. He needs peace and quiet. I'm looking to park him where very few people will be able to find and disturb him. Is it possible that I can hide him out at your farm? I'll pay you any reasonable rent."

Bergen, of course, was not telling the full story. Actually, the "visiting scholar" was Arnie, his brother-in-law. The "difficult research problem" was Arnie trying to figure out who had taken eight million dollars from B, H, and G. And the people who were looking for Arnie would not be content with "disturbing him"; they were trying to kill him. However, Bergen saw no need to burden Montego with an information overload.

"For you, old friend, whatever you want. I'll alert Mason to expect you. He will give you a set of keys for the main house. How long do you expect that this visiting scholar will wish to take advantage of our hospitality?"

"That's difficult to say," Bergen hedged. "It depends on how quickly he can complete his research problem. Suppose we leave it open ended with the understanding that, when he has worn out his welcome, you will tell me, and I'll move him somewhere else."

A small suspicion was beginning to grow in the back of Montego's mind. "This scholar wouldn't be some geopolitical refugee fleeing from his country's oppressive regime and their secret police, and now protected by the CIA, of which you are not a member, would he? If, in fact, there are agents who will be coming after this scholar to drag him back home, then I don't want to put Mason in the middle of such a dangerous mess."

Bergen answered with a laugh. "Of course not! You need to rein in that wild imagination of yours. There's already enough unpleasantness loose in the world without you dreaming up ridiculous new ones." He truly wanted to tell Montego the actual story, but he realized that, the fewer the people who knew it, the safer Arnie would be.

While Montego was reassured, the suspicion lingered. He relegated it to a dark corner of his mind. Then he telephoned Mason and alerted him that there was going to be a guest staying in the main house for the next few weeks. This guest would be looking for quiet and privacy. Mason should do whatever he could to accommodate the guest. Bergen Sawyer would be stopping by to pick up the keys. Finally, Montego gave Bergen the address for the farm and drew him a map so that he could navigate the boonies.

Their business concluded, they bused their trays and went their separate ways back to their offices. Both felt that the meeting had been constructive. Bergen came away with a new safe house for Arnie, one that was more secure than the previous one. Montego came away with a different way to view retirement, a subject that he was not yet comfortable wrestling with.

Chapter 25

Aunt Marcy

Her youngest child had just started college at the University of Wisconsin in Madison, intending to major in Abnormal Psychology. The nest was blessedly empty, and it was destined to remain so. Katie Carey now had the whole house to herself. There was no one to cook for and clean up after. There was no one to question her about where she was going and what time she would be back. She owned her schedule. She was responsible to no one. The quiet was a benediction. It was quite a change but glorious nonetheless. She reveled in her freedom.

The full-time position as restaurant critic for the Herald kept her busy and paid the bills. It also provided medical and retirement benefits. Plus, it was a labor of love. In her spare time, she functioned as GJ, the problem solver. Of the two, this was the more stimulating and, both mentally and physically, the more challenging work. However, it certainly paid much better than the newspaper did. This money went into her retirement account for she knew that there would come a day when she would no longer be able to handle the travel and/or the physical exertion. In addition, if the GJ operation was ever compromised, it gave her the means to run and hide.

The transition from Franklin to Carey as the independent contractor, GJ, occurred seamlessly. She preserved her anonymity just as Franklin had done with his. Jobs within a few hour's drive of Harrison were easily fit into her schedule at the newspaper. Those further away were accepted only when they could be made to coincide with her travel schedule for the paper. This rejection of choice contracts actually worked in her favor. It gave the impression that GJ was highly selective in "his" assignments and this increased the demand for "his" services.

It was in her second year as "Aunt Marcy" that Katie got the first opportunity to combine her two lines of activity. The paper sent her to Detroit, Michigan, to spend five days reviewing a half-dozen restaurants. Coincidentally, Mrs. Mildred Fletcher of Roseville, a Detroit suburb, solicited assistance in resolving a long-standing problem.

Mrs. Fletcher's nemesis was her next-door neighbor, Angela Bianco. The problem began many years ago when Mildred's husband, Michael, was still alive. At that time, the country was involved in what seemed like an endless war in southeastern Asia. Our country had abandoned the draft, but there were ominous signs that military conscription was soon to return. If it did, Michael was safe, having five minor children in house. However, Angela's husband, Tony, had not given her any children. Thus, if the draft was renewed, Tony was vulnerable and likely to be in the first cohort called. Angela could not allow that, and she was desperate to prevent it.

So, Angela seduced Michael, and he provided her with a child, and Tony with a rationale for a draft deferment. The child, a female, had features that were more Anglo-Saxon than Italian. Mildred suspected the truth and broke off her friendship with

Angela. Michael died young. He worked in the financial district and commuted by bus. One evening, as he was walking home from the bus stop, he was struck and killed by a hit-and-run driver. This driver was never identified. After a suitable period of mourning, Mildred moved on with her life.

After Michael's passing, Angela became increasingly aggressive and nasty. She never missed an opportunity to rub Mildred's nose in Michael's fall from grace. She accused Mildred of being a failure as a wife and lover. When no one else was watching, she spat on her. Mildred tried moving to a different neighborhood. Angela and Tony bought the adjacent property and they were neighbors once more, and Angela resumed the psychological warfare.

Mildred lacked the means to retaliate except in the more morbid of her fantasies. Then she found herself to be the beneficiary of a substantial inheritance from a favorite uncle. Now that she had the financial resources, she sought someone to put an end to Angela. Through the usual channels, GJ was offered the contract. After exhaustive research, Katie Carey deemed giving Mildred peace of mind to be a worthy cause. She accepted the commission.

Her destination was Detroit, Michigan. Whenever possible, she preferred to drive rather than fly. Her choice was influenced in part by the airline schedules, the delays for security checks, and the surcharge for baggage. Even if she flew, she would still need a rental car in Detroit. When there was serious driving to be done, she preferred her own vehicle, a 2017 Porsche Cayenne Turbo. She enjoyed driving; she was good at it; and she appreciated the quiet time to think. Finally, on her excursions, she usually brought back "souvenirs" that she didn't dare to expose to TSA scrutiny.

In Detroit, she checked in at the Westin Hotel and entrusted her Porsche to the care of the valet and the hotel's parking garage for the duration of her stay. Security at the garage was top notch and she was confident that her prized possession would be safe. She knew better than to take anything so valuable into sketchy neighborhoods and leave it parked at the curb, unattended. For her local travel in Detroit, she rented a Ford from Hertz. Since her expense account was courtesy of the newspaper, she attended to their assignment first. Business before pleasure! The paper had provided her with a list of ten recommended restaurants. Based on style of cuisine and location, she narrowed the list to a more manageable six. Two were steak houses, two featured seafood, and the other two, Italian food. Each restaurant received two visits, one for lunch and, on a different day, another for dinner. Routinely, she made reservations under the name of A. Burke.

She rated the meals on quality of ingredients, care in preparation, artistry of presentation, flavor, seasoning, price, and value. The staff was rated on knowledge of the menu, respectfulness, helpfulness, friendliness, and attention to detail. The establishment itself was rated on cleanliness, ambiance, noise level, décor, location, availability of parking, and, where appropriate, the view. After each meal, in the quiet of her hotel room, she wrote, in considerable detail, her impressions. Then, she exercised for two hours to burn off as many of the calories as possible.

After six days of restaurant tourism, she welcomed the change of pace that problem solving provided. Her research disclosed that Angela Bianco had become a pillar of St. Isaac Jogues' parish church and, this year, was Vice-President of the Women's Guild. She was determined to be President the following year. The only remaining hurdle was winning a popular vote. Thus, she was spending increasing amounts of time at church building her creds. A part of this was playing bridge three afternoons a week. She was a decent card player but hated the game. Still, her ambition drove her on.

GJ's records showed that Angela drove a black, 2007 Honda Accord. Katie Carey had no trouble locating the car in the church parking lot. Then, she left the lot and drove one street over, into a quiet residential neighborhood, shaded with a canopy of mature trees. She parked her rental car and gathered the tools that she would need. Locking the rental car, she walked back to the church parking lot.

Franklin's training program had included a tutorial on how to break into locked cars. With a wedge, a repurposed wire coat hanger, a little effort, and sufficient time, she popped the lock for the rear door on the passenger's side. Shortly before the scheduled conclusion of the card game, she entered the Accord, relocked the door, and lay on the floor behind the driver's seat, covering herself with a convenient blanket.

A short while later, Angela unlocked the car, got in, engaged the shoulder harness, and prepared to put the key into the ignition. Katie rose from her hiding place and lowered a rawhide loop over Angela's head and pulled it tight around her throat. She placed a wooden dowel in the loop and rotated it to tighten the garrote. Angela struggled, but the shoulder harness restricted her motion. Katie had the added advantage of being able to brace her knees against the back of the driver's seat for leverage. It was not a fair fight. *Always check the back seat before getting into your car.*

Just before Angela lost consciousness, Katie leaned forward and spoke into Angela's right ear. "Mildred sends you her greetings. She asked me to relay a message for her. May you rot in Hell!" That being said, Katie gave the dowel another turn and Angela began her journey to the netherworld. After Angela stopped breathing, Katie maintained the pressure for another five minutes before loosening the garrote. Then she spread the blanket over the back seat. Next, she released Angela's shoulder harness and muscled the body back onto the blanket.

Using Angela's key, she started the Honda and drove it off the lot and parked it in front of her own vehicle. She transferred the tools that she would need to the Honda. Then she cut off the lips, removed the tongue, and snipped off all ten fingers. Since she was not surgically trained, the operation was crude, but effective. The harvested body parts were encased in Ziploc bags and transferred to an insulated dry ice chest for transport in the rental car. Katie drove the Honda back to the school lot and parked it in its previous space. She moved Angela's body back into the driver's seat and used the shoulder harness to hold it in position. A Post-It note, with the initials GJ, was then pinned to Angela's blouse. Finally, with the key in the ignition, Katie set the locks and exited the Honda. She walked back to her car and drove to her motel. After a satisfying dinner and a good night's sleep, she transferred the ice chest to her own car, returned the rental, and drove home to Harrison.

Angela's body was discovered two days later. The Detroit police notified their counterparts in Harrison that the GJ serial killer had struck again. They acquiesced to the Harrison request that the body mutilation not be reported to the press. This information was being closely held to distinguish any GJ imitators who might spring up.

Mildred Fletcher read about the murder in the newspaper and was quite pleased with the results. It was money well spent. For miscreants, the message was clear: never mess with this widow.

Chapter 26

Arnie in the Boondocks

As reluctant as Arnie was to leave the comforting confines of Thornton University, the most recent attempt on his life had convinced him that he must relocate to survive. That being said, he was not altogether happy with the choice that Bergen had made.

They were on their way to Arnie's new quarters. Bergen was driving. Predictably, Arnie had buckled the lap belt and engaged the shoulder harness. He was not shy about expressing his feelings.

"Bergen, this new safe house is in the ass end of creation. If we drive much further, we'll be in the next state." His objection was approaching a whine. He was oblivious to the fact that Bergen had been taking an indirect route to make sure that they were not being followed.

Whining was no way to get on Bergen's good side. "Well, we tried hiding you in plain sight. In theory, it was a clever plan. Even Edgar Allen Poe might have approved. However, look how well that worked out for you in practice. So, now we're going to give total obscurity a try."

"It feels like I'm going to jail. I'm not the criminal here; I'm an innocent victim. And of all the people I might have gotten as a jailer, I draw you, my brother-in-law. Life is just not fair!"

"If you're looking for a pity party, you're talking to the wrong person. And, if you're displeased with my choice of location, you're absolutely going to hate my survival rules." If there was to be whining, Bergen was going to make sure that Arnie had something worth complaining about.

"What rules?" Arnie had not yet heard them, but he was already certain that he was not going to like them.

"There are several. First, you must not try to contact Gloria, or the children, in any way. No e-mail; no telephone! If you do, you'll put them all at risk. The people who are hunting you are ruthless. If they even suspect that your family knows where you are, or how to get in touch with you, they'll threaten them as a means of getting to you. I'm sure that you don't want their sufferings and deaths on your conscience." Bergen saw no reason to sugar-coat the situation. Arnie needed to realize that this was not a game, but truly a matter of life and death.

"That's harsh. I miss them terribly. However, I understand where you're coming from. I'll do nothing to jeopardize their safety."

That had been too easy, and Bergen didn't believe it for a moment. Which is why he had asked Max to loan him a technician for a couple of days. When Bergen kept Arnie out of the house for an afternoon, the tech bugged Arnie's cell phone and also tricked out Arnie's laptop computer so that all text messages, outgoing and incoming, also showed up on Bergen's computer. The tech repeated his magic with the land line and the computer at Montego's country home.

"Good! My second rule is that you must remain out of sight as much as possible. Stay indoors and avoid the windows. If you must venture out, confine yourself to the O'Higgins property. If they employ a sniper, you don't want to make it too easy for them."

"A sniper? Are you serious? Now you're trying to mess with my mind." Arnie was convinced that all this talk of a sniper was hyperbole to ratchet up the fear factor.

Bergen gave him his most sober stare. "If I was intent on killing you, I would use a sniper. It'd be my method of choice. It minimizes the risk for the assassin and it's neat, clean, and very dependable."

"Have you killed people that way?"

Bergen's only answer was "You don't really want to know," delivered with his most inscrutable smile.

They rode a while in silence. Periodically, Bergen checked Montego's directions.

Arnie broke the silence. "Suppose that I find your rules too Draconian and choose to ignore them? What'll you do?"

"If you insist on being a damn fool, I'll have two choices. I can kill you myself or I can look the other way while your pursuers do it for me. Either way, you're a dead man. Problem solved!" Bergen enjoyed watching Arnie process this information. Then he changed the subject. "How are you coming with the puzzle of figuring out who took the money? The sooner you solve that, the sooner we can end this game of house arrest."

"I've some suspicions but no hard evidence. This may be a problem I can't solve. If so, we may need to devise a different approach." Arnie's reluctance to give up on the problem was palpable.

They turned into a long driveway. A small bungalow sat 180 feet back from the street, on a two-acre lot. Behind the house was a large barn that housed the kennel. At first sight, Arnie found the house depressing. *If I am going to be confined to solitary, I was hoping for something more comfortable than this.* As they parked in front of the one-car attached garage, a man came out to meet them. He looked to be a generation older than Arnie, with a wrinkled face and a wild thatch of gray hair. His skin was deeply tanned and weathered, suggesting that he spent much of his waking life outdoors. His arms were heavily muscled and his hands well callused, indicating that he was no stranger to manual labor. For a man his age, he moved remarkably well. And, there was a mischievous twinkle in his gray eyes.

"Mason, I'm Bergen Sawyer. Montego phoned to alert you that we would be coming out here. This is my colleague, Professor Artemus Scott. He's going to be Montego's houseguest, and your neighbor, for a while. Artemus is looking for peace and quiet so that he can finish an important research project he's working on."

Bergen was glad for the opportunity to introduce Mason and Artemus. He didn't want either one mistaking the other for an intruder and doing something violent and irreversible.

"Well, yall've come to the right place," Mason drawled. "If it was any deader here, we'd have to put up gravestones." He handed Bergen a pair of keys on a ring. "Nobody uses the front door. I don't think it's been opened in years. Use the door off the deck in the back. The other key opens the garage. The place is ready for ya. If ya need anything, just give a holler."

As Bergen was about to put the car in gear and drive away, he was startled by a blur of gray, black, and white fur that streaked through the car's open rear window. He half turned to find an insouciant cat sitting regally in the backseat, casually preening itself.

Mason laughed. "Not to worry! That's just Phred. She's our official greeter. She comes with the property. She thinks that she owns all this." He waved his arm suggesting an indefinite expanse. "She's harmless unless yer a mouse, mole, chipmunk, weasel, or anything with wings. And, she's very fond of car rides."

Bergen shook his head and drove back to the main road. There he turned left and proceeded to the next driveway. This one extended much further back from the road and ended at a three-bedroom, split-level ranch with an attached garage, resting on the high-point of a five-acre lot. Flanking the entrance drive, were orchards of mature fruit trees: apple, cherry, peach, and pear. A small creek ran across the back of the property.

They left the car, went around to the back of the house, and ascended a short flight of stairs to the deck. As befitting a greeter, Phred led the way. The deck ran from the outer wall of the garage to the point where the house levels split. It was ten feet deep and held an eclectic collection of tables with umbrellas, chairs, loungers, and serving tables.

Bergen unlocked the sliding glass doors that led to the kitchen. When he opened the door, Phred was the first to enter and she quickly disappeared into the interior. Then, Bergen handed the keys to Arnie and told him to make himself at home and to behave himself. With that, he took his leave for the long drive back to Harrison.

Before Arnie could settle in, a loud "MEOW" reminded him that he was not alone. Phred was on the kitchen counter, sitting behind two empty metal bowls. Arnie understood the message immediately. He set down his bags and filled one bowl with tap water. A search of the cupboards revealed a supply of cat food. He half-filled the other bowl with dry food. "There you go, Princess! If you want anything more, you'll have to ask for it." Then, he caught himself. *What am I doing talking to a cat? Am I cracking up?*

He set out to familiarize himself with his new accommodations. The refrigerator and the freezer were well-stocked. So too was the liquor cabinet. He would not go hungry or thirsty. He commandeered the master bedroom for himself and left his suitcase there, on the bed. One of the other bedrooms had been converted into a home office and it was there that he parked his briefcase and laptop computer. Beneath the bedrooms was the family room. It was equipped with a state-of-the-art stereo system and an extensive collection of music that could be piped to speakers located in various parts of the house. It was not the Union's music room, but it was damn good. He could be comfortable here, but it would still be lonely. He missed Gloria.

Back in the kitchen, he found Phred sitting in front of the sliding glass door and staring out into the distance. She glanced over her shoulder at him with a beseeching look. Again, the meaning was unmistakable. He opened the door and Phred took off for parts unknown. *Eat and run! She could be one of my relatives.*

Before he left the kitchen, he picked a large Idaho potato and put it in the oven, set on low, to bake. He pulled a rib steak from the freezer and set it on top of the oven to thaw. There were greens for a salad and that would complete a reasonable dinner. Next, he queued up the two suites from Richard Strauss' "Der Rosenkavalier" and piped it into the study. He swung by the liquor cabinet and picked up a double shot of Jameson Irish Whiskey on the rocks. *After all, Bergen said to make myself at home.*

Then, he settled down at his computer, and for the tenth time, accessed the files at B, H & G, searching for any anomalies in the audits for the last five years. Once again, he found nothing. *The files were clean, almost too clean. Had you anticipated the audit and laundered your files, you could not have done any better.* He checked the personal brokerage accounts of his suspects, looking for matching transfers between the personal accounts and the clients' accounts. He found none.

One can only take so much frustration. He took a break and cooked dinner. The steak was broiled on the rare side of medium. The potato was baptized with a generous amount of butter. The field greens were anointed with a creamy Roquefort dressing. He washed it all down with a can of Molson's Golden Ale. It was a fine meal, and, in gratitude, he toasted his absent host, Professor O'Higgins. Letting his mind wander, he wondered where Phred was dining and what might be on her menu.

Reluctant to spoil his digestion with another round of frustration, he explored Montego's collection of DVDs. He found a copy of "Babette's Feast", a Danish film that had received an academy award for best foreign language film in 1987. Directed by Gabriel Axel, it was based on a story by Isak Dinesen. He had heard it much praised but had never had the chance to see it. It made for a delightful evening and, not once, did thoughts of grand larceny and attempted murder intrude on his enjoyment.

It was eleven o'clock when he turned in. Before he did so, he checked that the front door was deadbolted and that the rear sliding glass door was securely locked. Even so, he closed the bedroom door and wedged a chair underneath the door handle.

Chapter 27

The Broker and the Moneyman

I t had been ten days since the Moneyman had last talked with the Broker. The Moneyman was not long on patience and no amount of wealth could buy him more. He wanted results. They were what he was paying for. In the absence of results, he believed that he was entitled to regular progress reports. There had been none. He decided that it was time to give the Broker another dose of the Fear of God.

Using a burner phone, he dialed the number for the Broker's Las Vegas office. When the call was connected, the Moneyman launched into attack mode. "Where the Hell have you been? On vacation? In jail? Abducted by aliens? Given what I'm paying you, I've a right to timely progress reports. How are you coming with those loose ends we talked about?" The Moneyman had learned about the deaths of Hyrum Cassidy and Enoch Harris from the local newspapers. There had been no report of the passing of Barry Marsh.

The question was one of two that the Broker dreaded. But he could not duck this issue forever. "Harris and Cassidy have been dealt with. Unfortunately, Marsh has completely disappeared. My people are still looking. However, with each passing day, it becomes more likely that we'll never find him. On the bright side, so long as he remains missing, he's no threat to us." He spoke with a conviction that he did not feel in his intestines.

"Bright side, my ass! Don't delude yourself. So long as Marsh draws breath, he's a threat to both of us. It was a mistake not to deal with him first. The fellow in the hospital bed could have waited. He wasn't going anywhere. When are you going to learn to prioritize?"

There was a long pause while The Broker formulated and quickly rejected a series of witty replies to that rhetorical question. He knew that when The Moneyman vented, it was best to let him run his course and then quickly move on to other topics. To do otherwise was to risk prolonging the rant.

The Moneyman broke the silence. "Where are we with the hiring of GJ to solve our King problem?" He was desperate for any sort of encouraging news.

This was the other question that The Broker feared, and there was a quaver in his voice when he responded. "Well, I submitted our request through the usual channels. However, it was rejected."

"What the Hell! Who does this guy think he is? Is he so well off that he can afford to turn away paying customers?" The Moneyman's day was not getting any better and he was on the verge of losing control. "Do you think that he's just trying to hold us up for more money?"

"I don't think that money is his determining factor. This guy is good at what he does. He probably gets many more requests than he can possibly handle. I have no idea what criteria he uses to sift through the opportunities."

"Bullshit! Money rules the world. It always has, and it always will. Send our request back in. Tell GJ that we will double his usual fee. I'll bet that this gets his attention." This mindset had always worked for The Moneyman. Everything was for sale. It was just a matter of setting the price.

The Broker disagreed but he knew better than to argue the point. "I'll resubmit the request and call you as soon as I've an answer."

"Do that! If you don't have an answer in a week, call me anyway. We may have to examine alternative solutions to our problem. And if you can't handle simple assignments, I'll find someone else who can. I want King dead. I want to dance on his grave." The threat was delivered and understood. The Moneyman broke the connection.

The Broker sat quietly until his blood pressure returned to normal. Not for the first time, he regretted ever getting involved with the Moneyman. Then he composed a second solicitation for the services of GJ, this one at twice the going rate. He put it in the pipeline and sent it on its way.

* * * *

When Katie Carey received the second request, it had the intended effect. It got her attention. *Who is this guy who thinks that more money will persuade me to change my mind?* She rejected the bid for the second time. *Some people have too much money and too few brains.*

A week later, the request made its third appearance, this time offering to pay triple the standard rate. Considering that all the money that she earned as GJ went into her retirement account, she began to rethink the situation. *If this client is so foolish with his money, why shouldn't I be the one to relieve him of it? What is so special about this Mr. King that warrants such an extravagant send off?* The matter now had more than her attention. It intrigued her. She sent out an affirmative response but attached two conditions. First, she wanted to know everything that the client knew about Mr. King. Second, she asked for the complete details of any, and all, previous efforts to dispatch Mr. King. She was only guessing that there were such, but, given the circumstances, the guess was reasonable.

The client accepted the conditions. Katie worked her research into the occasional gaps in her schedule. Being Aunt Marcy by day and GJ at night left her precious little free time. In due course, GJ learned more about Mr. King than she cared to know. And she developed a rather low regard for the abilities of The Banned. *This type of work was not appropriate for amateurs.* Then she discovered that she was expected to deal with two problems rather than one. The first was that, since King had gone to ground after the two failed attempts on his life, she would first have to locate him before she could dispatch him. She was beginning to believe that she had sold herself short. On top of that, the Moneyman was pressing her for results. *If he thought that it was so easy, why didn't he go and do it himself? If he didn't ease up soon, she was going to have to tell him to take his business elsewhere.*

* * * *

For his part, the Moneyman was struggling to reconcile two different mind sets. He definitely wanted a professional job and GJ was judged to be the best in the business. However, he wanted the job done yesterday. GJ was moving at glacier speed, and the Moneyman worried that he might succumb to old age before King was put in the ground. In a close decision, common sense won on points. He had to cut GJ some slack, so he could work on his own time-table. Genius cannot be rushed. The careful, methodical man on occasion will win the day. He cut back on his nagging, but he was never happy about it. The partnership remained a very fragile one.

Of course, the one who was in the most uncomfortable position was The Broker. He was the most vulnerable and he had the most to lose. Neither principle knew the real identity of the other and they preferred that arrangement. But, the Broker knew the identity of both. Should the deal ever go South, the Broker, because of what he knew, could become a target for both sides. True, he was well compensated for his work, but you cannot spend it from the great beyond.

Chapter 28

The Search for Barry Marsh

Katie Carey recognized that Barry Marsh might be a valuable asset in fulfilling her assignment to eliminate Arnie King. So, she made a determined effort to accomplish what others before her had been unable to do, locate the missing Barry Marsh. The earlier failed attempts did not put her off. After all, she was a professional and the previous searchers had been amateurs.

She began her campaign by visiting Vera Marsh, Barry's wife at the time of his disappearance. The cover story that she used to gain Vera's confidence was that she had been commissioned to write a series of magazine articles on former NASCAR greats who were no longer in the public eye. The mystery of Marsh's disappearance made his story one that was irresistible. Was he dead and buried in a landfill? Or did he have one last blackout that permanently robbed him of his entire memory?

The two women got along surprisingly well. Vera cooperated fully. She had tried everything she could think of to track her missing husband, all to no avail. Now, she was so desperate that even the most unlikely approaches to solving her problem gave her a shred of hope. A feature article, in a magazine with national circulation, could be just the thing to induce someone with information to come forward.

As part of the visit, Katie got to see Barry's home office. Here, she quietly noted two clues. First, Barry was a long-time subscriber to Circle Track and to Motor Sport. The former was directed more to racers than to aficionados, while the latter was the original motor magazine, dating back to 1924. There were stacks of back issues everywhere. Barry never threw any of them away. Obviously, he valued them. Second was the fact that there were no recent issues. The latest ones all predated Barry's disappearance.

This suggested to Katie that Barry's subscriptions might still be active, just directed to a new address. If Barry had disappeared of his own accord, moving the subscriptions was exactly the thing that he would have done. So, she worked out a plan to con the publishers into providing her with Barry's current address. She spent some time writing out a script where she was the concerned wife whose husband had stopped receiving his magazines and who she was checking to make sure that the subscription department had their correct address. That there were two different publishers was a bonus. The effort paid off. The subscriptions were being sent to 32 Mound Street in Madison, Wisconsin.

Her next step was to persuade her editors that they should send her to Madison, Wisconsin, to review the restaurant scene of course. This was an easy sell. Since she was on a generous expense account, she elected to stay at the pricey Madison Concourse Hotel. It was centrally located, only a three-minute walk from the capitol. There were so many restaurants within easy distance that it was difficult to reduce her list to five. But the difficult had never stopped her before. Ian's Steak House was her first choice. Next came The Star, an upscale French Restaurant. Then Scion, another foray into fine dining. In the fourth spot was The Taste of Mexico. Closing the list was The Hamilton House.

She followed her usual routine, two visits each on different days, one lunch and one dinner if the hours permitted. Naturally, she began with Ian's. Here service and sophistication had been refined to the point that they threatened to eclipse the food. The attention was over the top, so much so that she began to wonder if she had been recognized and was being pampered to assure a glowing review. She finally concluded that her cover was intact. Ian's was praised for the level of its service but scolded for paying more attention to the service than to the quality of the food. A second scolding was issued for letting the prices get completely out of hand.

The Star ran into trouble immediately when it misjudged her as a granny who had lost her way. They seated her at a table just outside the door to the kitchen. This sin put her in a sour mood and would permit no absolution. Her scathing review was a body blow to the restaurant from which it never recovered. War with France was only narrowly averted.

Scion has delusions of becoming a threat to Ian's prestige. It still had a long way to go. On her second visit, she was seated adjacent to a table for a family of six, two parents and four pre-school-age children. The youngsters had never been taught any manners and the parents were blissfully unconcerned. Mayhem ruled! Complaints to her waiter and the Maitre'd were ignored.

The waiter might be excused for something that was beyond his job description. But, not so the Maitre'd. The dining room was his domain and his rule should be absolute. Given the ambient conditions, what was actually a very fine meal went undetected and thus unappreciated and unreported. She distracted herself from the mayhem by inventing, in great detail, gruesome deaths for the Maitre'd and for the clueless parents.

Mexican food had never been one of Aunt Marcy's favorites. She kept including it in her reviews because her readers and her editors expected it. At the time of her visits, The Taste of Mexico was experiencing an insurrection in the kitchen. The customers were collateral damage. Both hot and cold dishes were served lukewarm. Spicy food arrived either bland or blisteringly over-spiced. Dishes that should have been made with beef, contained chicken instead; the chicken dishes arrived made with pork. Orders for sides of sour cream or salsa were sometimes honored and sometimes not. However, the guacamole was exceptionally good!

The Hamilton House was a refreshing change of pace. It was not trying to be Ian's or Scion. It did not overreach in menu, service, atmosphere, or price. It was a family restaurant that knew its place. The staff, both kitchen and serving were well-trained and fairly-compensated. Aunt Marcy enjoyed two fine meals there and was not reticent when it came time to inform her readers.

In her free time, she staked out the home on Mound Street. A man fitting Barry Marsh's description was observed to leave early each morning. She followed him, and it soon became obvious that he was providing a taxi service. A little research revealed that the service was Uber and that he was using the name, Brandon Morris. She called Uber and arranged for Brandon Morris to pick her up the following morning at nine in front of her hotel.

Marsh/Morris was punctual. She asked to be taken to the Lake Windsor Country Club, ostensibly to make plans for a wedding reception for her daughter. When they arrived, she directed him to a remote area of the parking lot. Then, she touched the cold steel barrel of an automatic to his neck just behind his right ear.

"Mr. Marsh, keep both hands on the steering wheel, and remain still," she ordered. "I mean you no harm. I just want to talk with you. But, if you panic, I may, regrettably, be forced to shoot you."

"My name is Morris. I believe that you have me confused with someone else."

"Not very damn likely," she snorted. "You're the former racecar driver who twice failed an assignment to dispatch Arnold P. King into the hereafter."

"Who are you? Who sent you? And how did you find me?"

"You ask far too many questions! Many of the answers you have no need to know. Suffice it to say, I now hold the contract on Mr. King. I'm here to recruit you to help me. And, I do pay better than Uber. Are you interested?"

"Did the Pope used to be a Catholic? Hell yes, I'll sign on with you. How much are you paying and what do you want me to do?" He had learned very quickly that driving a hack was not how he wanted to spend the rest of his life.

"Why don't we go in to the Club Lounge and discuss the terms of your employment?"

The Lounge was paneled in Mahogany, with comfortable furniture, and dimly lit. It positively screamed Male Retreat and testosterone. Yet, no one challenged GJ. The bar was open and, despite the early hour, doing a brisk business. She ordered a Brandy Alexander and he, a Rob Roy. Then, she began to pick his mind for everything he knew about Arnie King.

Thus, she learned about Arnie's wife, Gloria, his bodyguard, Oscar, and Oscar's colleague, Bergen Sawyer. Indirectly, she also came to a better understanding of The Broker and The Money Man. The germ of a plan was planted, and she began to cultivate it.

She liked Marsh and, up to a point, trusted him. Even so, she still concealed her real identity and gave Marsh only as much information as he needed to complete his assignments. She provided him with a burner phone so that he could take her calls. At the end of the week, she drove back to Harrison. Still using the name of Brandon Morris, he followed two weeks later. He did not contact his wife. He suspected that the people who had terminated his two associates had not stopped looking for him.

Chapter 29

Arnie's Solitude

D espite all his faults, Arnie was a people person. He did not function well in isolation. Human contact was as essential to him as the air he breathed and the nourishment he ate and drank. Now, in the O'Higgins country retreat, comfortable prison though it was, he found himself in solitary confinement. Other than an occasional visit from Mason, there was nobody to talk to except Phred, the resident cat. Even after numerous attempts, Arnie had thus far been unable to engage the cat in an intelligent dialogue.

Arnie ignored Bergen's advice that he remain indoors and out of sight. It was too confining. Besides, he suspected that his brother-in-law exaggerated the risk. He reckoned that the odds on there being a sniper out there having a bullet with his name on it were vanishingly small. He was developing a serious case of cabin fever. In addition, he needed the exercise.

He started out cautiously by doing push-ups on the back deck. Afterwards, the lounger beckoned, and the sun felt good on his exposed skin. Phred seemed determined to find ways to amuse him. In one instance, she was stalking a low-flying butterfly. When the insect grew tired of the game and flitted to a higher altitude, Phred attempted to follow. She seemed to be climbing an invisible ladder that curved back over her head.

When she achieved her maximum height, she executed a graceful mid-air somersault and then stuck the landing. Always one to appreciate an artistic performance, Arnie applauded.

On another occasion, Phred was playing with a chipmunk she had caught. It was sport for the cat, but life and death for the rodent. Phred herded her captive, always keeping it in front of her. She would let it scamper a little distance toward freedom before playfully batting it back into the arena. After this torture had gone on for a few minutes, the chipmunk surprised everyone. Instead of running for the open yard, it charged directly at Phred. This move caught the cat completely off guard. David is not supposed to charge Goliath! The prisoner ran between Phred's legs and quickly climbed the mature lilac bush behind the cat. It did not stop until it reached the upper branches, well out of the cat's reach. Phred was one pissed pussy! She walked round and round the lilac bush, casting dirty looks at the escapee in the upper branches. From its safe perch, the chipmunk taunted her. She didn't take kindly to being outsmarted, especially by a chipmunk. Finally, she decided that it was a lost cause and she had better things to do. She wandered off. The chipmunk waited for the cover of darkness before descending. Arnie admired the animal's audacity but couldn't decide if it was the product of intelligence or desperation. He was tempted to applaud the rodent, but he didn't want to hurt Phred's feelings.

Arnie began taking daily walks around the periphery of O'Higgins five-acre parcel. He discovered a small creek running across the back of the property. It was too shallow for swimming and too wide to jump across. Thoughtfully, someone had taken an ancient corn crib, punched out the two end panels, and repurposed it as a charming covered bridge over the stream.

Today, while he walked, he kept turning over in his mind his puzzling predicament. *Who is it who wants me dead? And, why? Could it be personal? What have I done to warrant such animosity? My first guess at motivation was money. But that has led nowhere useful. It appears to be a dead end. Could the motive be revenge? Have I wronged someone so grievously that they now want me dead?* In great detail, he searched his past, including all of his client contacts. He found no transgression for which murder might be considered a proportionate response. *Could the motive be self-preservation? Was he a threat to someone's career, financial well-being, freedom, or life?* He could think of nothing that might fit. *Did he have something that someone else coveted? His position at the firm? His home? His wife?* Each new idea seemed more preposterous than the previous one. Finally, he gave up. He consigned the problem to his subconscious and backed off to give it room to do its thing.

Although his mind was preoccupied on his walks, he was still careful to remain watchful. His head was on a swivel; his eyes scanned everywhere, alert for any indication of a threat. He detected no glint of sunlight off a gun barrel. There were no unusual sounds. There were no signs of a stalker, except for Phred who seemed to be following his every move. *Perhaps she fancies herself a bodyguard and is here to protect me. Or, perhaps she is here to protect the property, to make sure that I don't damage it in any way.*

Today's circumnavigation done, they returned to the house and he followed Phred inside. He refilled her water bowl and helped himself to a second cup of coffee. Then, he settled down at his computer and began to catch up with what was going on in the outside world. He wanted desperately to e-mail Gloria, but Bergen had put the fear of God in him. The last thing he wanted to do was to put his wife's life in jeopardy. Phred followed him into the study and perched on top of a bookcase where she kept watch on him, eyes half-closed and as still as the Sphinx. She peaked Arnie's curiosity. *I wonder who she reports to?*

After lunch, Arnie explored the contents of O'Higgins' old barn. Among other things, he discovered artifacts of the original kennel, stored furniture, boxes of old files – the detritus of thirty years of academic life, an old tractor and snow blower, and a ten-speed bicycle with severely deflated tires. Nearby, he found a hand pump and was pleased to see that it still worked. He pressurized the tires and let them stand overnight. The next day he found that the pressure had indeed held. He rode the bicycle up and down the driveway several times to prove to himself that the vehicle was mechanically reliable. This finding buoyed his spirits immensely. *If someone comes after me here, I now have a way to escape this prison. It may not be as fast as I would like, but it is dependable and a mode of transportation that no one would expect.*

He began to take early morning bicycle excursions, building up his endurance while, at the same time, learning the pattern of the surrounding country roads. *If someone is chasing me, indecision could be fatal.* He was careful to avoid any contact with the pedestrians that he passed along the way. On his return to the house one morning, he found a dead animal on the deck, just outside the back door. For a brief moment, he wondered if his pursuers had found him and were sending him a Mafia-style message. Later that day, he had a chance encounter with Mason, the resident caretaker for the O'Higgins property, who had come to recharge the water softener. Arnie mentioned to Mason his discovery of the dead animal.

Mason laughed heartily. "That's a gift to you from Phred. It means that she likes you. She's a nocturnal hunter and she'll occasionally leave some of her trophies where Montego or I will be sure to find them. On a certain level, she's bragging about her hunting skills. You should be flattered that she's singled you out."

"That's all well and good, but what should I do with this trophy? If I bury it, she may think that I don't appreciate her gift. Yet, I can't bring it in the house and display it. What do you suggest that I do?"

Mason examined the trophy. "If I'm not mistaken, that's a Least Weasel. They are mean, nasty critters." He bent over and closely examined the weasel's mouth. "Look here, it has some fur between its teeth. The color of the fur is a good match to Phred's. The weasel may have lost, but it put up a good fight."

"Interesting, but not helpful. What am I to do with the carcass?"

"When I'm on the receiving end of one of Phred's gifts, I usually seal it up in a zip-lock plastic bag and put it in that freezer in the garage. Then, when Montego visits, he takes the specimens back to the University and donates them to the Biology Department for their collection.

"That sounds like a plan. Thank you."

Before Arnie's sojourn at the O'Higgins country home was finished, Phred gifted him with two more trophies. One was a long-tailed weasel. Google was a great help in making the identification. The other was a peculiar looking mouse. The forelegs seemed exceptionally short, while the hind quarters, including the tail, were enlarged and heavily muscled, reminiscent of a kangaroo. Eventually, it was identified as a jumping mouse, a species thought by most experts to be extinct in this corner of the state. It neatly filled a gap in the collection of Thornton's Biology Department and, in time, it earned Phred a letter of commendation. Montego O'Higgins framed this letter and hung it on the wall of his study where it remains to this day.

No account of Phred's exploits would be complete without a pair of stories that Mason, the O'Higgins caretaker and kennel supervisor, told Arnie. The first described how the cat delighted in teasing new litters of puppies. She would position herself on the serving shelf that stood beside the kitchen range and across from the kitchen table. Young puppies, who were just beginning to explore their surroundings, were given free run of the hallway and the kitchen area. Phred would dangle her tail over the edge of the shelf and wave it back and forth in front of the puppies, teasing them. They, of course tried to catch it. But Phred was fast and they were never successful.

The second story involved an incident that had taken place the previous year. It was early on a very cold morning. Mason, still in his pajamas and barefoot, was brewing his first pot of coffee. Outside the sliding glass door to the dining room, Sheila, the kennel's foundation bitch, but now very long in tooth, was taking care of her morning business. A large, male Rottweiler chose this time to stroll across the backyard. It belonged to one of the neighbors and was seldom allowed off their property, and then only on lead with a handler. Today, it was unleashed and alone. He seemed to be intent on some private mission and paid no attention to Sheila. Sheila may have been offended by this indifference, we shall never know. The fact is that she began to follow the Rottweiler as if they were forming a parade. Mason, not suitably dressed for a chase through the brush, opened the sliding door and called for Sheila to return. She ignored him. He might as well have been trying to call back the wind. At that point, Phred bolted through the opening and gave chase.

Quickly, she caught and passed Sheila. Then, ignoring the Rottweiler, she turned back toward Sheila and blocked the path. She would not let the bitch pass. This provided Mason with enough time to put on shoes and a coat and to get to the scene. He scooped up Sheila and carried her back into the house. Only later did Mason begin to wonder where Phred had acquired such intelligent instincts.

The more Arnie thought about his own predicament, the more he saw parallels with Phred's chipmunk. He was being hunted and, when the hunters finally caught up with him, they intended to kill him. Thus far, his strategy had been to evade the hunters and hide until a better strategy presented itself. But, suppose that this new strategy never materialized, what then? He could not hide forever. Perhaps he should imitate the chipmunk, do the unexpected, and go on the offensive. However, when you do not know the identity of your adversaries, it is difficult to plan an offensive. He might have to draw the hunters out into the open. To do so would require some irresistible bait. He shuddered when he realized that he, himself, would have to be that bait. It was not the role he had any desire to play, but then, he might not have any choice. None of this made for restful nights.

Meanwhile, he kept busy constructing in-depth profiles of each of his professional colleagues: Harold Boyd, Stephen Hunter, Jeffrey Gould, and Nicholas Gestas. He kept searching for anything that might suggest motive for what had been transpiring. Thus far, he had nothing. He put the question to Phred, but she remained silent and stoical.

Chapter 30

Constructing a Trap

Bergen, after many hours of reviewing, and rejecting, a variety of scenarios for resolving the Arnie King situation, finally decided that he and Oscar needed to have an extended talk about their strategy going forward. They agreed on Jedidiah's Restaurant on "the West Bank" the following Tuesday afternoon at 1:00 o'clock. When they arrived, they each scanned the collection of diners, searching for anyone who seemed out of place. While it was true that Enoch Harris, the would-be assassin from the Natatorium, was dead and buried, there could very well be a replacement. They saw no one pretending to read "Gilgamesh". No one appeared to be taking particular note of their arrival. They relaxed a bit, yet they still watched the front entrance, screening for any suspicious late arrivals.

Oscar opened the discussion with the question that had been haunting his waking hours: "How's our colleague, Artemus Scott, doing?" In their time together, Oscar had become fond of Arnie, much as he might have had he befriended a lost puppy.

Bergen grimaced. He was not yet comfortable with this alias. "About as well as you might expect. He's relatively safe so long as he behaves himself. He has the basic creature comforts. However, temperamentally, he's not well-suited for the role of either a prisoner or an exile. If forced to continue this way for an extended period, it may well drive him crazy."

"We can't have that." Oscar was simply belaboring the obvious. "We need him to help us figure out who is behind the plot to kill him."

Bergen had heard enough truisms to last him a lifetime. "What, then, do you suggest that we do?" The challenge in his tone was unmistakable.

Oscar's reply was prefaced with an eloquent shrug. "I've wracked my brain over that very question. I must admit that I haven't the slightest idea."

It was the answer that Bergen expected, but hoped not to hear. "Then, let me suggest a strategy. Until now, we've been playing defense. Thus far, we've been successful. However, we only need to fail once to lose the whole game. I think that it's time that we began playing offense. Let's take the fight to our adversaries; let them play defense for a while." Fundamentally, Bergen was a man of action. Sitting quietly and protecting the status quo was not his style.

"I approve of stirring the stew pot to see what happens," Oscar replied. "But, precisely how do you propose that we go about it?" He knew well that the mischief is always in the details.

"I suggest that we try to draw our opponents out into the open where we can see who we are up against. Otherwise, we're fighting ghosts and shadows."

Oscar was beginning to get a sick feeling deep in his entrails. "But, to get them to come out into the open, we're going to need to bait them with something they can't resist. Surely, you're not suggesting that we use Arnie? That's sick!"

"Come on, Oscar! They're not going to bite on anything less. I believe that we can do it while keeping Arnie safe. Hear me out."

"You've got the floor. Convince me!" Oscar folded his arms across his chest and his manner was defiant. He was beginning to think that Bergen was seriously unhinged. If that proved true, then it would be necessary for him to put an end to this dangerous folly.

Bergen laid out the basic framework. "Suppose we arrange a meeting between Arnie and Gloria. After all, they're both eager for this to happen. Then, we leak word that this meeting will take place at a given location, on a certain date, at a specified time. We stake out the meeting site and, when our adversaries come to take Arnie, we grab them instead. End of story." He paused for Oscar's reaction. It was not long in coming.

"You really are out of your goddamned mind. Not only would you be exposing Arnie, but now you would be putting Gloria at risk as well. I won't have any part of it!" Oscar's righteous indignation was building along with his blood pressure.

Bergen quietly applauded. "Bravo! I would expect nothing less from you. But, who said anything about putting these people in harm's way? According to my plan, neither one of them will even be there in person. We can use a pair of stand-ins. It will be a small theatrical production for a select audience."

Oscar was beginning to calm down. Clearly, Bergen had put a lot of thought into this and, wild though the idea was, it might just work. "The meeting site will be critical. Tell me that you've a place in mind."

Noting the tacit approval of the concept, Bergen plowed ahead. "It must be a place with very few people. They would simply get in the way, muck things up, and increase the risk that someone will get hurt. Besides, the fewer the witnesses, for what we're doing, the better. It should be a place where we can monitor all the access routes. We certainly don't want our opponents sneaking up on us. I think that it should be on campus. Our familiarity with the territory will give us an added edge."

Nodding his approval, Oscar said, "I'm impressed."

"Three sites came to mind rather quickly," Bergen continued. The first was the Nass Library. It'll be open late in the evening to give students who are studying for their mid-semester exams increased access. However, the sheer volume of student traffic makes the Library unsuitable. We must try to minimize collateral damage. My second thought was the Faculty Lounge. In many ways, it would be ideal. But, you never know when you're going to find an Accounting Professor asleep on the couch, snoring up a storm. My third choice was the Chapel of St. Tomas. That, too, will be kept open late to accommodate students who are preparing for their exams by imploring heavenly intercession. Here, one needn't worry about the volume of traffic. The Rathskeller is close by and its attraction easily eclipses that of the Chapel."

According to the sanctioned and authoritative history of the Order of the Sons of Bedric, St. Tomas, SOB, an early recruit in Bedric's order, was martyred in 974 A.D., killed by an angry, drunken mob when he refused to recant his faith. Death was said to be by drowning in the Berounka River.

As is often the case, the historical truth was less edifying and more prosaic. Tomas Pom (933-974) worked for Bedric's father, Zaclav, in the family brewery. Tomas was an apprentice brewer. At the time of his death, he was responsible for the addition of the hops to the wort. More specifically, he was charged with removing any foreign material that came mixed with the hops. He had spent much of that morning doing unauthorized quality control on a batch of Zaclav's lager, and it had adversely affected his balance. When he leaned into a vat to remove some twigs and leaves, he fell in and drowned. It was reported that, when his body was pulled from the wort, his face was frozen in a beatific smile.

"Of the three, the Chapel sounds like the best bet," Oscar observed. "A romantic reunion in the house of God. It smacks of Romeo and Juliet."

Bergen felt obligated to return Oscar's attention to the real world. "Remember that the Romeo and Juliet reunion didn't end well for either of them. Consider, too, that neither Arnie nor Gloria will actually be present. There is another reason I like the Chapel as our stage. It has that empty space that is intended to house a pipe organ once the President finds a donor who can be persuaded to earmark his gift for such an acquisition. That empty space is where you and I will conceal ourselves until our foes are within reach."

Oscar acted as devil's advocate, a role that he was born to play. "I can see that this might work, but how do we get the details of the meeting to the opposition since we do not know yet who they are?"

"You forget that they have a tap on Gloria's landline. We discovered it and decided to leave it in place to avoid alerting them that we knew what they were up to. Now, we'll use it to our advantage. Arnie, or more likely someone pretending to be Arnie, will call Gloria and inform her of the details of the meeting." Bergen was prepared to make the call himself if it proved necessary.

"I see one major problem," Oscar interjected. "If we're not going to have Arnie and Gloria participate in our little drama, how do we keep them off stage and out of harm's way? Can we keep them innocent of what we're doing? If they find out, then they'll want to be involved."

"You raise a worrisome point, one that has been bothering me," Bergen admitted. "With Arnie, it'll be best if he doesn't find out anything about what we are planning. I will arrange for someone to baby-sit him at the safe house and prevent him from leaving. As for Gloria, we may need to use her sister, Moira, to distract her and keep her occupied far away from the action. Shopping, dinner, and a show might do it." Since Moira was Bergen's wife, he was naturally reluctant to get her involved. But, stressful times often require uncomfortable choices.

"That begs another question," Oscar observed. "All along, we've presumed that the people who are hunting Arnie would have someone watching Gloria. It's what we would've done had our positions been reversed. If, in fact, someone is watching her, how do we spirit her away without them finding out?"

Bergen was pleased. The thought process behind the question showed that Oscar was buying into the whole scenario. "It won't be easy, but I think that it can be done. Personally, I prefer plans that are simple, with few moving parts. Unfortunately, this is not one of those. We will need an additional player, preferably a female. Let us call Gloria A, Moira B, and this other player C. B drives out to visit A. On the floor of the car, behind the front seat and covered with a blanket, is C. Since Arnie's car is still in the police impound lot, there's an empty space in the King's two-car garage, and it's here that B parks. The doors close and C enters the house unobserved. Later, when B drives away, it is A who is on the car floor, under the blanket."

"So, the sisters are safely off for shopping, dinner, and a show. I like it so far. Now what?"

"Later that afternoon, you drive out to the King house in your all too conspicuous car. You avoid the garage and park on the circular drive, directly by the front door. Shortly after, you and C leave in your car. C will have spent part of the afternoon trying to disguise herself so that, to a casual observer, she looks like A. It would help if, when you are leaving, she has a hand to her face so that the watcher cannot get a good look. A coat with a hood would also be useful. The two of you will drive to the Thornton campus and park the car well away from the Chapel. There, the two of you will part company. She'll go home, and you'll come and meet me in the Chapel. The two of us will then take up our hiding places." Bergen had deliberately left out a vital piece of information. He paused to see if Oscar would notice the omission. If he did, it was certain to provoke a serious disagreement. He steeled himself.

"My friend, you haven't yet said who'll be playing the part of C, the A stand-in. Who do you have in mind?"

Bergen decorated his face with a mischievous smile but did not answer.

Oscar got the point very quickly. "If you're thinking of involving my wife, Constance, then forget it. That's out of the question. It's not going to happen. I'll not allow it." He was working his way up to a full rant.

Bergen maintained the smile while he waited for the rant to crest and then begin to subside. When he finally spoke, he was almost apologetic. "Oscar, you're too late. I spoke with Constance this morning and explained the situation. She volunteered and is committed to doing it. At this stage, I wouldn't want to be the one who tells her that she's been written out of the script."

Oscar knew well the futility of trying to get his wife to change her mind once she had it made up. "You, sir, are a slimy bastard! One day I'll make you pay for this."

Over the years, people far more sinister than Oscar had threatened Bergen. He had never lost even a moment's sleep over any of them. "Look at it this way, aside from the time she spends in the King house, she'll never be alone. At the most sensitive juncture, she'll be riding with you in your car. What better protection could you ask for?"

Oscar's brow was creased with a deep frown. "Understand this! If any harm should come to her in this little adventure, I'll hold you personally responsible." Those were his last words on the subject. They never spoke of it again.

Before they went their separate ways, they agreed to stage the mock reunion at the Chapel one week hence.

* * * *

The telephone tap was still active and Gloria's invitation to a reunion with her errant husband was duly noted. Katie Carey shared this information with Barry Marsh/Morris. Initially, they were elated. They were going to get another crack at Arnie King. There were thoughts of celebrating with a party. But then, Katie's paranoid survival instincts kicked in. Suppose that this was a trap. They would need to proceed carefully to keep from screwing up.

Surveillance on the King home was doubled, going on high alert. One watcher was instructed to follow Gloria King every time she left the house, even if she was only going to church or to pick up the dry cleaning. The watchers were ordered to check in every hour by burner cell phones, even if they had nothing to report. Katie was convinced that, sooner or later, Gloria would be the key to finding Arnie. The game was on.

On the day of the reunion, Bergen's plan rolled out flawlessly. This fact made him uneasy. Only in fiction are detailed plans executed flawlessly. There must be something that they had overlooked. Moira delivered Constance to the King house undetected. Similarly, Moira left the house with Gloria hidden on the floor of the car, behind the front seats. Thinking that Moira was alone, the watchers did not follow. For all intents and purposes, "Gloria" remained alone in the house. Constance was careful to stay out of sight and to do nothing that might spoil the illusion.

Oscar arrived on schedule and picked up the supposed "Gloria". Constance was wearing Gloria's clothes and, when she made the transit from the front door of the house to the car, she feigned a sneezing spell and managed to hide most of her face in a large handkerchief. As they left the property, one of the watchers followed at a generous distance. After all, he knew where Oscar and "Gloria" were headed.

When Constance and Oscar entered the Chapel, she did a quick change into a nun's habit, The Order of St. Stephen, Stoned. She left the chapel and walked home. The wimple did a fine job of disguising her facial features. Nobody gave the nun a second look even though Katie Carey's people were watching the Chapel and had been since early afternoon. They were focused on identifying Arnie King when he arrived.

About a half-hour after the nun's departure, Bergen Sawyer and another man entered the Chapel. The watchers, who were equipped with night vision goggles, got a good look at the "plus one" and determined that it was not Arnie King. They stayed at their posts, checking everyone who entered the Chapel until, close to midnight, they received a call that Gloria had returned home. For Katie Carey and Bergen Sawyer, this sparring round was a draw. While there was no winner, now they each understood the other a little better.

Katie reviewed this transparent attempt to draw GJ out into the open. *"Nice try Professor Sawyer! Next time, bring the real Arnie King and perhaps we can do a little business"*. She put further thoughts of Bergen on the back-burner. She had a salary to earn and another road trip was in the offing.

Chapter 31

Aunt Marcy at Work

I t had been a month since Aunt Marcy last took her restaurant road show out of state. This time, the destination was Pittsburgh, Pennsylvania. As usual, she drove. It promised to be an easy trip. Katie Carey had no GJ business scheduled, so she would be able to focus all her attention on her day job.

Her list of recommended restaurants was far too long. After much work, she pared it to five, a number she was comfortable with. She always worried that, in the cutting, she had been arbitrary, capricious, or biased. Had she, unknowingly, eliminated a rising star from her list? She rationalized that, so long as it had been unintentional, there was no sin involved. Thus, she lost no sleep over her choices. But then, her actual sins, which were more grievous, did not keep her awake either.

The list of restaurants, not sins, included: Au Pair Frederick, a French restaurant in the Uptown area; Lamps of China in North Oakland; L'Auberge du Riviere, featuring a continental menu in the Southside Flats; The Wiltshire, a steakhouse in the downtown section; and Bidleman's, a seafood establishment in the North Shore area.

At Au Pair Frederick, the menu was authentically French and executed superbly. The wine list was unapologetically French and included some excellent, and expensive, vintages.

Impressive though that might be, what most intrigued Aunt Marcy was the service. The wait help had obviously been thoroughly trained, but it went beyond that. They almost appeared to be clairvoyant. After finishing one course, and taking some time to savor the afterglow, the mind inevitably turns to the next course. At that very instant, with no visible cue from the diner, the wait person would appear from wherever he/she had been lurking and begin serving the next course. The timing was surreal. *Did the staff read minds?*

Frederick was so deeply committed to providing the true French dining experience that, routinely, every August, he would close the restaurant for several weeks and, at his own expense, he would take his staff to France for a graduate course in authentic French dining. It was little wonder that the retention rate for his staff was so high.

The Lamps of China was a white tablecloth establishment. It was widely rumored to be financed by the Mafia. They dealt only in cash; no credit/debit cards; no personal checks; no promissory notes; no first-born children. The rumor of Mob backing may have been started by jealous competitors and was never proven. The cuisines were Cantonese, Hunan, and Sichuan. Here one found all the favorites, including Beef with Oyster Sauce, Barbecued Honey Garlic Spare Ribs, Dong'an Chicken, Mao's Braised Pork, Kung Pao Chicken, and Tea-smoked Duck. It was an expensive night out and most people reserved it for a celebratory occasion. None the less, it was a good value.

For L'Auberge du Riviere, the river in question is the Monongahela. The Inn is charming; the menu, written on a chalk board mounted high up on the wall at one end of the main dining room, is continental. There are some staples that are immutable: Lobster Bisque en croute, Coquilles Saint-Jacques, Filet de boeuf Wellington, Veal Medallions with Lobster, Shrimp, Scallops, and Asparagus in a Normandy Wine Sauce, Lemon Cheesecake, and Raspberries Romanoff. Then there are the variable listings that change with the season, with the availability of the ingredients, and the whim of the head chef. One might find an intense Pumpkin Soup, Escargot Basilic, Lobster/Shrimp Ravioli, Snapper crusted in almond meal and topped with sautéed apples, Cherries Jubilee Francois, and Bananas Foster.

Aunt Marcy had dined at L'Auberge six years earlier, when it was under a different ownership. She remembered it for two quite different reasons. The first was that the meal had been magnificent, one that was imprinted on her gastronomic memory. The second was that, engrossed as she was with the dining experience, she had come away afterwards leaving behind her very expensive camera that she had put underneath her place at the table. By the time she missed it, it was too late to go back. Instead, she alerted the management by telephone and they found the camera and locked it away for her. She came back for it the next day, arriving in the late morning. At that time, the restaurant was not open for lunch. She was escorted in through the kitchen. There, on a stainless-steel table, she saw a regiment of uncooked Beef Wellingtons lined up with military precision, as if standing for inspection by a visiting commander-in-chief. It was a grand sight and the memory of it never failed to bring a smile to her face and an accompanying rumbling in her stomach.

The Wiltshire had been a fixture on Claremont Street since 1902. The restaurant is in a long, narrow brownstone. The original lighting used 35 gas lamps. These were still in place but had been converted to electricity. Cherry-framed mirrors line the two long walls, contributing to the illusion that the room is much wider than, in fact, it is. The furniture is substantial mahogany. The atmosphere is such that it would be easy to believe that one had been magically transported to an exclusive men's club, circa 1933.

Appropriately, steaks and chops, whether beef, lamb, mutton, or pork lead the voluminous, but idiosyncratic, menu. Following closely there is a staggering variety of crustaceans, headed by Oysters, Clams, Lobsters, Scallops, Shrimp, and Crabs. There are a dozen varieties of fish. Where else can you find a menu that includes frogs-legs, stirred eggs Treblow, and four kinds of Welsh Rarebit. Before it became illegal to sell turtle or whale meat for consumption, green turtle soup and a whale steak were menu fixtures. Not so in this more enlightened age. However, if you enquire discretely of the waiter, you may get lucky.

Quite arbitrarily, Aunt Marcy chose to begin her restaurant tour with Bidleman's. Thus, on Monday, at 12:30 p.m., she drove her rental Ford to the North Shore. Parking was scarce, but she finally found a spot three blocks away. The lunch crowd was beginning to thin and she was seated promptly. On the menu, the promise of an "authentic" Salade Nicoise spoke to her. She added a glass of the house Chardonnay to her order.

To be kind, the meal was a great disappointment. While the salad was edible, it was far from authentic. Even the wine tasted as if it was poor quality supermarket swill. In her head, she was beginning to compose a damning review, when the Manager stopped by her table.

"Aunt Marcy, what the Hell are you doing here?" Tobias Woodford, the Manager, was making routine rounds of the tables, doing his best to promote good public relations. Wherever he went, he carried with him a glass of Vodka and Tonic, sipping from it occasionally. It was part of the persona he was projecting.

"Tobias, please lower your voice, and refrain from using my name," scolded Aunt Marcy who went to great lengths to remain anonymous. "Please sit down and join me for a few minutes."

Tobias accepted the invitation and let his mind drift back in time. He and Aunt Marcy had crossed paths just once before, in Harrison where he was managing a restaurant. The encounter, while brief, was unforgettable. At that time, he had not known who she was or the power that she wielded. Her review damned the restaurant brutally. The only thing that she reported liking about the establishment was its attractive menu. That review had cost Tobias his job and the restaurant its existence. In the heat of the moment, Tobias had threatened to kill Aunt Marcy if he ever got the opportunity.

"You're looking well Tobias. I see that you landed on your feet and that you're still involved in the food service business."

She appraised Tobias with a critical eye, on the lookout for any indication of impending violence.

"Yes, I was quite fortunate. I own this place and we're doing well. I assume that you are here to evaluate our operation for your paper. How was your lunch?"

"I really regret that you asked me that. But, since you did, I'll be direct. She ticked off the gastronomic failures on her fingers. Your "authentic" Salade Nicoise was anything but. You should be sued for misrepresentation. The tuna fish was not fresh, but frozen. The anchovies and beans came from cans. You substituted Kalamata for the Nicoise olives. The potatoes were reconstituted, and the chervil was dried, not fresh. Finally, the Chardonnay tasted as if it came in a box from the supermarket. I hope that this wasn't an example of one of your better efforts."

Tobias fought down the rage that was building and fueling the urge to strangle Aunt Marcy with his bare hands even in front of a room full of witnesses. He managed a laugh. "Same old Aunt Marcy. You catch everything. You haven't changed a bit." He sipped his drink. "Most of our clientele aren't so astute. You must come to dinner one evening and let us show you what we can do when we put our minds to it."

"You really don't need to go to all that trouble. I will not be bribed. A favorable review cannot be bought with an extravagant dinner. Since my cover is blown, my paper will not be publishing a review of your restaurant. Given the quality of the Salade Nicoise, I'd say that you have caught a lucky break. Accept it for what it is."

Although his mind was contemplating murder, Tobias laughed exuberantly. "Dear Lady, bribing you was the farthest thing from my thoughts. Let us fix you a fine dinner for old time's sake. What do you say?"

"Well, my schedule is rather full. How about Friday evening at seven? Should I bring my personal food-taster? I seem to remember that you once threatened to kill me." She made light of the threat, but, in her mind, she still regarded it as genuine and serious.

He laughed again. "No need! I'll be your food taster. My threats were rash words made a long time ago in the heat of a very difficult moment. When I calmed down, they disappeared completely, like the morning dew. You've nothing to fear from me. In fact, I've become a great admirer of your work." He lied most convincingly. "Dinner on Friday at seven it is then. I'm looking forward to it."

Aunt Marcy paid her bill and went on her way. Given this unexpected encounter with Tobias, she now had some shopping to do. Her first stop was at a nearby plant nursery where she spent some time admiring their collection of oleanders. The owner noted her interest and engaged her in conversation. She enquired about the dos and don'ts of raising oleanders. Patiently, he answered her questions. It wasn't often that he had the opportunity to spend time with someone who took such a serious interest, and he was pleased. She enquired about the problems of raising the plants from seed. He pointed out that, while it was not easy, when successful, it was most rewarding. She told him that it was something she wanted to try. He sold her a small package of oleander seeds, enough to get her started.

Next, she visited a liquor store and bought a pint of Everclear's 190-proof Vodka. Then, she located an apothecary and purchased a small agate mortar and pestle, a package of plastic disposable syringes, a dozen two-inch test tubes, and a pair of neoprene gloves.

That evening, back in her hotel room, wearing the gloves, she carefully opened the package of oleander seeds. She knew that they were a source of cardiac glycosides. In the mortar, she crushed them and then ground them into a fine powder. Adding a few milliliters of vodka to the mortar, she ground the powder again. When the undissolved solid had settled, she decanted the liquid with a syringe and put it into a small test tube. She repeated the procedure with fresh Vodka several more times. The extracts were combined and let stand for most of the solvent to evaporate.

Aunt Marcy prided herself on being a shrewd judge of human nature. She knew Tobias Woodford to be a complete scoundrel and no passage of time was going to change that. Thus, she trusted him not at all and she was determined to launch a preemptive strike before he had an opportunity to kill her. It was nothing personal, just enlightened self-preservation.

For his part, Tobias sprang into action as soon as Aunt Marcy left his restaurant. From the kitchen, he summoned the assistant sous-chef, Salvatore Stavola. Sal often padded his take-home pay by performing wet-work for Tobias.

"Sal, have a seat. What would you like to drink?"

"Bourbon, on the rocks, please."

Tobias placed the order and, while they waited, they discussed trivial matters. With the arrival of the drink, Sal toasted Tobias' health, sampled his drink, and then, since he sensed that this was not a social occasion, brought the focus back to business. "What's on your mind, boss?"

"This coming Friday, at seven p.m., I am hosting a dinner for Aunt Marcy, just the two of us. She isn't one of my favorite people and I've a score to settle with her from bygone days. When she leaves here, I want you to follow her. When she gets to her car, I want her to be the victim of a mugging. During this encounter, things go terribly wrong for Aunt Marcy. She is shot and killed by the mugger. Most unfortunate! Do you think that you can handle this? I'll double your usual fee."

"Boss, it's as good as done. Don't give it another thought." Sal drained his glass and returned to the kitchen.

Tobias took another sip of his drink and basked in the warm glow of a plan well-conceived. He was very pleased with himself.

Chapter 32

Showdown at Bidleman's

O rdinarily, Aunt Marcy scheduled one last restaurant evaluation, a dinner, on Friday evening before decamping for Harrison with her notes and the first draft of several reviews. However, tonight would be rather different since no review of Bidleman's would be written, much less published. It should have been a stress-free, enjoyable social evening. Alas, such was not to be the case.

She arrived five minutes before the appointed hour. It might have been earlier except that parking was more of a problem than it had been on her previous visit. She was lucky to find a space four blocks away from the restaurant. Tobias had planned an intimate dinner for two. The table was in an alcove set in the right-hand wall, about halfway between the main entrance and the kitchen. There was no clear line-of-sight from the kitchen into this alcove, so Sal switched roles with the busboy and came out to pour the ice-water. He got a good, close-up look at Aunt Marcy and committed her features to memory. She reminded him of his grandmother. He would have no trouble identifying her later.

Carefully, she put her clutch purse and her gloves down next to her water glass. Tobias, still sipping his vodka and tonic, asked her if she would like a cocktail. She paused before responding, weighing the possibility that the bartender might have been instructed to poison her. She finally decided that Tobias lacked the balls for such a direct attack and ordered a Brandy Alexander. It was a drink of which she was especially fond. While it was more commonly ordered as an after-dinner drink, she thought of herself as a trend-setter and did not feel constrained by outmoded tradition or what other people thought.

When she commented on the absence of menus, Tobias told her that he had designed a special dinner to showcase the skills of his chefs and to impress his distinguished guest. It was the least he could do for a friend of long-standing. He was piling it on so deep that Aunt Marcy was forced to reconsider the possibility that he actually did intend to poison her.

At six minutes past the hour, the Maitre'd materialized at Tobias' elbow and whispered a message in his ear. As she watched her host's facial expression, it changed from irritation at the interruption, to curiosity, and then panic once he heard the full message. As he started to rise from his chair, he made his excuse. "It's a telephone call about a matter of life and death. I must take it. Please excuse me for a few moments." He hurried off in the wake of the Maitre'd.

Aunt Marcy feigned disappointment as she waved him off on his way. Inwardly, she was quite pleased. She had arranged with the concierge at her hotel for the telephone call. The call had been timely and, obviously, convincing. It was all precisely as she had planned it. She made a mental note to increase the concierge's gratuity.

Tobias had been so distraught that, in his haste to get to the telephone, he had left his drink behind. It was a bit of luck, something that she had hoped for, but dared not count on. Depending on luck was a loser's game plan. But, when it fell into your lap, you would be a fool to ignore it.

Moving with the speed and dexterity of a master illusionist, she reached into her purse and removed a hypodermic syringe loaded with a few milliliters of the concentrated solution of oleander seed extract in vodka. She squirted it into the drink that Tobias had left behind. She used the syringe to give the mixture a few quick stirs. Then the syringe disappeared back into her purse. She didn't touch her own drink but sat quietly waiting.

When Tobias returned, he was in a foul mood and muttering to himself. She was at her most solicitous. "Is everything all right? I hope that the call wasn't bad news." When she wanted to, she could give a most convincing impression of empathy.

"It was just some drunk claiming to be my girlfriend's former lover. He was threatening to kill her and himself. I've dealt with it. He'll not bother us again. Now, where were we?"

"I was about to propose a toast," she said, raising her glass. "Here's to the beginning of a long and mutually beneficial friendship!" Neither one of them believed that anything like that was actually going to happen, but they both participated in the toast and drank deeply.

Almost immediately, Tobias became flushed and began to sweat profusely. He started to retch, got up from the table, and headed for the men's room. He only made it six paces from the table when he lost consciousness and pitched forward, landing face down on the tile floor. Respiratory paralysis and death followed shortly after. When the emergency rescue squad arrived, they tried to resuscitate him, but it was far too late.

During the ensuing melee, Aunt Marcy calmly finished her drink, put on her gloves, gathered up her purse, and headed for the door. Her work here was done.

From his post at the window in the door to the kitchen, Sal had missed the doctoring of Tobias' drink. But he did observe the rest of the action. When Aunt Marcy headed for the exit, he stripped off his apron, put on his jacket, and followed.

She walked slowly to her rental car. She was not about to spoil a good performance by calling unwanted attention to herself with unseemly haste. Casual was the order of the day. The neighborhood was a changing one and the streets were dark and deserted. When she reached her car, she searched in her purse for the key fob, which often acted as if it had a mind of its own. It was particularly mischievous and tended to run off and hide in a remote corner of her purse.

At that moment, she felt the barrel of a gun pressing between her shoulder blades. "Just be quiet, Aunt Marcy, and do as you're told, and no one will get hurt." It was a male voice, one that she had never heard before. However, given that he knew her name, it had to belong to one of Tobias' henchmen. "Bugger! What do you want?" She managed to work a quaver of fear into her question.

"I want three things: your car, your money, and your credit cards. Hand them over and I'll be on my way." He backed away two steps, but he kept the gun in his right hand, aimed at the back of her head. At this distance, he couldn't possibly miss.

She turned to face her assailant, her right hand still in her purse where it had been rummaging for the key fob. "I can never find anything in this damn purse. Bear with me for a moment." When her hand did come out of the purse, it came out quickly, holding a can of Mace. Sal caught a large charge of capaicin full in the face.

Sal reacted instinctively, but stupidly. He dropped the gun and raised both hands to his burning eyes, screaming profanities as he did so.

"My friend, you should clean up your language when you're in the presence of a lady." In a smooth motion, she scooped up his gun. She checked it and found that it was fully loaded, and that the safety was off. While she could never be called a gun enthusiast, and did not ordinarily carry one, she knew well how to use one.

She inserted the muzzle into Sal's right ear. "Give my regards to Tobias when you see him." With that, she squeezed the trigger. The body dropped to the ground, shuddered a few times, and then was still. She checked Sal's carotid to make certain that he was dead. Once that was verified, she returned the gun to Sal's right hand. Then she removed the used syringe from her purse, wiped off here prints, and put it into the breast pocket of Sal's shirt. After giving the tableau one last look, she got into her car and drove away. *Darwin had been correct. Survival of the stupid was never part of the divine plan.*

In a park bordering the Allegheny river, she parked in a deserted section and spent a few moments emptying the contents of her purse onto the passenger seat. Then, she removed her gloves and put them in the purse. She got out of the car and found a rock of an appropriate size and added it to the purse before snapping it closed. She walked down to the river's edge and then threw the weighted purse, as far as she could, out into the river. With her mission accomplished, she got back into the car and drove back to her hotel.

That night, there were no violent dreams to disturb her rest. She slept like a baby and awoke quite refreshed the next morning. Since she had missed dinner the evening before, she treated herself to a full breakfast. Then, she returned the Ford to Hertz, reclaimed her favorite ride from the hotel's parking garage, and drove back to Harrison. She harbored only one regret. She had not had the opportunity to collect souvenir body parts.

Chapter 33

King Moves Again

I
t was Saturday morning and things were quiet in the Sawyer household. Moira had driven the boys to soccer practice. It was her turn. When there were league games, they both made an extra effort to be present. Bergen lived a life that, on occasion, was intense and dangerous. Thus, he appreciated and savored these all too rare interludes of relaxation and peace.

He was sitting at the kitchen table with a pot of tea steeping in front of him. Before he got to the tea, he was working his way through a small selection of fruit juices. Rarely did he eat solid food before noon. He had learned that his stomach was quite content to sleep until noon. However, once awakened, a piece of toast was insufficient. Instead, his stomach demanded a full meal.

As he sipped his juice, he worked his way through the Harrison Herald in his own peculiar way. He started with the comics, or as he liked to refer to them, the Intellectual Pages. Then, he read his horoscope. Not that he believed any of the drivel he read there, but it was always good to start the day with a laugh or two. Then, it was on to the Cryptoquip and the Cryptoquote. On a good day, he could decipher these without putting pen to paper. On the occasional bad day, he couldn't even find a foothold. Next came the daily Chess Problem, the Jumble, and the Bridge Hand. The multiple Crossword Puzzles he left for Moira. Once he had his brain awake and functioning, he moved on to the Sports Pages. Next came the Obits and the Local News. Finally, he reached the front section with the National and International News. In a very real sense, he read the newspaper back to front.

In the Local News section, one article grabbed his attention. A major case in the Federal Court had been concluded. A local mob boss had been convicted on multiple felony counts and sentenced to consecutive long terms in the Penitentiary. Naturally, his lawyer announced that they would appeal. Very likely, it would be many years, if ever, before the felon served any time behind bars. The star witness against the mob boss had been his accountant. Bergen knew that, for the duration of the trial, the accountant had been cloistered at a safe house provided by Max Greenfield, on the city's west side, up near the lake. Now, with the witness disappearing into the Federal Witness Protection Program, the safe house should once again available.

Bergen was reluctant to leave someone in his protection at any location for extended periods. Arnie King had been sequestered at Montego O'Higgins' suburban retreat for too long. Mason, the custodian for the O'Higgins' property had reported that Arnie was showing signs of restlessness. He'd been seen out walking the property in daylight despite cautions to the contrary. More alarming, he'd been observed out on the neighborhood roads, riding a bicycle. For someone with a target on his back, this was unacceptable behavior.

A simple telephone call to Max reserved the safe house for Arnie. Now, it was only a matter of moving him undetected.

Bergen got dressed and took the car out. As was his habit, he set off in the opposite direction from the O'Higgins' property. He drove an irregular pattern, on the alert for a tail. Until about ten days ago, he always had one. Losing the tail became an amusing game, but one that Bergen always won. Then, suddenly, the tail was no more. This made Bergen uneasy. Had they tired of the game or had they found some other way to follow him? He searched, in vain, for small fixed-wing aircraft, helicopters, and even drones. Problems that he could not solve irritated him.

Satisfied that he had no tail, he drove to the O'Higgins' country house. He came up the driveway and parked in his usual spot behind the house. There were no other vehicles and no sign of life. He crossed the deck and came in through the sliding glass door to the kitchen. The door was unlocked and that was a clear violation of the orders he had given.

Quietly, he crossed the kitchen, passed through the dining room, and made his way down the corridor toward the bedrooms. The third bedroom had been repurposed as an office. It was a good-sized room, almost square. There was only a single window, set high in the middle of the wall opposite the door to the corridor. This plus the shade from the large overhanging trees made the room dark and inherently uninviting. Montego and Syn had solved that problem by painting the walls Aztec Yellow. It contrasted nicely with the baseboards and the closet doors that were deep chestnut. The yellow color almost screamed the falsehood, "I glow in the dark".

The desk and its ergonomic chair were opposite the window, just to the right of center, facing the left-hand wall. Like poor relations, two straight-backed side chairs sat across from the ergonomic one. Behind the desk, at the ends of the right wall were several filing cabinets. Against the left wall, facing the desk, was a three- cushion couch. It called seductively to whoever was seated at the desk, saying that it was time to put work aside and take a nap. High up over the couch, and running the full width of the wall, was a shelf. It held a crowded display of the trophies won by the dogs from the O'Higgins kennel. There were sterling silver loving cups, plaques, plates, bowls, and obelisks, along with framed, color photographs of their triumphs. In the center, just over the couch, holding the place of honor, was a three-foot high ceramic vase, done in what can only be described as godawful colors. Given its size and its prime position, it had to represent a major win at a national, or a specialty, show.

Bergen entered the room quietly. Arnie was absorbed by his computer work. Bergen poked his right index finger into the back of Arnie's neck while at the same time lifting Arnie's left ear piece and calling out in a loud voice, "Bang! You're dead."

It'd be little exaggeration to say that Arnie raised up a foot off his chair. In a tremulous voice, he said "Don't do that! You could give me a heart attack."

"It's what you get for leaving the back door unlocked," Bergen countered. "How many times do I have to tell you that you must keep it locked? Why do I even bother? Perhaps I should just let them kill you and be done with it. You obviously don't care."

Arnie had had enough of Bergen's criticism. "When are you going to stop trying to dictate every moment of my life? You are not my mother! Stop acting as if you were."

They were both so focused on their argument that they failed to notice the figure that appeared in the doorway. Marty Harold was a foot-soldier for God's Judgment, most recently assigned to following Professor Sawyer wherever he went. He spoke for the first time, "If you two ladies are done with your cat fight, you should pay a little attention to me and my friend here." He was referring to the forty-five that he had leveled at them.

Arnie was speechless. Bergen resorted to Syn's favorite expletive, "Shit". Then, ignoring the gun, he challenged the intruder. "Who are you? How did you get in here? What do you want?"

Marty smiled. "Professor, all questions will be answered in time. For now, all you need to know is that I'm in charge. You will be quiet and do exactly as I say. Turn those straight-back chairs to face the couch and place them side-by-side. Then, sit down." He, himself, backed up and sat in the middle of the couch.

Bergen had learned two things. First, by calling him Professor, their intruder had signaled that he probably worked for God's Judgment. Second, he wasn't too bright. It would take longer to get up off the couch and into a fighting stance than it would from the chairs. Had it been his show, Bergen would have arranged it the other way around. On the other hand, he had to admit that possession of the gun cancelled out a lot of stupidity.

There was a fourth presence in the room. Phred had been sleeping, curled up on the right end of the trophy shelf, taking advantage of what little sunlight leaked through the single window. The activity in the room had awakened her. She stretched languidly and began cleaning herself.

"As I am sure you have already figured out, I represent G. J." Marty was inclined to be talkative when he believed that he was in control of a situation. "I have already phoned in my report. Unfortunately, G. J. is out of town and it may take some time for a reply. I asked if I have authorization to dispatch you or whether the boss wants to handle it personally. As to how I got in here, someone left the door to the deck unlatched. Very careless!"

Arnie and Bergen exchanged murderous glances. Bergen believed that it was to their advantage to keep their captor talking. He was watching for any opportunity to overpower the intruder and take control. He needed a distraction. "How did you find us? I was certain that there was no tail."

"We finally gave up on the chase car strategy and went high tech," Marty responded. "We placed a GPS locator in the right rear wheel-well of your car. We knew within ten feet where the car was at any given time. I could stay back out of sight until you parked the vehicle. It was easy peasy."

Bergen mentally kicked himself for overlooking such an obvious tactic. Then, out of the corner of his eye, he caught sight of Phred beginning to move. She picked her way slowly and carefully, intent on not disturbing any of the clutter on the shelf. Her progress was maddeningly leisurely. Bergen had to discipline himself so as not to stare at the cat and give the game away. He waited for Phred to knock something from the shelf and provide him with the distraction he craved.

"I didn't hear you drive up. How did you manage that?" Bergen was buying time in the only way he could.

"I know what you're doing Professor. You're stalling, waiting for an opportunity to overpower me. Don't waste your time. I'm a crack shot and, no matter how fast you are, the bullet is faster. To answer your question, I parked my car on the berm, just north of the driveway. You would be able to see it from the front window if that stand of trees was not there. Then, I walked up the drive." Marty was growing more loquacious. "What about you, Arnie? Why so quiet? Surely you, too, have questions you're dying to ask me."

Arnie gave him his best blank stare. Dying was something that he really didn't want to think about. He subscribed to the Woody Allen stance on death. "I have nothing against dying. I just don't want to be there when it happens." "My name is Artemus C. Scott. I think that you have me confused with someone else." His delivery was letter perfect.

Marty laughed. "You're good, but I know better. You are Arnold King, a wanted fugitive with a price on your head. And, I'm going to collect it."

"Bergen, do something! He intends to kill us." Arnie's wail was plaintive.

Bergen turned toward Arnie. "This is all you fault. If you'd followed my instructions, this never would have happened. What an ass-hole you are. I'll never understand why my sister-in-law married a loser like you." He was goading Arnie into a fight. He was beginning to believe that expecting Phred to provide a distraction was a lost cause. Any cat who had earned the title of Mighty Hunter was unlikely to be clumsy afoot. In that case, he might have to create his own distraction.

Predictably, Arnie rose to the bait. "The omniscient Professor falls into the trap of a common hoodlum and then blames it on the poor Accountant. When are you going to grow up and take responsibility for your actions. Your carelessness is going to get us both killed." Bergen and Arnie had turned toward each other, and it looked like the disagreement was about to get physical.

Marty was following the dispute intently. "I take offense at being called a common hoodlum. Since I hold the gun, you should show me some respect. Now, I want you two ladies to shut up and behave. Otherwise, I may have to shoot you just for the fun of it."

Phred had reached the middle of the trophy shelf and had disappeared behind the oversized ceramic vase. She turned to face the vase and stood up on her hind legs. Reaching up with her front paws, she found the rim of the vase and pushed it forward. The ceramic tumbled off the shelf and scored a direct hit on Marty's skull, caving it in. In a last reflex action, Marty squeezed the trigger, getting off a single shot.

Bergen, who had been trying hard not to stare at the cat and its movements, only caught the last part of the action. With his right hand, he pushed Arnie's shoulder as hard as he could, toppling King and his chair over sideways. A split second later, he leveraged his body up out of his chair and toward their captor. The bullet grazed his right shoulder and then his body plowed into the gunman, bowling him over on the couch. He wrested the gun from Marty's hand. When he had a chance to examine Marty, it was clear that he was dead. Looking up, he saw Phred sitting in the space recently vacated by the vase, nonchalantly washing herself. Bergen's manners were impeccable. He straightened up, looked the cat in the eye, and said, "Thank You. I owe you one."

Arnie was shivering uncontrollably. Bergen helped him up, righted the chair, and sat him down. Arnie stared at the body on the couch. "Is he dead?"

"The answer is Yes, and you have Phred to thank for it. She saved us both. But, I'm afraid that the big, ugly ceramic vase will never be the same again."

"What happens now? Should we call the police?" Arnie had really not thought through their situation.

"No police!" was Bergen's stern response. "I need you to pull yourself together. We've work to do. Your idyllic sanctuary has been compromised. I'm going to move you to a safe house. Gather up your things and put them in my car. Leave no evidence that you were ever here."

"What about the body?"

Bergen was accustomed to having his orders obeyed without question. "We'll take care of that in due time. He isn't going anywhere. Now do as I asked." While Arnie was gathering his things, Bergen had work to do. First, he stripped the body of all identification. Then, he went out to his car and removed the tracking device from his right rear wheel-well. To be thorough, he checked the car for other tracking devices. He found none.

Then, he walked out to the road and, using Marty's keys, he drove that car back behind Montego's deck and parked it next to his own vehicle. Taking nothing for granted, he searched Marty's car for tracking devices. Again, he found none.

Next, he went to Montego's barn and brought a wheel-barrow and two shovels back to the house. Arnie had finished his assigned chore and was waiting for further instructions. Bergen did a walk-through on the house to convince himself that Arnie had not missed anything.

Together, the two of them carried Marty's body out to the wheel-barrow. They gathered up as much of the broken ceramic as they could find and added it to their load. Several hundred feet behind the O'Higgins' house, there was an orchard of Montmorency sour cherry trees. They buried Marty's body, along with the ceramic shards and the gun, deep in the middle of the orchard. Phred looked on approvingly. Arnie wanted to say a few words of dismissal over the grave, but Bergen objected that they did not know how much time they had before Marty's colleagues came looking for him. Any delay could be fatal.

They locked the door to the deck and drove off, with Bergen leading the way in Marty's car and Arnie following. Doubling back to the Interstate, they headed west and paused at the first rest stop. Bergen prowled the ranks of long-haul trucks that were waiting their turn to refuel. When he found one with California plates, he went down on one knee and pretended to retie a shoe. In fact, he was planting the tracking device on the truck.

Then, he surveyed the collection of passenger cars in the parking lot in front of the restaurant. It took a while, but he finally found a convertible with the top down and wearing Vermont plates. Reaching in, he buried Marty's cell phone deep in the space next to one of the rear seats.

To make Marty's disappearance complete, there was one last detail to take care of. In the eastern suburbs of Harrison, they stopped at a Wal-Mart Super Store. In the parking lot, well-removed from the store's entrance, they parked Marty's car, leaving it unlocked with the keys in the ignition. The message could not be clearer had they placed a hand-lettered sign, "Please Steal Me", on the windshield. Before he left, Bergen wiped the car clean of all finger prints.

Finally, Bergen took possession of his car again and drove them to the safe house. It was a small detached bungalow in a very old neighborhood, one that had been overlooked for gentrification. He stashed the car in the garage and then found the house key where Max had said it would be.

Chapter 34

Arnie and Bergen

The two of them inspected the house. Arnie was clearly disappointed. "It's ancient and not nearly as comfortable as the O'Higgins' ranch. I'm going to be claustrophobic and there's no cat. Can't you do any better than this?"

On the other hand, Bergen was pleasantly surprised. Max had gotten someone to restock the pantry and the refrigerator. "Don't complain to me. If you'd behaved yourself and followed my instructions, we might not be here. Count your blessings that you're still alive."

"No thanks to you. It was the cat who saved both our lives. And, as I recall, it was you who compromised my hiding place. I'd be better off with Phred as my bodyguard." It almost seemed that Arnie was trying to pick a fight.

Bergen saw what was happening and shrewdly changed the subject. "I'm hungry. How about pizza? What do you like for toppings?"

"Pizza is fine with me," Arnie replied. "I vote for sausage and pepperoni."

At last, Bergen thought, *something that we agree on! There may yet be a future for this partnership after all.* On the wall next to the phone, he found the number for the local pizzeria and called in an order. While they waited for the delivery, he cracked open a bottle of Ruffino Chianti Classico. Arnie dealt out the napkins, plates, glasses, and cutlery.

They made small talk until the pizza arrived. They didn't realize just how hungry they were. Near death experiences can do that. Together, they finished a large pizza and emptied the entire jug of Chianti. It promised to be a mellow evening.

Bergen had no intention of leaving Arnie alone just yet. He wanted to make certain that his charge was settled in and behaving himself. After clearing the table, they picked up their glasses and adjourned to the living room.

"Arnie, it's been a while since we talked about the origin of your predicament. I gather that following money as a motive has proven unproductive. Where does that leave us?" Oscar had been providing Bergen with periodic updates.

"I have looked exhaustively for any sign of a money trail. I can't find one.Either it doesn't exist, or it is very cleverly camouflaged." Arnie was almost apologetic that his search had proven fruitless. "I'm beginning to consider other motives."

"Once you eliminate greed, what do you have left?" Then Bergen began to answer his own question, ticking them off on his fingers. "There's pride, envy, lust, gluttony, anger, and sloth, if I remember my catechism correctly. We can probably eliminate gluttony and sloth from the present puzzle." Arnie nodded his head in agreement. "The remaining ones all suggest that this may be personal. Pardon me for being indelicate, but who've you antagonized lately?"

"I think of myself as a mild-mannered, easy-going person. It's difficult for me to believe that I've offended anyone to the point that they would want me dead." Arnie's tone was almost plaintive. "But, day-by-day, the world is becoming a stranger place. Everyone seems to be so hypersensitive."

Bergen was sympathetic, but only up to a certain point. He remembered many occasions when he, himself, would have cheerfully strangled Arnie. "Remind me again who are the in-house persons of interest?"

"Well, first there's Harold Boyd, the founding, and managing partner of B, H, & G. The senior partners are Stephen Hunter and Jeffrey Gould. Among the junior partners, Nicholas Gestas stands out. But, I can't see any of them as the villain of this soap opera." Arnie was, himself, an associate.

"Let's start with Boyd," Bergen suggested. "Have you ever done anything to piss him off?"

Arnie gave it a few moments thought as he drained his wine glass. "A few months ago, I discovered one of his secrets. When he finally retires, he's going to dissolve the firm. In conversation with him, I kidded him about his plan. It was then that I found out that, when it comes to business, Harold has no sense of humor. Joking like that with the boss was a dumb thing for me to do but I had no idea that he was so humorless. However, does stupidity warrant a death sentence? Is he that vindictive?"

It was not a question for which Bergen had a diplomatic answer. "Talk to me about Hunter."

"Steve is an interesting case. He's a young man aggressively on the make. He has his eyes fixed on the top position. How to get there is never far from his consciousness. A standing joke in the firm is that, when he gets dressed in the morning, he doesn't decide the color of his socks, or pick out his tie, without considering whether it will help him become the Managing Partner. On several occasions, Boyd has given him a problem to solve and each time, after going through strenuous mental contortions, he arrived at a solution that offended no one, but didn't satisfy anyone and, more importantly, didn't really solve the original problem." Arnie was warming up to his subject.

Bergen interrupted him. "Arnie, give me an example of the situation you're talking about?"

"Sure! In one case, Steve chaired a committee that was charged with suggesting ways to improve the firm's image in the community. This committee met many times and discussed the question *ad nauseum*. Finally, they produced a report that contained only a single recommendation: That the firm revise its letterhead! Even harder to believe is the fact that Steve came away from this project openly proud of the fine job he had done."

"So, after great labor, the elephant gave birth to a mouse." Bergen shook his head in disbelief. "But, how do you fit into this story?"

"After the report was issued, Boyd asked me what I thought of it. Foolishly, I answered bluntly and honestly. Then, I tried to soften the criticism by making excuses for Steve and suggesting several reasons why he had not done a better job. In retrospect, it could've looked like I was tearing Steve down to build myself up. But, so help me God, that wasn't my intention. Later, I learned that this exchange was reported back to Steve. He has never forgiven me. He barely speaks to me".

Bergen listened soberly. "I can see how he might have revenge on his mind. However, murder seems to me to be just a tad extreme."

"There's a great irony here. Had our positions been reversed, and he was the one making the intemperate remarks, then, it's quite likely that the motivation he ascribed to me, would have been his. He's accusing me of acting as he would have under the same circumstances. It would be rich, if it wasn't so sad. Steve had so much talent, so much promise. What a waste!"

"How about Jeffrey Gould?" Bergen had the feeling that Arnie would talk about Hunter all night if allowed to do so.

"Now there is a genuinely nice guy. Whenever I have a problem I'm struggling with, I go talk to Jeff. No matter how busy he is, he always makes time for me and usually points me toward solutions to my problems. The man is exceptionally bright. There are times that I think he's smarter than all the rest of us combined." Arnie was almost effusive in his praise.

"So, you and Jeff have never had a rough patch?" Bergen knew that even marriages made in heaven sometimes have their troubles.

"Your mention of rough patches does remind me of one incident. It happened in 2011. Jeff was sidelined for several months with quadruple coronary by-pass surgery. During his absence, I inherited his client list as an overload. Ordinarily, this is not a problem. It just means that I work longer hours and see my wife less often. Unfortunately, Jeff's leave coincided with a major correction in the Stock Market. The Dow lost almost twenty percent and the dip lasted for five months. His clients began to panic and practically beat down my door demanding help. I did my best to calm them down and help them rebalance their portfolios. When the recovery clicked in, they all wanted to leave Jeff and have me manage their holdings. To Jeff, and a few others, it looked like I had taken advantage of his hospital stay to poach his clients." Arnie paused for breath. "I did no such thing. Even if I wanted to, B, H, & G has strict rules against such behavior. Naturally, I refused to take these clients. Some left for other firms, and others went back to Jeff. When Jeff returned to work, he had to rebuild his stable of clients. Things between us were tense for a while. Then, he began to understand that I had done nothing wrong. We have been fine ever since. Both of us have pretty much forgotten about it."

"No good deed goes unpunished," Bergen observed. "That brings us to Nicholas Gestas."

"Now, there is a fascinating individual. He's unlike any of my other colleagues. He's had a much tougher life than the rest of us. He didn't come from wealth or privilege. Everything he has, he had to work and fight for. It's an admirable success story. However, I think that it has scarred him. Just below the surface, there is a seething resentment toward his co-workers. It's the sort of thing that may keep him from ever making partner in the firm." Arnie truly liked Gestas although, at times, this was extremely difficult to do. "Then, there's his personal life. He's been married and divorced more times than I can count. I know that this instability doesn't set well with Boyd."

"So, Gestas is an anomaly," Bergen said. "How do you and he get along? Any friction there?" He placed a mental bet that there was something.

"Aside from being the focus for more than my share of the resentment, I have no problem with Nick." Arnie was trying to be honest. However, self-criticism was not his strong suit. "But, the resentment is real. It is palpable."

Bergen saw that he needed to force Arnie to dig deeper. "Why do you think Gestas resents you?"

"Well, for one thing, my performance reviews are consistently better than his. Then, even though I've been with the firm a shorter time than he has, I seem to have the inside track for making partner." Arnie was not being entirely forthcoming, and it showed.

"Is that it?" Bergen asked. "Is there nothing else?"

"There is one other thing, something that I was reluctant to mention. I believe that Gestas has eyes for Gloria, my wife. But that would make his motivation jealousy, rather than resentment. Of course, I may be misreading the whole situation." Arnie was almost apologetic.

Bergen shook his head in disbelief. "Are you bucking for sainthood? There's someone out there who wants you dead. Until proven otherwise, everyone is a suspect. No plausible motivation should be dismissed out of hand. Those two cautions should constantly be front and center in your mind. Your survival could well depend upon it."

"Finding out that there is someone who wishes you dead is truly depressing. That it might be one of my professional colleagues is actually painful." Had there been more wine, Arnie was ready for a refill.

Bergen summarized. "So, each of your colleagues may have a personal ax to grind with you. However, no one of your actions seems to rise to a level that would make murder a logical reaction. But, there's one other possibility that we have not considered. What if these four colleagues got together and pooled their resentments? Cumulatively, there might be enough to make murder an attractive option for the good of the firm."

Arnie's reaction was immediate and impassioned. "That's obscene! What a twisted world you live in! When did you join the ranks of the conspiracy theorists?"

Bergen shrugged eloquently. "If we're ever going to solve your problem, we must be objective and consider every possibility."

They agreed to call it a night. There were two bedrooms. Arnie retired first, closing the bedroom door. Bergen made the rounds, checking the locks on the doors and windows. Then he took the second bedroom. He left his door ajar and he slept lightly. He needed to know if Arnie tried to go off the reservation.

Bergen stayed at the safe house for three days and nights. He had to convince himself that Arnie had settled into a routine and wasn't about to do anything monumentally stupid. Bergen had a very good reason for leaving after three days. Arnie was driving him nuts!

Chapter 35

Aunt Marcy Takes the Offensive

It was Saturday night and Bergen Sawyer was alone at home, catching up on some paper work. It was not his preferred method for passing a weekend evening, but, when one keeps putting off mind-numbing chores, eventually there comes an immutable deadline. Moira, his wife, had gone to meet her sister, Gloria, and the two were off to a leisurely dinner and then a movie. The children were spending the weekend with his in-laws.

The quiet reminded Bergen of stories Steve Madigan used to tell. Steve had been a classmate in graduate school. When Steve was an undergraduate student in New York City, he paid his way through school by working for a prestigious law firm on Wall Street. To make up his quota of hours, he often worked a shift from 1:00 pm until 11:00 pm on Saturdays. He would describe the terrible loneliness he experienced on those evenings, standing at the window of the reception area, looking down twenty-eight floors at the completely lifeless sidewalks and the totally empty streets. It could be mistaken for a city of the dead. The first time he had this experience, he wondered whether perhaps the Rapture had taken place and he had missed it. *Why had he received no invitation? Had he been judged unworthy to be "gathered up into the cloud"?* Quickly, Steve banished such fantasies.

Bergen had begun his working evening by grading a set of examinations from his large freshman class. The papers had been sitting here on his desk for five days. They must be graded and returned to the students at the next class meeting. Otherwise, he would be in violation of his policy statement for the course. While he was doing this binge grading, he kept reminding himself that it was insanity to continue to ask essay questions. The short answer variety would see him finished much sooner. Yet, there was some information that could only be obtained in the essay format. So, however much he might swear that he was going to change, he never did.

The tests done, he rewarded himself, in part, by putting some music on the CD player. Prolonged silence can do serious harm to the mind. Recently, he had obtained the complete set of Sibelius' symphonies on compact disc, and this was his first chance to immerse himself. Music, although necessary, was not sufficient. He poured himself a generous portion of 12-year old Jameson Irish Whiskey.

Thus fortified, he turned to his second project. The lead journal in his field had recently accepted one of his research manuscripts for publication. In return, he was obligated to acting as a referee on two papers submitted by other authors. It was a fair system of peer review, and it worked. However, he still begrudged the time it took. The music and the alcohol served to make the experience less unpleasant.

He was about half-way through the first paper when the telephone rang. As he marked his place in the manuscript, he mentally blessed the yet unknown caller for rescuing him from a sea of murky prose and twisted logic. He answered with a cheerful "Hello."

"Professor Bergen Sawyer?" a female voice asked.

"Yes. Who's calling?"

"My name is not important. I am calling on behalf of God's Judgement. Think of me as God's Messenger. He'd like to meet with you."

"If this is some sort of joke, it's in very bad taste."

"I assure you, Professor Sawyer, that this is no joke. In fact, it's deadly serious."

"Why does he want to meet with me? What business do we have that can't be conducted over the phone?"

"Come now, Professor, don't be obtuse. You are a bright fellow. You have something he wants, and we have something you value. He wants to arrange a simple trade."

"I know that he wants Arnie King. However, I am at a loss to see what I would get in return."

"How's your wife Moira? Will you put her on the phone so that I may say hello?"

Bergen began to get a sick feeling deep in his gut. "She's not available just now. Give me your number and I'll have her call you back."

"Nice try Professor. Why don't you telephone Moira? Until next time, goodbye Professor."

His hand was shaking as he punched in the number for Moira's cell phone. After three rings, the call was answered. A familiar voice said, "Hello again, Professor Sawyer."

"How did you get my wife's cell phone?" He knew that Moira never went anywhere without her phone. It would take a major cataclysm to separate the two.

"You're being obtuse again, Professor. It's not becoming."

Bergen's temper was building. He raised his voice. "What've you done with my wife. Let me speak to her."

"Professor, you're in no position to make demands. Your wife is unable to come to the phone, but I assure you that, for the moment, she's unharmed. Whether that condition persists depends on your cooperation. Your next task is to telephone your sister-in-law, Gloria. Do it now." With that, she abruptly broke the connection.

It took him a few moments to look up Gloria's number. As he keyed in the digits, he was rather sure that he knew who was going to answer, but he hoped that he was wrong. The phone rang a maddening six times and then it was answered. "Very good, Professor! You follow directions well. Keep that up and we may be able to conclude our business with a minimum of unpleasantness."

"You don't know who you are dealing with. If any harm comes to either of those women, I'll hunt down you and your boss and kill you both very, very slowly." He was venting, threatening to spiral out of control.

"Save your bravado, Professor. You don't scare us. Are you a poker player? We've the winning hand. In the absence of wild cards, two queens beat a solitary king every time. What we propose is a simple trade: the women for Arnie King. It is two-for-one trade. Such a deal!" She affected a Yiddish accent. Having the upper hand, she was almost smug.

"You seem to have thought this through rather thoroughly. When and where do we make this exchange?" There was no harm in pretending to go along. It might provide him with useful information.

"We propose that the meeting be tomorrow morning at 3:00 am. On the beach at East 178th Street, there's a picnic pavilion. We'll rendezvous just north of the pavilion. You and Mr. King are to come in one car and alone. Park in the lot at East 178th Street and proceed on foot. If we see any sign of the Police, we shall abort the meeting. So, don't try anything foolish. Do I make myself clear?"

"Crystal," he answered through gritted teeth. "However, you've set a very tight schedule. Suppose I'm unable to gather up Arnie in time to make it to this meeting?"

"Don't be disingenuous, Professor. You have more than enough time. Failure to meet as scheduled would have most unfortunate consequences. Don't even consider it. Goodbye Professor."

Bergen sat looking at his phone for a good five minutes as if he was expecting it to spring into life and magically solve his problems. Meanwhile, his mind was working furiously. *Can I get the women back without giving up Arnie? Most unlikely! GJ and his people have planned well. At three in the morning, the beach will be deserted, so no witnesses. With all that open space, any reinforcements I might bring will be detected long before they can get close enough to be useful. Will I be able to persuade Arnie to cooperate? I must! Failure is not an option. Certainly, we're going to find out how much Arnie loves Gloria. I've been told to bring Arnie and no one else. But, I never agreed to that and abiding by this condition would be a stupid thing to do. My adversaries have been brilliant in giving me very little lead time. They are presuming that I will not have enough time to organize a serious defense. Once again, they underestimate me.*

He pushed the two manuscripts to one side. A matter of higher priority had surfaced, and the refereeing would have to wait. He topped the papers with his unfinished drink. For what he was going to be doing, he would need a clear mind and quick reflexes.

Then he sent the first of a series of text messages, this one to Arnie King at the safe house.

"Arnie, there have been some developments with your situation. It's something that we must discuss in person. I'll come to see you about eleven tonight. Be ready." It was a confrontation that he was not looking forward to. But it was a necessary one, and something better done in person rather than electronically.

His second message was to Oscar.

"Sorry to bother you on a Saturday night, my friend, but I need your help. Are you up for a little adventure? The people, who're after Arnie King, have kidnapped Moira and Arnie's wife. They want to make a trade tonight. I'd like you to accompany me. I'll come by and pick you up at about ten o'clock. If you have a gun, bring it with you."

The third text went to Montego O'Higgins.

"Montego, I have a situation and I need your help. Moira and her sister, Gloria, have been kidnapped. I have something of value that the kidnappers want. I'm meeting them on the beach at East 178th Street at three tomorrow morning, for an exchange. I'd like you to be parked on one of the side streets, off Beach Drive, where you can see them arrive and watch when they leave. Don't try to apprehend them, just follow them at a safe distance. I need to know where they go."

When he had confirmation from all three, he telephoned Max in Atlanta. He caught him during the intermission of the Atlanta Symphony. He explained the problem in broad strokes and asked if there was a drone operator in Harrison. Max knew of three such people and gave Bergen the names and their contact information.

The top name on the list was Artis Crawford. Bergen called him and used Max's name as an entry. Artis and his drone were available on short notice for a twenty-percent bonus on his regular fee. The job was to be simply photographic surveillance of a meeting that was going to take place at 3:00 am Sunday morning on the beach at East 178th Street. The surveillance was to follow discretely any vehicle leaving the scene that was not a black 2017 Mercedes-Benz-S-Class Sedan. Artis assured Bergen that this was not a problem and that the people on the beach would never know that they were being watched.

With those arrangements completed, Bergen went out to his car and set off to fetch Oscar. He muttered a prayer for the safety of the two women.

Chapter 36

The Meeting on the Beach

S ince both he and Oscar lived on the east side of Harrison, near the University, the first leg of Bergen's trip was a short one. He spent much of the travel time mentally flaying himself. *I should've seen this gambit coming and done a better job of protecting the women. It was a novice's mistake. Yet, I'm supposed to be a seasoned professional. If any harm comes to them, I'll never forgive myself.* Then, he thought more deeply. *Could it be that this is G.J.'s ploy to get inside my head, to make me waste my time making futile recriminations when I should be trying to figure out how to get the women back and still deny him Arnie?* Then, he reviewed the plans that he had made for counter measures. *Given the compressed time scale, they're the best I could do. Now, I must find a way to make them work.*

He arrived at Oscar's house shortly before ten. Oscar was waiting at the side of the road, near his mailbox.

"Oscar, thank you for being available on such short notice. I hope that I haven't pulled you away from anything important."

Oscar replied with a snort. "Important? Hell, you rescued me from another depressing evening. You are a Godsend. Once a month, we are scheduled to play Bridge with the Jansens. Don't get me wrong, they're nice people and I love them dearly, but we play on into the small hours of the morning and they never lose.

It is humiliating. Wouldn't you think that, every so often, they'd throw a game, just to make us feel good? Not a chance!"

Bergen couldn't keep from smiling. *If only all problems were so petty!* "Could it be that they're using a marked deck? Or, perhaps you or your wife have a tell that they've discovered?" This leg of the drive, to the northwest side of Harrison, was longer and gave Bergen time to get around to giving Oscar a detailed report on his communications with the kidnappers.

"How horrible! Is nothing off limits for these animals? What're you going to do? What can we do?" *Quietly, Oscar thanked God that the kidnappers had not targeted his wife, Constance.*

"I've taken certain precautions. Inviting you along is one of them. Our adversaries won't like it, but they'll have to permit it. Our more immediate problem is this: how do we persuade Arnie to allow us to trade him for the women?" It was a question for which Bergen had not yet been able to find a satisfactory answer.

Oscar turned philosophical. "Altruism is a virtue that we often admire in others, but one we find repulsive when we're expected to practice it ourselves."

Bergen nodded stoically. "Very true, my friend, but not really helpful."

With each engrossed in his own thoughts, they drove on in silence. They arrived at the safe house about fifteen minutes before eleven. Arnie invited them in and they gathered at the kitchen table for their discussion. They passed on Arnie's offer of refreshments. This was a business, and not a social, meeting. Slowly, and in great detail, Bergen reviewed the events and their time line.

The early part of the review was a story that Arnie knew well. He had lived it. He was comfortable, relaxed. It was only when Bergen got to his back-and-forth with God's Messenger, that he became agitated. "They've kidnapped my wife?"

Bergen responded. "It appears so, and mine also. We cannot be absolutely certain. However, it is most likely. We must proceed on the assumption that it's true."

"I've avoided any contact with Gloria to keep her safe. A lot of good that did. Bergen, this is all your fault. What're you going to do about it?" Arnie was distraught and was lashing out. As usual, when that happened, Bergen was his favorite target.

"Arnie, would you agree that recovering the women unharmed is our highest priority?" Bergen fixed him with a penetrating stare. It was time for Arnie to step up. The silence continued while Arnie processed this information.

Finally, he answered. "Absolutely! We should be prepared to pay any price they ask." There was another long pause while Bergen and Oscar waited for him to make the next connection in the logic train. When he resumed, his tone was quite sober. "I expect that the price they are demanding is me. If that's true, then I think that we must give them what they want. I don't like it, but I'm resigned to the fact that we have no other choice."

Bergen breathed a mental sigh of relief. *Thank God that I don't have to force him to cooperate.* "That's most noble of you! But, why would you do such a thing?

When his answer came, it was heartfelt and gut wrenching. "I take my marriage vows very seriously, and I do love that woman."

Bergen found himself actually beginning to admire Arnie. "Understand that we'll do everything in our power to keep these people from harming you, and we won't rest until we free you."

"Thank you for that." However, Arnie's mind was moving in a different direction. *You promise that, but it is unlikely that you'll be able to deliver on it. It would be a mistake for me to count on you. I'm going to be on my own. God help me!* Arnie had the look of a man heading toward the gallows.

"Alright then, let's head on out." Bergen was eager to survey the meeting site. On the way out to his car, Bergen took Oscar aside and told him "you and Arnie should sit in the back seat. I want you to be close to him in case he has a last- minute change of heart and tries to renege on his commitment."

It was nearly 1:00 am when they arrived at the agreed upon location on the beach. They parked in the East 178th street lot, at the eastern end. The beach appeared deserted. The pavilion was shrouded in shadows and, from a distance, looked foreboding. Up close, it was simply a roofed wooden structure, open on all four sides, and now a repository for old, weathered picnic tables and a few rusty grills. Two restrooms, one male and one female, occupied the southwest and northeast corners. Close examination revealed that there were no evildoers lurking in the shadows.

Bergen looked for any evidence that the drone and Montego were at their appointed posts. He found nothing. Since there was a chill in the air, the three of them elected to wait in the car to take advantage of the heater. To kill time, Arnie and Bergen regaled Oscar with stories about how they had met and courted their wives. These memories helped them maintain their focus on the critical nature of the upcoming meeting.

When the end of the story-telling was in sight, Bergen changed the subject. "Oscar, did you bring along a gun as I suggested?" When Oscar answered in the affirmative, Bergen surprised him. "Give it here and I'll lock it in the glove compartment."

Oscar was confused. "Didn't you want me to bring it along for self-defense? How's it going to do us any good when it is locked away?"

"I expect that one of the first things the kidnappers will do is to pat us down for weapons. I don't want the gun to fall into their hands. I want it somewhere safe where we can get to it if we need to." Then Bergen turned his attention to Arnie. "Are you still carrying around that pig-sticker?" When Arnie refused to respond, Bergen answered for him. "Of course, you are. Give it here." He contributed his own gun to the collection and locked all three weapons in the glove compartment.

At 2:45 am, two more cars arrived and parked at the western end of the lot.

Bergen exited the car and led the way to the beach. Arnie followed, with Oscar bringing up the rear.

The two groups faced off just north of the pavilion. God's Messenger had sent Aunt Marcy and a muscular male companion for protection. She introduced him as Mr. Marsh. He brandished a hand gun and gave every indication that he was looking for an excuse to use it. She was clearly unhappy. "Professor Sawyer, I told you to bring Arnie and no one else. What didn't you understand about "no one else". I have a good mind to terminate our meeting immediately."

Bergen hastened to reply. "Let's not be too hasty. Meet my colleague, Professor O'Flahertie. He's my Rabbi, my bodyguard, and my food taster. I don't carry out any substantive negotiations without first conferring with him. If you find him unacceptable, then the three of us will leave right now."

Marsh appraised Oscar and quickly concluded that he was no threat. He decided that Oscar was not the hero type, and would be hard put to defend himself, much less a colleague. Marsh displayed a self-satisfied smile and a perfect set of dentures. He finally spoke, "Aunt Marcy, go check them for weapons."

She fixed him with her most disapproving look. He had been told not to use her name. If looks could kill, Marsh would have died a moment ago and already be moldering in his grave. Very soon, any record that he had ever lived would be expunged. Dutifully, she followed his orders, patted down the guests, and found no weapons.

Bergen needled her. "See, I really do know how to follow directions."

Aunt Marcy laughed. "You are a very funny fellow, Professor. There are two very persuasive reasons for you to stay and negotiate. First, that is a very big gun my associate has leveled at you. Second, you won't leave without securing the release of the women. So, why don't we cut the bullshit and get down to serious discussion?"

Bergen was spinning out the dialog. He used the time gained to memorize the features of both kidnappers. He also filed away what he gleaned from their speech: the timbre, the accent, the placement of the pauses, and the vocabulary. Finally, he studied their mannerisms and their movements: how Marsh held the gun and how Aunt Marcy patted him down in her search for weapons. He was convinced that this was not going to be their last encounter and he wanted to be certain that he would recognize them on the next occasion.

"Since you brought up the subject, where are the women? Why didn't you bring them with you?" Without proof of life, Bergen was reluctant to make any deal.

"We didn't bring them because I don't trust you, Professor. However, they are close by and, when we left them, they were alive and well, although somewhat uncomfortable. Once you have turned over Mr. King to us, I will tell you where to find them." She was almost smug in her delivery.

"That's not the way this was supposed to work," Bergen complained. "All the hostages were supposed to be here, and we would then make the exchange."

"I never said any such thing. I never agreed to that." Aunt Marcy knew that she had the stronger hand and she was not about to make any concessions.

The stand-off ended in a most unexpected way. Arnie walked past Bergen and headed for the kidnappers. Marsh shifted his aim from Bergen to Arnie. Over his shoulder, Arnie called back to Bergen "Let's get this deal done."

As the others watched, Aunt Marcy cuffed Arnie's hands behind his back. He did not resist. Then she locked on ankle cuffs that were connected by eighteen inches of chain. If he limited himself to short steps, he could walk. But he would not be able to run, climb stairs, of kick anyone. Once Arnie was secure, Marsh swung the gun back toward Bergen.

While giving Aunt Marcy and Marsh high grades for their planning and execution, Bergen was becoming more, and more, exasperated. "You got what you wanted. Now, tell us where to find Moira and Gloria!"

"Fair enough, Professor!" Aunt Marcy answered. "About a mile east of here, at East 200th Street, there is an old refreshment stand that has been abandoned and boarded up. Start at the stand and proceed one hundred paces north, toward the lake. You'll recognize the spot. We marked it with two long-handled shovels sticking up out of the sand. There you'll find the two women. They were bound and gagged and buried up to their pretty necks in the sand."

Bergen couldn't restrain himself any longer. "What a sadistic monster you are! If I ever get the chance, I'll make you pay."

Aunt Marcy grinned. "Professor, this is no time for idle threats. You have no time to spare. It was low tide when we buried the ladies." She made a great show of consulting her watch. "Unless I'm mistaken, high tide is in another half hour. You shouldn't linger here. You have work to do."

Bergen and Oscar turned and sprinted for their car. Aunt Marcy and Marsh each took one of Arnie's arms and half walked and half dragged him from the beach toward their waiting vehicles.

Chapter 37

More Beach Action

Fortunately, there was no traffic on Beach Boulevard at this small hour of the morning. Equally welcome, there were no traffic police issuing speeding citations. Bergen and Oscar followed the kidnappers' directions and had no trouble finding the shovels. As promised, the wives were there. Physically, they were unharmed but emotionally, they were verging on hysteria. When the gags were removed, Moira spoke for the two of them. "What the Hell took you so long?" Gloria was nearly catatonic. Bergen did his best to cover up the anxiety he had been feeling. He also knew what was expected of him – he was supposed to be the stable, unemotional partner, there to comfort his wife. "Well, your kidnappers were asking too high a ransom, and we had to negotiate it down to something we could afford. As a lawyer, you should know how tedious and time-consuming such discussions can be. But, be of good cheer! I'll subtract your family discount from my usual fee for rescuing damsels in distress. And, you are in luck. Today we are featuring a two-for-one deal." Had her hands been free, she might have hit him with one of the shovels. As it was, she had to settle for a scathing reply, "You can be such an ass-hole! Your court jester act doesn't fool me for a minute. But I love you just the same."

Although the shovels may have been appropriate for digging the original holes, removal of the sand was a chore better accomplished by hand. It helped that the women had been put into the holes in kneeling positions. Holes to allow them to stand erect were probably too much work for the kidnappers. With two sets of hands to lift them from their prisons, it wasn't necessary to remove all the confining sand.

Once freed, the women spent some time in pacing back and forth on the beach trying to improve their blood circulation. With his fear and frenzy put to rest, Bergen had the opportunity to assess the surroundings for the first time. The holes that the kidnappers had dug for the wives were a good twenty yards above the high tide mark. This was contrary to what Aunt Marcy had implied. One possible explanation was that she had misjudged the reach of high tide. This seemed unlikely since she paid such close attention to all the other details. A second explanation was that she never had any intention of letting the women drown. The mention of the high tide then was simply to propel Bergen into rescue mode, where he would ignore everything else. This gave the kidnappers time to escape with their prize. Her scheme had worked beautifully.

Next, Bergen reached out to his appointed watchers. His first call was to Artis Crawford, the drone pilot. The word from Artis was not good. His drone had suffered an unfortunate collision with an overly amorous lake gull. This encounter had utterly destroyed the drone and the mangled remains now rested under thirty-feet of Lake Katherine. The gull had not fared any better. Artis was most apologetic about letting Bergen down in his time of need. Bergen was glad that he was not being asked to compensate Artis for his property loss.

His call to Montego O'Higgins went directly to voice mail. This suggested that Montego was busy and could not pick up. Bergen told his colleagues that they should not waste any more time. They needed to go and see what sort of trouble Montego had gotten himself into. Bergen's plans appeared to be coming apart at the seams. He was beginning to get yet another sick feeling in the pit of his stomach.

* * * *

After Bergen and Oscar rushed off, Aunt Marcy and Marsh wasted no time in hustling Arnie off the beach and to the parked cars, where the prisoner was unceremoniously thrust into the back seat of a blue four-door sedan. It was a 1998 E46 generation of the BMW 3-Series. It had been modified for street racing before Marsh bought it. It was no longer much to look at, but he was confident that he could outrun almost anything else on the road. Marsh got into the front seat, while Aunt Marcy made for her own car, a white Acura. When the vehicles began to move, Marsh headed west at top speed. Aunt Marcy went east.

Montego had watched the scene come together and now was faced with a dilemma – *which car do I follow?* There was no time to think it through. He needed to act. His gut told him that he should stick with Arnie and Marsh, so he did. But, it was no simple matter. With essentially no traffic on the Shore Road, he had to leave an uncomfortably large separation between his car and the BMW to avoid giving the game away.

Unlike Montego, Arnie did have adequate time to observe and to think. The BMW had been modified with no thought to transporting prisoners. There was no heavy mesh screen separating the front and back seats. However, with his hands cuffed behind his back, there was no way that he was going to be able to use them effectively to overpower Marsh. Arnie tried to work his hands down over his rump so that he could pass his legs through the space above the wrists, thus bringing his hands in front of him where they would be more useful. To his dismay, he found that there were two problems. First, the cuffs were so snug that most movement was painful. Second, over the years he had accumulated sufficient fat in his derriere that the intended maneuver was no longer possible. He cursed himself for spending too much time sitting, and too little time exercising.

Then, he looked down at his ankles, studying the way that they were hobbled. This sparked an idea that he began to test. He slid far to his left so that he would not be visible in the driver's rearview mirror. Then he slouched down in his seat and raised his legs. Straightening them at the knees, he could, if he strained, touch the ceiling of the passenger compartment. The position was a most uncomfortable one. Essentially, he was laying on his back, his cuffed hands beneath him, with his legs stretching straight up in the air. It was not a position that he could maintain for very long. He spread his legs as far as the connecting chain would allow and then moved them forward, over the driver's head. Next, he bent his legs at the knees. The feet came down and so did the tether. When the back of the front seat prevented him from lowering his legs any further, he abruptly drew them back. The tether caught the surprised Marsh just below the chin. Arnie continued to pull his feet back with all the strength he could muster. If he was to remain alive, this was a battle he had to win.

With the chain cutting off his air supply, Marsh acted instinctively. He took his hands off the steering wheel and tried to get them under the chain to relieve the pressure on his windpipe. He attempted to steer the rapidly moving vehicle with his knees. Trying to do two difficult jobs at the same time taxed his considerable skills beyond their limit. The BMW began to swerve wildly from side to side. Soon after, the vehicle left the road and crashed head on into a mature sugar maple tree. Although the air bags did deploy, the force of the impact drove the motor into the passenger compartment, pushing the steering wheel deep into Marsh's chest. He was dead before the car stopped moving. Nor did Arnie escape unscathed. He had been knocked unconscious, his right leg was broken, and he had possible spinal injuries. But he was alive! Once again, he had beaten the odds and survived.

Montego watched the crash unfold in front of him. He parked at the curb just behind the wreckage. It was hard to believe that anyone could have survived such a horrendous crash, however he was obligated to check. As he suspected, the driver was beyond help. But, Arnie was still breathing. Not knowing the extent of Arnie's possible injuries, Montego was reluctant to move him. There was no sign of fire. There was no smell of spilled fuel. So, there was no urgency. Using his cell phone, he called in the accident, and asked that the Emergency Rescue Squad be dispatched. While he was waiting for help to arrive, he searched the pockets of the dead driver, looking for the keys to Arnie's shackles. He found them in a vest pocket and used them to remove the restraints, being careful to move Arnie's body as little as possible.

He transferred the shackles to the trunk of his own car. Trying to explain them to the ERS members would just complicate matters unnecessarily. While he waited for the Rescue Squad, Montego telephoned Bergen and gave him the location.

Bergen arrived just before the Rescue Squad. He and his passengers clustered to one side and gave the paramedics room to do their work. They confirmed that Marsh was dead. Then they moved on to Arnie. They slid him onto a back board, immobilized him, and extricated him from the wreck. When they started questioning Montego to get information for their report, Bergen intervened. He claimed that Montego was just a Good Samaritan who had been in the right place at the right time. After that, he stuck mainly to the truth. He identified the injured passenger as his friend, Arnie P. King, who was the victim of a botched kidnapping plot. He introduced Moira and Gloria as pawns in the plot, who had themselves been kidnapped and held hostage by the late Mr. Marsh and his associates. Since the women might also need medical attention, he suggested that they ride with Arnie in the ambulance. He and Oscar would follow in their own car. Their destination was St. Jude's, the nearest trauma center.

As they were leaving, a police squad car arrived to secure the scene and to deal with Marsh's body.

At the hospital, Moira was examined and released. Gloria, on the other hand, was kept overnight for observation. Bergen made a complete police report. Also, he suggested that the hospital put the Kings in the same double room and post a round-the-clock guard on the door. It was possible that, thwarted once, the kidnappers might make a second attempt. For that reason, the ERS and the hospital agreed on a total news blackout of the accident and the new admissions.

Bergen and Moira drove a euphoric Oscar home. He counted the adventure a major success: two hostages rescued, one kidnapper dead, and one kidnap victim rescued, although a little the worse for wear. Bergen resisted the temptation to burst Oscar's balloon. But, when he viewed the results, he was more sanguine. The extent of Artie's injuries was unknown. The damage done to Gloria's psyche by her ordeal was yet to be determined. GJ and Aunt Marcy, whoever the Hell she was, were both still at large. Also unknown was the prime mover, the person who was the driving force behind the attacks on Arnie. Oscar might be content with half-a-loaf, but not Bergen. He knew that much work remained to be done. However, they now had something that they had not had before. The name, Aunt Marcy, had to mean something. The look that she had given Marsh when he called her by that name suggested that it must be important. It could be the clue that he needed to unravel the entire puzzle.

After they dropped off Oscar, Bergen and Moira drove to their own home. On the way, he asked her to give him a full account of what had happened to her the previous evening, up until the time he had sprung her from her sandy prison. It was not something she was eager to revisit. However, she knew that the longer she put off the telling, the fewer the details that she was likely to remember.

"I picked up Gloria about four in the afternoon. We had dinner reservations at the Green Turtle. Once there, we had two leisurely rounds of cocktails and a nice selection of hors d'oeuvres". She was considerate to avoid all details about the menu. She didn't know when he had last eaten, and she didn't want a growlingstomach to distract him. "After dinner, on the way to my car, we were attacked by two thugs wearing ski masks. We were overpowered and drugged. When I regained consciousness, I found myself bound hand and foot, gagged, and blindfolded. I was in a moving vehicle, probably a car, but I can't be sure. Once I was conscious, my captors fitted me with ear plugs. If there was any conversation, I wasn't allowed to be party to it. When the vehicle finally stopped, I was carried a fair distance and then dropped on what I now know to be the beach. Then there was a maddening interval where nothing seemed to be happening. In hindsight, it was likely that the holes were being dug. Then I was lowered into the hole in a kneeling position. After that the hole was filled with sand up to my chin and the ear plugs were removed. I could hear the surf breaking on the beach and, off in the distance, the call of the lake gulls. Otherwise, everything was quiet. I struggled to get free, but it was futile. After a while, I slept intermittently. Then, you and Oscar arrived to free us." Just recounting the action gave her the shakes. She needed a stiff drink.

"So, you never heard your kidnappers speaking. You would not be able to identify them by their voices." The regret was obvious in his voice.

"Correct! However, I might be able to recognize them by smell. The person who carried me from the car onto the beach was a male. His aftershave was distinctive. There were traces of juniper, rosemary, and sandalwood in the aroma. It reminded me of Cade from L'Occitane, a scent that one of the partners in our firm uses."

"Great, now all I have to do is round up the suspects and have you smell them." He was being facetious. The information could be useful He would have to find out what brand of aftershave Marsh favored. "What about the other one?"

"I think that the other one was either a female or a very effeminate male. Whenever that person drew close, I caught the odor of lavender, the sort of perfume favored by elderly maiden aunts. It wasn't overwhelming, but it was there. Beyond that, I can't think of anything that would help you. Now, why don't you tell me what this is all about?"

By this time, they had reached home. They put the car in the garage, went inside, got comfortable, and Bergen fixed them each a drink. Then, he rolled out the complete story as he knew it, sparing nothing and no one. Moira took it all in, stopping him from time to time to ask a question. It was dry work and, when he had finished, he freshened their drinks.

She was quiet while she sorted the pieces of the story in her mind. Finally, she spoke. "What a godawful mess. These people are ruthless and will stop at nothing. None of us are safe. What do you propose to do about it?"

He gave a wry smile. *Why is it that I am always the one called upon when serious action is required? And they always make it sound so easy.* "To begin, in the morning, I'll contact Max and have him provide two protection details, one for our family and the other for Arnie and Gloria. Then, I'm going to try to track down Aunt Marcy. It isn't much of a lead, but it's the only one that we have."

Moira kissed him goodnight and went off for a long overdue shower and a restful night's sleep. As for Bergen, he brewed a pot of strong coffee. Then he fetched his gun and sat in their most uncomfortable chair, positioning himself where he could watch both outside doors and many of the downstairs windows. *Thank God, most of the night is behind us. Still, dawn cannot come too soon.*

* * * *

Making sure that she was not being followed, Aunt Marcy went back to her headquarters. She waited for Marsh to bring Arnie to her. As the hours rolled by with no sign of Marsh, she began to suspect the worst. A few hours after dawn, she got back into her car and traced the route that Marsh would have followed. She found the wreck, marked off with yellow crime-scene tape. After parking in the next block, she walked back and joined the small knot of curious spectators. She talked to anyone who seemed to have information. The word among the spectators was that the driver had died on impact and that the passenger in the back seat had been taken to St. Jude trauma center.

She left the group, crossed the Shore Road, and sat on a bench where she could look out over Lake Katherine. For two hours, she sat there and reformulated her plans. Potentially, she had some very serious problems and she needed to be prepared.

Chapter 38

The Search for Aunt Marcy

A t 9:00 am, Bergen called Max in Atlanta. He arranged for two security details, one for the King family and one for the Sawyers. Next, he telephoned the University and told them to postpone his classes for the day. He would reschedule them for a later date. When asked for a reason, he responded "Family emergency." No one ever took issue with that explanation. While he was waiting for his security to arrive, he did a computer search on Google, for any reference to Aunt Marcy. He was aware that the name might be a red herring and a total waste of his time. But, he did not believe this, and so he had to search. The profusion of Aunt Marcy references in Metropolitan Harrison blew his mind. Either the name was more popular than he was prepared to believe, or there was a unique Aunt Marcy who was an astonishingly prolific woman. Under that name, he found: a day care center for pre-school children, an antiquarian book store, a dog grooming shop, a center for holistic healing, a school for aspiring bartenders, an event planner, a retail outlet for pork products, a restaurant reviewer, a café, a retail shop for decadent baked goods, a retirement community, a nail salon, and a marriage counsellor.

He felt himself drowning in a flood of information. He needed to narrow his focus. Next, he telephoned each establishment and asked to speak with Aunt Marcy. The dog groomer and the school for bartenders told him plainly that their Aunt Marcy had died some years ago and that they continued to use her name to celebrate her memory. Furthermore, the cost to revise their advertising would be prohibitive. Bergen crossed them off his list. Four others, the holistic healing center, the pork store, the café, and the retirement community, all admitted, some grudgingly, that there never was an actual Aunt Marcy. They had chosen the name for the warm and cuddly feeling it conveyed. These were also removed from the list. Now, he was down to seven possibilities, a much more manageable number.

He debated whether he should ask Max to collect pictures of the seven remaining candidates for Aunt Marcy, or should he visit them in person. He decided that he needed the exercise and it was time for a road trip. Besides, if he was successful, he had some unfinished business to conduct with Aunt Marcy and it was the sort of thing best done in person.

When he visited the daycare center, his request to talk to Aunt Marcy was greeted with much amusement. The proprietor asked him if he was perhaps in the wrong place. When Bergen stood his ground, the proprietor summoned a child who was barely old enough to walk and introduced her as the resident Aunt Marcy! He began to explain the convoluted genealogy behind the naming, but Bergen stopped him, apologized profusely, crossed the establishment off his list, and moved on.

Next on the list was the Antiquarian Bookstore. Here the proprietor was a stooped, gray-haired woman who looked to be much older that most of her stock. She answered to the name

Aunt Marcy. She claimed that no one else with that name was connected to the business or her family. She had named the business after herself and was proud of it. Bergen thanked her for her time, resisted the invitation to browse, crossed her off his list, and continued his search.

The Event Planner was a male, Marion Freemont, who was exploring his female alter ego. He had gone so far as to change his name legally to Aunt Marcy. Once it became clear that Bergen had no actual event to plan, Freemont lost all interest. Bergen crosses him/her off his list and, somewhat dejected, went on his way. He began to wondered if perhaps he was on a fool's errand.

His list now led him to the editorial offices of the Harrison Herald. When he asked to speak to Aunt Marcy, he was questioned about the nature of his business. He had not prepared a back story, although he should have anticipated the need. On the spot, he improvised, and invented a plausible story. He was a free-lance writer who had been commissioned to do a profile of Aunt Marcy for a magazine with a national circulation. He was here to find out if Aunt Marcy had time in her busy schedule to sit down and talk with him at length.

The gate-keeper disappeared and returned a few minutes later to say that Aunt Marcy could spare him fifteen minutes. Following the gate-keeper's direction, he had no trouble finding Aunt Marcy's office. He rapped smartly on the frosted glass in the door and was invited in. He stopped in the doorway and eyed Aunt Marcy who sat behind a large desk and was busy reading copy. When she looked up, it was clear to Bergen that he had finally found the Aunt Marcy that he was searching for. That face was etched on his memory.

When she saw who her visitor was, she uttered the traditional invocation of the Irish Royal Family, "Oh Shit!" Then, she broke into a broad smile. "I've been expecting you, but not this soon. I greatly underestimated your tracking skills, Professor Sawyer. Please come in. Shut the door behind you and have a seat." She gestured toward the two side chairs.

Bergen was momentarily disconcerted by her calm reaction and her hospitality. He had expected surprise followed by fear or panic. The surprise was there and was genuine, but the other two were nowhere to be seen. By now she should be facing the decision of fight vs. flight. She was alone and there was no sign of a weapon, although there might be a gun in a desk drawer. Thus, the fight option appeared unlikely. His seat was between her desk and the door, blocking her escape route. So, flight seemed even more unlikely. Yet, she was complacent and that worried him. *Does she have resources that I am unaware of?*

She tilted her chair back and laced her hands behind her head. "Tell me, have the wives recovered from their little adventure?"

Why the Hell are you asking? It was a lot more serious than an adventure. Furthermore, you don't give a damn about their wellbeing! "Give me one good reason why I shouldn't call the police, and have you arrested for kidnapping, reckless endangerment, and attempted murder. Trust me, you won't look good in orange."

"That would be a terrible mistake. You misunderstand the situation. I'm as much a victim here as is Mr. King." She favored him with another smile, this one very self-assured.

"Bullshit! What sort of mental contortions did you have to go through to conclude that you're a victim?" He was unpersuaded, but her confidence made him uneasy.

She really did not want to go into detail, but she had no choice. "I have three children, two girls and a boy. They are now adults, away at out-of-state schools. I am still very fond of them even though we are estranged. G.J. tracked them down and threatened to kill them unless I joined his operation and followed his orders. What choice did I have? G.J. did not make empty threats. I was unwilling to stand by idly and watch my flesh and blood get slaughtered. So, I became one of the Devil's disciples." She hoped that Ed Franklin, wherever he was, would forgive her for playing so fast and loose with the truth, and making him out to be an evil monster.

Bergen was busy processing this new information. It was a plausible story. Given such a choice, most people he knew would have made the same decision.

Aunt Marcy watched him wrestle with this new reality. She decided that, while she had him off balance, she would give him another push. "I am really glad that you came to see me. I was afraid that I wouldn't get the chance to thank you for freeing me from G.J.'s captivity. You saved not only my life but that of my family as well."

Now, Bergen was even more confused. "What? How did I do that? What are you talking about?"

"Why, when you killed Barry Marsh. Didn't you know that he was G.J.?" She delivered her lines cleanly, as if it was truth that everyone else, other than Bergen, already knew.

Bergen shook his head, attempting to clear the cobwebs. He was approaching the point where truth and fiction were beginning to merge and become indistinguishable. "Let me set the record straight. I didn't kill Barry Marsh. Arnie King gets all the credit for that. I must admit that I didn't think that he was capable of it, but life-threatening stress can reveal previously hidden strengths. You're telling me that Marsh was G.J.? How can I tell if this is the truth? Where's the evidence?" It was a blatant challenge.

Aunt Marcy recognized it for what it was. She knew that Bergen was wavering and now was the time for the knock-out blow. "If you want concrete evidence, I cannot help you. However, if you're willing to be patient, you'll see that G.J.'s killing spree has stopped. There'll be no more corpses turning up with signature post-it notes pinned to their clothes. The Devil is indeed dead."

"I would like to believe that. But, how do I know that you, for example, are not G.J.?"

Clearly amused, she laughed scornfully at the suggestion. "A woman as G.J.? Preposterous! Do I really look to you like a criminal mastermind? Your cup of paranoia is overflowing."

"Tell me, what does a criminal mastermind look like? I've never met one. In the absence of evidence to the contrary, anything is possible." He was playing the ultimate skeptic, but it was a mind-set that was beginning to weaken.

"What'll it take to convince you?" This, too, was a challenge and she delivered it with aplomb. She had been reading his face and she had watched as Doubt insinuated itself into his brain. She was confident that she knew the information that would convert him into a believer. However, she should not be the first to name it. That request must originate with Bergen.

"When did Marsh bring you on board? How much of his operation were you privy to?" Even though it was not the ultimate question that he longed to ask, he had to start somewhere.

It pleased her that he had replaced the G.J. with Marsh. She counted one-half of the battle as won. She paused several heartbeats before answering his questions. It was to her advantage that she appeared reluctant to provide information. "He recruited me three years ago, in June," was her sober reply. "Once he had my family as hostages, he knew that I wouldn't betray him. He let down his guard and let me inside. I got to see everything. What would you like to know?"

"How did he get his contracts?"

This question amused her. She knew the other question that he was dying to ask. However, he could not bring himself to jump directly to it. He had to stalk it, as if it was some wild animal. "He worked through an out-of-town broker who collected the job overtures. All communications were electronic. The two never met. The broker weeded out the obvious hoaxes, the trivial matters, and the delusional requests. The rest were forwarded to Marsh. He always had the final say. Once he had chosen, he worked through the Broker. To protect himself, the client never knew Marsh's identity."

Bergen processed the information. It was an intelligently organized operation. It provided Marsh with maximum anonymity and protection. Aunt Marcy's account begged the next question. "Who is the Broker?"

Again, she feigned resistance. 'Why do you need to know? Why is that so important?"

"If I'm to believe your story, I must know everything. Who's the Broker?"

"Suppose I told you that he, too, is dead."

"That would be too much of a coincidence and would make me inclined to disbelieve your whole story. Give me the name of the Broker!"

She finally admitted "Marsh was always careful never to use the Broker's name. All that I was told was that he was a lawyer working in Las Vegas, Nevada. In time, I learned that the e-mail was addressed to

www.striplawyerwm@gmail.com.

Without Marsh becoming aware of what I was doing, I tracked the e-mail address back to Wil Malone, Esq. Wil was not the name he was given at birth. Nor was it Wilbur, a name that he detested. His original name was Wilberforce. Not knowing when such information might become useful, I tucked it away for future reference. You're welcome!" As Bergen would find out, Wilberforce Malone was a real person and was indeed the Broker. Aunt Marcy gave him up without any regret. He was showing signs of wanting to take over the entire operation. From her perspective, he had outlived his usefulness.

"What about the payments? How were they handled?"

It was a shrewd question. Aunt Marcy admired Bergen's practical mind set.

"The Broker collected the payment. After subtracting his fee, he deposited the balance to Marsh's account in the Caymans. It was never allowed to stay there very long. Marsh was careful to move it to another offshore bank. He used several and I was never able to track the funds after they left the Caymans. Marsh was not exactly a trusting soul."

"Now, we come to a more serious subject, who's the client who wants Arnie P. King dead?" It was the ultimate question. It was the reason he was here.

"We don't refer to these people as clients. We use the term, Bankers. After all, these people are the source of the money." She had established a pattern of passive resistance and she was not going to give the game away by abandoning it now.

Bergen's patience was beginning to wear thin. "I want a name! Give me a name!" He raised his voice in frustration.

Outwardly, she showed fear at his outburst. Inwardly, she smiled. *How predictable!* "**IF** I tell you, what'll you do with this information?"

Bergen favored her with his most disarming smile. "Knowing what I will do is above your pay grade. **WHEN** you tell me what I want to know, I will deal with this Banker, whoever he is."

"What makes you think that the Banker is male?" She watched his reaction and knew that she had him. This was a possibility that he had never considered. "What would you say if I told you that the Banker is Gloria King?"

His reply, "Bullshit", was predictable but lacking in conviction.

"But it makes perfect sense. He is a nebbish who ignores her, in favor of his job. Once he is gone, she will inherit a fortune, and can go anywhere and do anything she pleases."

"I don't believe it. Without supporting evidence, I won't believe it."

"Good! Because it isn't true. I was just testing you. The actual Banker is Nicholas D. Gestas, Junior Partner at B, H, & G."

"Gestas! But why?"

"Is there no end to your questions? Do I have to do all your work for you? Since Mr. Gestas has not shared his motives with me, I am left to speculate about them. My first guess is that he has a thing for Gloria King. Beyond that, perhaps he also covets Mr. King's house, possessions, position at the firm, and/or his future prospects. Or it might be that Mr. King has wronged him in some unforgiveable way, some sin that cries out to heaven for vengeance. I leave that for you to figure out. Now, get the Hell out of my office and let me get back to work. I have a salary to earn."

Bergen went to his car and sat there for the better part of an hour without starting the engine. In his mind, he replayed his conversation with Aunt Marcy. Her story hung together well. But how much of it could he really believe? She had been almost too good, as if she had rehearsed the scene. He was going to need to check every purported "fact". He had a lot of work ahead of him. However, he now had the names of four of the players, Barry Marsh, Aunt Marcy, Wil Malone, and Nicholas Gestas. Four places to begin his research.

He started the car and drove home. *Perhaps Max and his staff can help me with my research.*

Chapter 39

Bergen Assigns Homework

It finally occurred to Bergen that he had, at hand, his own little research group. Each member had an agile mind and a personal incentive. He decided that it was time to put them to work.

He began with his wife, Moira. After breakfast, before she set out for work, he discussed the matter with her.

"I'm still trying to sort out who is responsible for the attack on Arnie. Ultimately, it led to your abduction and ordeal. I could use your assistance." He did not wait for a verbal reply. The nodding of her head was sufficient. "There's been a suggestion, preposterous I know, that Gloria masterminded the whole thing."

"You've got to be kidding! Tell me that you aren't serious! You've been reading too many penny dreadfuls." The response was entirely predictable and delivered with passion.

He shrugged. "We must examine all scenarios, no matter how far-fetched they may seem. After all, Arnie did desert her and then remained silent for a long period. Part of that, I admit, was my doing. Then you and Gloria are put in, what is meant to look like, mortal jeopardy even though it was not. Could it be that she was tired of him and wanted to be rid of him and get his money, without going through a messy and expensive divorce?" She would not be the first woman to take this way out of a dead-end marriage. Neither would she be the last. But, he didn't believe it of Gloria, not even for a moment. Still, the question needed to be reexamined with a fresh set of eyes before it could finally be put to rest.

"For you I will do it," Moira replied. "However, my questioning must be subtle, delicate. If she even suspects that I am cross examining her, she will shut me down. I can't believe that I am agreeing to do this to my own sister."

"Somebody must do it. And, who better than you?"

* * * *

Bergen moved down to the second item on his mental do list. He telephoned Oscar and arranged for lunch today at 1:00 pm, at their favorite spot on the "Gaza Strip."

Over king-sized corned beef sandwiches on kosher rye bread, washed down with superb beer, Bergen made his pitch. "Oscar, you have developed a close and trusting relationship with the local constabulary. I want you to work that connection and do a bit of research. See if you can get a complete record of all the murders attributed to G.J. We need dates and locations going all the way back to the first one reported."

"I can try. But, in case they ask, I'll need a convincing reason. Do you have any suggestions?" He had a good working arrangement with the local police and he did not want to risk damaging it. Besides, he knew Bergen well-enough to know that he never showed all his cards up front.

"In fact, I do. I've given the matter considerable thought. You could tell them that you're thinking about writing a scholarly work about our most recent serial killer. After all, it's part of our local history. You intend to picture the police in a positive light, and you want to be sure that you have your facts straight." Bergen was aware that the authorities, on occasion, withheld details from the press. Short of G.J. himself, the police figured to be the best source for the complete story.

Oscar thought about it as he finished his sandwich. "I'll give it a go. In all such writing, it is crucial to have an accurate time-line." But there was a question, nagging from the back seat of his mind, that he had to ask. "Tell me why this information is so important."

"My colleague, you are growing more astute day by day. You may yet make a serviceable Dr. Watson. There's been a suggestion that the late Barry Marsh was, in fact, G.J. We need a data base to test if this is even remotely possible. Personally, I think that it's unlikely, but we dare not dismiss it without supporting evidence." Bergen began to contemplate dessert.

"Where did this wild suggestion come from? How credible is it?"

"Good questions. My source is Aunt Marcy." Bergen leaned back and watched Oscar's reaction. He was not disappointed.

Oscar's jaw dropped. "You found her? How? Where? Tell me all about it."

"Yes, I did! We had a long talk. She paints herself as another victim. She told me an elaborate and convincing story. I'll give you all the details once we get this mess cleaned up. Our present job is fact-checking to see how much of her story we can believe. You are working one piece of the puzzle and a very important piece it is. So, stay focused. Other people will be doing other pieces."

They each ordered a piece of cheesecake and black coffee. After they settled the bill, they parted, each off to work on his own puzzle piece.

* * * *

That evening, Bergen drove to Thornton University and sought out Montego O'Higgins in his third-floor office, adjacent to his research laboratory. Through the open connecting door, he could see six students at work in the laboratory. Montego was behind his desk, drafting an article for the journals.

Bergen wrapped on the office door. "Do you have time for a visitor?"

A look of relief passed across Montego's face. "Thank God! Someone has come to rescue me from this drudgery." He was quick to pile his work papers off to the side.

Bergen smiled. "The research not going well?"

"To the contrary, the research is going marvelously well," Montego replied. "It's the damn writing that won't flow. I need a break. Come in, have a seat, and tell me your troubles." The interruption was most welcome. It could not have come at a better time.

"What makes you think that I have troubles?" Bergen delighted in demolishing preconceived notions.

"Unless Moira is pregnant again, or you won the Mega Lottery, what else would bring you to my aerie this late in the day? Furthermore, you are rarely without problems. What is it this time?"

"I am looking into Arnie King's situation, trying to determine the prime mover, the person who wants Arnie dead. Who hates him enough that he would pay big bucks for G.J. to dispatch Arnie? One approach to an answer is to identify G.J. and persuade him to tell us who paid for the hit. There has been a suggestion that G.J. was none other than the late Barry Marsh."

Here, Montego interrupted Bergen. "You mean that fellow who was making off with Arnie, after your beach meeting? The fellow who didn't survive that horrendous collision with the sugar maple tree? That former race car driver?"

Montego was incredulous.

Bergen regained the floor. "I know. I, too, find it hard to believe. But, before we can dismiss the suggestion outright, we need some hard evidence. Will you help me?"

"Of course! Just tell me what you would want me to do." The response came without hesitation.

It was the answer that Bergen had expected but, even so, hearing it cheered him. "We need to know much more than we do about Barry Marsh. Who were his parents? When and where was he born? Where did he go to school? Did he have a job prior to his racing career? When did he start to race on the circuit? Most importantly, where and when were his races? When and where were his major wrecks? What hospital admitted him and how long did they keep him? When did he retire from racing? Was he employed post-racing? When and by whom? Did he marry? Are there children?"

Montego nodded. "You want a detailed profile on Marsh. You want to compare it with what we know of G.J.'s activities to see if it's possible that G.J. and Marsh are the same person."

"Precisely!" Bergen commented. "Will you do it?"

"Certainly! I've a former student who is a racing nut. Once, he was deliberately absent from a set of qualifying examinations so that he could go watch the races at Watkins Glen. Now, he works in the Sports Department of the Harrison Herald. He'll be a valuable research resource."

"Excellent! I really do appreciate your assistance. I owe you one."

Montego was not about to let him get away with this. "You already owe me quite a few. This is just one more. One of these days, I am going to come around to collect."

Bergen left, and Montego returned to his manuscript.

* * * *

The following evening, Bergen drove over to the Kings' house and spent some private time with Arnie. Considering that Arnie had recently survived being kidnapped by Marsh as well as a horrendous automobile accident, he appeared surprisingly centered and in good spirits. Being reunited with your wife and children, sleeping in your own bed, and being restored to familiar surroundings, can do wonders for one's mental health.

It was about this time that the Fourth Estate learned that Arnie King was back in circulation. Banner headlines announced, "Missing Investment Counselor Discovered Alive!" In an interview with reporters shortly before he was released from the hospital, Arnie claimed that he had no memory of any events between the time of his accident at the retention pond and awakening in this hospital. In so doing, he was following Bergen's advice to claim amnesia and suggest that what was brought on by a terrible traffic accident was cured by yet another one. Several doctors who were interviewed admitted that such a thing was possible.

"Arnie, I am continuing to work on your problem. I have developed several new leads and I could use your help. I know that you have been through a hellish experience and you may need more time to recover. Are you up to some work?" If Arnie was mentally fragile, Bergen did not want to do anything that might push him over the edge.

The reply came with no hesitation. "I'm ready! Just tell me what you want me to do."

Bergen nodded his head in agreement. "Good man! I know that, during your exile, you worked up profiles on your former colleagues at B, H, & G. I need you to revisit the one on Nick Gestas. This time, I want you to dig deeper and find out everything. No fact is too trivial. What does he like to eat for breakfast? Does he favor blondes or brunettes? Does he have any tattoos? Where and how many? Is he superstitious? If so, in what ways? Is he religious? Does he have any criminal associates? Where does he have his wealth invested?" He watched Arnie closely for his reaction. He realized that he was asking a great deal but no one else knew Gestas as well as Arnie did.

"Does this mean that Nick is the one responsible for what happened to me?" The delivery was flat and emotionless.

"I'm not prepared to go that far," was Bergen's answer. "However, he's certainly a person of interest and we need to learn absolutely everything we can about him. Are you up to it? What do you say?"

"Count me in. I'll do it!"

"Remember, thoroughness is more important than speed."

They shook hands and Bergen went home and slept the sleep of the just.

* * * *

The following morning, Bergen telephoned Max in Atlanta. Again, he was asking for a favor. He wanted Max to put some of his research people to work on constructing a detailed history for another person of interest, Aunt Marcy. He might have done it himself, but he knew that Max had superior resources at his disposal. Besides, he had other things to do.

He had left one puzzle piece for himself. The Broker, Wil Malone, was his. To begin, he did the obvious thing. What better way is there to catch a crooked lawyer than to use a much smarter one? He telephoned Carleton Dunn and set up an appointment.

Chapter 40

Assembling the Puzzle Pieces

C arleton Dunn had read the newspaper accounts of Arnie's resurfacing. He sensed that there was much more to the story than the reporters had provided, and he was curious. When Bergen called for an appointment, he saw this as a chance to learn the full story. He agreed readily to the meeting.

It was scheduled for the middle of a Thursday afternoon in the offices of Gray, Arnold, and Young. The firm occupied the 30-32nd floors of the Third Federal Building in the heart of Harrison's Financial District. The space provided offices for ninety associates, thirty partners, ancillary secretaries, and service staff. It also accommodated a steno pool, a file room, a mail room, a Law Library, a switchboard, a small cashiers cage, and a cadre of messengers.

A bank of six elevators serviced the 31st floor. None of them stopped at the 30th floor. Just one elevator was programmed to stop at the 32nd floor and then only when summoned by the senior partner, Wilhelm Young. Young had outlived both Gray and Arnold. He was well into his nineties and, while his gait was a slow shuffle, his mind was as agile and alert as the brightest student fresh out of the best law school. He looked like a hybrid of the oldest man alive and a mischievous cherub. But his adversaries had learned, sometimes painfully, not to be deceived by appearances. Wilhelm had two secretaries, the younger of the two was a beautiful Latino woman who had once been chosen as Miss Rhode Island. Young might be old, but he was still full of life. Of the beauty that God had created for us to admire and enjoy, none escaped his notice.

Dunn had a roomy corner office that commanded a magnificent view of downtown Harrison, with Lake Katherine beyond, and Canada off on the horizon. Dunn told his secretary to hold all calls until further notice. He and his visitor were not to be disturbed for any reason short of a full-scale Martian invasion.

Bergen accepted the proffered handshake, chair, and authentic Havana cigar. It amused him that he was being treated in a much more deferential manner than he was the last time he and Dunn were together. Clearly the lawyer had concluded that he was no threat and, perhaps, that they were both on the same side after all.

Dunn began their dialog on a conciliatory note. "A while back, I denied knowing Arnie King and helping him in any way. As I am sure you have determined, that was an untruth. I was concerned that an enemy might exploit my involvement to bring charges of collusion as well as those of aiding and abetting a fugitive. I regret misleading you. I prize Arnie as a friend. Please tell me what has happened to him."

Bergen made a mental note that it would be a serious mistake ever to regard Carleton Dunn as a friend. A useful acquaintance, yes. A helpful business associate, perhaps. But, a friend, never. Not unless you welcomed the idea of being thrown beneath the bus when the going got tough. "I will tell you the whole story, or at least as much of it as I know. However, it comes at a price. I want something in return."

At the suggestion of reciprocity, Dunn's guard went up. "What is your price? What is it that you want?"

Bergen blew a perfect smoke ring and then spent a moment admiring his artistry. Then he smiled. "Don't get your knickers in a knot. I've a lead on one of the conspirators in the plot against Arnie. He's an out-of-state lawyer. I need someone to assemble a complete dossier on this character, so I know what I'm dealing with. My guess is that you have access to resources that I could never touch. For Arnie's sake, will you help?"

Dunn took a few moments before he answered. He used the time to trim the ash on his own cigar. He concentrated on the task as if the survival of the free world depended on it. "Yes, with the understanding that I am not committing to anything illegal, immoral, or fattening. What's the name of this lawyer?"

"Noted," Bergen responded. "This fellow has the unlikely name of Wilberforce Malone. For understandable reasons, he prefers to use the shortened version, Wil Malone. On more formal occasions, he has been known to sign himself as W. John Malone, hiding that given name behind the initial. He operates out of Las Vegas, Nevada, where, rumor has it, he serves as a discrete Broker for contract murders. You would do well to keep your information gathering below his radar."

Dunn's complexion turned two shades paler. "Mr. Sawyer, you are an endless source of amusement! You want me to put my life on the line while you lurk in the shadows. You, sir, are a scoundrel! Have you ever considered a career, in Law? As it happens, I have a former classmate who is practicing Law in the Las Vegas area. He owes me a couple of favors. He should be able to get us all the information we need, while we both remain in the shadows. Now, tell me all about this plot to kill Arnie."

If I am a scoundrel, that makes two of us. Bergen proceeded to recount Arnie's saga. He told of the time Arnie spent at Thornton University as a guest of Professor O'Flahertie; the near-fatal incident at the Natatorium; the relocation to the O'Higgins suburban retreat; the third attempt on Arnie's life, this time by Marty Harold, that failed because of the intervention of Phred, the cat; another move, this time to the Safe house on the West Side; the attempted prisoner exchange on the beach; the rescue of the wives; and the almost miraculous survival of Arnie from the horrific car crash that killed Barry Marsh.

He saw no need to recount Oscar's attempts to mislead Arnie's pursuers or Aunt Marcy's involvement. Frankly, he, himself, was not yet sure which side she was on.

Dunn asked an occasional question, but, for the most part, he was engrossed in the account. When Bergen had finished, Dunn asked the key question, "Do you know who's behind all of this?"

Bergen shook his head. "Not yet, but we are pursuing some promising leads. One pathway to an answer goes through Wil Malone. That's why your contribution is so important. I suspect that Malone knows who financed the hit. I'm going to make it my business to find out."

"Suppose he refuses to tell you what you want to know?" Dunn was still trying to take Bergen's measure.

"Counselor, you are a sworn officer of the Court. That's a question that you really don't want to ask me and one that you certainly don't expect me to answer."

Dunn nodded soberly. *My instincts were correct. Sawyer would have made afirst-class lawyer.* "Give me a couple of days and I'll have your information. Call me."

Three days later, Dunn called Bergen. "I've some information for you. Your Wil Malone is a most interesting character. He refuses to use the name Wilberforce unless it is legally required. He absolutely hates the diminutive. Wilber. He once thought seriously about going to court to change his given name. But, his mother likes it, and he stands to inherit a bundle when the old lady passes. So, he can't afford to antagonize her, lest she change her will.

Wil owns a three-bedroom townhouse in Henderson. It is in a gated community on the shores of a 300-acre lake, Lake Vista. It has 4660 sq. ft. and a market value of $826,000. I'll send you the address. He's not married but has a live-in girlfriend, Sophie Viagra, who works as a blackjack dealer on the Strip. Neither of them has any ongoing credit card debt. Neither are there any outstanding wants or warrants. There is no mortgage on Wil's house. Among other things, he has a hunting lodge in Canada, and an estate on Tortola in the British Virgin Islands. The motor vehicle records show that he owns a red 2016 Ferrari LaFerrari, but his everyday ride is a white 2017 Audi R8 Coupe. I'll send you the plate numbers. So, clearly, he's not hurting for money. Most of his banking seems to be done off-shore. His investment accounts are heavily encrypted. If you wish, I can get a thorough analysis of his finances, but it may take another week.

He conducts his business out of an office on the third floor of the MGM Grand, on the Strip. He doesn't have a permanent secretary, preferring to use a revolving collection of stenographers. That suggests to me that he has something to hide. He's a long-time member of the local Bar Association, but it's been a stormy relationship. On four different occasions, charges have been brought against him. In two cases, the charges were abruptly withdrawn. In the other two, the Bar Association dismissed the charges without explanation. What that tells me is that Wil has some serious juice in high places. Further digging revealed that his mother's second husband is a long-time member of the governing board of the Bar Association. Wil is Teflon-coated. No charges against him will ever stick.

With the other material I'm sending you, I'll include a recent photograph of Wil Malone. Good luck with your investigation. I look forward to hearing all about it."

Bergen was pleased with the amount of detail in Dunn's report. He arranged for someone to cover his classes, booked a flight to Las Vegas on Pegasus Airlines, and reserved a rental car at his destination.

* * * *

Wil Malone had fifteen clients, from ten different cities, in four countries. He subscribed to the primary newspaper in each of the cities and spent a good part of his working day scanning these papers for any mention of his clients and their "problems".

Thus, it was that he, too, read about Arnie's abrupt resurrection. It would be an understatement to say that the news did not thrill him. Instead, it gave him a very queasy feeling in the pit of his stomach. *The Banker will not be pleased with these results. And, when he's not happy, bad things begin to happen. But, my hands are clean. He asked for God's Justice and I put the two of them in touch. I did my part. However, I know from experience that, when the Banker gets angry, he lashes out in a very wide arc. I must be on high alert to stay clear of the flailing and the fallout.*

* * * *

Bergen left Harrison on an 8:00 am flight. The plane was filled, many of them dreamers headed for a long, profitable weekend in the casinos. The flight arrived on schedule at 9:30 am local time. He picked up his rental car and drove directly to the MGM Grand. There he entered the subterranean parking garage and found a parking space. On foot with his carry-on bag, he made his way to the level reserved for tenant parking. After a half-hour of searching, he found Malone's 2017 Audi. He checked to make sure that no one was watching and then, fixed a tracking device in the right rear wheel well. It was a trick that he'd learned from the late, and unlamented, Marty Harold. He checked his receiver to make sure that the transmitter was working properly.

He retreated to his own car and left the garage. It took considerable searching, great patience, and a bit of luck to find an outdoor parking space with a clear view of the ramp leading up and out of the garage. After a long break for a leisurely lunch, he verified that Malone's car was where he had left it, returned to his own car, and got to work. He began by using his mobile phone to call Wil Malone. When Wil picked up, Bergen used his best imitation of a Brooklyn hood. "Wilber, dis is Geno. I'm in Vegas takin' care of a little business for da Boss. He asked me to talk wit' you about da Arnie King situation. When can I cum an' see ya?"

The call shook Wil to his core. He suspected that Geno was one of the Banker's enforcers. The "little business" he spoke of was probably the tying off of loose ends. *And I, myself, may be one of these loose ends.* That thought caused him great distress. "Tell Mr. Gestas that there's nothing here to connect him to the King hit. He can trust me to keep my mouth shut."

"That's good, but da Boss said we gotta meet. What time is gud fer ya?"

"This afternoon doesn't work for me." He tried to keep the tremor out of his voice and he was only marginally successful. "I've got a full slate of meetings." He needed to buy time to beat it out of town. "How about 9:00 o'clock tonight in my office here at the MGM Grand. It is quiet then and we won't be disturbed."

Bergen sensed what was going on, but he played along. "Yur our office den, at 9:00 pm. Stay well!" He broke the connection and smiled. If he could find someone to cover the wager, he would bet that Wilber intended to be several states away by the agreed upon hour. He relaxed his body, but continued to stare intently at the exit from the underground garage. His vigilance was rewarded when, a half-hour later, Wilber's Audi came barreling up the ramp and out into the parking lot. Clearly the driver was in a hurry. Bergen started his Nissan and followed the Audi out onto the strip.

By the second red light, Bergen had managed to maneuver directly behind the Audi. He anticipated that, by now, Wilber would be a little jumpy. To add to this nervousness, Bergen flashed his lights twice at the Audi. Wilber panicked and jumped the light, racing down the avenue as if pursued by the hounds of Hell. Bergen let him go. He wasn't going to outrun the tracker.

When Wilbur reached the bedroom community of Las Vegas, he turned off the main road and sought cover in the residential neighborhood where the houses all looked alike. Several blocks in, he pulled into the circular driveway of a darkened house and turned off his lights. It was twilight and soon it would be dark. He hoped that he would pass as another commuter returning home from the rat race. He was bitterly disappointed when, a few minutes later, a car stopped in the street in front of the house next door. That driver flashed his lights three times. Once again, Wilber chose flight.

Returning to the main road, he turned right, doubling back in the direction from which he had come. About a mile up the road, he pulled into a Friendly Gas filling station. There were sixteen pumps, and business was brisk. He pulled up to pump nine and killed his lights and the engine. He made no move to get out of the car but watched the rearview mirror intently. After a few minutes, a car pulled in behind him at pump ten. The driver flashed his lights four times. By now, Wilber was close to losing his mind. He started the Audi, left the station, and fled south on the main highway.

Bergen was in no hurry to follow. He had the tracking device and, he expected that Wilber was heading for home, to gather up a few things before he skipped town. On his screen, he watched as Wilber turned onto the shore road that rimmed Lake Vista. It followed the shore line faithfully except where there were bridges to bypass inconvenient inlets. The original real estate covenants forbade any building on the lake-side of the road, so as not to ruin the view from the gated mansions on the other side.

After making the turn, Wilber slowed and watched the rearview mirror, looking for his pursuer. He saw no one and this pleased him. Whoever it was might not be infallible after all. He began to relax.

Before making his turn onto the shore road, Bergen killed his headlights.

Once he had completed the turn, he was faced with a long straightaway. He gunned the engine. Fortunately, there was no other traffic on the road at this hour. He soon overtook the Audi and braked just short of a collision. Then he turned on the headlights, switched to the brights, and flashed them five times.

Taken by surprise, Wilber was scared witless. He gunned his car forward, mashing the gas pedal to the floorboard. He spent too much time checking the rearview mirrors for any sign of pursuit, and not enough watching the road ahead of him. He missed the approach for a bridge and the Audi left the road in a high arc, before crashing into the Lake. It settled into the water and sank quickly.

Bergen arrived in time to see the last of the Audi slip beneath the surface. He could detect no sigh of life within the car. For just a moment, he thought that he should get out of his car and try to rescue the driver of the Audi. But then, he thought better of it. He had gotten what he came for, the name of the Banker. Moreover, Malone's demise was dripping with irony and completely appropriate. *What a shame Arnie King wasn't here to witness this climax. He would've been delighted. There is even a bonus. I didn't have to kill Wilber. I never met him; I never touched him. It was his own guilty conscience that did him in. A guilty conscience can be a terrible burden.*

Chapter 41

The Case Against the Banker

Bergen flew back to Harrison from Vegas on Saturday morning. The length of the trip gave him ample time to analyze his role in the demise of Wilberforce Malone. He had not intended Malone's death. To the contrary, if he had his preference, Malone would still be alive. There were questions that he wanted to ask him. Now he would never, at least in this life, have that opportunity.

However, Malone did not die by Bergen's hand. There was never any physical contact. One brief telephone conversation was as close as they ever came to meeting. Yet, it was clear that Bergen's surveillance had unhinged Malone to the point that he behaved irrationally. So, Bergen could be accused of being an accessory in the lawyer's death. Except that there were no witnesses, no one to implicate him.

Some people take an almost orgasmic pleasure in wallowing in guilt. Bergen never had that problem. He rationalized that Malone had already been on the edge of the abyss, staring down into it. All Bergen did was to give him the last little nudge that sent him toppling forward. How could anyone know that he was so close to the edge? The real guilt rested with the people who had pushed him to that edge.

Whenever Bergen began to feel remorse over the tragic ending of Malone's life, he reminded himself that Malone had not been an innocent victim. He had been the traffic manager for a large, but uncounted, number of contract killings. While Malone, himself, had not been a ruthless killer, he had enabled many other people who were. If they knew all the facts, few law-abiding citizens will mourn his passing. With him gone, there might be a momentary decline in the homicide rate, but it will only be a matter of time before someone else moves up to take his position.

Bergen marked his Malone folder closed and filed it away in his mental archives. Then, he turned to what he had learned in Vegas. Two different sources now had implicated Nick Gestas as the driving force behind the attempts on Arnie King's life. It was not proof, but it suggested that Gestas should be the next focal point in his investigations. He needed to learn everything he could about Gestas. Fortunately, he already had Arnie compiling the data.

After dinner that evening, Bergen and Moira lingered over another glass of wine. The children had gone their separate ways. His wife spared him the trouble of creeping up on the topic most on his mind. "I had a long talk with my sister, Gloria. I pushed her as hard as I dared. There's absolutely no way that she could be the mastermind behind the attempts on Arnie's life. I'd stake my professional reputation on it. To begin with, she's a carload of gray cells short of being a criminal genius. Then, even though I know that you've little use for Arnie, Gloria actually loves him. He's good to her, and for her. If he should die tomorrow, she wouldn't last a week without him."

Bergen listened closely. "Independently, we've both reached the same conclusion. I needed that corroboration. Thank you."

"Did you have any luck in Vegas?" She knew that he hadn't gone there to gamble, but rather to get information. Her questions were guarded. Over the years, she had learned that there were certain things that it was better not to know.

"I wasn't able to get everything I wanted, but I believe that we're one step closer to identifying the person responsible for most of Arnie's troubles." He drained his wine. "Tomorrow, I'm going to have a talk with Arnie. His is the next puzzle piece."

* * * *

The following afternoon, when Bergen arrived at the King home, Gloria let him in. Her greeting lacked warmth. He was not sure whether this was because of Moira's visit, or because of Gloria's ordeal on the beach. Either way, it was probable that he was being cast as the villain. He expected that this attitude would be of short duration. He was prepared to live with that on a temporary basis.

Arnie was in the sun room, working his way through the book review section of The New York Times. He waved Bergen to a seat and greeted him with more bonhomie than he felt. "Back from the wars so soon! Did you learn anything useful?"

Bergen grimaced. "A few more bread crumbs but not the grand prize." He wanted Arnie to stay focused and not get sidetracked, so he was reluctant to go into details.

But, Arnie persisted. "Did you get a chance to meet with that lawyer we have been calling The Broker? What the Hell is his name?"

"The name was Wil Malone. He and I spoke once on the telephone but never had a chance to meet face-to-face. Before that could happen, he died in a one-car automobile accident." He knew that Arnie would not let him stop here, so he continued. "He was driving recklessly, missed a turn, and went into Lake Vista. He never made it out of the car."

With his own escape from what could have been a watery grave fresh in his mind, Arnie's complexion turned ashen. "Now that's a spooky coincidence!"

Bergen did not believe in coincidence. He was beginning to wonder if a pattern was emerging. But, this was not the time for such speculation, there were other subjects that needed to be discussed. "Bring me up to date on what new information you have uncovered on Nick Gestas."

It took Arnie a moment to transition from the land of the dead back to that of the living. "I knew that he was obsessed with numbers. He could quote from memory all sorts of trivia: the price per pound of a leg of lamb in 1954, the cost per gallon of gasoline in 1960, and how much he tipped his newspaper carrier last year. But, he's turning out to be a much more interesting character than my earlier, limited study, suggested. For one, he appears to have a serious gambling habit. Once a month, he travels to Vegas, Atlantic City, or one of the Indian Casinos. His game of choice is Black Jack. And, for someone who is reputed to be a mathematical wizard, he doesn't appear to be very good at it. He loses regularly.

So, even though B, H, & G pays him well, he always seems to be strapped for cash. Routinely, he makes only partial payments on his credit card debts."

"Which could give him motive for siphoning off funds from your clients' investment accounts," Bergen interrupted. "It's suggestive but not probative. What else do you have?"

"Unlike every other upper management type at B, H, & G, he does not keep his own personal investment accounts in house. Gestas has his with an Atlanta firm, Greenfield and Associates."

At the mention of the name Greenfield, a cold chill ran up Bergen's spine. *Max and Gestas were business associates? It was quite likely that they knew each other. Now, this was getting spooky.*

"So, it's difficult for us to get a fix on Gestas' net worth. These files are heavily encrypted, and I haven't yet been able to penetrate them." Arnie was almost apologetic.

"Why not put that problem on the back burner for the moment. I may have a way of getting around the encryption." *A talk with Max might solve the problem.* "What else do we know about Gestas? What makes him tick? What does he want more than anything else in this world? What really gets his motor going? You worked with the man for several years. You had the opportunity to study him up close and personal. What did you learn?" Bergen was pressing him to dig deeper.

Arnie frowned. "What expertise I have is in financial analysis Psycho- analysis is beyond my skill set. As an amateur, all I can give you is my impressions. They may be completely off the mark."

Bergen encouraged him. "I'll take whatever I can get. Have at it."

"Nick has had to work hard for everything he has. He believes, wrongly, that all the rest of us were somehow divinely entitled, and never had to work for anything. Thus, he has a chip on his shoulder. With that chip comes a heavy load of resentment. He's not good at hiding this and it shows up in his work. He desperately wants to become a partner in the firm. For him, it would be the ultimate vindication, proof that he's without peer. Sadly, it's unlikely ever to happen. Up until the time of my recent accident, I think that I had a better shot at partnership than he did." Laying all this out was not easy for Arnie. It was clear that the whole matter depressed him.

"So, if Nick came to the same conclusion, he would've had a powerful motive for bringing you down. You stood in his way." Bergen was simply stating what was for him obvious.

Arnie was unconvinced. "C'mon Bergen, get real! It's an awfully long leap from professional jealousy to attempted murder."

"You're the one who needs to get real," was Bergen's response. "People have been murdered for much less. There's someone out there who wants you dead. Unless we can find him and stop him, he'll keep trying. If we don't stop him, eventually he'll be successful. It's imperative that you understand that!" He was exasperated with Arnie and needed to change the direction of the conversation before one of them said something that couldn't be taken back. "You said that Nick was unlikely ever to make partner. Why is that?"

"When you are invited to become partner, you are expected to make a "buy-in", to become a share-holder in the firm. At last report, for B, H, & G, the amount required is $400,000. Given what we know of the state of Nick's finances, unless he has some secret source of funds, he could never afford the ante. So, it's never going to happen." Arnie's answer was delivered with morbid finality, as if he was pronouncing a death sentence.

It fell to Bergen to remind him, "Unless, of course, he has the loot that disappeared from the accounts of your investment clients." He made a mental note to check with Max and find out how much was in the Gestas accounts. "Anything more on Gestas?"

"I don't know if it has any relevance, but I discovered that Nick suffers from sleep apnea. He bought an expensive, custom-made sleep mask. It showed up in his credit card statements."

Bergen shook his head. "It's a curiosity, but I doubt that it'll be useful." He had gotten what he had come for, but he could not leave without raising one more issue, a personal one. "How're you doing?"

"Physically, I'm fine. The bruises from the crash that killed Barry Marsh have pretty much healed. Mentally, I'm still on edge, waiting for the next attack. The round-the-clock security details do help. Legally, I seem to've dodged a bullet, but I'm still under a cloud. The police have accepted my story that I've no memory of the time between my car going in the retention pond and then waking up in the hospital after the Marsh crash. I get the impression that they don't believe it, but they can't produce evidence to refute it. Professionally, I'm in Limbo. Harold Boyd is still holding my job open, waiting for the legal cloud to disperse. However, he can't do this indefinitely. If we don't solve our mystery soon, my job will go to someone else."

"I understand. I am working as fast as I can." Bergen sympathized with Arnie. "But, these things take time. We're making progress. I believe that we're close. Meanwhile, keep digging on Gestas."

* * * *

That evening, Bergen telephoned Max, at home. He apologized for bothering him on a weekend. He explained, "Max, I think that we've an unexpected problem. You will remember that I am trying to unravel the plot against Arnie King. During this investigation, the name of Nick Gestas has come up several times. If I remember correctly, he's a friend of yours who has his investment accounts with your firm. Now, he's a person of interest to us and I've some questions about these investment accounts. Given how scrupulous you are about protecting the confidentiality of your clients, this could pose a conflict of interest. Is there some way we can avoid that?"

For several minutes, there was silence on Max's end of the line, save for the sound of him sucking on his pipe. "You know, you've an unpleasant habit of presenting me with sticky problems. Let me begin by correcting you. At one time, Nick Gestas was a friend of mine. But, that time has passed. At present, I would call him an uncomfortable acquaintance. He's not the same fellow I once called friend. Plainly put, I don't trust him."

"That's good to know! If my suspicions are correct, he's been involved in some very serious mischief and I may have to deal with him." Bergen smiled. His job had just gotten a bit easier.

Max employed Bergen from time to time as a very selective hit-man. He knew that Bergen had a rule against operating in Harrison, his home town. However, with sufficient provocation, he had, on occasion, been known to bend that rule. "As for my ethical code, you have given me fair warning. Let me worry about that. Moreover, you are listed on my payroll as a "Special Consultant" and that makes you a member of the firm. With that, you are entitled to access some information that isn't available to the public at large. What I suggest is that you ask me specific questions, and I'll answer them up to the point where you begin to intrude on privileged information. There, I'll stop you."

"Fair enough!" It was more than he had hoped for. "How many accounts does Nick have with us?"

"There are four. I won't tell you the specific holdings or the current balances."

"Are all of the transactions electronic, or does he still receive paper statements?"

"They're electronic only."

"Does he put new money in on a regular basis?" Bergen was trying to develop a behavioral baseline.

"No, he doesn't."

"Did he begin to add to these accounts about September of last year?" Bergen had chosen the week when the first attempt was made on Arnie's life, at the retention pond.

"As a matter of fact, he did. They were unusually large deposits. I became suspicious and I asked Nick about them. He laughed it off. He said that Lady Luck had finally decided to smile on him. He claimed that he was running a hot winning streak in the casinos. I had a hard time believing him. Nobody has a streak that hot for that long. If it ever happened, the casinos would, at the very least, shut him down. Then, there was the fact that these deposits weren't coming from a bank in Harrison. Instead, they were wire transfers from the Cayman Islands. My guess was that the money had been laundered off shore and was now returning home. However, my suspicions were all circumstantial. I had no proof." Max was almost apologetic.

Bergen was sympathetic. But, he sensed that there was more to the story. "What did you do?"

"I was on the verge of telling him to take his money somewhere else. But then, it became clear that he knew about our E.P funds. He wanted to hire us to hunt Arnie down and make him disappear permanently." In all the previous conversations Bergen had with Max, the person who wanted Arnie dead had always been referred to as "a client". Now, for the first time, that client had a name. "That's when I got you involved. Ultimately, we turned down his request. So, if you are looking for the person behind Arnie's troubles, I would put my money on Nick Gestas."

"Max, many thanks. You have been most helpful. Let me digest what you just told me, and I'll get back to you."

At this point Bergen was ninety-percent certain that Gestas was the person responsible for Arnie's misadventures. However, before he acted, he needed to be one hundred-percent sure. That rule was deeply ingrained in his behavioral patterns. He thought about it long and hard.

The following evening, Bergen again called Max at home. "I agree with your assessment. I'd like you to do me a favor. Contact Nick Gestas and tell him that you've changed your mind. You'll take the contract on King after all, if it is still available. Having failed to kill Arnie on at least four different occasions, if Gestas is our man, he should be most anxious to get it done. I expect that he'll jump at the chance for a final solution to the King Problem. If he does, charge him top dollar."

"What're you going to do?"

"Until I hear back from you that he has taken the bait, nothing. But once Gestas commits, then I'll act. You can promise him that I intend to put an end to the King Problem. You really don't want to know how. But, if I were you, I would collect my fee in advance."

"Be careful, my friend!" Then he broke the connection.

Chapter 42

Killing the Banker

While he was waiting to hear back from Max, Bergen arranged to meet with Oscar. Once again, they were off-campus, at Jedidiah's Restaurant in the Gaza Strip. They were becoming such regulars that the waitress knew them by sight and guessed in advance what they would order. *Such creatures of habit!*

After they placed their orders, Bergen began the serious discussion. "Well, Oscar, what've you learned so far about the career of the serial killer known as G.J.?"

"The police like the idea of the book. They're at a point where they need all the favorable public relations they can get. They're cooperating and being most helpful." Oscar reached into his briefcase and extracted two identical, green, pressboard binders. He kept one and passed the other across to Bergen. "Here is what I have so far. This is not the time nor is this the place to read the whole thing. Let me give you the Executive Summary. To begin, we've a time line for the local killings that were marked with a post-it note bearing the initials G.J. There could've been killings before the killer began claiming credit for them. We may never know."

Bergen noted that the list began twenty years ago and that it included the names of the victims, when such were known, and the sites where the bodies were discovered. *Somebody on the force had taken a serious interest in tracking G.J.'s career.*

Oscar continued, "The second section lists all of the killings attributed to G.J. in the rest of our state and in eight nearby states. You'll note that the total is smaller than in the previous section for the same period."

"This could be due to incomplete reporting or it might mean that G.J. was reluctant to travel." Bergen was making a preliminary analysis of the data.

Oscar nodded agreement. "The third section has photocopies of most of the post-it notes that were pinned to the bodies. Notice the firm hand and the consistency of the writing style up until about two years ago. The hand is now less steady, and the style begins to slip. This might mean that G.J. had a minor stroke."

"Or, it could mean that the old G.J. is gone and we've a copy-cat taking his place," Bergen added.

"Coincidentally," Oscar continued "about two years ago, our killer seems to have evolved. Now the bodies all show signs of mutilation. The missing pieces have never been recovered. This piece of information hasn't been released to the press. But, my police sources swear that it's true."

"Either our killer has slipped deeper into his madness, or we have a new player," Bergen concluded. "It makes an interesting puzzle."

Then, as if on cue, their lunches arrived. Bergen put his folder aside for a later, in-depth, study. The morbidity of their discussion did nothing to kill their appetites.

* * * *

During his many conversations with Arnie, Bergen had learned the workings of B, H, & G in considerable detail. He'd noted the day and time of the weekly General Meeting, the one that no employee dared miss. He was certain that he knew where Nick Gestas would be on Wednesdays at 10:00 am. That was information he could use. The coming Wednesday was too soon, but the one a week hence could be made to work. True, he had a class on Wednesday mornings. However, if he wrote an exam for that day and had one of his research assistants administer and proctor it, he could be busy elsewhere.

Thus, at 7:30 am on the Wednesday in question, Bergen was sitting in his car fully a block away, and on the other side of the street, from Gestas' home. As he watched, Nick left for work. Bergen had done his homework. There were no servants and the cleaning lady was not scheduled until Friday. Nick's estranged third wife was in Seattle, attending a conference. There were no children, and, at this moment, Nick wasn't seeing anyone on a regular basis. The house should be empty. Bergen heard it calling to him.

The front door lock proved no challenge. There was no alarm system. *For such a clever man, one would've thought that he'd be more careful about his security. Arrogance perhaps!* Bergen let himself in, donned neoprene gloves, locked the door behind him, and began to explore. Illicitly violating another's private space when they weren't at home never ceased to give him a frisson of excitement. Some might call him a closet voyeur. He spent considerable time in Gestas' study, going through his private papers. He found no paper record of any financial transactions. Max had been correct. Gestas preferred to do his investment business electronically. There were no signs of thumb drives backing up his data, so the obvious conclusion was that everything was kept on the hard drive. *Typical, but neither smart nor safe. Then, again, Gestas was known to be a gambler.*

Next, Bergen moved on to the upstairs bathroom. *Bathrooms and bedrooms always have a story to tell.* The medicine cabinet held the usual array of salves, creams, ointments, and analgesics. He was disappointed to find no opioids. However, he took note of the presence of the prescription medication, Temazepam, used for inducing sleep.

Then, he made his way to the master bedroom. It was a large, comfortable room furnished with a king-size bed, a plasma TV, a writing desk and chair, a low dresser with mirror, several small tables, a few casual chairs, and wall-to-wall carpeting. Two of the tables flanked the head of the bed. On one of the tables was a small pile of books. Gestas' reading tastes ran to John Grisham, Tom Clancy, and Anne Rice. On the other side of the bed, the table held a sterling silver serving tray on which stood two inverted low-ball glasses, a Styrofoam ice bucket with lid, a small pitcher of water, and a fifth of Jack Daniel's Sinatra Century. *A pretty pricey drink for a man with money problems. However, it did speak to his priorities.* The seal on the liquor bottle had been broken but it was still nearly full. This suggested that Gestas had devised his own cure for insomnia. *Who needs pills?*

Bergen's attention was drawn to the dresser. On the top, centered in front of the mirror was a ceramic bust similar to those that milliners use for their displays. The image was androgynous, but handsome all the same. While it was hatless, it was dressed in Gestas' custom cpap unit. The full mask fit snugly over the face. The air intake was through a piece of 5/8 in. plastic tubing and was powered by a small motor to maintain a positive pressure and keep the nasal passages open. It appeared well-constructed and was an attractive piece of equipment. However, Bergen doubted that he, himself, would ever be able to sleep with such a mask over his nose and mouth. *To each his own!*

A plan was beginning to come together in his mind. He sat down at the desk, closed his eyes, and watched it play out in his mind's eye. It was not foolproof, but it should work. He liked the simplicity of it. It was appropriate and had a certain inherent elegance. He returned to the bathroom and collected a handful of the sleeping tablets. Back in the bedroom, he uncapped the bourbon bottle and added the Temazepam. He swirled the mixture to speed up the dissolution. Then he recapped the bottle. There was nothing else he could do at this time, so he left and drove back to campus.

At Thornton, he didn't go directly to his own office. Instead, he paid a visit to Montego O'Higgins in the Chemistry Department.

"Montego, do you have a few minutes?

"For you, Bergen, anytime. But, if you want my final report on the life and times of Barry Marsh, you will have to wait yet a little while. My teaching, my research, and my wife come first."

Bergen smiled. "I'm sure that Syn appreciates where she ranks in your cosmic hierarchy. No, I haven't come to bug you about your assignment. Rather, I'm here to ask for a small favor." Without waiting for an answer, he plowed right ahead. "I want to make a wash bottle similar to those your students use in General Chemistry. The mouth of my reservoir is 28 mm in diameter."

Montego had heard many stranger requests. "For that you'll need a number six, two-hole rubber stopper. C'mon into the lab and I'll get you one." He continued talking as they headed for the lab. "You'll also need a few lengths of pyrex tubing, 8 mm. outside diameter, as well as several lengths of Tygon tubing, 8 mm. inside diameter." As he was talking, he found a suitable stopper and kneaded it between his palm and the bench top. Then he lubricated the openings with a little glycerol. Next, he took a three-inch length of glass tubing, wrapped it in many folds of towel, and inserted it easily into the stopper. "I do recommend using the towel. A Stigmatis isn't a good fashion statement this season!" Just as easily, he inserted a foot-long length of glass tubing in the other hole. Then, he handed the assembly to Bergen along with a couple of lengths of Tygon tubing.

"Thank you, my friend," Bergen said. "However, I didn't intend for you to do all the work."

"No problem! I like to keep my hand in and demonstrating is usually quicker than giving someone else directions. Also, I didn't want you to hurt yourself. Besides, sometimes I just like to show off.

Bergen politely turned down Montego's invitation to join him for lunch. Instead, he took his glassware, wrapped in the towel, back to his office.

In the middle of the afternoon, he left again. He made one stop, at The Stone Oven, for a take-out order of a small salad and a sandwich, rare roast beef and Emmenthaler cheese with a spicy horseradish dressing on Miller's Multigrain bread. Then he resumed his observation post near the Gestas home. He needed to know whether Nick brought anyone home with him. He watched the Lord of the Manor arrive home at 7:00 pm. He was alone. There were no late arrivals. Gestas was spending another solitary evening. Bergen ate his salad and the sandwich, washing them down with bottled water. When dinner was finished, he turned on the car radio. It was perpetually tuned to WHAR, Harrison's fine arts station. Tonight, they were featuring the Harrison Symphony Orchestra in a concert performance of Wagner's Die Gotterdamnerung. *Perfectly appropriate!*

At 11:00 pm, the downstairs lights winked out. Then the light came on in the master bedroom. *I hope that Nick is enjoying a generous nightcap.* At midnight, the bedroom went dark. Bergen waited another hour and then he slipped on his latex gloves and picked up the drawstring bag that held his tools. Once again, the lock on the front door presented no problem. Knowing the layout of the house, he negotiated the stairs up to the bedroom in the dark without difficulty.

Now came the moment of truth. He switched on his flashlight and played it on the bed. Gestas was indeed alone and he never moved. He was soundly asleep. He was wearing his cpap, and the motor was whirring quietly. Bergen observed that one of the glasses had been used. It sat upright, and the dregs of the Jack Daniels were visible in the bottom. He uncapped the bottle and inserted the rubber stopper, with its two glass tubes, into the neck of the bottle. The shorter tube just cleared the stopper on the inside. The longer tube reached almost to the bottom of the bottle. Next, he turned off the cpap motor and separated it from the air delivery tube. Gestas didn't stir. Then, Bergen connected the external portion of the long tube to the air inlet hose. Finally, he put the motor on its lowest setting, connected it to the external end of the shorter tube, and turned it back on. He was pleased to see that the pressure didn't dislodge the stopper from the bottle. Had that not been the case, he came prepared to wire the stopper in place.

As he watched, the pressure inside the bottle slowly forced the whiskey up the long tube, out the top, and into the air inlet hose. Bergen pulled up a chair. He needed to make certain that this worked perfectly. If there were any glitches, he wanted to be present to correct them.

The liquor ran into the mask. When it began to submerge Nick's nose, the body gave one great spasm, followed by two lesser ones, and then it became still. The mask filled completely. The air was forced out through a one-way valve at the mouth. Bergen waited a full five minutes. Eventually, the booze began to leak out through the mouth vent. At that point, Bergen turned off the pump. He checked Gestas for a pulse and found none. Gestas was now enjoying an endless sleep.

Had Bergen been a more religious man, he might have muttered a few appropriate prayers over the body. He did believe in a Supreme Creator. The Universe, and the Laws of Biology, Chemistry, and Physics, were just too intelligent and orderly to believe otherwise. Further, any Being with the intelligence and power to create and set in motion our Universe could do pretty much anything It pleased. But, as far as an afterlife, with a system of rewards and punishments, was concerned, that was just asking for too much. It struck him as an ecclesiastic fairy tale, fabricated to keep the masses in line, a dogmatic carrot and a stick if you will. Of course, it was possible. However, he knew of no evidence supporting a Heaven, a Hell, a Purgatory, or a Limbo. To him, it smacked of wishful thinking. Yet, he continued to wrestle with this conundrum. His belief system was a work in progress.

It was time to get to work again. Bergen disconnected his glass tubes from both the air inlet hose and the one to the motor. Next, he removed the rubber stopper from the bottle, wrapped the whole device in the towel, and put it in his bag. Then he put the open end of the air inlet tube into the Jack Daniels bottle, so that, when gravity drained the whiskey out of the mask, it wouldn't make a mess. *Neatness always earns style points.* He returned the chair he had been using to its original position. Finally, he took a few minutes to study the room to make certain that he had left no trace. As he stared at the body on the bed, he sent a silent message to the deceased. *Nobody messes with my family.* When he was certain that the scene was clean, he left the house, locking the door behind him, and returned to his car.

On Friday, the cleaning lady discovered the body. The police were called, and they made the obvious call that it was a crime scene. With the front door locked and no sign of forcible entry, they had second thoughts. They dusted for prints and found only four sets. The first two belonged to the deceased and his cleaning lady. The other two belonged to a pair of male prostitutes. However, both of these men had unimpeachable alibis for the night of the death. One had spent the week with friends in San Francisco and the other had been in the drunk tank at the central jail, sleeping off a world-class binge.

The report of the Medical Examiner did nothing to dispel the confusion. Gestas' lungs were filled with expensive whiskey. Death was by drowning. Some suggested that it was a suicide. But, could one really inhale that much booze? If it had been suicide, then it was one of the most unusual ones on record. The later finding that the whiskey had been laced with Temazepam, tipped the scales again in favor of murder. It is said that everybody likes a good mystery. The newspapers picked up the story and ran with it. It sold a lot of papers. To this day, it remains an unsolved police case.

Chapter 43

Making B, H, & G Whole

Bergen followed the progress of the Gestas Murder/Suicide investigation in the Harrison Herald. He likened the procedures to a dog chasing its tail. The authorities still had not reached a conclusion as to whether it was murder or suicide. If, indeed, it was murder, they were still mystified about how it could have been done. They were still a long way from the question of who did it. He was rather pleased with his performance but not to the point where he would make a careless mistake.

His next project was getting Arnie reinstated with B, H, & G. To do this, he would have to replace the money. *Where was he going to find $8 million laying around?* When at such an impasse, he usually found it helpful to talk with Max.

He called Max on Saturday morning and asked if there was a time and a place where they might sit down and have a long talk. Max congratulated him on his exquisite timing. The following day he was scheduled to fly on the corporate jet to a conference in Aspen, Colorado. He could come by way of Cincinnati and arrange for a three-hour lay over. Why didn't Bergen meet him at the Greater Cincinnati Airport at 9:00 am.?

The Cincinnati airport is actually in Hebron, Kentucky. Bergen decided that, given the early meeting time, it made more sense for him to drive from Harrison to Hebron. Max arrived on schedule and the two of them retired to the VIP lounge.

Fortified with good strong coffee and a plate of assorted pastries, they settled in. Max opened up the discussion. "Tell me everything you know about the Gestas mystery."

Bergen gave him the full story. He finished his account with "If Gestas was the prime mover behind Arne's troubles, then this should end it. We'll have to wait and see."

"I think that you've put a stop to it." Max said. "But, this does leave me with a couple of problems. Nick Gestas paid us a handsome sum to put an end to the Arnie King problem. By that I'm sure that he understood that we would kill Arnie. You, on the other hand, found a different way to solve the problem. What do you want me to do with your fee? Should I deposit it to your retirement account in the Caymans?" Max was baiting him. He suspected that he knew what Bergen's answer would be.

"Not this time. I would rather see it go back to B, H, & G. It would be a nice gesture if you did the same thing." In his own way, he was challenging Max.

"That is what I intended to do. However, it will fall far short of the $8 million that went missing. Which leads me to my second problem. As you already know, Nick Gestas had four investment accounts with us. Their total value at the close of business on Friday was well north of $8 million. I checked his application the other day. He never listed a beneficiary.

Bergen saw where this was headed. He resigned himself to playing the straight man. "Wouldn't it be lovely if we could find some way to channel this money back where it belongs?"

Max smiled and helped himself to another cup of coffee. "Well, there is always Rule 27, Section B, Subsection 3."

"What in God's name is that? It sounds like some arcane set of Bylaws."

Max sipped his coffee. There was a twinkle in his eye. "It's real. It's buried deep in the fine print of the agreement each client signs before we take them on. I know because I put it there myself. Basically, it says that if there is a sudden shift in the market, and we cannot get in touch with the client in a timely fashion, then we are empowered to move the funds to a safe-haven of our choice."

Bergen was stunned. "I never knew that."

"That's because you never read all of the fine print. Don't feel bad. Damn few ever do."

"At one time, I started to read it. However, I fell asleep before I finished the first page."

"Writing like that is how some lawyers earn a living."

"Sweet!" commented Bergen. "All we have to do is wait for the next big hiccup in the stock market, and then reinvest that money in shares of B, H, & G.

Is that legal? Can we get away with that?"

Max replied, "Probably not. But, there may be a better way."

"You are a devious bastard, Max." Bergan made sure to smile when he said this. "I can't wait to hear what you have in mind."

"When Gestas opened his accounts with us, it was my impression that this was not his personal money, but rather funds from his firm." Strictly speaking, this was a bold-faced lie and they both knew it. However, there was no one left on this earth who could prove the statement false. "That being so, with the death of Mr. Gestas, we have an obligation to return this money to the rightful owners." It was to Max's credit that he could complete this statement with a perfectly straight face.

"Bravo, Max! That was a performance worthy of an Oscar. Are you prepared to follow through on this?"

"If you haven't already, I expect that you'll soon make an appointment to meet with Harold Boyd for a serious conversation. When you do, please give him my best regards. I know him from bygone days." Then Max reached into the inside pocket of his suit jacket and withdrew a white legal-sized envelope. He passed it over to Bergen. "Also, give him this."

The envelope was not sealed. Bergen looked inside and found a cashier's check for $8 million. A tremor crept through Bergen's usually steady hand. "Is this real?"

Max reassured him, "Absolutely! But, be careful with it. If you lose it, you are in big trouble. You'll be working for my firm for the next five hundred years with no pay. Properly employed, that envelope should give you all the leverage you need with old Harold."

"What will you do if Gestas' heirs come looking for his wealth?" Bergen was imagining what six ex-wives, a gaggle of children, plus half-a-dozen hungry siblings might do for a chance at an inheritance like this.

Max chuckled. "It would be a circus. There's some money left in the accounts but gambling certainly took its toll. The balances are plausible, but they won't make anyone wealthy."

"Is this legal?" Bergen gestured with the envelope.

"Probably not," Max answered. "But it's the right thing to do."

On his drive home, Bergen marveled at what a clever fellow Max was, and how blessed he was to have him as a friend.

* * * *

The following morning, he called B, H, & G and made an appointment with Harold Boyd for 4:00 pm on Friday next.

Later Monday afternoon, he received the final report on the life and times of Barry Marsh from Montego O'Higgins. Barry had been born in Indianapolis, Indiana, to Birchford and Willomena Marsh. He grew up in the shadow of the Motor Speedway. While racing was not in his blood, he had been baptized with it, and one aspect of his future was preordained. He began competitive racing before he was old enough to have a legal driver's license.

Montego's report included a detailed time-line showing every race that Barry had participated in, where it was run, the date on which it occurred, and how Marsh finished, if, in fact, he did finish. Bergen pulled out the list that Oscar had provided of the body dumps attributed to G.J. He began a side-by-side comparison of the two lists. This new time-line clearly showed that Marsh was still actively racing when G.J. began leaving dead bodies marked with his signature post-it notes. It was difficult to imagine that Marsh was multitasking. Indeed, on the date that one of the bodies was deposited in Nashville, Kentucky, Marsh was winning a race at Watkins Glen, New York. On another occasion, when G.J. left a body in Flint,

Michigan, Marsh was racing at Daytona Beach, Florida. A third mismatch was a corpse in Bean Blossom, Indiana, while Marsh was in a hospital in Columbia, South Carolina, recovering from a broken leg, incurred in a pile-up at the local track. The obvious, inescapable conclusion was that Marsh could not possibly be the serial killer known as God's Justice.

Bergen was pleased to have a definitive answer to the question whether Barry was G.J. But, it still left open the issue of who G.J. really was. The field was wide open. Aunt Marcy was automatically reinstated as a candidate.

* * * *

On Friday, promptly at 4:00 pm, Bergen was shown into Harold Boyd's office. Harold rose from his seat behind an oversized desk that was free of any clutter and extended his hand. "Professor Sawyer, have a seat. Tell me what I can do for you."

Bergen had the perfect ice-breaker. "To begin with, I bring you greetings from Max Greenfield."

Boyd was pleasantly surprised. "Is that old rascal still alive? We had lost touch. The last I knew, he was running a wealth management firm in Atlanta."

"He is in good health, and still at it," Bergen replied. "From time to time, he employs me as a consultant on special projects." He didn't dare elaborate.

"When next you see him, do extend my best wishes." Then, as a man who knew that his time was money, Harold got down to business. "Now, specifically, what can I do for you?"

"I am here to provide you with some information that you may find useful." Without giving Boyd a chance to interrupt, Bergen launched into his exposition.

"Several months ago, $8 million went missing from a group of your investment accounts. At the same time, so did Arnold P. King." It was clear to Bergen that he now had Boyd's full attention. "The obvious conclusion, one that most people reached quickly, was that Arnie had absconded with the money. However, the obvious answer is not always the correct answer. There is another possible explanation: that someone else took the money and set Arnie up as the fall guy. In fact, that very Friday evening, on his way home from work, someone ran Arnie's car off the road and into a retention pond, trying to drown him. It's rather difficult to defend yourself against charges of theft if you are dead. But Arnie didn't die. Miraculously, he escaped from the car and the pond, and ran for his life. Any intelligent person would have done the same. With help from a small contingent of friends, he has been on the run ever since. After the incident at the retention pond, there have been at least three additional attempts on his life, all unsuccessful."

"Professor Sawyer, that is a fascinating story, and one well told. But, if Arnie did not take the money, who did?" Boyd was a skeptic and he would need some convincing.

Bergen reclaimed the floor. "I was about to get to that. In the interest of full disclosure, I must tell you that Arnie is my brother-in-law. However, I really don't like him very much." That announcement shocked Boyd but it raised Bergen's credibility. "The real thief was Nick Gestas."

"Professor Sawyer, you do know that Mr. Gestas is dead, don't you? It's easy, and despicable, to accuse someone who is unable to defend himself. What proof do you have?"

Now Bergen had a dilemma. He had to be sufficiently forthcoming to convince Boyd that what he was saying was true, while not saying so much that he exposed the operation of Max's E.P. fund. It was a fine line that he had to walk. "But that's exactly what people have been doing to Arnie! I will tell you this: after the most recent failed attempt on Arnie's life, one of his assailants confessed to me that Gestas was the person who had paid for the hit. If that doesn't convince you, consider this. Gestas, himself, reached out to me and offered me a substantial sum of money 'to make the King problem disappear'."

"Incredible!" Boyd commented. "What possible motive did Gestas have?"

"Since he and I never discussed this, I can only speculate. My guess is that, fundamentally, it was jealousy. He saw that he, himself, was never going to make partner at your firm, while Arnie was rather likely to. Then, there's the suspicion that Gestas coveted Arnie's wife. Either way, Arnie was an obstacle in his path, and he wanted the obstacle removed. Of course, it could be that he simply needed the money. You do know, don't you, that he had a serious gambling problem? He was addicted to Blackjack and was not very good at it."

"No, I never suspected a gambling problem. My God, what a disaster! And, it all happened on my watch." Boyd was on the verge of self-flagellation and it was not a pretty sight.

Bergen interrupted him. "He hid his addiction well. You had no way of knowing. Don't beat yourself up over it. However, you may want to review the procedure you use to vet prospective employees."

While Boyd was adjusting to the new reality, the hard-headed businessman in him still had additional questions. "What happened to all that money?"

Bergen smiled. *I was wondering how long it would take him to get around to that.* "Max had the same question. So, he followed the money trail. The path was a convoluted one, but Max was finally able to track the money to four active accounts." Diplomatically, he did not add that these accounts were with Max's own firm. At this point, he produced the envelope containing the cashier's check. He passed it across the desk to Boyd.

"What is this?"

"It's a gift to you from Max. Open it."

Boyd stared incredulously at the check. "What? How?"

"It's the money that Gestas stole from your firm! Why not put it back where it belongs? Quite likely, it was never actually lost, but simply misplaced. As for the how, that's more information than you need to know."

"You should get a finder's fee for the recovery of the money." Boyd was reaching for his checkbook.

Bergen stopped him. "That won't be necessary. However, I do have a favor to ask of you."

Boyd knew better than to agree without first knowing what the favor was. "Name it."

"We'd like you to reinstate Arnie and pretend that this whole unfortunate incident never happened." The use of the plural was deliberate. Bergen paused for Boyd's reaction.

"You ask an awful lot. There's still a chance that he was the thief. Besides, I thought that you didn't like him. Yet you ask me to show him compassion. You're a very strange fellow." Boyd was beginning to think that he had been suddenly transported to Wonderland. Was the Red Queen very far away?

"Arnie will probably never be one of my favorite people, but, in this case, he is as much the victim as are you and your firm. He shouldn't have to live the rest of his life under a cloud of suspicion. We're simply asking you to do the right thing, the honorable thing." It was Bergen at his most sincere.

Boyd sat in silence with downcast eyes for several minutes. Bergen worried that he had fallen asleep. Finally, Boyd lifted his eyes and spoke "Done, and my thanks to you and to Max."

Chapter 44

Aunt Marcy's Just Desserts

T he following day, Bergen drove out to the King home once more. He needed to have a serious, heart-to-heart talk with Arnie.

"Congratulations on being reinstated with B, H, & G." Bergen began.

Arnie was surprised. "How did you hear about that? It seems that sometimes good news can travel as fast as the bad."

Bergen ignored the question. "When you return to work, a lot of people will ask you many questions. You need to be circumspect in your answers. Think of all the friends who helped you during your odyssey: Carleton Dunn; your wife, Gloria; Fingal O'Flahertie and his wife, Constance; Montego O'Higgins; my wife, Moira; Maxwell Greenfield; and, of course, myself. You don't want to put any of these people at risk. It's now clear that Barry Marsh wasn't G.J. So, that means that, whoever that rascal is, he's still out there somewhere, lurking and watching. We don't want to highlight possible targets for him."

Arnie nodded soberly. "How do you suggest I handle these questions?"

"There are many ways to deflect unwanted questions without being combative. There's also a wide variety of evasive answers. Sometimes, merely asking a question in return will suffice. Let me give you some examples:

Q: "Did you actually steal $8 million?"

A1: "Why do you want to know?"

A2: "Of course not. Why would you think that I did?"

A3: Delivered with a furtive look over your shoulder, "Ssh! Someone may be listening."

Q: "If you didn't take the money, then who did?"

A1: "What money?" Accompanied by a bewildered look.

A2: "Didn't you? I heard that it was you."

A3: "Why? Is there a reward?"

Q: "Did you really kill Barry Marsh?"

A1: "Who is Barry Marsh?"

A2: Delivered with a sly smile and a wink, "We may never know."

A3: "I thought that it was you who did it."

Q: "Are you the serial killer known as G.J.?"

A1: "What an evil mind you have. Did you get it from your parents?"

A2: Delivered with a dramatic shrug, "Your guess is as good as mine."

A3: "If I told you, then I'd have to kill you."

You get the idea. I'm sure that you can think up more of your own."

"So, I'm to be a whimsical man of mystery?"

"If you want to play it that way," Bergen answered. "However, if you don't think that you'll be able to pull it off, then it might be better to stick with the story that you have no memory for the months that you were on the run. It hasn't come back. It may never return."

"I still have very many questions. Was Gestas murdered? If so, who did it? How was the missing money recovered? Who convinced Mr. Boyd to reinstate me? How can I be sure that there's no one out there stalking me?" These were all relevant questions and the lack of answers troubled Arnie.

Bergen tried to ease his mind. "There are some questions for which you are much better off not knowing the answers. Frankly, I think that your personal storm has passed and that you are in safe harbor now. However, the security that Max provided will remain in place until we are certain. Meanwhile, you have a group of close friends who will continue to watch out for you. Try to resume your normal life as if this trouble never happened." Bergen knew that this was easy to say, but difficult to practice.

"Bergen, for whatever part you played in it, I am sincerely grateful."

"Don't get all sentimental on me! You can't get on my good side so easily." With that, Bergen left. He had classes to prepare.

* * * *

In Monday's afternoon mail, Bergen received a thick envelope from Max. Inside was the research team's final report on Aunt Marcy. It was organized into three sections. One dealt with her personal life. The second outlined her work history, and the third was an in-depth study of her finances.

The first section tracked her from her entry into the world as Aphrodite Burke, to her marriage to Eric Carey, and her self-rebranding as Katie Carey. Given the date of birth, she was fifty-nine years old. The account noted the arrival of three children and the untimely passing of her husband. Her estrangement from her children was reported. There was no mention of Uncle Byron or Ed Franklin.

Katie's first job with a catering firm was listed. Marriage and children explained the following disconnect in her work history. Her return to the work force as a novice reporter for the Harrison Herald was marked. Since this happened more than two years after Eric's death, the report raised the question of how she had supported herself during this intervening time. Whatever the details were, they might just as well have disappeared into a black hole. Eric's death benefits and insurance could not have stretched for two years. There was no trace of her in the regular work force. She filed no Federal Income Tax returns. She made no contribution to Social Security. Yet, she made regular mortgage payments and paid her property taxes. She held a valid driver's license, paid her utility bills, and, presumably, bought groceries. The report provided no answers, but it speculated that, in some unspecified capacity, she had been a part of the vast underground economy where everything is off the books.

The report went on to chronicle her success at the Herald, her promotion to restaurant reviewer, and her canonization as Aunt Marcy with her own column, "Food to Die For". Her awards, achievements, and travels were well documented. There was a clipping for every time her picture appeared in the paper or her name was mentioned. It was a veritable scrapbook.

The third section was rather bland. She still lived in the same modest house that she had shared with her husband, and where she had raised the children. There remained a mortgage, but it was close to being paid off. There was no evidence of lavish spending. In the interest of full disclosure, she had recently remodeled the master bath and installed an up-scale hot tub. But, to be fair, the plumbing in older homes does wear out, and old bones do appreciate a soak in a warm tub. There were no indications of sudden wealth. Her checking account held less than five thousand dollars, and her Money Market account, less than ten thousand dollars. She had a bank credit card with an outstanding balance of two thousand dollars, and the records showed that she paid the balance off in full every month. No evidence was found of stock or bond activity. She was getting by but she was far from wealthy.

For all the world, she appeared to be a sweet, harmless old lady who had lived a tough life, and then, in her later years, got lucky when she happened upon a decent job for which she was well-suited, and one with good fringe benefits.

Bergen was unconvinced. The gap in the employment record bothered him, as did the fact that Katie had admitted being an accomplice, willing or unwilling, to G.J. and his work. The report had been a tasty hors d'oeuvre, but it did not slake his appetite. He hungered for more information.

Now that he had all the reports from his collaborators, he constructed a composite time-line. It revealed several curious things. For one, the discovery of the first mutilated G.J. body, in a highway rest area south of Harrison, occurred about six weeks after Katie Carey's husband's death. The victim was never identified. Then there was a lapse of over two years before another such mutilation was reported. After that, they appeared with regularity. Why the lapse? Was G.J. not ready for this escalation the first time?

Then, too, once Aunt Marcy began travelling to more distant cities for her restaurant reviews, the mutilated bodies began to show up for the first time in the cities she visited. Of course, this could all be an unfortunate coincidence. However, Bergen did not believe in coincidence. Even if he did, coincidence does not prove causality.

On rereading the report from Max's people, he noted that Aunt Marcy had developed a pattern to her out-of-town trips. Every one of them occurred during the third week of the month. Moreover, whenever possible she drove her personal car, and avoided air travel. Clearly, Max's research staff had a pipe-line into the Harrison Herald. He called Max and asked to be informed the next time Aunt Marcy scheduled an out-of-town business trip. A few days later, Max's secretary telephoned to tell him that Aunt Marcy was expected to spend the following week on assignment in Milwaukee, Wisconsin. Bergen estimated that this was a full day's drive from Harrison. This meant that she would probably leave on Saturday morning so that she would have Sunday to rest up for her work week. Her house in Harrison should be empty on Sunday evening. A perfect time for a nocturnal visitor.

That Sunday evening, Bergen parked his car on the next street over from the one where Katie Carey lived. He approached her house through the alleys and back yards. Since the front door to her house was bathed in full lamplight, his target was the back door. It was less well-lighted, and he expected that it would have an inferior lock. He was not disappointed. The lock on the back door was child's play. He donned his neoprene gloves and entered first the mud room and then the kitchen. The house was in darkness and there was not a sound. However, following his custom, he took nothing for granted. He proceeded quietly and cautiously until he had convinced himself that he was indeed alone. Then he used his penlight sparingly to find his way.

On the first floor there was little of interest. Oh, to be sure, the kitchen was furnished with high-end appliances. But that was to be expected for someone who was professionally involved in food and its preparation. He climbed the stairs to the second floor and spent a long time in a spare bedroom that had been converted into a home office. Once again, he was disappointed to find nothing incriminating.

He moved on to the master suite. The remodeling of the bath had required eliminating a closet and taking over part of the hallway for added space. The result was quite attractive, and the hot tub was the focal point, the first thing that one saw when one moved from the bedroom into the bathroom. In the hands of a less talented designer, it might have dominated the room. It was set in a stone frame and defined tasteful luxury.

A search of the medicine cabinet revealed no opioids and no sleeping medications. Clearly, Aunt Marcy's conscience, if she even had one, did not keep her awake at night. The bedroom itself was sparsely furnished. There was a queen-sized bed, a side table with a reading lamp, a plasma television, and wall-to-wall carpeting.

Bergen leaned against the doorframe and took stock. *I've found nothing that contradicts the impression that Aunt Marcy is who she appears to be, an elderly widow, whose children have deserted her, who lives alone, and who is navigating very well in a male-dominated workplace. This whole evening may have been a complete waste of time.*

He had just one last place to check, the attached garage. As expected, her car was gone. There was a large hot-water heater on a platform against the back wall. Underneath were shelves with cans of paint, gardening tools, plant food, and bug repellent. Against the near wall were a push lawn mower, a small snow blower, and a set of storm windows. But, his attention was drawn to the far wall where stood two 25 cu. ft. Frigidare chest freezers, both plugged into wall outlets and running quietly. He opened the one on the left and found it to be nearly full of frozen meat, poultry, and fish, uncooked casseroles, and covered containers with leftovers, exactly what one might expect for a serious cook. He closed the first freezer and moved on to the second.

Even before he opened it, this one appeared to be much more interesting. Unlike the first one, it was secured with a stout chain and a padlock, such as one might purchase in the local hardware store. *What was so valuable?* He set to work with his tools and, in a matter of minutes, he had defeated the lock. *Why don't people who have something to hide or protect, invest in more serious security?*

On opening this freezer, he found that it contained a large collection of Ziploc plastic bags. The bags were filled with what looked like frozen meat. Each bag was marked only with a numerical code, that appeared to be a month-day-year identification. If that assumption was correct, they were in date order. The oldest was from about a year ago; the most recent from just a week ago. *Could these be souvenirs of G.J.'s mutilations?* He took time to make a list of every one of the numerical codes. Then, he checked to make sure that all the bags were back exactly as he had found them. Finally, he closed the lid and relocked the chest.

Bergen locked up the house and returned to his car. He sat behind the wheel for a few minutes before he started the motor. *I've some homework to do, but perhaps tonight wasn't a complete waste of time after all.*

* * * *

The following evening, after his last class, he sat down with his list of codes from the Ziploc bags and his composite time-line. Very soon, it became abundantly clear that each date on a Ziploc bag approximated the date of the discovery of one of G.J.'s mutilated victims. The uncontrollable variable was how long after the murder, the body remained undiscovered. When such could be determined, the time of death as fixed by the medical examiner, gave a much better correlation. It was powerful circumstantial evidence. It might be sufficient to get a conviction in a Court of Law. But, it still fell a bit short in the Court of Bergen.

He enlisted Oscar's help. They quietly alerted their contact in the Milwaukee police department, to be on the lookout for a mutilated body bearing the G.J. signature post-it note. About a week later, a body, fitting the parameters, was found. It was that of a liability lawyer by the name of Cosmo Reinis, who left behind a small army of dissatisfied clients and several pending law suits. There were few mourners at his funeral. The medical examiner placed the time of death late in the week when Aunt Marcy was in town. Once again, the evidence was suggestive but not definitive. However, now Bergen was another step closer to becoming a believer.

Aunt Marcy's first week back at work after her Milwaukee trip was a rather hectic one. The volume of work in her in-box appeared to have reproduced in her absence. Deadlines were huddling closer together like penguins in the face of an Antarctic blizzard. Staff meetings threatened to go on endlessly like an insomniac's worst night. She began to wonder if she was getting too old for this work. However, she couldn't yet afford to retire. Perhaps she should hire an assistant.

On Friday evening, she dragged herself home, too tired even to fix a meal. She readied the hot tub and prepared a carafe of Brandy Alexanders chilled in an ice bucket, essential components of her unwinding process. The ice bucket and a long-stemmed cocktail glass were arranged on a wooden serving tray that she carried into the bathroom and set on the side of the hot tub. Then, she stripped and eased herself into the water. She folded a hand towel lengthwise several times and draped it around her neck. This cushioned her neck when she rested her head back on the edge of the tub. The first cocktail went down smoothly, and she lost no time in pouring herself a second. She imagined that she sensed her tensions dissolving and her troubles washing off into the hot water. She was beginning to feel quite mellow.

* * * *

The light in the upstairs window alerted him that Aunt Marcy was home. Bergen put on his neoprene gloves and let himself into the house via the back door. He didn't use his penlight since he remembered the layout from his previous visit. Moving quietly, he crossed the kitchen and entered the garage through the connecting door. He unlocked the second freezer. The light from the freezer was sufficient for his work. There was a new Ziploc bag that hadn't been there on his earlier visit. It bore the date that the Milwaukee Medical Examiner had assigned to the death of Cosmo Reinis. Unzipping the bag, he checked the contents. There were a pair of lips, a tongue, and ten fingers.

In a whisper, Bergen greeted the body parts, "Counselor Reinis, I presume." When he received no answer, he closed the bag, returned it to its place, and locked the freezer. He was now a true believer and he knew what he had to do. *Others may see little difference between what Aunt Marcy does and what I do. But, I'd beg to disagree. Her actions are for material gain. They've nothing to do with the guilt or innocence of her victims. In my case, material reward is not my motive. I target only people who are certainly guilty of despicable crimes and who have earned this extreme treatment. They must be removed so that they cannot repeat their actions. In a sense, I'm weeding God's garden and taking out the trash.*

He left the garage and headed up the stairs to the second floor. He avoided the squeaking third step and was careful to make no sound that might alert Aunt Marcy to his surprise visit. He stopped in the doorway to the master bath and surveyed the scene. Aunt Marcy was in the tub with her back to him. Her arms were stretched out along the edge of the tub. Her head rested back on the edge of the pool apron, and she was snoring softly, almost melodically. On the serving tray, the carafe was empty and lying on its side. The cocktail glass was likewise empty, except for a milky film.

Bergen removed his shoes and left them by the door to the bathroom. Quietly, in two quick steps, he was at the edge of the tub. Crouching down, he took hold of the ends of the towel around Aunt Marcy's neck. He wrapped the towel under her chin and he pushed her head under the surface of the water. She struggled briefly but she was in no condition to put up a fight. She was elderly, tired, and very drunk. Moreover, he had all the leverage. Using minimum force, he held her under for a full five minutes, trying not to leave bruises. When he checked for a pulse, he found none. God's judgement had been visited on Aunt Marcy. He released his hold on the towel and launched her body further out into the tub. *Bon voyage, Aunt Marcy!*

Being careful to leave no trace evidence, he reclaimed his shoes, left the house, locking the door behind him, and returned to his car. As he headed for home, he decided that now it was his turn for a nightcap. He had earned it.

* * * *

When Aunt Marcy failed to report for work on Monday, and her home telephone went unanswered, the authorities were alerted. They found her body in the hot tub. There were no signs of forced entry at the house. There were no bruises on the body. The empty carafe and the single cocktail glass were noted. On autopsy, her blood alcohol content was measured at 0.20 percent, more than enough to indicate insobriety. The cause of death was ruled as accidental drowning.

Those attending the funeral were primarily co-workers at the newspaper. None of her children made the trip home. Arnie King was present, hoping that it would give him some closure. Katie Cary was buried next to her husband, in a simple ceremony.

* * * *

It was about two weeks after the funeral when Bergen had time to review his documents from the King Case before he dispatched them to his Archives in Atlanta. He only kept them because he had this vague idea that, in his dotage, he might keep himself busy by writing his memoirs. Max was providing better security for his papers that any bank could.

Ever since Aunt Marcy's death, he had felt the fingers of his subconscious gently tugging on the sleeve of his memory. There were unresolved issues that needed to be dealt with. One had to do with Aunt Marcy's collection of souvenirs. It was a well-documented fact that the mutilated bodies had been turning up for well over two years. Yet the freezer in her garage had held only the souvenirs from the most recent year. *Was it possible that, in that first year the killer was someone else who was then replaced by Aunt Marcy? Did Aunt Marcy have, at some remote location, another locked freezer with the missing collection of body parts? Or, had they been lost or disposed of in some way?*

He was in the middle of re-reading the report on Aunt Marcy from Max's research staff. He was at that point where they listed her honors, accolades, and every time her picture appeared in the paper, something he had earlier dismissed as scrapbooking. There was a clipping from the Harrison Herald describing a luncheon that Aunt Marcy had catered for her co-workers to celebrate the second anniversary of the birth of her column in the paper. The meal was well-attended, and the main course had been a savory meat stew, that she had personally prepared. It drew raves from her assembled colleagues. Everyone ate second helpings. Many asked her for the recipe. Politely, she turned down all such requests, claiming that it was a secret family recipe.

At that point in his reading, Bergen paused and leaned back in thought. Then his face creased in a broad grin. *Aunt Marcy, you didn't...*

The more he thought about it, the more it made perfect sense. *Secret family recipe indeed!*

Acknowledgements

Once again, my first reader was my wife Ann. Her comments, criticisms, and suggestions were spot on and useful in improving the manuscript. However, Ann reads primarily for the story. I know that some others are gifted proof-readers who are sensitive to lapses in spelling, punctuation, grammar, syntax, and continuity. Blessed be you all for your work is vital and, sadly, under-appreciated. Still others look deeper and analyze character development and motivation; the time line and the continuity; the logic and pacing of the narrative; and the realism of the action sequences. You are a rare group, far too few in number. Yet you perform an essential function and I, for one, would be lost without you. Finally, there are the guardians of good taste who prevent me from embarrassing myself by reminding me that "…you can't say that."

For the present work, Chuck Wilkie, Jeullee and Richard Greff, and Ingrid Standish critiqued the manuscript. I took their suggestions seriously and made the appropriate changes. They have my profound gratitude.

As usual, none of the people mentioned above bear any responsibility for whatever errors may survive in the text. The blame for them rests entirely with me.

The photo of the author is the work of Bill Pappas of Pappas Photography, Inc., Cleveland, Ohio. The photographs on the front cover and on Page iii were taken by the author.

The rest of the layout and design of the book was accomplished by Eli Blyden of CrunchTime Graphics, Tampa, Florida. I am constantly awed by his artistic ability and his insight. Thank you, Eli!

Printing and Binding by A & A, Inc., Tampa, Florida.

Biographical Sketch

James Walsh was born and raised in Brooklyn, New York, the eldest of three children. His mother was a housewife and his father a member of the New York City Police Department.

Walsh is a product of the parochial school system. He completed Grammar School at St. Patrick's in Brooklyn. High School was at St. Francis Xavier in Manhattan. After short stints at Notre Dame and New York Universities, he earned his B.S. in Chemistry from Fordham University in the Bronx. He paid his way through school by working for the law firm of Cravath, Swaine, and Moore then on Wall Street. He acknowledges that another significant part of his education came from the three hours he spent each day commuting on the New York City Subway System.

His graduate training was at Purdue University where he earned his M.S. (Physical Chemistry) and his Ph.D. (Organic Chemistry). While at Purdue, he spent three years as a full-time Instructor. There he met two of the major influences on his life: his future wife, Ann Marie Nicklas, and his mentor, friend of long standing, and most forthright critic, the late Professor Derek A. Davenport.

In 1963, he joined the faculty of John Carroll University (JCU) in Cleveland, OH, as an Assistant Professor on tenure track. He "retired" from JCU in 1999, as a tenured full Professor. Then he taught three-and-one half summers as a Visiting

Professor in the Chemistry Department at Case Western Reserve University in Cleveland. So much for retirement. He prefers to call it a "career transition".

Jim and Ann now live on Treasure Island, a barrier island in the Gulf, off St. Petersburg, Florida. Neither of them misses the winters of northeastern Ohio. Occasionally, Jim will chuckle over the weather and traffic reports on WCLV-FM. He is still a member of the American Chemical Society but, in his mellow old age, he's quite content to let others wrestle with the governance issues of the Society. When he is not writing, he can be found walking the beaches along the Gulf of Mexico, or swimming in the pool at their Condo Association.

Currently, Dr. Walsh is at work on yet another Entertainment, this one tentatively titled, "Second Acts". He has also started writing what he hopes will be a collection of short stories under the title of "Tales Told by the Blind Man."

www.ingramcontent.com/pod-product-compliance
Lightning Source LLC
Chambersburg PA
CBHW051521050726
47503CB00014B/424